The Heir

Darcie Wilde is also the author of:

The Secret of the Lady's Maid
The Secret of the Lost Pearls
A Counterfeit Suitor
A Lady Compromised
And Dangerous to Know
A Purely Private Matter
A Useful Woman

The Heir

DARCIE WILDE

KENSINGTON
PUBLISHING CORP.

kensingtonbooks.com

KENSINGTON BOOKS are published by

Kensington Publishing Corp.
900 Third Ave.
New York, NY 10022

All Kensington titles, imprints, and distributed lines are available at special quantity discounts for bulk purchases for sales promotion, premiums, fund-raising, educational, or institutional use. Special book excerpts or customized printings can also be created to fit specific needs. For details, write or phone the office of the Kensington Special Sales Manager: Attn. Special Sales Department, Kensington Publishing Corp., 900 Third Avenue, New York, NY 10022. Phone: 1-800-221-2647.

Library of Congress Card Catalogue Number:

ISBN: 978-1-4967-5068-6
First Kensington Hardcover Edition: September 2025

ISBN: 978-1-4967-5070-9 (ebook)

10 9 8 7 6 5 4 3 2 1

Printed in the United States of America

The authorized representative in the EU for product safety and compliance
Is eucomply OU, Parnu mnt 139b-14, Apt 123
Tallinn, Berlin 11317, hello@eucompliancepartner.com

To all those who are just tired of waiting.

Author's Note

There's a lot we don't know about Queen Victoria.

This is a strange thing to say about one of history's most documented human beings. Hundreds of books have been written about her, not to mention the movies and TV series made about her. She also left behind hundreds of journals and thousands of letters. It's estimated that she wrote around sixty million words during her lifetime.

But there's a problem. For the past two hundred years, the queen's writing has been meticulously and constantly censored. Those sixty million words have been repeatedly judged by her family and her archivists. They've been edited, rewritten, locked away, and burned. Whenever someone thought Victoria's version of her own life might make her (or them) look bad, her words were altered, sequestered, or destroyed. This means that the woman herself has been cut down, burnished, and fit to the fashionable frame.

So, what's left of Victoria is the official version. More recent historians have tried to look behind that frame, to find more of the woman who was Victoria. But there are still a lot of gaps.

What follows isn't a history. It's a story sparked by the gaps in the recorded life of Princess Alexandrina Victoria of Kent, the girl who became Queen Victoria. Some of the events in this story actually happened. Some of them are guesses. Some of them are entirely made up. Some of them are probably mistakes that didn't get caught, and for that, I apologize.

I hope you enjoy.

A Note About Names

I frequently joke that nineteenth-century England labored under a name shortage.

A quick Wikipedia search shows that the historical John Conroy married Elizabeth Fisher and that they had two daughters—Elizabeth and Victoria. Since this story already had Victoire and Victoria, to avoid (further) confusion, I changed Victoria Conroy's name to Jane.

The aristocrats, and the royal family, on the other hand, had a plethora of names. These names could change throughout a person's lifetime. One person might have their given name, their family nickname, and a whole set of different titles that they assumed at different times. And, of course, women's names changed when they got married and rose (or fell) through the ranks of society.

King William IV's brothers, the "royal dukes" are a case in point. To (hopefully) reduce confusion, I've referred to each of the dukes by their title (Sussex, Cambridge, etc.) even when their family probably would have called them something different.

Prologue

SIDMOUTH,
1820

*H*e's dying.

Victoire, Duchess of Kent, sat on a hard stool at her husband's bedside and willed him to keep breathing.

The room was dark, except for the fire that sputtered fitfully in the hearth, trying in vain to match the roar of wind and surf outside, trying also to warm the room and bring some small chance of life to the man who lay so still in the narrow bed.

The doctor—William Maton—was speaking. Dr. Maton was a fussy, fat, pale, bald man. He had spent the past four days swearing as to the unfailing efficacy of his knives, cups, and leeches. Now he was saying something far different. Victoire's mind was too dulled by exhaustion to fully translate his English into her native German, but she understood his tone. "We have done all we can," he was saying, or something like it. "Now we must wait." Or something like it.

Perhaps there was also something about trusting in a merciful God.

Victoire ground her teeth to shut in the sob that threatened to escape her.

The doctor fell silent, but a fresh noise insinuated itself into the room's chill—a thin, insistent bawling. The baby, tucked up in her cot in the adjoining room, was crying. She was cold, or she was hungry. Or she simply wished to protest that she was alone in a dark cottage, surrounded by a foul winter storm, while the man who loved her most in the world was dying.

Drafts curled around Victoire's neck. She imagined them like the fingers of a ghostly hand. She imagined that hand dragging itself up the quilts to caress her husband's cheek. To cover his mouth. To stop his breath.

Dr. Maton was speaking again. A second voice answered. That was Conroy, her husband's equerry and assistant. Victoire had forgotten he was even in the room. Their English whispers fluttered around her ears. Victoire made out *hope* and *strong* and *hour*. She tried to understand the rest, but it was no good.

She turned her face toward the window, but there was nothing to see. The shutter had been closed. For all the good it did in keeping out the cold or the sound of the storm.

The baby was still crying. Where was the nurse? Where was Lehzen? Or even Feodora? She would have to do something. Give an order. Make herself understood.

She could not even make herself move.

"Victoire."

The sound of her name was less than a whisper, but she still heard it. Her heart thumped. Edward's eyes were open and searching for her.

"Yes, my heart, I am here," Victoire said in German. She seized his hand. It was hot and light, as if his bones had already burnt to ash. Or perhaps it was because he had been drained dry of blood. Dr. Maton said he'd taken only a pint this time. It looked to her as if it had been a gallon.

"Victoire," Edward said again.

"Rest, my heart. You must regain your strength." She spoke lightly, praying that he would not notice the tears slipping down her hollow cheeks.

Edward had always been so strong, and so proud of that strength. Let all his royal brothers drink and debauch themselves. Let them carouse with their wastrel friends and squander their fortunes. Edward would not follow their examples. He would keep to strict, simple habits, eat a plain diet, and get plenty of exercise. Oh, the sight of him on horseback or on the driver's box of a carriage! It was enough to stop any woman's heart.

Even her heart, which had been withered by her first marriage, her two children, her poverty, her fear for her future. *The future Edward saved me from.*

He had driven her out of her tiny, trampled German kingdom all the way to England. She had protested that she was too far gone in her pregnancy to make the journey, but he had insisted. Their child must be born on English soil. He hadn't wanted anyone to be able to question whether the babe really belonged to him or whether it could very well be the future of English crown.

He had installed them in Kensington Palace and dared his brothers to protest his right to rooms in the royal residence, especially once the baby—their pocket Hercules of a princess—was born.

But now where are we?

Fat George squatted in Windsor and rubbed his greedy hands at the bedside of his blind, mad father. He debauched his mistresses, railed against his legal wife, swilled his wines, and gambled away England's treasury. But Fat George lived and, to all appearances, would continue to live.

Freddy, the grand old Duke of York, had grubbed under

his mistress's skirts with one hand and stolen from the public treasury with the other and died far earlier than anyone had imagined he might.

Silly Billy, Duke of Clarence, walked the streets without remembering to put on his hat, heartsore for the whore-actress he'd thrown over so he could marry a princess even poorer than Victoire and get himself at least one legitimate heir.

Augustus, the Duke of Sussex, had decided to stick a thumb in the eye of the entire family by refusing to marry anyone acceptable, but that marriage had failed. Now he puttered uselessly about the ruin that was Kensington Palace with his collections of clocks and Bibles.

And all the while, Ernest—the lecherous, damnable, scarred, half-blind Duke of Cumberland—leered at his brothers from his wife's palace in Germany and waited to see which of them fell first.

But Edward? Strong and plain-living Edward had taken Victoire and the children away from London because Fat George would not advance him the money he needed to live there. They had come to this dreary seaside town and huddled together in this tiny hovel of a cottage.

And Edward had gone for a walk in the December rain and had gotten his feet wet.

That was all. How can he be dying when that was all that happened?

Victoire pressed her hand against her eyes.

And still the baby was crying. And her husband wanted to speak to her.

"Conroy," she said.

"Yes, your grace?" John Conroy was a tall man with a long face, bright blue eyes, and thick, dark hair. Ladies blushed and batted their eyes at him. The more vicious gossips wondered what kinds of services he performed for the duchess now that the king had brought her to England.

"Go see to the baby," she said. *Conroy is a father. He does not fear a nursery.* "Go talk to the nurse. See that Feodroa and Karl are still asleep. I . . . I cannot."

"Yes, ma'am."

If he bowed, she did not turn her head to see it. She rinsed the linen cloth in the basin on the nightstand and dabbed at Edward's forehead. His skin was too dry. His eyes were too bright, and yet his cheeks were far too pale.

Bloodless.

"You are not crying, Victoire," he said in German. He tried very hard to teach her English, but still, they always spoke German when they were alone together.

"No, of course I do not cry," she lied. "I never do. You know that."

"I know." His fingers curled around hers, feather soft. Her heart twisted inside.

"I will show them yet," he told her. "I have done what they could not. I have found a good wife. I have fathered a healthy child. You and I will take up the crown together, my heart. We will make a place for our Alexandrina Victoria. We will see them all bow their heads to her and to us. To *us*."

Victoire held her husband's burning hand and willed herself to believe. But if he had been hollowed out by the fever and the bloodletting, she had been made equally hollow by fear. All the belief she could muster did not fill even an inch of her emptiness.

"Now, it may take some little while for me to get better," he went on. "In the meantime, you may rely on Conroy. He has been with me these many years. I trust him absolutely."

"Yes, my heart." She wished he would stop. He was so weak. This talk was doing him no good. But she had not the strength to tell him so.

"And do not let them take our daughter." By *them* he meant his family. His mad father, his ridiculous mother, he spidery spinster sisters and, most of all, his greedy brothers. "They will try, but they want only to turn her against us and use her for their own purposes. You must hold her tightly to you."

"They will have no chance to take her." She meant to speak lightly, but her voice broke. "You will be better long before they can do any such thing."

"Yes, yes. I have promised, haven't I?" His eyelids fluttered closed.

Dr. Maton was back. He maneuvered daintily around her. She was a duchess, after all, and could not simply be elbowed out of the way. Instead, he took himself to the far side of the bed, coming to stand between Edward and the wall. He lifted Edward's wrist and stared at his watch.

Fresh fear bubbled up in Victoire. As Edward weakened, Dr. Maton was all the hope that she had. He had scarcely left her husband's bed, ceaselessly battling the encroaching fever with his knives and his glass cups and his jar of glistening leeches. He was so attentive, so unstinting. She tried to look at him now and believe he had succeeded.

He must succeed. He was all that they had left.

"Well," said Dr. Maton softly. "Well. His fever has increased. Yes. I think we may bleed him one more time."

"*Bleed*?" she breathed, ashamed of her weakness, her irrationality. "He surely has no blood left."

From the way Dr. Maton stared at her, Victoire knew she'd spoken German. But she could not now summon her English.

"Ma'am." Conroy stepped out from the shadows. "We must listen to the doctor."

Dr. Maton was staring past her at Conroy, clearly uneasy. Afraid, perhaps, the duchess had gone mad with her grief and was spouting gibberish.

Edward's hand twitched in hers. His eyes opened again.

"Edward?" she cried.

"Sir?" The doctor bent close. "Sir, we must bring your fever down! I must bleed you once more."

Edward's tongue pressed against his lips, trying to wet them. Victoire snatched up the cloth and rinsed it again and dabbed it against his mouth.

Edward's eyes closed. He swallowed. Victoire felt her heart creak, like ice in the last moment before it shatters.

"Let it be done," Edward said in English. His eyes opened, and she saw the spark in them. Her heart cried out with hope, and the pain was worse than despair.

"Conroy," Edward breathed. "Conroy, look after my wife and my daughter."

"Of course, sir." Conroy bowed crisply, like the soldier he was.

Then in German Edward said, "Fear not, my heart. I am still strong. Maton will drain this fever out of me." His fingers curled around hers again. "Then we will show them. You and I and our daughter. We will show them a true queen, and they will all kneel."

Chapter 1

"Keep up, Jane, can't you?"

"I'm trying!" whined Jane Conroy. Perched uncomfortably on Smokey, her plump mare, the girl had already fallen a full length behind.

"It's a beautiful day!" Victoria tried, even as the wind snatched at her hems and the edge of her bonnet. The chill air smelled of soot, mud, and rain. This late in July, it should be hot and dry, but it had been raining for three days straight. As a result, Victoria had been stuck inside. She was not going to waste this clear spell, however brief it might prove. "Don't you long for a gallop?"

"You mustn't, Your Highness." Hornsby, today's groom, looked positively panicked. "Your mother would never allow it."

As if I were not fully aware of that.

But Mama was inside the palace, and Victoria (and Jane

and Hornsby) were outside. They had already ridden beyond the gardens' straight paths and formal hedges. The Round Pond, with its honking geese and suspicious swans, was likewise behind them. Ahead was nothing but an unbroken carpet of grass and low hills stretching to the gate that divided the palace grounds from the park beyond.

Prince felt Victoria's restlessness. He shifted underneath her, letting her know he wanted to run as much as she did.

Jane tipped her head back to look at the lumpish gray clouds that obscured the sky. From the way the other girl screwed up her face, one might have thought they were about to drop down and smother her. Instead, a single raindrop fell and smacked her in the eye.

"Ouch! Oh!"

Victoria ducked her head and tried hard not to smile.

"We can't," Jane mumbled as she wiped at her eyes. "Father will be angry. I promised to bring you back at the first sign of rain!"

She had, in fact. That promise and Jane's dreary presence were the only reasons Victoria had been able to ride out at all today.

It was not fair. But it was all a part of the "Kensington System." That system dictated how Victoria's life was to be lived. It required that every minute of her day be accounted for and, worse, that she never be alone. So, if Mama could not ride out, Victoria was stuck with Jane or stuck indoors.

She had tried to remain patient today. She had sat dutifully through having her hair done and had stood still while being dressed. She'd attended to her lessons in geography and history and penmanship and music (not that this last was any great trial). She'd stayed quiet while Mama inspected her journal and her books and examined her tutors as thoroughly as her tutors examined Victoria.

After her journal had been pronounced satisfactory, Mama

had gone to confer with Sir John about some one or the other of the plans for the tour of the northern counties they had declared she would undertake in September.

This resulted in Victoria having a rare ten minutes with nothing to do and only Lady Flora Hastings and her own governess, Louise Lehzen, watching over her.

And, of course, Jane Conroy. Jane slumped sullenly in a chair with her needlework in her lap and a copybook beside her. Jane was hopeless on horseback, hopeless with a needle or a piece of music or a sketching pencil or a paintbrush. Hopeless in the face of her father's endless commands.

Victoria tried to muster some sympathy for the other girl. Jane did not want to be here any more than Victoria wanted her, and yet, like Victoria, here she was. Today and every other day.

Victoria stood in front of the windows with her spaniel, Dash, in her arms. She looked out across the gardens. At least she tried to. Streaks of grime obscured the view. When she was six, she'd been asked what she wanted for her birthday. She'd answered that she would like to have the windows washed. She remembered the startled faces of the adults around her and their nervous laughter. But nothing had come of it. Victoria had received dolls and books and an enamel brooch rather than what she had actually wanted.

The sunlight—when there was any—remained blurred by a film of dust and soot. The view—what there was of it— turned into a spoiled watercolor of green and gray, so that the whole apartment remained gloomy even on the brightest of days.

Even Dash knew it wasn't right. He whined softly and pawed at the window.

You want to be out, too, don't you? She kissed the top of his head.

It was true that Kensington Palace was a palace. It was

huge, filled with rare and precious things, and housed a changeable cast of persons belonging to the royal family. It was also true, however, that the doors creaked and stuck, that mice had nibbled the edges of the fine carpets, and that damp bloated the trompe l'oeil murals lining the king's staircase until the painted faces of the people depicted there bulged and cracked.

Mama told her that when they first arrived, there had been mushrooms growing in their rooms. As a very little girl, Victoria had been fascinated by the idea. It made her think of fairy rings. She'd hunted for mushrooms in all the corners, but she only ever found shadows and spiders and blossoming stains of thick black mold.

"Do not let yourself be fooled, Victoria," Mama told her (and told her and told her). "We are lodged in this dingy hole because his family hates me, and they hate me because I will not let them get hold of you. You will never be their hostage and plaything, romping about with their bastards and cronies until you are spoilt as rotten as the rest."

"Enough," muttered Victoria to herself. She could not, she *would* not, stand here anymore, waiting for the next instruction, order, or direction.

Victoria hugged Dash quickly. Then she faced the room.

"I shall go for a ride," she declared. "Prince needs the exercise."

"Certainly not in this weather, ma'am!" cried Lady Flora, as shocked as if Victoria had suggested she was going to dance naked in the gardens. "You mustn't think it."

Jane Conroy just pulled a face. "It's going to rain."

"Not for hours yet," said Victoria, as if her words could make it true.

"Shall I go speak with your mother for you, ma'am?" asked Lehzen.

Victoria imagined saying, *She is busy with Sir John. I will*

only be gone for a little while. She would then simply go into
her dressing room, have the waiting maid bring out her habit,
and give orders that the groom saddle Prince and bring him
to the courtyard. It was what another young woman might
do. Other young women could move without asking permission and without hands to hold.
*Hands to hold them back. Hands to keep them from going
anywhere at all.*
Because those other young women were not Princess Victoria, heir to the throne of the United Kingdom. If she left
these rooms without Mama's permission, there would be a
scene, and she would be locked in her boudoir for days.
Sir John and I are only trying to protect you.
"You need not bother, Lehzen. I will go to her myself."
"What is it Lehzen need not bother with?"
Victoria started. She could not help herself. Mama had returned.
Victoire, Duchess of Kent—Mama—was a tall, elegant
woman. *How could I have such a short, plump little girl,
hmmm? It is the influence of your father's blood.* Her dark
hair fell in dramatic ringlets, much thicker than Victoria's
own blond hair. *Sit still, Victoria. You cannot be seen with
your hair hanging down like a wild thing. What will people
think of you?* She had wide-set eyes that could take in every
detail of a room, or a person, with a single glance. *Pay* attention, *Victoria. If the dean sees you drift away in the middle of
a conversation, what will he think of you?*
Dash squirmed in Victoria's arms, and she set him down.
He immediately ran for his basket and wriggled under the
blanket. It was as if he could already sense a very different
sort of storm coming.
"Victoria, why are you standing there?" Mama's voice
could contain equal amounts of weariness and anger. It was
her finest accomplishment. "Come away at once. How many

times have you been told not to linger about in front of the windows? What if someone on the road was to stop to gawp at you? What would they think?"

"They might think that I am looking to see if the weather is good enough to go out for a ride," Victoria replied. "Prince needs the exercise, and I have finished my journal and my letters." *And my workbooks and my piano practice and . . .*

"No, Victoria," said Mama. "It is a foul day. What if you got wet and took cold? Besides, we must make sure you are prepared for the dinner. Prince Liechtenstein in particular should see you at your best. You are aware that he will report on your behavior to—"

"I will just go around the grounds," said Victoria. "I will be no more than one hour. It will not rain before then, and I will be back in plenty of time for you to quiz me for the dinner." *Again.*

"I said no, Victoria. Now, come along." Mama held out her hand for Victoria to take. Under the Kensington System, Victoria could not walk anywhere alone. Especially not down the stairs. She must be held. She must be steered. She must be managed and instructed and ordered.

But she had been kept inside for three days by the rain, and this might be her only chance for some air.

"I will go riding, Mama. I will not stay here so you can listen to me recite the names and histories of your dinner guests for the hundredth time."

Mama leaned down and gripped Victoria's chin in her strong white fingers.

"I see what you have been doing." Her breath was hot and smelled of Madeira wine and licorice. "You have been standing here, idle, staring out windows, rehearsing all your wrongs. Disparaging your mother to your governess, to your ladies, and your friend."

"Jane is not my friend." Victoria forced the words through clenched teeth. Mama's grip hurt her. She should be still.

I will not be still.

"Jane comes because Sir John makes her, and you let him," Victoria grated. "It is not fair. I would never treat anyone in my family so poorly!"

Mama's grip on Victoria's chin tightened. Dash poked his nose out from under his blanket and barked once.

"I did warn Your Highness." Lehzen murmured under her breath.

Mama's head jerked up. Her grip loosened. Victoria twisted her chin away. Dash slid out of his basket and scampered to her side.

"What did you say, Lehzen?"

"I beg your pardon, ma'am." Lehzen lifted her own chin, as if she herself was a duchess rather than the daughter of a Prussian schoolmaster. It was an attitude that never failed to infuriate Mama. "It's only that I had already told Her Highness that an outing on such a day would be quite inadvisable."

"Well, yes, I am sure I am always grateful for your advice in how to best care for the health and safety of my child!" Mama's words oozed condescension and a thick, oily suspicion. "You may say that you warned her, but I know your ways. I'm sure it was you who put this notion of a ride into her head!"

"This is not Lehzen's idea!" shouted Victoria. Dash pressed closer against her shin. "You will not blame her!"

"Well, now. What is this?"

Sir John breezed into the room. Jane immediately looked around her in panic, clearly trying to discover what she *should* have been doing. Mama, however, plunged into an attitude of dramatic relief.

"Victoria is determined to go riding!"

You say it as if I had been planning to burn the stables down.

"She has been plaguing me this half hour!"

"I did tell her that riding on such a filthy day was not to be thought of, Sir John," said Lehzen. "But she has insisted she will go out with Jane."

It was, of course, entirely wrong that Lehzen should lie to Mama or to Sir John. But now she had, and—Victoria could not help but note—Lehzen's addition of Jane to the story made Sir John smile down from his great height. His eyes were a brilliant blue color and showed every emotion that flitted through his mind. Or rather he could make you believe that they did. That, in turn, made people of all stations want to trust him. Some because they believed he was open-hearted. Some because they believed they could keep ahead of him.

But neither thing was true. Victoria watched him, and she knew better. When he was not exerting himself to charm, Sir John's clear blue eyes examined the person in front of him carefully, seeking weaknesses he might expose. His seemingly easy smile was in reality an expression of his smug satisfaction. It sent chills down Victoria's spine that were far worse than when he frowned.

"Well, I see no harm in it, ma'am, if Her Highness will take Jane." As he looked to his daughter, Sir John's smile stretched to show his teeth. "She'll make sure they return at the first sign of rain. Won't you, Jane?"

Jane looked as if she would rather be banished to the Outer Hebrides. But she got to her feet, her gaze pointed resolutely at the floor.

"Yes, Father," she murmured.

Dash growled. Sir John's head jerked around. Dash barked. To Victoria's horror, Sir John drew his foot back just a little, just enough to aim a kick.

Heart thumping, Victoria snatched Dash up in her arms. Sir John seemed to re-collect himself, and he smiled.

"Yes, I think a ride with Jane would be very beneficial," he said.

He pretended nothing had happened, but Victoria had watched and she had seen and she would not forget.

But that was all before. Now she was out of doors, in the fresh air. Prince trotted determinedly across the green. Dash barked happily and nosed about the grass, far too smart to get himself in the way of the horse's hooves. A raindrop thumped against the back of Victoria's glove. Another smacked Prince's head, causing him to shake his ears.

"We need to go back," whined Jane. "My father will be furious we were out this long."

Your father maybe, thought Victoria. *My father was a horseman. My father would have loved to ride with me.*

Her father also died from a chill he'd caught in the rain. Another drop hit the edge of Victoria's bonnet, and another. Victoria had been told the story a thousand times. A hundred thousand. The recitation had taken on the shape of catechism. Only instead of saving her soul, it was meant to keep her trembling indoors when the weather turned gray.

The thought of those hundred thousand lectures dissolved the last of Victoria's patience.

Prince snorted. As if it was the starting gun, Victoria slapped his dappled flank with her crop. The gelding laid his ears flat and sprang forward.

"Ma'am, no!" cried Jane.

"Your Highness!" wailed Hornsby.

But they were too late. Prince was fast, and Victoria could ride him to the ends of the earth. *And why not?* She bared her teeth, as if to dare the world to try to catch up. *Why shouldn't I?*

The gates were closed, but the walls were really only a suggestion between the grounds and the park (a fact that her mother pointed out endlessly to further frighten her). Victoria could take the jump. Prince could do it easily. They would vault over the wall and land firmly on the other side. Dash would wriggle right under the gates. Together, they would make for the carriage drive.

The wind whistled in her ears—an urgent, exhilarating sound. Victoria leaned low over Prince's neck, his reins gathered up in her gloved hands. She laughed. Because they could not stop her. They could not even catch her. Not poor, dreary Jane or pinch-faced Hornsby. She would leave them behind—them and this whole miserable day.

The gallop filled the whole of Victoria's senses—the speed of the world whirling past her; the thunder of Prince's hooves and the heat and life radiating from him; the work of keeping her seat, keeping Prince from stumbling, keeping control of the reins, keeping her eyes ahead to watch for rabbit holes or hillocks.

Freedom.

Victoria's bonnet flew backward and dangled by its ribbons. Her hair uncoiled down her back. Rain pattered against her scalp. Jane and Sir John and Mama, the palace, the system, the dreaded dinner—they were all miles behind now. Not one of them could be shocked by her bare head.

Freedom!

Rain stung her face and eyes, but she did not pull Prince back. If he did not mind a bit of rain, why should she? She shouted for pure delight and touched Prince's flank with her crop again. Let them try to catch her. Prince would outrun them all. He'd carry her away.

Away from Mama and her lectures and her pinches and her tears.

Away from Sir John Conroy and his shouting and his speeches and his demands that she obey his system without question.

Away from Jane, their limp, reluctant spy.

They'd topped the rise. Prince's breathing was growing labored; the ground underfoot was slick with fresh rain. Dash barked in the distance, letting her know he would catch up soon. The downslope ahead was steep. Victoria's pulled back the reins to slow Prince down, disappointment welling up in her. But her wish for flight was not worth the risk of his legs and her neck and . . .

And Prince shied.

The gelding screamed. Victoria screamed. The world slipped and spun and slammed against her. For a moment, there was nothing but sparkling stars and one great howl of pain that ripped through her skull and bones. She couldn't see. She couldn't breathe.

Then, ever so slowly, came the realization that she was lying on her back. On the slope. In the wet grass. Icy rain filled her eyes and trickled into her nose. Dash was barking in frantic distress, but the sound seemed very far away.

Victoria sputtered and twisted, trying to right herself and perhaps quiet the ringing that filled her ears.

And found she was staring down at a dead man.

Chapter 2

Jane saw Prince rear up. She saw the princess fall. In that instant, all her breath stopped in her throat.

They will blame me.

She looked to the horizon, wondering how far she could get before they fetched her back again. Would they lock her in the Tower?

While Jane sat frozen, barely holding on to the reins, Hornsby raced past her on his bony brown mare and disappeared over the rise.

Dash was barking wildly, demanding that someone, anyone, come and see what had happened.

See what Jane Conroy let happen!

"Miss Conroy!" Hornsby hollered. "You're needed, miss!"

Despite the fear raging inside her, Jane found herself reflecting distantly that no one had ever said such a thing to her before. She slid awkwardly from Smokey's back and stumbled up over the hill.

The princess was sitting up on the sloping ground. Dash

stood beside her, barking like it was the end of the world. Mud and water soaked into her skirts, and rain fell on her bare head. Her face had turned green with nausea and blue with cold. She blinked stupidly at the dark hillock below them and then up at Jane. The familiar sharp young woman was entirely missing from her wide eyes.

"There's a dead man," said the princess.

Jane stared. First at the princess and then down the slope toward the hillock that seemed to command her attention. Hornsby had dismounted to catch hold of Prince's reins. With the horses and the groom in the way, it was impossible for Jane to see anything clearly.

"He's dead," the princess told Jane. "I saw it."

Dash whined and pawed at her skirt. The princess did not look at him. Jane, not knowing what else to do, scooped Dash up into her arms.

Hornsby had managed to calm Prince and was now leading him back up the slope. His mare remained where he'd left her, and looking between the horse's legs, Jane could see a lumpish black shape. Hornsby glanced behind him—once, twice—as if he thought his mare might bolt or someone might be following.

"Is Her Highness all right?" Hornsby's face was almost as ashen as the princess's.

"I . . . I don't know."

Jane and Hornsby stared at each other, both understanding that they were alone with the most important person in the world, and that if anything happened to her, it was their fault.

Hornsby broke the stalemate first. "Miss Conroy, you must get Her Highness indoors. I'll . . . deal with things here." He took Dash from her and set him down on the sodden grass.

"There's a dead man," said the princess again.

Hornsby, however, was an experienced servant. He knew there was only one possible answer when one of the higher-ups spoke in this way.

"As you say, Your Highness. Now, if I may, I think it would be best if you were not on the damp grass. Perhaps Miss Conroy . . . ?"

Jane forced herself to move. She grabbed the princess's shoulders, and heaved her to her feet. Hornsby held Prince's reins with one hand and the stirrup with the other. Between them, they wrestled the princess up onto his back. Prince danced and shuddered and seemed determined to have done with them all. Thankfully, the princess was able to keep her seat, even though she could not seem to tear her eyes away from the green.

Hornsby boosted Jane unceremoniously onto Smokey, then handed up her reins and the princess's reins.

"Hurry, Miss Conroy," he said. "But for God's sake, be careful."

Jane gritted her teeth and urged Smokey forward. Dash followed, issuing the occasional bark, which the horses ignored. Thankfully, now that the horses realized they were heading back for their dry, warm stables, they were more than ready to comply with her awkward commands. In fact, it was difficult to hold them to a walk.

If Prince begins to canter, the princess will fall again. What will I do then? She'll break her neck this time!

The rain was increasing. Jane had forgotten to put the princess's bonnet back on. Rain trickled down her gray face, and she huddled in her saddle, her eyes still staring straight ahead. She didn't even look down at poor little Dash loping dutifully beside her, stopping every so often to shake the rain from his ears.

Can someone go blind from hitting their head? No. Don't think it.

There were days when Jane hated the princess. She hated her acid tongue and her determined rebellions, hated the way she constantly needled Father and the duchess. She hated the arguments and disorder, and most of all, she hated the gleam that came into the princess's eyes when she invented some fresh defiance.

But this dead, dazed look terrified her.

"Say something, ma'am," Jane begged. "Please, just . . . say something."

The princess blinked. "I . . . I'm cold."

Now Jane could hear her teeth chattering. Panic cracked open that much farther. The Duke of Kent had died from cold. Jane knew that. Everybody knew that. If the princess took ill, if the princess *died*—even if they didn't lock her in the Tower, Jane would be thrown out of the palace, out of her home, and left in the street to starve. Father wouldn't even look back. Mother wouldn't stop him. Her sister, Liza, might not even bother to watch it happening. Her brother, Ned, definitely would not.

"If we can go a little faster," Jane tried.

Prince snorted and tossed his head. Jane's words might not reach the princess, but the horse's unease did. The princess blinked and shook her head, and some semblance of her normal self seemed to seep back into her demeanor.

The princess reached for her reins but saw that Jane held them, and frowned with annoyance.

"Give me my reins," the princess ordered.

Jane thought she might dissolve from sheer relief.

"We must get back. I have to tell Mama. And I'm perfectly fine." Her pinched, pained face and chattering teeth gave away this blatant lie. Still, Jane was perfectly happy to pretend.

She handed over the reins and pulled Smokey back just far enough so that the princess could take the lead. That would make things look less like a disaster. Like there was less to blame useless Jane Conroy for.

A shout went up from in front of them. They'd been spotted. Now that Jane had attention to spare, she could see the palace gardens and the yard were filled with shifting figures. People surged toward them. The duchess or Papa had grown worried, and the palace staff had been turned out to find them.

Her. They are all out to find her.

A flock of grooms and what seemed like half of Kensington's footmen surrounded them. Everyone was crying and exclaiming and shouting orders. The footmen—begging their pardon, moaning over the state of them—pulled them off the horses. They were then handed off to the flock of uniformed maids and cloaked ladies-in-waiting, who surrounded them and whisked them back inside.

Of course the duchess was there in the sitting room. In fact, the duchess stood in the same spot by the windows where the princess had been earlier. Father stood there with her, holding her hands as she gazed, panic-stricken, through the blurred glass. Louise Lehzen, the princess's governess, and Lady Flora hovered in the background.

The cluster of maids herded Jane and the princess—who hugged Dash to her chest—into the room. Lehzen charged forward to pull the princess away from them. Jane was left beside the doorway. Victoria was shaking badly. So was Jane.

The duchess dropped to her knees in front of the princess. "You little fool!" She wrapped her arms around her daughter, wailing in grief and outrage. "I begged you! I pleaded with you! Oh, my God! She will die! She will die like her father died!"

Jane thought no one had noticed her. She was wrong. Father strode forward, brushing past the princess and the duchess. When he reached her, he raised his hand. His fingers curled. Jane blinked.

Father struck her across the face.

Jane's head snapped back and slammed against the wall, barely cushioned by her ruined bonnet, and for a moment, she could see nothing but stars.

"Stop!" shouted the princess. "It was not Jane's fault!"

There was silence, except for the ringing in her ears. Jane brought her head upright again gingerly. The movement hurt. The room seemed oddly blurred, as if she still peered through the rain.

The princess twisted herself out of her mother's arms. "*I* was the one who decided to gallop. Jane's Smokey cannot keep up, and I got ahead of her. I fell because Prince was startled and he shied. Jane had no part in it! You have no reason to treat her so!"

Her jaw throbbed with pain. Her tongue was coated with a weak slime that tasted of salt and warm copper.

Blood.

She did not want to swallow but had no choice. Her kerchief had been lost somewhere, and if she moved, she would be noticed, and there would be another glare, another order, perhaps even another blow. She might topple over and this time be unable to rise.

The princess had turned to the kneeling duchess, deliberately cutting Father from her notice. "Mama, there is a dead man on the green."

The duchess lurched to her feet. "*What?*"

"There is a dead man on the green," the princess repeated. "I saw him. That was why Prince was startled. The guard should be sent."

The duchess, genuinely alarmed, stared at Father. Father's expressive eyes went briefly blank and distant, as they usu-

ally did when he heard something unexpected and unwanted. Jane's cheek throbbed as if in answer, and she swallowed more of the slick copper taste. He'd forgotten her,
forgotten the blow and all the sins that merited it. He was
somewhere else entirely, and Jane was grateful. And she was
frightened.

"Hornsby saw him, as well," the princess announced.

"I'll go look into this." Father bowed, sharp and crisp,
and marched through the door. He did not spare Jane so
much as a glance.

Jane, trembling, was grateful all over again.

"If you please, your grace," said Lehzen to the duchess.
"We must get Her Highness out of these wet things before
she catches cold."

The duchess turned dead white at the mention of a cold.
"My God, yes, yes, yes, at once. She is ill! That is why she
says such things. She is delirious!"

Led by Lehzen and the duchess, the fluttering ladies and
maids enfolded the princess and bore her away to the boudoir to be changed and warmed and plied with sugared tea.
Perhaps a spoonful of brandy.

Jane stood against the wall. She was alone. Not even Dash
remained. Tears blurred her eyes, but they would not fall.
Her jaw ached, and she was certain it had swelled. Her hands
and feet were ice cold. She felt sick. She wanted to sit down,
but somehow she couldn't make herself move.

She had no idea how long she stayed like that, but eventually a voice spoke.

"Here, now, Miss Conroy."

Hard, competent hands steered Jane to a stool and pressed
on her shoulders until she sat down. Her own hands were
lifted and wrapped around something lusciously warm. Jane
inhaled. Tea. A mug of tea had been put into her hands. She
trembled. Someone removed her bonnet, which dangled down

her back, and pulled her dripping hair away from her face. Jane blinked and saw Lehzen looking down at her.

Are you all right? That was the question in Lehzen's eyes. Jane nodded.

Lehzen nodded in return and strode back into the boudoir, leaving Jane alone with her tea. Jane drank. The tea was painfully hot and very sweet. Her mouth burned, but at the same time, her trembling eased and tingling life returned to her hands.

Jane drank again.

She remained on her stool for a long while. Her sluggish blood quickened, and something like normal movement returned to her thoughts. A man, one of the doctors, came into the room and quickly disappeared inside the princess's boudoir. Jane heard the duchess's hysterical exclamations and the doctor's calm responses.

Jane's tongue prodded cautiously at her teeth. One—no, two—had been loosened.

Jane finished her tea. The boudoir door opened again, and the doctor emerged. For a single instant, Jane looked through the doorway, and her gaze met the princess's. In the next heartbeat, Lady Flora slammed the door shut.

Some more time passed. Jane finished her tea. She blinked at the floor, and to her shame, she realized what she wanted most right now was to curl up and fall asleep.

Perhaps she did doze some. The next thing she knew was the touch of a hand on her shoulder, and she found she was looking up at the new doctor.

"Are you all right, miss?" he asked her.

Jane nodded.

It was plain from the doctor's expression that he did not believe her. However, his only response was to shrug, as if to say that if she wished to be a fool, it was not currently his business to stop her. He left.

Voices were raised in the boudoir. The princess was once again arguing with her mother.

Of course she is.

Before Jane could think anything else, Father returned. He ignored her as he marched past and instead glowered at the closed boudoir door. Father ruled any room where he was present, but in the end he was a man of rank—not a doctor or footman or body servant. As such, he could not enter the princess's closed bedchamber.

He turned and glared down at her, angry and suspicious, as if she was the one who had arranged for the door to be shut against him. Jane found herself too tired to cringe.

"How long since the doctor left?" he asked. "What did the man say?"

Thankfully, Jane was saved from having to admit her ignorance. The boudoir door flew open, and the duchess darted out.

"Oh, Sir John!" The duchess collapsed against him and pressed her forehead to his shoulder like a small girl or . . . or . . .

Jane felt her stomach turn over. She tried to look away and instead found herself looking through the doorway into the boudoir and directly at the princess, who looked directly back at her. Jane saw her anger and her sadness. Saw the frank, open urge to break something and scream out loud.

"Go home, Jane," Father snapped.

Jane put down her empty mug. She stood carefully, making sure her legs were steady and that the room did not spin. She walked to the bell rope and rang for her maid, Betty. Betty brought her bonnet and coat, both still damp, probably ruined entirely. Jane let herself be dressed and took her reticule when Betty handed it to her.

Father watched every movement. She could feel his gaze, even when the brim of her bonnet blocked him from her view. Jane made her curtsy. Father gave no sign he regarded Jane at all. He just curled his arms protectively around the duchess and patted her back, crooning to her as if she were the child.

He had never held Jane so. Or their mother. Or her sister or her brother.

Or, or, or . . .

Jane turned and walked out the door.

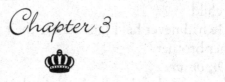

Chapter 3

The doctor, of course, had been summoned. It was not the familiar Dr. Maton who came in when the door opened, but a new man.

"Dr. Clarke, ma'am," he said as he bowed crisply, polite and businesslike. He had a frank manner about him, and when he looked her up and down, that examination was entirely objective. Victoria found herself pleased with this. Dash sniffed around his shoes and trouser cuffs and must have been satisfied, because he returned to Victoria's side without a sound.

"Where is Dr. Maton?" Victoria asked. The "medical household" attached to the palace and her family was extensive. But since she was a child, Dr. Maton had always been the one to attend her.

"Dr. Maton is ill, I'm afraid." Dr. Clarke set his bag down and brought out his watch and stethoscope. "He has been suffering from a stomach complaint. Now, if Your Highness will hold still while I take your pulse . . . Thank you. Now. If I may see the back of your head . . . Thank you." His fingers were hard and impersonal as he prodded her scalp. Victoria winced and bit the inside of her cheek to hold herself still.

"Is she fevered, Dr. Clarke?" Mama wrung her hands. "Is there cough? Oh, what will I do? What will I do?" She turned to Lady Flora, but not without a swift glance back at the doctor to see how he responded.

Dr. Clarke's demeanor did not change. Victoria decided she liked this man.

"We shall know shortly," he said. "Did Your Highness faint at all? Does Your Highness see stars now? Face me, if you please, ma'am, so I may see your eyes . . . Thank you. Will Your Highness do me the favor of standing? Of walking to the other side of the room? And back . . . Thank you. Now, I must ask if Your Highness's dresser may loosen the gown so I may observe the back and spine . . . Thank you." Again, the touch on her back was firm, impersonal, unsparing. "Yes. Yes. Is there any pain here? Perhaps here? If I may, I will listen to Your Highness's breathing . . . yes. Thank you. Your dresser may do the gown up again."

"How is my daughter?" demanded Mama. "Must she be bled? Is there fever?"

"Her Highness is very well, your grace." The doctor returned his watch to his pocket and his stethoscope to his bag. "I think we may count ourselves quite lucky, and thankful to God, for soft grass and perhaps the reputed hardness of the family heads. Ha ha. Ahem." He coughed. "I detect no sign of fever nor any obstruction of the lungs. There will be some bruising, which is likely to turn a number of alarming shades before it is finished healing. But ribs, spine, and skull are all quite sound."

"But surely she should be bled," said Mama. "Dr. Maton would recommend an ounce at least to restore the balance of the humors after such a horrible fall."

"With all due respect to Dr. Maton, I see no occasion for it. Her Highness is young and healthy and has sustained no serious hurt. She will be sore and has perhaps had a bit of a scare. That combination, in my opinion, can be beneficial for any rider."

"Any other rider, perhaps, not the heir to the British throne!" cried Mama.

Dr. Clarke bowed. "I would not presume, ma'am, to comment on the heir to the throne. My recommendation for Her Highness is plain food, plenty of rest, and a slower pace going down hills." He winked at Victoria.

"Thank you for your kind attention, Dr. Clarke." Victoria put extra warmth into her voice, which made Mama frown harder, as she had known it would.

He bowed once more. "Your Highness. Your grace. I am, of course, at your command should Her Highness have any further complaint."

Mama nodded coolly, by which Dr. Clarke understood— quite correctly—that he was dismissed. He left with as little fuss as he had arrived. Through the open door, Victoria saw Jane huddled alone on her stool with a mug of tea, staring into it, looking as if she was starved to death.

Mama gestured to Lady Flora, who immediately shut the door.

Victoria braced herself. The muscles in her back cried out as they tensed. She winced again. She couldn't help it. Mama noticed, and her eyes glittered, but Victoria could not tell whom the tears were for.

"What on earth were you thinking, Victoria?" demanded Mama in German. "Were you trying to kill yourself? To ruin me?"

"Is that all?" Victoria shot back. "Your aria has one note, Mama—What have I done to you? Will you for once listen to what happened to me!"

"I know what happened! You were disobedient, petulant. You risked your life—"

"I *saw*—"

Before she could get any further, Victoria heard another voice out in the sitting room. The words were not clear, but they all knew who it was. Sir John had returned.

Mama gave a grateful cry and ran out to meet him.

Victoria watched Mama fall against Sir John and weep on his shoulder. Her teeth ground together as his arm curled protectively about her shoulders. Victoria glared daggers at him, hoping he would see and let her go.

But Sir John's attention was elsewhere.

"Go home, Jane."

Jane made no protest. When did she ever? She simply stood and rang for the maid. Sir John watched as Betty arrived to bring her rain-dampened things. All the while, he held Mama close. Mama wept noisily, wretchedly, as if she was the one who might die. Sir John, satisfied his daughter was doing as she was told, turned his attention fully to the woman who cried her eyes out against his chest. He curled his arms protectively around Mama and patted her back, crooning to her as if she was the child.

Jane turned and walked out the door. Victoria sincerely wished she could do the same.

At last, Mama appeared to regain her strength. She pushed away from Sir John's shoulder, and he, as if indulging a delicate child, let her go.

Victoria found she could no longer remain silent. She moved to stand in the threshold between the rooms. "Sir John. Did you speak with Hornsby? What did he say?"

In that moment, Victoria realized she had made a mistake. Sir John was smiling and perfectly at ease as he answered.

"Hornsby, in fact, took me out to the place where you fell. There was nothing there, and he told me when you fell, he saw nothing at all."

Chapter 4

Mama pressed a hand against her mouth. Pain rippled up Victoria's back.

"That is not possible. I saw the man." She remembered it clearly. If she had paper and pencil, she could sketch the curve of the skull, the line of the shoulder in the rumpled black coat, the limp, unmoving hand.

"Then who was he, this man you claim you saw?" asked Sir John.

"I did not see his face."

"No." Satisfaction filled that single word. "I expect not."

"Sir John?" breathed Mama.

He faced Mama and took her hand again. "There was no dead man, your grace. It may have been a hillock, or a pile of stones, perhaps. A shadow on the grass. But there was nothing else there, and I cannot think why Her Highness continues to speak such nonsense."

"It is not nonsense!" cried Victoria. Startled, Dash barked.

"You will control that creature!" shouted Mama. "Or it will be removed!"

Victoria went cold as ice. She picked Dash up and handed him to Lehzen to take to his basket in the boudoir. When she turned back, it was to see that Sir John had laid his hand on Mama's shoulder. Together, they looked down at Victoria.

Sir John smiled.

"If your story is not a lie, then what is it?" inquired Mama.

"It is the truth," replied Victoria.

"The truth?" Mama's brows arched. Sir John did not move. He stood there, his smile never wavering, his caressing hand on Mama's shoulder. "The truth is you chose to go for a gallop after being expressly forbidden to do so. The truth is that you lost control of your horse. Then the truth is that to cover over your carelessness, you invented this outrageous story!"

"That is not how it was!"

"Then why does your groom contradict you?" inquired Mama. "Why didn't Sir John find any sign of this . . . this . . . *thing* you claim you saw? Did the dead man get up and walk away? Did he magically turn into a pile of stones?"

It was too much. Words, swollen by feeling and memory, clogged Victoria's throat. She could not answer quickly enough.

But Sir John could. Sir John always could.

"Your Highness is either lying or imagining things," he said. "Which is it?"

"I am not lying! I did not imagine it. I *saw*—"

"Victoria, stop!" Mama started forward.

"I will not—"

But Mama had her by the shoulders and shook her once, hard. "You will stop! You must stop, or you will make yourself ill!"

Sir John loomed behind Mama. He gazed down at her, entirely satisfied with their work thus far.

And they were not done.

"She cannot stop. She is incapable of controlling herself or her temper. It was inevitable that the breakdown would come sooner or later."

"But we have done everything possible." Mama leaned toward him.

"I know, I know," he breathed. "But it has always been in her."

"I am not mad!" screamed Victoria.

The words rang in the air. Sir John and Mama both faced her. Mama on the verge of tears, Sir John smiling, cold and smug. Separate individuals again.

Victoria knew her face was flushed. She felt the hot tears, harsh against her skin.

Sir John watched her cry and was so very happy.

"How are we to know?" he breathed. "When you cannot control your temper or stand upright without growing dizzy, when you talk of seeing ghosts—"

Those words froze her. "I said nothing of ghosts." *I did not. I am sure I did not.*

"You saw a dead man who was not there. What is that but a ghost? And you stand here, screaming like a banshee, insisting on the truth of a story that has already been contradicted. That is foolishness, or it is madness."

Mama dropped both hands onto Victoria's shoulders. "No. It is not so. It cannot be. I have watched. I have taken every precaution—"

"No one can blame you." Sir John spoke to her gently, lovingly, and entirely. It was as if Victoria had dissolved and was no longer there. "No one can have shown more care. It is the family taint."

"Her father showed no sign!"

"But there is her grandfather," said Sir John. "And her uncles and her aunt Sophia," he added, as if he had just thought of it, as if he had not repeated this slander a thousand times previously.

"You will stop this at once!" shouted Victoria.

But of course they did not stop. They were caught up in each other and their mutual imaginings.

Mama clasped her hands together. "What will we do? What can be done? We cannot tell the doctors! They will talk. This new man, Clarke! What will he say? We cannot know!"

Victoria felt her anger crumble as the panic burned through. Without thinking, she sought out Lehzen. Their eyes locked. She saw her governess willing her to resist the storm building inside her.

Be strong. You must be strong.

But she also saw how worried Lehzen was. Victoria suddenly felt acutely aware of how her back and head both ached. Her knees trembled.

No matter what Sir John might or might not do, she knew that she must lie down, or she would grow dizzy again. She had already shown him far too much weakness. She could not let him see her balance fail.

Victoria closed her mouth. Her back hurt, but she drew herself up. Her vision blurred from the pain. She forced herself to ignore it.

"I beg your pardon, Mama," she said. "I should not have spoken so."

Mama lifted her head and turned. Victoria arranged her features into an expression of calm regret. She dropped her gaze and made sure her hands were folded neatly before her.

You are not the only one who can play your part.

"I am tired. I believe I shall lie down a little before dinner."

She raised her eyes. She made them wide. She made herself small. Made herself the Victoria that Mama wanted to see.

"Oh, my child." Mama folded her in a close embrace. Victoria shut her eyes. "You must not frighten me like that!"

She loves me. She is afraid because he makes her afraid. She would not be so if he was not here.

Victoria shoved that thought roughly down into darkness.

Mama finally released her, and Victoria faced Sir John. Sir John frowned. He always did when she became this other thing—this little girl whom he could not fault.

"So, tell me, Your Highness . . ." His words dripped with acid mockery. "What did you see on the green?"

On the green, Sir John? What about in these rooms? I saw you strike your daughter. A weak, whey-faced creature trembling with cold and fear. You hit her so hard she was left with blood on her mouth, and her face was swollen and bruised. I know who you are, Sir John Conroy. I know what you are.

"I saw a dead man," Victoria said. "He wore a black coat and had a bald head. Then Prince shied, and I could see nothing more. Now, as I said, I am tired, and I will go lie down before I dress for dinner. Unless, Sir John, you find some reason to object to that?"

Before Sir John struck Jane, he'd had a look in his eyes, a cold calculation, as if he already knew where he would strike but needed to decide how hard. Victoria saw that same look about him now, and for a shameful moment, she wanted to hide behind her mother.

Perhaps this once even Mama saw that the scene had gone too far.

"Let her go lie down," said Mama. "She will be able to talk more sensibly after a rest."

"Very well," said Sir John. "Perhaps with rest, she will think the better of telling such an outrageous story."

Victoria turned and walked toward her boudoir. Lehzen followed and closed the door.

Chapter 5

"Miss Conroy?" bleated Betty. "Miss? Where are you going?"

"I want a walk."

Jane should have left the palace using one of the side doors in the central wing. She should have walked through the clock courtyard and out to the street, and from there made her way between the curious onlookers who always clustered about the gilt and iron gates.

Instead, despite Betty's protests, Jane had ducked out one of the many back doors and hurried down the garden's straight central path.

Betty continued to protest, but Jane ignored her. Even so, her heart was in her mouth.

What if I'm seen? What if I'm stopped?

But that was ridiculous, of course. Who cared where Jane Conroy went?

Father would care.

Jane saw him again, towering over her. Saw his hand rise up and the fingers curl into a fist.

I'm a fool. I will be in such trouble.

But she did not turn back, and no one came to stop her. She left the gravel path and struck off across the green, following roughly the same route that she and the princess had taken on horseback. Conveniently, it was also the shortest route home, as long as she chose not to worry about ruining her shoes or getting her hems dirty.

Father had taken, or been granted, a house near the palace so that he would be available whenever the duchess chose to call upon him. Or so he said. There were doubtlessly other reasons. With Father, there were always other reasons.

Jane was almost certain that one such reason was that the proximity allowed her to be dispatched home on errands—or dismissed in disgrace—without anyone having to trouble about the carriage.

The grass was damp from the latest burst of rain. Water puddled in the hollows. Wind grabbed at Jane's hems and her bonnet ribbons. The princess's general restlessness was well known, and therefore, most days Jane was dressed for the possibility of time spent out of doors. As a result, her boots had low heels and were somewhat sturdy. Her skirts were plain stuff, and her sleeves narrow cut. Her corset had been laced to allow for some freedom of movement.

The current fashion was for dramatically ballooned sleeves, a cruelly diminutive waist, and voluminous skirts. The whole was unrelentingly heavy and cumbersome, requiring as it did all manner of pads and supports to keep the fabric properly puffed. Pale pinks, blues, and sunny yellows were the colors of the day, and the whole was to be adorned with plenty of ribbons.

Such a dress, and the firmly laced corset it required, would have made it impossible to walk across the grass. As it was, Jane found herself gasping painfully as she slogged up the ridge, and stars crept into the edge of her vision. But she kept walking. Behind her, Betty huffed and groaned and threatened to tell.

What am I doing?

Jane had been struck before, of course—slapped by Mother when she wouldn't behave. Smacked across the knuckles by Cook with a wooden spoon if she was caught dipping her fingers into the cake batter, or by her governess with a wooden ruler when she did not attend properly to her lessons. Pinched on the arms and kicked in the ankles by her brother and sister for any reason or no reason at all. And, of course, Father boxed her ears and slapped her face when he was displeased.

That was simply part of life. But it had never been like this. She had never been struck so hard that she could taste the blood and feel her loosened teeth. But it wasn't the blow itself that left her so broken. It was the calculation in his eyes as his fist came down, and the disdain as he turned away.

That was what made her burn as she swallowed bitterness and salt. That was what clung to her heels now while she slogged her way across the sodden green.

It was easy to find the spot where the princess had fallen. The gouges in the turf where Prince had reared up showed clearly against the silver green of the damp meadow grass. Jane stood in the middle of the disorder and turned in a slow circle.

She saw the grass and the mud, hoofprints from the horses and footprints from people. A few wildflowers nodded their heads here and there. A cluster of round gray stones waited in a nest of weeds.

And that was all. There was no dead man in a black coat, and no sign that there had ever been such a thing.

Jane was relieved.

Jane was profoundly disappointed.

"Miss!" Betty had not followed her down the slope. She stood at the top of the rise. "I'm done, miss! I'm going straight home, and I will tell your mother what you've done!"

Mother would probably not care all that much. But if Betty made enough of a fuss, Mother might be moved to complain to Father. Jane touched her bruised jaw.

"All right, I'm coming!"

As Jane turned, her gaze caught on something—a glint in the mud that was neither a puddle nor raindrops. Jane bent down and stripped off her glove so she could dig out the object. It was a pair of gold-rimmed spectacles. The right lens was cracked, and a filthy black silk ribbon dangled from the frame.

"Now, miss!"

"Yes, Betty. All right." Jane tucked the spectacles into her bag. Now she saw something else—twin ruts in the mud, as if someone had hauled a cart to this place.

Jane turned her back and trudged up the rise. "Let's go home, Betty."

Chapter 6

The rooms Victoria and Mama had been allotted on the first floor of the palace were a closed circle that began and ended at the stone stairs. The space that was now the boudoir had once been Victoria's nursery. The moss-green paper that covered the walls had faded and thinned over the years. The carpet had once been a shade of deep emerald but was now a nameless pond-water color. The ceiling was stained with fireplace soot the way the windows were stained with dust. Only the furnishings were new and comfortable—the chairs, the chests of toys, the beds, a large one for Mama, a smaller one for Victoria, and two plain ones for Lehzen and Lady Flora.

Victoria might be sixteen years old, but Mama insisted her old dollhouse be kept out on its table. The white wooden boxes that held her dolls stood beside it.

Anyone who saw this room would think that Victoria still played with these toys. They would also look at her little bed situated next to Mama's great one and think she could not stand to sleep apart from her mother. At least they would if no one bothered to mention it was Mama who dictated this arrangement.

No one did mention it. And an alarming number of people saw this room. Mama made sure of that.

Victoria sat cautiously on the edge of her bed. The pain was everywhere. Dash left his basket and came to sit on his haunches beside her. She started to pick him up but winced.

Lehzen picked Dash up and set him on Victoria's lap. He immediately licked her face and wriggled down to make her skirts into a comfortable nest.

Lehzen sat beside them and took Victoria's hand.

"What happened to you during your ride, ma'am?"

"Just what I said."

They spoke softly, both of them angled so that they could see the door and be ready to close their mouths should the handle turn.

"Prince shied, and I fell," Victoria told her. "And there was a dead man on the green." Her voice turned pleading. "You believe me, don't you?"

"Your Highness would not lie to me," said Lehzen. She spoke without artifice and without doubt. "But is it possible—"

Something inside of Victoria snapped. "I was *not* mistaken!" *I'm sorry, I'm sorry. It's that my back hurts, and Sir John . . . and Mama . . .* "I saw what I saw. Why is it so impossible that there should be a dead man on the green? Why is everyone acting as if I said I saw—I don't know what—pink elephants singing opera?" An idea struck her. "Hornsby!"

"The groom?"

"Yes. I know what Sir John said, but that could very well be a lie. If you went to Hornsby and talked to him without Sir John to hear, he might have a different story."

Lehzen opened her mouth and closed it again.

"Will you go, please, Lehzen?" said Victoria. "It can't do any harm, can it? If Hornsby didn't see anything . . ." She paused. She petted Dash's silky back. His presence soothed her and allowed her to think more clearly. She needed to be calm now. "If he didn't see anything, then, well, perhaps I did imagine it."

But I did not. Sir John lies. He may not have even gone to talk to Hornsby at all.

Lehzen blew out a long breath. "Very well. I will see if I can go speak with him as soon as I can get away."

"Thank you, Lehzen."

"Now, ma'am, you must lie down and rest. I will make a poultice for your back. It will keep the muscles from stiffening and make it easier for you to stand straight for the dinner tonight."

"I don't think I can manage the dinner," murmured Victoria. Shame filled her, and fear.

"I'm afraid you must. If you try to beg off, your mother will say you invented this story of seeing a dead man to get out of your duties. And Sir John . . ."

Lehzen did not finish. She did not have to. They both knew what he would say. He had already said it.

It is the taint of her father's blood.

Victoria let herself be undressed and lay down on her bed. Lehzen unlaced her corset and shift to bare her back. Dash was absolutely forbidden to be on the bed, but he stretched out on the floor beside her and rolled over onto his back so she could lay her hand on his warm belly.

Victoria squeezed her eyes shut. She made herself picture the grassy slope, the gray sky, the rippling curtains of rain. Made herself remember how she pulled back the reins to slow Prince, how she felt his gait falter. She remembered that she struggled to keep her seat, to guide her horse, to look ahead for holes, for stones, and other hazards.

She remembered the world turning over. The pain and the stars. She remembered twisting around to try to sit up.

It was then she saw the black figure crumpled on the ground. It was unmistakably a man. It was not a hillock. It was not a shadow. She saw the man's head, saw the blue-gray skin through the disheveled, thinning hair. Saw the hand flung out at an unnatural angle. Saw the way the whole body seemed deflated.

I saw it. I did see it.

Except she now also saw a mound of dirt and a pile of gray stones stained green with lichen. Involuntarily, she imagined how they might lie close to each other, creating the illusion of a prostrate man.

Sir John said it could be. So, her treacherous mind now wondered how it might be, and tried to construct it. And the more she thought about it, the clearer the construction became. The memory—the true memory—began to blur, like the view beyond the dirty windows.

I must think of something else. I must not deceive myself because Sir John has lied. But . . . could he be right? If Hornsby didn't see anything—No. Sir John was not there. I was. I saw it. She squeezed her eyes more tightly closed.

Lehzen was humming and moving about the room. A warm towel, thickly plastered with herbs and goose grease, was laid on her aching back. Victoria, exhausted and lulled by the warmth and Lehzen's familiar, secure presence, felt the world begin to slip away.

I did see it. Him. I did.

She kept repeating this to herself as darkness dragged her down into sleep.

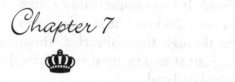

Chapter 7

"Jane? Is that you?"

Jane had hoped that once she reached home, she'd be able to run straight upstairs to the rooms she shared with her sister. Unfortunately, the door to the blue parlor was open, so Mother heard her entrance.

"Jane?"

"Yes, Mother!" Jane called back.

"What are you doing home?" called Mother. "Where's your father? Oh, do come in here. I'm too exhausted to be shouting."

Betty's smile was triumphant, and her pointed glance at Jane's muddy hems and soiled boots was positively pitying.

Betty whisked away Jane's coat, bonnet, gloves, and bag with smug efficiency, leaving Jane to bat feebly at her skirts. Her hair was surely a ruin, as well.

She told herself not to worry. Mother disliked any sort of bother, and the list of things that bothered her frequently included her younger daughter. She would make a few dismayed remarks and then let Jane go upstairs.

"Jane?"

Jane slunk into the parlor.

Somehow, Mother always managed to look like a painting. Just now, she lay back on the sofa, as prostrate as her corset permitted. A froth of ocean-blue skirts spread out all around her. Despite her seeming swoon, her hair remained fetchingly arranged, with her curls draped perfectly across one white shoulder.

Mother lifted her head just a little and opened her limpid eyes.

"Good heavens, Jane! Your face! You're swollen! And the color! Was it a beesting? Did you fall?"

"No, Mother," mumbled Jane. She was suddenly enormously tired. She was shivering again. Both her tongue and her mind felt feeble and slow.

"Well, you can't be seen like this." Mother waved one long white hand to shoo her away. "Oh! I'm too tired to deal with you. I had my card luncheon today, and you know how that always fatigues me. Get yourself upstairs. I'll send Meg to you."

Jane hesitated. "Why Meg? Where's Susan?"

Mother gave a wordless groan of frustration. "Susan has been dismissed."

"What! Why?" Jane had been counting on Susan's help, and her silence.

"She upset my best tea tray," said Mama, more to the ceiling than to Jane. "And broke every piece of china."

"Oh."

What do I do now? Jane needed help, but she could not trust Betty or Meg. And Liza . . . Liza might be willing to keep a secret, but only if it amused her.

Thankfully, Mother completely misunderstood Jane's discomfort. "Yes. It is a tremendous nuisance. Now we shall have to find another maid. But where one is to find any sort of trustworthy girl these days is beyond me. Still, what else could I have done?" Mother threw up her hands, but only for a moment, before allowing her arms to collapse delicately back against the pillows. "How I do wish we could get through one day without some sort of trouble!" Her eyes drifted closed. "Go and hide yourself, Jane. Meg will know what to do for you."

Dismissed as easily as Susan had been, Jane took herself upstairs.

It was futile to hope that the rooms set aside for her and her sister might be empty when she arrived. The sitting room was, but the door to the dressing room had been left open, so Jane could see Liza at her mirror, tying up her curls in a yellow ribbon.

Liza took after Mama. All pale pink and gold, she was the picture of the delicate English female. When they were out in company, the men's eyes, and not a few of the women's, always followed Liza.

"What are you—" began Liza. Then she, too, saw Jane's face. "Good grief, Jane! You're a mess. What did you do?"

"Nothing." Jane sank onto the sofa. Her jaw throbbed. Her head felt muzzy, and her stomach ached. She could not tell if she was hungry or simply sick. "I wanted to walk home across the green."

"Did you fall out there? Your face is a disaster! Look at yourself!" Liza, with far more than the necessary energy, ran over and thrust a hand mirror in front of Jane.

It was the first time Jane had seen herself since the blow. She could understand why her mother had asked about a beesting. Her cheek was badly swollen. Rain and cold had left her pale and pinched. Dirt smeared her cheek and mingled with the deepening blue gray of the bruise. Dark circles under her eyes added a finishing touch.

She was, in fact, just as Liza described. A disaster.

Jane handed the mirror back. She did not want it.

"And you've managed to end up with your hems and good boots an inch deep in mud," Liza went on in angry disbelief. "Well done, Jane. That was an excellent thought, taking a walk on such a day."

Jane ignored this. What, after all, was there to say? If she tried to blame Father, she would only be asked what she'd done to make him angry. She let her gaze drift to her own dressing table, which stood beside Liza's. Her reticule lay there, ready for her, should she need to retrieve something from inside.

Such as a pair of broken spectacles trailing a muddy ribbon. Jane hoped her melting relief did not show in her expression.

Liza sighed sharply. "Well, we'd better get you out of those things before Father sees you looking like that."

Father has already seen me. "Don't bother. Mother said she'd send Meg up."

"Yes, and we all know how well Mother attends to details. I am not going to spend the night with you snoring because your nose has swelled up with cold. Come along." She gestured for Jane to stand up.

While Mother truly was indolent, Liza merely played at it. Liza would complain when asked to undertake any form of exertion, but she could be remarkably brisk when it suited her. The two sisters acted as each other's dressers most days, so Liza had plenty of practice wrestling Jane out of a walking costume, even one that was unusually muddy and damp.

"What happened to Susan? Mother said she's been dismissed." Jane was curious to hear Liza's version of events. It was not that Mother would lie, exactly. But she might choose to simplify events to avoid the strain of answering questions.

"Lord, I don't know. I was out leaving a card with Mrs. Ashford, and then I went to call on Greta Schumann. By the time I got back, Mother had already sent Susan packing. She said the tea tray was upset and there was a dreadful commotion, and that was that. Susan always was clumsy and sulky. Perhaps that's why you two got on so." The insult was casual, a normal part of Liza's conversation when she was talking with Jane. "But personally, I don't think it had anything to do with the tray."

"Then what . . . ?"

"I think Mother wanted Susan out of the house before Father noticed that Ned had already paid her too much attention." Liza drew out the last word significantly.

"Do you mean she was increasing?"

"Well, if she wasn't, she would be soon."

Jane's words dried up.

It was a thing that happened. Everyone knew it. Jane herself had been pinched and handled by men at the palace. Like all the other women, she learned who to avoid and where not to walk alone.

But to find out their brother had been so careless with another person's life . . . Anger stirred. Helplessness made it stronger.

But, of course, there was nothing to be said, because there was nothing to be done.

By the time Meg arrived with the second-best tea tray, Liza had Jane out of her sodden dress. They had changed her muslin petticoat for one of flannel and, blessedly, loosened her corset stays so Jane could breathe more easily while Liza wrestled her into her plain blue house dress with the straight sleeves and white cuffs and collar.

"Leave the tea, Meg, and take these." Liza dumped Jane's discarded things into Meg's arms. "Also, I think we will need a warm compress. As you can see, Miss Jane has somehow managed to damage herself." Liza went into the sitting room and cast herself upon the chaise lounge in a fair imitation of Mother's customary fainting pose. "We'll do something with your hair in a minute. Pour the tea, Jane, would you? And tell me how things are at the palace."

Jane sat down and did as she was told. "Things are as usual. Another scene between the princess and her mother." *She says she saw a dead man on the green. She fell from her horse and might now be dying of cold and shock.*

"Well, at least all you had to do was sit and watch." Liza held out her hand, and Jane put the teacup in it. "I swear, it almost makes me want to change places with you."

Anytime you like. Jane drank her own tea. The fresh warmth was a shock to her empty stomach. "And what was so strenuous about your day?"

"If you think running Mother's errands and paying Mother's calls and writing Mother's letters—not to mention giving the orders to Cook and Mrs. Pullet because she simply cannot be bothered—is a grand way to spend your time, you're welcome to try it. No. Wait. Forget I said that." She waved her own words away as Jane opened her mouth. "You'd only make a mess of it."

Jane reached for the bread and butter, and then she froze. The sound of boots on the stairs reached them.

The door opened.

Father had arrived.

"Hullo, Father!" Liza jumped to her feet, all sunshine and smiles. She ran to him and stretched up on her tiptoes to kiss his cheek.

"Hullo, Liza." He beamed at her proudly. "That is a very pretty ribbon." He touched her curls, but he was already looking at Jane. Jane felt pinned in place—drab, small, gray.

"Your mother wants you," Father told Liza.

This was probably not true, but Liza didn't question it. None of them would. Liza kissed him again and skipped away like a much younger girl.

Father closed the door.

"Come here, Jane."

Jane stood and walked over to stand in front of him. Father cupped her chin in his calloused hand and turned her cheek toward the light. He pressed his thumb against the swelling. Her loose teeth shifted. Jane winced. She couldn't help it.

"If that swelling has not gone down by tomorrow, you will stay home," he said. "Liza can go in your place this once."

"Yes, sir."

"Now." He sat on the chaise Liza had vacated a moment before. "Tell me what you saw today on your ride."

Jane blinked. Surely, he had already satisfied himself as to what happened.

"Don't stand there like a block, girl. Tell me what you saw."

"I . . ." Bile welled in Jane's throat. She swallowed. "The princess wanted a gallop. I tried to stop her, Father. I promise I did—"

Father's eyes darkened. He did not like displays of emotion. Or, rather, he did not like displays of emotions he disagreed with. Plainly, he saw no reason for Jane to become agitated by such a simple instruction.

"I'm sorry, Father," said Jane. She tried again. "Well, I . . . she . . . Prince, rather, began to gallop away, and Hornsby went after her, and I tried to keep up, but I couldn't, and the reins kept getting muddled, and I was afraid I might fall."

Father's made an impatient sound. "And the princess went up the rise, and then Prince shied, and she fell?"

"Yes, sir."

"And that was all you saw? You have not left anything out?"

"No, sir."

"Well, that's something, anyway," he muttered. "Jane, you must do better with the princess. We all of us must do our part if we are to elevate our family to the position we are owed. This is not only for me or for your brother. You understand that when Victoria takes the crown, I am to become her personal secretary, yes?"

I understand that's what you always say.

"When that happens, you will become an official lady-in-waiting. Keep that post, keep your influence with the princess, and you will eventually make a brilliant marriage. You'll be a rich and influential woman all your life. But if you fail, if you cause *us* to fail, you will be nothing but a ridiculous spinster shut up in her rooms, like the Princess Sophia."

Princess Sophia was one of Victoria's aunts. There were six elder princesses in total, but Sophia was the only one who lived in Kensington Palace. The rest had been married off, mostly to German nobles. Nobody talked about why no husband had been found for Princess Sophia and why she had been sent away from St. James's to live in absolute retirement at Kensington.

"But we need for you to be her *friend*, not just another lady at court," Father went on. "*That* is why I let you go out with her today. To give you a greater chance to enter into her confidence. You should know this by now. You must make her trust you and your judgment. She must *depend* on you—on all of us—to act in her interests. She must come to trust us more than she trusts herself."

Father rose and went to stand in front of the window. He gazed out toward the palace, lost in daydreams and stubborn pride.

"We deserve our position, Jane. You must not ever forget that. We are not merely connected to them but bound by the closest possible ties. Her grace, the duchess, understands this. That is why she trusts me—trusts *us*—to protect her daughter from those influences that might corrupt her before she can ascend the throne."

Jane felt as if she was in the midst of a yellow fog. Distant shapes moved and shifted in the sickly vapors, and she was filled with a nagging curiosity to know what they might really be. There were whispers, too, as vague as the shadows. All of them twisted together in the uneasy depths of her dull, restless mind.

Father was looking at her, expectant. Jane realized with a jolt, she'd heard nothing of what he'd just said. Then, worse, she realized it didn't actually matter, because she knew the answer required of her.

"Yes, sir."

Father nodded. "Now I must return to the palace. I'll be home late tonight, and tomorrow morning we can judge if you are fit to be seen."

She could let him go. Her silence would be taken for obedience. He did not need to know she'd found anything on the green. She could quietly dispose of the spectacles on her own. That would be easiest and best.

"Father?"

He paused on the threshold. His grim expression warned her that his patience was at an end.

"I only tried to do right, Father."

Jane lifted her eyes to his. Her jaw throbbed. She felt suddenly aware of every part of herself—of the breath in her lungs and the beating of her heart.

Let him say he loved her.

Let him say he needed her.

Let him mean it. This once, let him mean even one word of it.

If he did, she would bring out the spectacles she had found and hand them over. He would thank her and praise her foresight and cleverness.

"Well, you must try harder." His eyes were flat and distracted. Jane knew his mind had already traveled elsewhere—back to the palace perhaps, to the duchess and the princess and his own private dreams.

Jane felt herself fade slowly back into the yellow fog. It closed over her, cradling her—cold, foul, and dangerous— and whispering in her ear.

In her mind, Jane turned and let herself listen.

Chapter 8

To call the royal household an organization was to grant it too much credit or, perhaps, too little. It was a living, breathing entity comprised of nearly a thousand souls, each with their own very particular job. Those jobs were grouped into departments and subdepartments that amounted to fiefdoms of varying sizes. The powers, privileges, and duties of the office holders in these departments had been contorted and complicated by the ever-expanding requirements of the monarchs and their families, not to mention by centuries of intrigue, failed reform, and royal whim.

For example, Louise Lehzen, now Baroness Lehzen, was nursery governess for Her Royal Highness, Princess Alexandrina Victoria. This meant she attended to the princess inside her private apartments and accompanied her on all unofficial occasions, such as her walks about the grounds.

For all official and state occasions, however, Lehzen must give way to the state governess, Lady Charlotte Florentia Clive, Duchess of Northumberland. In practical terms, this meant that Lehzen could not attend the dinner with the princess and her mother and was very much at her leisure until the evening's concert.

On such evenings, Lehzen normally stayed in the princess's apartments—mending, tidying, working at her account books and journal, or possibly stealing a moment to sit with some of the palace staff for a drink and a cozy bit of gossip.

After all, one never knew what one might hear if one simply took the time to listen.

Tonight, however, Lehzen had different business to attend to.

Once Lehzen had ceded the princess and her mother to Lady Charlotte's care, she sat down to write a very particular letter to her private friend Mrs. Martha Wilson. This she entrusted to Peter, a footman to whom she paid a sweetener so regularly it could well be considered a salary.

That done, Lehzen wrapped herself in her oldest woolen shawl and set out for the stables.

Properly, she should have taken her questions directly to the master of the horse. He had ultimate charge over the stables and all the persons who served there. There were, however, two problems with this. The first was that His Lordship was currently away in Ireland, seeing about some new breeding stock. The second was that His Lordship was very deeply in Sir John's pocket. Even if he were here and knew anything, he would be off tattling the moment she poked her nose into the stable yard.

If Lehzen was to find answers rather than betrayals, she must seek them elsewhere.

The stables had a walled yard to themselves. While it might appear to be only a short walk from the palace, this was an entirely separate neighborhood, if not a separate world. These buildings housed not only the horses and carriages but also all the works required to maintain them. Here were the barns and the grainery, the blacksmith, the farrier, the saddlery, the wheelwright's shop, the upholsterer, and a great deal else. The damp night air was thick with the smells of horses, iron, hay, dust, and ripening manure.

Like the rest of the palace buildings, the stables were made from red brick. They had been built as strong and as snug as any of the places meant for human habitation. They were also, Lehzen thought peevishly, better maintained.

This was one matter on which she and the duchess agreed. Kensington Palace was sorely neglected. That the old king, George, had kept them there was no surprise. His resentment of Princess Victoria had snapped and crackled like a halo of lightning whenever they'd been in his presence. No amount of drink or laudanum could fully dull the energy of it.

But George IV was long dead. The current king, William IV, could easily have found them better quarters or, at the very least, arranged for the palace to be repaired. But he did not. While this frustrated Lehzen, it enraged the duchess. Which was most likely the point. The duchess did not like the king, and the sentiment was more than reciprocated.

As she made her way up the gravel path, Louise felt her gaze stray to the great iron gate. Torchlight glinted on its gilded decorations. The gate hung open, so that the guests might come and go easily, and Lehzen could see the pale band of the carriage road cutting through the darkness.

For an odd, strained moment, Lehzen remembered standing in her mother's parlor a thousand miles and a thousand years ago. The window was open to the fresh breeze and the rich green smells of spring. It had been years since that same breeze carried the smell of gunpowder, but some part of Louise was still surprised by its absence.

This was the day the letter had arrived from the woman who would become the Duchess of Kent. At the time, she was still the princess of tiny, impoverished Leiningen and in need of a governess.

"Do you think I should go, Mama?" Louise had asked.

Mama was writing. Mama was always writing. Even on the days when her knuckles were swollen and her shoulder ached, she would sit in this room, laboring over some page or the other—Papa's accounts or the household's, or letters to the parents of Papa's students, reminding them of unpaid bills. Once all that was done, it would be time for her to take up her correspondence to her friends and her family.

"One should write a letter every day," she'd told Louise. "It helps organize the thoughts and reminds one of what is truly important in life. Otherwise, it all becomes nothing but a muddle."

Even when the roads were blocked by soldiers or snow, Mama wrote her letters. She would tie them into bundles with butcher's twine until they could be sent. Louise had once accompanied Mama to the postal office carrying a full year's worth of letters that she had not been able to send because of Napoleon's invasion.

"Should your mama ever decide to become a modern woman and run off from her husband, I will be informed by return of post," Papa teased.

Mama took the princess's letter and smoothed it out on her desk. She always ran her fingers down any page she read, as if it were their tips that absorbed the information rather than her eyes.

"It is a reasonable offer," said Mama. "But being a governess is a hard business, no matter how grand the family. You know that."

Louise did know. Friends had done it. Young women like her—of sound but not exceptional families, educated but not wealthy—packed their bags and climbed into carriages and coaches, heading to all points of the compass. Eventually, they returned home, bitter, frightened and, if exceptionally unlucky, pregnant. They unpacked their bags and their stories of mistreatment, overwork, and unwanted attentions.

But the bills did not care about contentment, and families still needed help. Years of war had taken the lives of so many sons, leaving only daughters to care for parents and siblings. So, the girls put out their advertisements, packed their bags, and left again.

Now it was Louise's turn.

"I will not deny the money would be useful," Mama told her. Louise's father was a schoolmaster. When times were lean or unsettled, the pupil's fees were frequently delayed or simply never arrived. Boarding pupils might have helped make up the difference, but those had been scarce of late. Families were sending their boys to larger, more prestigious schools. Papa's reputation was excellent, but families wished their boys to make connections, not merely pass exams.

If Louise went to be a governess, not only would she be earning an income, her parents would no longer have to bear the cost of her keep.

"But is it what you want, Louise?" Mama was asking her. "Our home is always yours, my heart, and we will always manage, as we always have, you know." She touched the letter again. Her hands were very bad today, the joints so swollen it looked as if there were marbles stuffed beneath her skin. "These grand houses, they are sometimes easier to get into than they are to get out of."

Oh, Mama, thought the woman who had once been Louise. *You were right. And palaces are even worse.*

And yet here she was.

And I will be damned if it is Sir John Conroy and his machinations that make me break my word. Especially now.

The princess might be subject to occasional flights of fancy, like any young lady. But not this kind. Something had happened out on the green.

The stable yard was bright with the lamplight that poured from open windows. Warm laughter rolled out into the damp night, along with the loud, cheerful talk of those who lived and worked with the snugly kept horses. This was no surprise. The barracks must be full of the drivers and outriders who had arrived with the duchess's dinner guests.

Lehzen could not help but think how Princess Victoria would have much preferred to be down here rather than in the red salon with her mother's guests.

Lehzen's personal connection with the men who served in this department was tenuous. She did not ride and, therefore, kept no horse of her own. The idea of her having her own carriage was laughable. But the groomsmen and pages had direct contact with the princess, and therefore, Lehzen took it on herself to at least know their names and something of their histories and, most importantly, to whom they answered.

The skinny page at the barracks door smelled as much of beer as he did of horses. He lolled on a pile of empty sacks, his head back and his mouth open in a loud and steady snore. Lehzen shook him by the shoulder, and when he blinked awake, she sent him scrambling to fetch the head groom, whose name was, incongruously, Arthur Saddler.

Saddler was a solid brick of a man who had worked with horses all his life. He had a keen sense of his own worth and did not stand on any ceremony, no matter who was in front of him. In fact, he was still pulling on his coat when he came out to meet her.

"Well, now, ma'am." His bow held no more respect than his greeting. "What brings you here to my doorstep?"

"I was hoping to speak with you about the groom Clyde Hornsby."

"Oh, yes? It wasn't enough that Sir John sent him packing, then? You need to come down here and *talk* about him?"

So.

Lehzen had suspected she would find that Hornsby had been dismissed. Sir John believed he played the game of politics deeply. Perhaps he did out in the wider world. But inside the palace, his play was blunt and shatteringly obvious. When somebody knew something or said something that might become inconvenient, Sir John's first move was to bribe them. If he could not bribe them, he sacked them.

"I am sent here by Her Highness personally," Lehzen told Saddler. "Princess Victoria wished it to be known she thanks Hornsby for his service. She has long said he was one of her favorite grooms, and she appreciated the care he took with her horses. If it happens that he should need a character reference, he should come to me, and I will arrange it. She also asked that Hornsby be given this." She reached into the pocket at her waist and pulled out two sovereigns. This amount was a significant portion of a groom's quarterly wage.

"One of Her Highness's favorite grooms?" Saddler gave a sharp bark of a laugh. "Not what Hornsby said. Said she called him 'Pinch-face' when she thought he couldn't hear. But as you like. I'll see he gets the message. And the money." He held out his hand.

Lehzen dropped the coins into Saddler's leathery palm. Most likely, Hornsby never would see them, but that was beside the point. Saddler's demeanor had shifted from open suspicion to burgeoning curiosity, and that was what she needed.

Saddler tucked the coins away in his waistcoat pocket. "Tell me, m'lady, why's Her Highness taking such an interest in Clyde Hornsby?"

"She fears he has been done an injustice."

"Now, that does surprise, since the great Sir John himself said Hornsby was being sacked for his insolence to her royal personage."

So.

"Sir John does not speak for Her Highness," she said.

"Somebody ought to tell Sir John that."

"It is my hope—indeed, it is my expectation—that this information will eventually be communicated to him by the appropriate persons."

Their gazes locked, and silence stretched out between them. Saddler's mouth twitched.

"Well, we shall have to put our trust in our betters, then." He bowed.

There was irony in both the tone and the gesture. Lehzen chose to ignore them.

"How did this matter unfold between Hornsby and Sir John?" she asked. "What did Sir John see when they went out to the green?"

Saddler's expression twisted, as if he was trying, and failing, to work through some particularly difficult equation. "What do you mean, when they went out to the green? They didn't go nowhere. Sir John just storms in here, bellowing for Hornsby. Doesn't even take him to one side. Gives him a dressing-down in front of God and all about his slovenly conduct and his gross insolence. Says Hornsby insulted Her Highness, told her lies to frighten her, and endangered her life with his neglect of her." Saddler stopped. "Her Highness was right. Hornsby *is* a pinch-face, but he's a good man with horses and knows his duty. He looked after Her Highness like she was his own daughter."

"I know it," said Lehzen.

"It ended in Sir John telling Hornsby to clear out. At once. With night coming on and all. Said that his things would be sent on."

Lehzen bowed her head. "I am sorry. But please believe me, Sir John's orders did not come from Her Highness or from anything Her Highness said about Hornsby's conduct."

"Then what was it?" demanded Saddler. "Because—and

you'll pardon me for speaking plain—Hornsby and the rest of my men need their jobs. Most of 'em, they ain't got friends in the palace or anyplace else. They may be shoveling shit in a stable, but it's better than starving in a ditch."

"I do understand. And if it becomes possible to help return Hornsby to his post, I will see it done."

Saddler did not entirely believe her but did not entirely doubt her, either, which was something. "Anything else you wanted? Ma'am?" he added as an afterthought.

"I have detained you long enough. Thank you."

He bowed again. There was a shade more courtesy in the gesture this time. She returned that courtesy and began the long walk back to the palace, where, she felt sure, Sir John was already waiting for her.

Chapter 9

Victoria loved music. She always had. When there was music, she could feel—feel deeply, feel truly. Not even Mama or Sir John could fault her if she sighed or if a tear escaped during an aria or concerto. But it was more than that. As long as the music played, she could set the princess aside. No matter how many people surrounded her, she, Victoria, could simply *be*.

But not tonight. Madame Dulcken's beautiful music filled the room, but Victoria could not let herself soar. It wasn't just the pain in her back and her head that kept her spirits depressed. It was the uncertainty.

Lehzen had not returned. She should have been here when the ladies filed into the pillared music room from taking their after-dinner tea, but there had been no sign of her.

Where is she? What did she learn?

Has something happened to her?

Victoria felt her brows knit. She told herself not to be ridiculous. Nothing could have happened. But the fact remained, Lehzen was not there. Neither was Sir John.

They were still missing when the men came in from their port wine and cigars, and when Madame Dulcken arrived and settled herself to play.

This, despite the beauty of Madame Dulcken's piano, kept Victoria's spirits rooted to the ground. She wanted to twist in her seat, to watch the doors. But of course she could not. Mama was right beside her. Mama's eyes might be fixed ahead, as if she were fully absorbed by Madame Dulcken's virtuosity, but she was really paying attention to the gathering itself. She was judging how Victoria—her dearest daughter, her hope, all she had in the world—was being judged by her carefully selected group of guests.

Victoria had spent hours in the red salon, sitting at the dining table. Mama had moved to each empty chair in turn and rapped out her questions.

"Who sits at the head of the table?"

"Paul III Anton, Prince Esterházy."

"And who is he?"

"Ambassador to the Court of St. James's." *And if given half a chance, a man who will talk your ear off about the intricacies of sheep farming. And, not incidentally, so happy to be flirted with by a pretty woman that he will faithfully pass on any story you choose to tell to Their Majesties.*

"And at his right hand?"

"Emily Clavering-Cowper, Countess Cowper." *Who thinks she's still eighteen and dresses accordingly. And who will be keeping those sharp eyes of hers on you and me so she can tell Lord Melbourne how we are doing, because Lord Melbourne does not entirely trust Sir John, so you want to make sure she sees us all happy and united.*

"And at her right hand?"

"Prince Johann Joseph of Liechtenstein." *And to hear him tell it, he is also the man who single-handedly won the Battle of Austerlitz against Napoleon.*

"And why is he in England?"

"He is addressing Parliament regarding the constitutional reforms being implemented in Liechtenstein." *And, incidentally, keeping one eye on us for your family in Leiningen, so you can tell him how matters stand without having to put anything on paper.*

"And at his right hand?"

"Countess Sebastiani."

"And who is she?"

The woman who writes regularly to Princess Lieven, who passes on whatever she knows to Prince Metternich and, incidentally, to Tsar Nicholas, which allows you to keep a private line of communication open. . . .

And on and on, all around the table, not once or twice, but three times. From Prince Esterházy down to Lord and Lady Cowper, to Lord and Lady Norreys, to Monsieur Van der Weyer and, at last, to tiny Aunt Sophia.

Because of her rank, Aunt Sophia would be seated at the foot of the table, although, Victoria felt sure, Mama would just as soon see her confined to her rooms with a bowl of bread and milk.

During her quizzes, Mama never asked who Princess Sophia was or what she might be doing at the table. Victoria sometimes wondered if that was a mistake.

Madame Dulcken finished the delicate concerto with an intricate, rising flourish. The audience, even those who had to be elbowed awake by their neighbors, returned enthusiastic applause and shouts of "Brava!"

"Brava!" agreed Victoria, and for once, Mama smiled approvingly. Mama was in a benevolent mood. The dinner had gone off without incident. Victoria had comported herself as expected and had correctly remembered every guest's name and position. She had made small talk. She had not frowned when served her mutton and potatoes as the richer, more elaborate dishes were handed round to the others.

Victoria stood, which allowed the guests to stand. She approached the virtuosa and said her thanks.

"I do hope you shall be able to return to play for us soon," Victoria told her.

"Indeed, Your Highness, it would be my honor and my pleasure." Madame Dulcken curtsied again.

Now that Victoria had broken the silence, the other guests could circulate. Victoria moved away so Madame Dulcken might speak to them and receive her due. Prince Johann cornered her at once, which would surprise no one as the musician was young and pretty.

Mama steered Victoria to the edge of the room. Here they would stand while the guests approached them in decorous ones and twos to make their polite remarks and better inspect their princess.

Victoria had been dressed to Mama's specifications in white silk and tulle. She had given up protesting that she should have at least some say in what she wore. If she ever tried to give directions to her dressers, Mama would simply overrule them. If she insisted on wearing some item Mama did not specifically select for her, the dress (or ribbon or pair of stockings) would then disappear from her wardrobe, never to be seen again.

Victoria imagined turning to her and saying, *Where is Sir John? Do you think he has gone out to dig a secret grave? Or did he already pay someone to have that done?*

Mama's reaction would surely be unforgettable.

Unfortunately, so would the aftermath.

Victoria did not sigh at this thought. She did not show any expression at all. She stood as she had been taught to stand, her face a gentle, perfect mask, as Mama discreetly motioned her guests forward.

Victoria was perfectly aware she was meant to remain

blind to the contradictions that filled her life. Here was one of the most glaring. Mama and Sir John would spend hours bemoaning her unfitness, her childishness, the madness that surely must simmer in her veins. At the same time, they paraded her before all manner of people to show how fit, how demure, how intelligent and engaging she was.

"Which am I?" she'd shouted at them. "Am I the shining hope of the nation or a feeble baby who cannot walk down stairs on her own? Which one?"

In return, she'd received blank stares.

But Mama was certainly not contemplating any such contradictions now. Her glittering eyes were focused on the guests. If they came forward to measure Victoria, they were each of them measured by Mama—for their taste, their wealth, their future usefulness, and their past behavior. Victoria wondered if any of them realized that.

Probably. We all know how this game is played.

Except me, of course. I am not to know that it is a game at all.

Lord and Lady Cowper approached, made their reverences, received their nod from Mama. With this, the key was turned, and Victoria the Princess was set into motion.

"Did you attend the opera much this season, Lady Cowper?" she inquired.

"Yes, indeed, ma'am. And we are very much looking forward to the opening of the new season. Grisi will be appearing. I believe Your Highness is also very fond of opera?"

"Yes, I am always delighted at the chance to hear Signora Grisi sing. I understand she will be performing Rossini's opera seria *Semiramide* for her opening, will she not?" *She wants to see if I can pronounce the Italian correctly, if I am attentive to the meaning of the opera.* "I find her interpretation of the aria 'Bel raggio lusinghier' so wonderfully delicate."

Lady Cowper proceeded to gush, lauding Victoria's taste

and education. There was no need to listen closely. She let herself focus on the room over Lady Cowper's shoulder. There was one advantage to the position Mama had chosen, Victoria realized. She could see the doors. She would know the moment Lehzen returned.

Where is she? What has happened?

All around them, the guests continued performing as expected. Prince Liechtenstein busied himself with telling Lady Norreys about Austerlitz. Monsieur Van der Weyer made a bad job of hiding his contemptuous smile as Lady Norreys tried to pretend she had not heard this story fifteen times over. Aunt Sophia tottered through the gathering, greeting everyone whether she recognized them or not, her surprisingly deep voice cutting through the decorous chatter.

"Johann! You made it. Tell me, how many times are we to hear about Austerlitz tonight? Anne! You are looking surprisingly well. And your man is still with you. Well, well. What a surprise that is!"

Mama turned just a bit paler, even as she laughed at something Lord Cowper said. The Cowpers withdrew, to be replaced by Lady Norreys.

Victoria smiled her well-rehearsed smile and spoke her lines. "I believe, Lady Norreys, that you are recently returned from Ireland?"

"Yes, indeed, Your Highness. A most interesting and informative trip. Tell me, do you form any opinion on effects of the emancipation bill?" Lady Norreys was a troublemaker. She wanted to see if Victoria dared to form any opinion at all on a law the king had signed only with great reluctance.

"My uncle, the king, pays the greatest attention to developments in Ireland as well as in the capitol, and I believe he is being most soberly advised on the current state of affairs."

The countess looked openly disappointed and quickly

withdrew. Victoria glanced toward the doors again. Her gaze caught Aunt Sophia's, and Aunt Sophia winked.

Victoria smiled.

A pinprick of pain shot up her arm. Mama pinched her. Victoria dropped her smile at once. No one noticed. Except possibly Aunt Sophia, who shook her head and turned away.

"Mr. Van der Weyer!" Aunt Sophia boomed. "How do you find yourself? We were all so sorry to hear about that business with your sister—"

Motion caught the corner of Victoria's eye. Finally, *finally*, the doors opened. But it wasn't Lehzen. Instead, Sir John slipped through.

Victoria's shoulders drooped from disappointment.

Sir John was very much in his public persona. He smiled and glided effortlessly between the milling guests until he reached her and Mama. He bowed.

"Sir John," said Mama. "You have been playing the truant this evening."

"I beg your pardon, ma'am," he said. "But there is a matter on which I must report to Her Highness."

The conversation in the room dropped to a bare murmur. Even Aunt Sophia stopped talking. He drew himself up. Victoria felt her heart thump. *What is this?* Her eyes reflexively searched the room for Lehzen, but Lehzen was not there. Whatever was about to come next, she must face it alone.

Then Sir John bowed to her, very low. "I fear, ma'am, I owe you an apology."

Chapter 10

Apologize? Victoria stared at Sir John. He remained in his deep bow, and his face, what she could see of it, was filled with contrition.

Victoria stared, frozen. *How do I answer this?* Sir John did not apologize. He blustered, he excused, he circumnavigated, but never once did he say he was sorry.

Even Mama looked startled. As for the rest of the gathering—they didn't even pretend not to hear this extraordinary declaration.

"Why, Sir John!" Mama exclaimed. "What can you possibly have done?"

"Indeed," boomed Aunt Sophia. "I can't wait to hear this." She toddled forward until she stood directly beside Mama.

This was the moment the door opened, and Lehzen slipped quietly into the room. Victoria's heart leapt into her throat. But however much she wanted to, she couldn't run to her governess or even call her over. Lehzen must take her place against the wall with the other waiting ladies and women, and Victoria must stay where she was, caught between Mama and Sir John and whatever game he was playing now.

Because it was a game. It must be. Sir John straightened and gave them all a thin smile. It was meant to look sheepish, but Victoria saw the knife-edged gleam in his eye. He was set to deliver a move he was certain would mean checkmate for her.

"I am afraid that after Her Highness informed us this morning that she had seen a corpse on the green, I did not believe her."

Victoria's heart thumped. *What is happening?* Sir John apologizing . . . and apparently accepting her story. And this after he had tried so hard to convince her she'd been imagining things.

"A corpse, Sir John!" cried Lady Cowper.

"Yes. It is shocking indeed. But, you see, Her Highness fell from her horse—"

This announcement was met with a chorus of horrified gasps, some of which might even have included genuine feeling.

"Let me say at once there is no cause for alarm," said Mama. "As you can see, Her Highness is quite well." Mama's gaze bored into Victoria's own. The message was plain. She was to do her part to reassure the assembly.

Victoria lowered her lashes and made herself murmur, "In fact, Dr. Clarke said distinctly no material harm came of it." Hopefully, her display of decorous self-effacement would soften Mama's glower. "Indeed, he commented that members of our family in general are blessed with sturdy constitutions and hard heads."

The laughter was general and nervous. The guests, clearly, were not certain it was correct to appear amused at such a joke.

"I cannot count the number of spills I took as a girl," remarked Lady Cowper. "I was quite the despair of my parents."

"That one can readily believe," quipped Mama. The party laughed again, much more heartily this time—all except for Lady Cowper and Victoria herself, who felt her cheeks coloring as she blushed for Mama.

Aunt Sophia didn't laugh. She kept her watery eyes fixed on Sir John. "Do continue, Sir John. We are all on pins and needles to hear what has happened!"

"When the princess was returned to the palace, she told us that she had seen a dead man on the green and that was what had startled her horse." He paused to allow for another collective gasp and a ripple of murmurs. *Just like an actor on the stage.* "Having experience with my own daughters and the . . . energetic imaginations of young ladies, I have to admit I doubted that this could be true. I was wrong, Your Highness, and I ask that you accept my apology." He bowed yet again.

Mama looked set to speak, to turn away from Sir John and the whole of this conversation. But Victoria spoke up first.

"And what has happened to change your mind, Sir John?"

"I spoke with the head groundskeeper," he told her, told the whole room, really. "I learned that Your Highness had unfortunately happened upon a simple, everyday tragedy. The man you saw was one of the under-gardeners. He had been walking home to his supper. He was quite elderly, and it seems his heart gave out."

Various pious murmurings filled the air. Victoria found herself looking very hard at Sir John. He appeared relaxed and confident, as he generally was when he was sure of his audience and his subject.

Could he be telling the truth?

"The poor man," Mama was saying. "We shall remember him tonight in our prayers."

"Yes, of course," said Victoria gravely.

"Ridiculous!" snapped Aunt Sophia.

"I beg your pardon?" Mama's words were pure ice.

"There is no dead gardener. I would have known. You are making up a story, Sir John. What on earth do you mean by it?" She reached up with her ivory fan and slapped him hard across the arm.

The entire gathering had gone silent. Mama's face was paper white. And yet no one moved. There was no protocol for this, no person of rank sufficient to intervene with the princess.

Except one.

"You are right, of course, Aunt Sophia." Victoria stepped forward and slipped her arm through her aunt's. "And I am sure that as soon as the steward has looked into the matter, he will come see you at once, and everything will be cleared up. I'm surprised at you, Sir John," she added with a delicate frown. "That you should come here before you had all the facts in hand and disturb Her Highness so."

Sir John's face remained bland, but behind his blue eyes, anger boiled.

"I do apologize, ma'am," he said to Aunt Sophia. "It was only that I was in a hurry to correct my previous error."

"I hope Your Highness may find all her advisers so diligent," said Lady Cowper.

Victoria smiled politely. "It has gotten late. We should retire, do you not think, Aunt? Mama?"

"Yes, indeed." Mama gestured for Sophia's anxious maid to come forward. "Lady Charlotte, Lehzen, Her Highness will retire."

As Aunt Sophia was led away by her own attendants, the whole gathering made their reverences. Victoria saw how the guests' eyes gleamed with pity for Princess Sophia and with greed at how they would have so much to tell all their friends. But she saw something else, as well. As Aunt Sophia turned away, Victoria caught a glimpse of a swift, satisfied smile on the old woman's face

What just happened here?

Victoria let herself be walked away, with Lehzen beside her and her other ladies and maids behind. Mama would stay behind and close the gathering and try to ensure that the gossip and news were steered in the proper direction.

With Sir John's able assistance, of course.

When the doors were closed, Victoria squeezed Lehzen's hand, and Lehzen squeezed hers in return, signaling she understood. They might be leaving the party, but their evening was not yet done.

Because of the music party, all the rooms in this wing of the palace were well lit. Lamps and candles and footmen had all been stationed at regular intervals. Victoria swept past until they reached the stone stairs. There Victoria paused. "I believe I should like to go say good night to Aunt Sophia," she told Lehzen. "It may help settle her mind."

"An excellent idea, ma'am," agreed Lehzen at once. "Lady Charlotte, might I suggest that you take the women to Her Highness's rooms and make sure all is in readiness? Perhaps some hot milk would be in order?"

Lady Charlotte did not like Aunt Sophia, so she was perfectly ready to accept any excuse to avoid such a visit. "An excellent idea, ma'am." She made her curtsy and her escape, taking the remainder of the maids and waiting women with her.

With no one now to see, Lehzen let go of Victoria's hand. Freed, Victoria ran up the stone stairs, her slippers making fluttering echoes against the walls.

Uncle Sussex and Aunt Sophia both resided in the farthest wing of the palace. There was no proper corridor between their apartments and Victoria's, only a long, straight succession of doors that opened between unused chambers.

Drafts curled across the bare floorboards. No guests were expected here, only the family, so these rooms had not been lit. All the windows were shuttered, allowing just the faintest smear of moonlight to shine on the floorboards. The only other light was from the lamp Lehzen carried. The patter of their slippers combined with the soft scratching of the mice and other vermin that lived in the walls.

Safe in these thick, rustling shadows, Victoria asked, "What kept you so long, Lehzen? What did you learn at the stables?"

"Very little. By the time I was able to speak with Mr. Saddler, Sir John had already dismissed your groom Hornsby."

"Dismissed him! Why?"

"He said it was for insolence toward Your Highness."

"Ridiculous," snapped Victoria.

Lehzen's silence said that she agreed on this point.

"You heard Sir John's story?" Victoria asked. "That it was an elderly gardener I saw? That the man had been walking home, and his heart failed him?"

This time, Lehzen's silence was less easy to read. The lamp threw more shadows than light across her face and hid her expression.

"I do not believe it," Victoria told her.

"I dare say," muttered Lehzen.

"Don't tell me you do believe?"

Lehzen shook her head. "I lost my ability to believe Sir John long ago." Her attention seemed to drift to the darkness around them, as if she sensed something looming just beyond the circle of lamplight. "Ma'am," she said. "Why are you doing this?"

"I want to talk to Aunt Sophia," Victoria said, deliberately misunderstanding Lehzen's meaning. "She knows more than she lets on, and there was something behind her scene in the music room, and I want to know what it is."

Lehzen did not look happy about this, but neither did she argue. She simply said, "Yes, ma'am," and held the lamp higher so Victoria could see her way.

Chapter 11

Aunt Sophia's apartments were very much like the princess herself—out of date, threadbare, and perpetually befuddled. The furniture was all higgledy-piggledy. The ornaments and pictures were constantly being rearranged according to some scheme that Sophia could never quite finish to her satisfaction. Sewing boxes with their tops open and their threads hanging over the sides rested on footstools and chairs. A spinning wheel stood sentry between Sophia and the hearth. It was a rainy day, but it was still summer, and the rooms were warm and stuffy, so no fire had been lit.

When Victoria and Lehzen were let in, Aunt Sophia was bent near double over her prayer book. But she was not alone. When the door opened, Uncle Sussex turned away from his contemplation of the empty hearth.

"Victoria!" he cried. "Shouldn't you be in bed, my child?"

Uncle Sussex was a tall, round-faced man. Like most of his brothers, he possessed an ample belly and stooped shoulders. His hair was so white he joked he would have no need of powder, even if that was still the fashion. He was often shabby, preferring to wander about the palace in an old coat, threadbare breeches, and slippers that Victoria felt sure were older than she was.

Mama did not often let Victoria visit her uncle's rooms, but Victoria always found them a kind of wonderland. Where Aunt Sophia indulged herself in knickknacks, prayer, and needlework, Uncle Sussex collected books. His shelves were lined with ancient volumes, and more were stacked on the tables, even piled on chairs. Any surface not covered in books was filled with antiquities of all sorts, but primarily clocks. One of Victoria's dearest possessions was a Christmas gift Uncle Sussex had given her—a tiny gilt clock with a dancing bear that came out to strike the hour.

Somewhere on the Continent, Uncle Sussex had a wife and a pair of children. The marriage, however, had been declared illegal and the children illegitimate, because Uncle Sussex had not gotten the king's (and Parliament's) approval before he took the lady to church. Unlike his brother King William, however, Uncle Sussex had never remarried. Instead, he had let himself be moved into Kensington Palace, choosing exile from court over his place in the line of succession. It was impractical and romantic, and Victoria had always liked him better for it.

"Hello, Uncle." Victoria turned her cheek up so Uncle Sussex could kiss her. Lehzen retired to a place beside the door, along with Aunt Sophia's waiting woman and Uncle Sussex's man. "I wanted to say good night, Aunt Sophia."

"That was very kind of you." Aunt Sophia closed her book. She wore her massive spectacles, which made her look perpetually goggle-eyed. "She is a good girl, is she not, Sussex?"

"As she has always been," he said fondly.

Victoria took her aunt's hand. "I was worried that you might be ill after—"

"After that little scene I made at your concert?" said Sophia. "Yes, well, I can understand your feeling that way. I confess, I behaved very badly, even if it was only to Sir John."

Victoria's skin prickled. She did not like this swing into cheery calm.

"It seems, though, that you are well now?" Victoria pressed her hand.

Aunt Sophia glanced at her brother before answering. "A little prayer and reflection was what was needed," she said. "That, and a dose of my brother's good sense."

Uncle Sussex chuckled. "I'm afraid good sense is not an attribute many would accuse me of possessing."

"That is because they do not understand you as I do."

They were smiling at each other, but the expression did not reach their eyes. Victoria watched them, aware of a tension in the air and also of a kind of silent communication.

"Aunt, why did you say Sir John's story was impossible?" Victoria asked her. "That it could not really be a gardener out on the green?"

"Caprice," answered her aunt promptly. "I admit it. I was bored, and some little imp got into my brain." She shrugged. "Being old as I am is rather like being a young girl again. Sometimes one does things just to do them."

Victoria regarded her aunt for a long moment. But Aunt Sophia was very practiced in the art of waiting and showed no impatience with the silence. If anyone seemed restless, it was Uncle Sussex.

And Lehzen. She wanted to leave this room now. Victoria swallowed. Something was wrong—with her aunt, with her uncle, with her governess.

And I cannot tell what it is.

"I am glad you are well, Aunt," said Victoria out loud. "I will wish you good night."

"Give me a kiss, Vickelchen." Aunt Sophia used the cheerful nickname bestowed on Victoria by her German-speaking family.

Victoria bent and kissed her cheek. Aunt Sophia patted her shoulder. "Such a good girl, is she not, Sussex?" she said, as if she did not know she'd said the same thing just a moment ago.

Uncle Sussex beamed. "All I could wish in a daughter of mine."

Of course, Uncle Sussex did have a daughter, somewhere. Did he ever see her? Or even write to her? What about his son?

"I'll say good night, as well, sister." Uncle Sussex kissed Aunt Sophia's cheek, as well. "Come along, Victoria." His waiting man picked up a lamp and opened the door so Uncle Sussex could shepherd Victoria and Lehzen back out into the dark.

"I trust you'll forgive Sophia, Vickelchen," said her uncle once the door was closed behind them. "She didn't mean to cause trouble. She just . . . wandered a little far afield tonight."

Victoria stood in front of him, in a circle of lamplight, in the middle of a palace filled with darkness and tried to understand him. This was a simple man, a sad man. That was the uncle she had always known. But now she glimpsed something more hidden behind his benign demeanor, and she could not comprehend it. She knew instinctively, however, that she did not like it.

"Uncle," she said carefully, "if there was something I needed to know about Aunt Sophia or anything else, you would tell me, would you not? We are family."

Uncle Sussex spread his hands. They were badly discolored with inks and dust. "What could I know, Victoria? I am a doddering old fool, sequestered away from the world with his clocks and his books." He smiled again, as kind as ever, but his eyes remained distant.

Victoria felt her heart break.

"Well, good night, Uncle."

"Good night, my girl." He gave her a furtive smile and turned away, then strode quickly through the long line of doorways, following his waiting gentleman and the lamplight.

Victoria said nothing as she brushed past Lehzen, heading in the opposite direction, back down to her own rooms. Back through the shadows that would wrap her up and hide her from prying eyes.

Lehzen followed, holding the lamp up high.

"I don't believe her," said Victoria. Her words sounded dull and harsh in the empty rooms. The doorways seemed to make an endless tunnel from nowhere to nowhere. "But why would Aunt Sophia lie? Especially when she made such a scene, telling Sir John it could not possibly have been a gardener I saw."

Lehzen was silent. She walked stiffly to keep the lamplight steady.

"She knows something," insisted Victoria. "She said something to my uncle."

Silence. Silence and footfalls and the hiss of the lamp burning and the soft scratching in the walls.

"How can we find out what it was? What can we do?" *Answer me, Lehzen. Please.*

"I do not think you should do anything," said Lehzen.

They had reached the stone stairs again. One flight down waited her apartments, waited the lights and all her waiting women and Mama. Victoria felt exposed. There was only a thin railing between her and the long, straight drop down the empty stairwell.

"Ma'am, you must understand," said Lehzen. "If you

continue to ask questions about . . . about whatever it is that you saw, it can only lead to more arguments with your mother. This will give Sir John more and stronger criticisms of your behavior and temperament. Ones he can take to the Kensington Board."

The Kensington Board was a committee of men—lords and members of Parliament—who oversaw Victoria's household and Victoria herself. Sir John reported to them on a regular basis.

"I do not think that would be good for Your Highness," Lehzen concluded. "Especially now."

Victoria felt her brow furrow. "Why now?"

"That was what delayed me from coming to you this evening." Lehzen paused. The silence pressed closer. "I was waiting for an answer to a note I had sent to my friend Mrs. Wilson."

Victoria frowned, confused and not a little frightened. Mrs. Wilson attended Queen Adelaide. She served as a channel for news from St. James's Palace, one that could not be diverted by Mama or Sir John.

"She, Mrs. Wilson, had previously communicated to me some . . . stirrings concerning you," Lehzen went on. "I wanted to confirm them so you might better be able to judge how to approach the next few days."

"Stirrings?" echoed Victoria. "What sort of stirrings?"

Lehzen paused again. She was listening and looking down the stairwell, alert for any movement. All remained still. Nonetheless, she moved closer to Victoria and dropped her voice to the lightest whisper.

"Their Majesties are talking about your future. Queen Adelaide has been pressing the case to His Majesty that as you are now sixteen, you should have your own household. One in keeping with your status as a young lady and heir to the throne. One which Their Majesties and Parliament organize."

Victoria felt her mouth go dry. "Would that mean . . . ?"

"That would mean that the queen would choose your staff and your attendants," said Lehzen. "And they would most certainly not include Sir John."

Victoria could barely speak the next words. "And Mama?"

"That would be up to you—"

She could not finish. Down the stairs, a door flew open, and light burst onto them.

"There you are! What is the meaning of this!"

Mama. Mama still in her evening gown, but with her hair in disarray. She grabbed up her hems and climbed up the stairs, puffing and red in the face. Two footmen with lanterns raced behind to light her path. She looked ridiculous, but she also looked dangerous.

"I'm sorry, Mama," said Victoria. "I only wanted to—"

"To frighten me half to death!" Mama grabbed her elbow, pinching her hard. "To go skipping off through the palace, playing hide-and-seek like a naughty little girl and giving no thought to how I would feel when I got back and found your rooms entirely empty!"

"Mama, Lady Charlotte was there—"

"Lady Charlotte was *not* there. No one was there!"

Lehzen opened her mouth and closed it again. After all, what could she say? That she'd sent Lady Charlotte on ahead so she and Victoria could talk secretly?

"I just wanted to say good night to Aunt Sophia and make sure she was feeling better," said Victoria. "We were on our way back. I had thought you would be staying with the guests for a while—"

"You mean you thought I would not catch you out!" Mama's fingers pinched tighter. "What do you mean, Lehzen, encouraging this behavior! No, no, don't bother. I cannot bear to listen to any more of this." She snatched Victoria's hand and began to pull her behind as she started down the stairs.

"Let go, Mama! I can walk by myself! I am sixteen!"

"Sixteen, but only the size of a girl half your age!" Mama spoke to the stairs, to the walls, to the empty air, pouring out her rage to the palace itselft. "What if you should fall? What if someone bent on our ruin should come to push you out a window or down the stairs? Alone in the dark here. The gates were open for hours! Anyone might have gotten inside!"

And so Victoria's hand must be held, and Mama—enumerating every possible danger, all of Victoria's ingratitudes and reckless acts—must haul her from room to room all the way back to her boudoir so she could be locked safely inside.

It had been a long time since Victoria had seen Mama in such a rage. She thought again about Sir John's story of the gardener, about Aunt Sophia's little "caprice."

She also thought about what Lehzen had said—that she might finally be given her own household.

That would mean that the queen would choose your staff and attendants. And they would most certainly not include Sir John.

And Mama?

That would be up to you—

And she listened to Mama's scolding and endless list of dangers. Mama who knew everything, who should have been down with her guests, who had friends inside St. James's Palace, just as Lehzen did.

And Mama?

That would be up to you—

And Victoria wondered what it was that truly frightened her.

Chapter 12

Victoria was not surprised that the ghosts came to her that night. With the day she'd had, and all its revelations and up-endings, how could they fail to rise?

Kensington Palace was haunted. Victoria had always known this. She had begun to see the ghosts when she was still a child. Even then she'd known they could not possibly be real, but she'd seen them nonetheless.

It began as it always did, with Victoria opening her eyes to darkness. Was she awake or only dreaming? She never knew. She stood. She walked. She felt the carpets under the soles of her stockinged feet, felt the palace's eternal drafts across the backs of her hands. But no one stirred as she passed their beds, not Mama, not even Lehzen.

Did she open the doors? She must have, because she was at the top of the stone stairs or in the queen's wing or in the clock yard, walking. She would turn a corner or descend a stair or step into a patch of moonlight, and there she would be, that other queen.

Elizabeth was easy to recognize by her bright red hair and

her heavy gown. Mary Tudor showed herself sometimes, as well—small and gaunt, dressed in black like a widow, with her bony hand held before her eyes, as if she could not bear to see what was to come. Little Lady Jane was most often found huddling in a corner, as if she could hide from her approaching doom.

None of them had ever lived in this house, but it didn't matter. They were here because she was here. They haunted Victoria because she was one of them.

There was one pair who walked arm in arm, holding tight, as if they could not bear to let go of each other. This was Mary Stuart and her sister Anne.

There were others whom she did not recognize and who were not to be found in any portrait in the galleries. One sturdy, pale girl with dark waving hair, who pressed both hands against the wall, as if she meant to shove her way straight through it, her mouth open in a silent scream. And the other one—painfully thin, with her fair hair cropped so short, Victoria at first thought this shadow must be a boy. Later, when Victoria saw her bent over, weeping and retching, Victoria realized she was simply horribly ill, perhaps even dying.

Victoria understood them, all these other shadows of women and girls. She knew what they were doing. They were crying, screaming, trying desperately to void themselves of their unbearable feelings before someone could see. Before someone could scold or judge or—worse, infinitely worse—make use of that little bit of weakness.

She wondered if one day, one of them might come across some dream shard of Victoria, huddled in a dark corner, tears spilling down her cheeks, terrified that Mother, that Conroy, that anyone at all would see her crying.

Tonight, though, Victoria walked only as far as her dressing room. She stood in front of her white and gilt table and stared into the darkened mirror.

Inside, she saw the dark paneled rooms of the queen's wing. Saw a tiny, pale young woman. It was Jane Grey, the girl who had worn the crown for just nine days before she was toppled and beheaded. Lady Jane stood with her forehead pressed against the wall, bowed over a prayer book she clutched in both hands. Her mouth moved.

Help me.

Victoria reached toward her, but she was too far away.

Save me.

Hot tears spilled down Jane Grey's cheeks and down Victoria's cheeks.

Please, begged Lady Jane. *They will take me away.*

"Come away, ma'am."

They will lock me up. Please.

"Please."

And Victoria was herself, was standing in front of her dressing table, was in her nightgown and stockings. Lehzen stood over her, her face drawn tight with worry.

"I—"

Lehzen embraced her, pulling her close, as if she was nothing more than a girl who had had a bad dream. Victoria let herself be held, let herself be returned to her bed and tucked in. When Lehzen told her to close her eyes, she obeyed. But she still heard Lady Jane.

Please. They will take me away.

Please.

It was a very long time before Victoria was able to fall asleep.

Chapter 13

Jane and Liza were both woken at half seven by a flustered Betty. "Your father sent word from the palace, Miss Jane. He wants you ready to go by nine o'clock. He's going to come fetch you himself."

"Himself?" Liza peered out from under her covers. "Why would he do that?"

"He didn't say, at least not to me. Up you come, miss." Betty drew back Jane's covers.

Liza studied Jane as if she were some complete stranger plopped in the middle of the boudoir. "Well, it looks as though you're going to have an interesting day."

Jane said nothing. She was afraid her voice might shake.

Liza groaned and kicked her way out of her bed. "Let's see that face."

Jane obediently turned toward her. Liza prodded at her bruised cheek. "Much better. We can risk a little powder to damp down the bruise, and you'll be just fine."

"You just don't want Father changing his mind and dragging you off to the palace instead," muttered Jane.

"Clever girl. Now, stand there." Liza hauled Jane out of the bed and shoved her into position in front of the long mirror. "And let's see what can be done."

With Betty's help, Liza did Jane up in pale green silk with an acceptable amount of puff to the sleeve and an acceptably tight waist. Then she selected a pair of not entirely impractical green slippers.

"Keep her boots hidden, Betty," warned Liza. "Otherwise, she might be tempted to go gallivanting off again." Jane pulled a face at her sister.

"I'll have the pink reticule today, Betty," she said.

"But, miss, it won't go with the rest."

"I'll have it, anyway."

Betty looked to Liza, who rolled her eyes. "Oh, let her have her way. I'm hungry, and if she fusses, we won't get downstairs until everything's gone stone cold."

Jane had the distinct feeling that what Liza really wanted was extra time to quiz her on what was happening inside the palace, but if that was her aim, she was doomed to disappointment. When the sisters reached the breakfast room, they found it already occupied by their older brother, Ned.

Generally speaking, Ned looked like a younger version of Father—dark, curling hair, blue eyes, and pale Irish complexion. But something had been lost in the translation. The looks that on Father combined to create charm and authority seemed mismatched on Ned. His brow was too high, and his nose too long. His hands dangled awkwardly at the end of his thin arms, and his legs had no calves. Liza called him Matchsticks, and Jane had to admit it was an apt name.

Their brother had gone to school and on the grand tour. There he had accomplished nothing as far as Jane could tell and had come back. He'd gone into the army as a lieutenant and come back. Then he'd gone to Brussels as a ministerial attaché and come back.

Now he was a determined presence at local social events and had a large circle of acquaintance. Every so often, Father called him into the study, and they talked, or probably Father talked. Then Ned would go away for some days or weeks and come back, and all would go on as before.

"You're up early, Ned." Liza helped herself to a fillet of sole from the sideboard.

"Don't I know it." There were circles under Ned's bloodshot eyes, and the dark, viscous concoction in front of him was like nothing to be found among the platters and chafing dishes Mrs. Pullet had set up on the sideboard.

"So what brings about this extraordinary behavior?" Liza drew herself a cup of coffee and sat down next to him.

"Walters and I are going to look at a horse he has his eye on."

"For buying or betting?" inquired Liza.

"Both, probably." Ned held his nose and downed half of the potion in his glass.

Father believed that a man should keep a generous table, and Mother complied, or rather, Mother ordered the housekeeper, Mrs. Pullet, to order Cook to comply. It was an area in which Jane was unambiguously grateful to her father. Breakfast was the only meal she had at home where she could eat what she liked without Mother sighing over her unladylike appetite.

This morning, however, Jane looked at the array of eggs, kedgeree, fish, kidneys, and mutton chops, and her stomach roiled.

She sat down at the table and took some toast from the rack. Her brother looked down at his potion, grimaced, and took another swallow. Jane thought about how Susan was no longer part of the household, how not one of them knew where she might be or what might happen to her next without a reference or firm prospects, and how that was his doing.

"Susan's been dismissed, Ned," said Jane.

"I'd noticed. I told Mother she shouldn't have done it, not over something so small, but you know how Mother gets." He looked green around the gills, but he still drank off the second half of the beverage. "Get me some coffee, won't you?"

"That's all you did?" asked Jane.

"Leave it, Jane," said Liza. "It doesn't matter."

"What else should I have done?" Seeing no one was going to obey his orders, Ned got to his feet and slouched to the coffee urn. "What are you even talking about?"

"As if you don't know," muttered Jane.

"As it happens, I have no idea."

Jane forced herself to swallow her toast. She couldn't look at Ned just now, so she turned to her sister. "Liza. That book Aunt Cathleen sent you, with the etchings of the country-side in County Clare . . . Do you know where it is?"

"What do you want with that thing?" Liza's question was unusually sharp. Clearly, it was beginning to dawn on her that something had shifted in Jane's manner, and she did not trust it.

Jane suppressed a shiver and took another bite of toast to cover her discomfort. "The princess is reading Irish his-tory," Jane mumbled. "I thought she might be interested in seeing it."

"An excellent thought."

Father stood at the room's threshold. Liza, Ned, and Jane all stood up, just as they had been taught to do as children. He ignored them. Or, rather, he ignored Ned and Liza.

"Are you ready to go, Jane?"

"I thought—" she began, but he was already frowning. "Yes, of course." She hadn't even had time to finish her toast, but of course she could not keep Father waiting.

Liza fetched Aunt Cathleen's book while Betty bundled

Jane into coat and bonnet. And handed her the pink reticule. Jane bit her lip hard to keep from showing the relief she felt.

The carriage was waiting. Jane was glad to be driven today, although it meant being closeted with Father. The morning was already warm and damp. With the sun shining through the haze, the day promised to be hot and close.

Papa drew back the curtains and gave orders for the coachman to walk on.

Jane folded her gloved hands over her book and did her best to keep her eyes fastened on them. She tried not to look at the reticule on the seat beside her. She'd had no chance to look inside to see if the spectacles were still in there. Betty or another maid, perhaps Meg, might have gone through her bag, looking for crumpled handkerchiefs or dirty gloves in need of laundering. They might have seen the strange object with its muddy ribbon and removed it.

Jane knew Father was watching her. She felt it in the way her skin prickled under her cuffs and in the way her jaw burned.

Oddly, she thought about the princess then and the way she could shout her disapproval to the world. The princess did not look for a fight. She demanded one.

Why am I thinking about that now?

"There is something you need to know, Jane. A story you will hear today."

Jane was jolted out of her thoughts. Her gaze—guilty, frightened—flickered to her bag lying on the seat beside her and then widened in horror, in case Father had noticed.

But he had turned away from her to contemplate the world outside the window.

"The man that the princess saw yesterday when she fell off her horse was a gardener who had died on his way home."

But you said there was no corpse. You said it was her imagination yesterday. Why is it not her imagination today?

"Oh." Jane concentrated on keeping the slump of disappointment out of her shoulders. She thought she'd been clever. She thought she'd found out something that would actually put the lie to one of Father's stories. But as usual, he remained one step ahead.

"There will surely be rumors spread about what happened during your ride yesterday and about the identity of the corpse, which, by the way, has been returned to the family," said Father. "It will be your duty to help contradict any such stories you hear and supply the true facts. Do you understand?"

"Yes, sir."

"And you will tell me anything the princess has to say about the matter. Anything and everything."

"Yes, sir." Saying those words was easy as breathing. Which was a good thing, because disappointment had swamped her thoughts. Had a more thoughtful response been required, Jane was not sure she could have supplied it.

"Now, let me see that book."

Jane handed it over. Father turned over the pages, leaving her a moment to sit with the knowledge that she was, in fact, useless and foolish.

A gardener. An accident. That was all. And Father knew, and the princess knew. She had thought for a moment that just once, she had a secret of her own that she could use for . . . something. Anything.

"This was a very good thought," he said, indicating the book. "You should do more little things like this. The princess loves such attentions."

The princess did not. The princess saw straight through them. But Jane had wanted some excuse to sit with her, so they could talk without being overheard.

"It is important you stay close to her today," Father continued. "She must not be left alone."

"She is never alone." That was the point of the Kensington system. Or one of its points.

He handed the book back, and as he did, he finally looked at her. "I will also need you to pay special attention to the duchess today."

"The . . . the duchess?"

Father nodded. "This business with the dead man has her grace jumping at shadows. I must know if her fears are driving her to any . . . rash decisions. Like saying she wants to cancel next month's tour, to keep the princess safe at home."

"But you will be there?" *You are always there.*

"As much as I can, but I also need to speak with the Kensington board and the clerk of accounts. Just to head off any of those rumors." He leaned forward and took both her hands.

"I need you today, Jane," he said softly. "I am trusting you."

Jane's breath stopped. Her father pressed her hands and leaned back.

"I know how painful it is for us to have to constantly dance attendance on . . . the family, without the fullness of our rank and connections being acknowledged. And I know you have been made impatient by this state of affairs. I understand that. I feel it keenly. But I ask you to be my eyes and ears today." He chuckled. "More so than usual, that is."

Jane sat in a state of utter bewilderment. *What is this? What's happening?*

Father was asking for her help. He couldn't possibly mean it. Father did not ask her things. He ordered. He demanded. He insisted. She stared at her own hands, which he'd pressed with affection just a moment before. Her cheeks burned with a flood of confusion and embarrassment.

And something else. There was an odd thrill inside her. "I need you today, Jane," he said. "I am trusting you."

Part of her believed him, or at least wanted to. Because if he trusted her, if he needed her, it might mean that somewhere, somehow, in the depths of his heart, he did, in fact, love her.

Jane felt her mouth flutter into a tiny smile.

"I . . . I'll do my best."

"I know you will, Jane. I *know* it." He was smiling at her now, and that smile shone in his blue eyes. Her father was looking on her with approval. With admiration even.

And despite every other disappointment, despite the whispers from the fog in the back of her mind, Jane wanted to stay in this place of warmth and light.

It is not love, murmured those treacherous voices. *Not really.* But another part of her found she did not care.

Do not trust him. Everything he's giving you now, he'll take it away again. You know he will.

Except this once, she had the means to keep his regard. All she had to do was open her mouth and tell him what she knew, what she'd found and kept.

"Father?"

"Yes, Jane?"

Her throat tightened. She swallowed, and the movement in her throat made her jaw ache where his blow had landed.

Perhaps this was what determined all the things that happened next. Jane would never know what imp or presentiment took hold of her in that single moment.

"Nothing," she said, and she turned her face away.

Chapter 14

That morning, Mama was in a foul mood.

Victoria was not surprised by this any more than she was surprised by the appearance of her ghosts the night before. It was, after all, her fault for being caught out in the stairway when she should have been safe in the boudoir. And she acknowledged that. To make up for it, she attempted to be a model of obedience. She held perfectly still while being dressed and having her hair done. She ate only a tiny bit at breakfast. She made a decorously sentimental sketch of Dash in his basket, nothing that could be even mildly construed as rebellious.

Or interesting. She then felt obliged to ruffle Dash's ears to show that she did not mean he was not interesting.

When Sir John arrived, with Jane trailing nervously in his wake, Victoria smiled politely.

"Good morning, Sir John. Good morning, Jane. What have you there?"

Jane clutched the book she was carrying like it was the only thing holding her upright. Sir John beamed down at his daughter. Victoria shivered at the power and the poison in his expression.

"A . . . book, ma'am," Jane stammered. "Some etchings of Ireland. I thought — "

Lord. She'll look at her father now to see if it is all right to think anything at all.

But this once Victoria saw she was mistaken. Jane did not look to Sir John. She met Victoria's own gaze. In fact, Jane was staring hard, as if willing her to understand . . . something.

"Jane thought that as you are reading Irish history, ma'am, you would be interested in seeing something of the country." Sir John sounded for all the world as if he was describing a dog who had just done a particularly clever trick.

"How very thoughtful," said Mama. "Is it not, Victoria?"

Victoria kept her gaze on Jane's. "I look forward to seeing what she's brought."

Jane let out a long breath, and her father shooed her to her usual corner.

An unfamiliar and distracting curiosity bubbled up inside Victoria. But, of course, it was not possible to talk with Jane now. It was time for lessons, and the system demanded she attend only to her tutors.

It will turn out to be nothing, she assured herself as she opened her grammar book. *Jane has always been her father's puppet. What could she possibly have to say that he hasn't put into her mouth?*

But Jane had never looked at Victoria in such a way before, and Victoria found herself itching to know what it meant.

The clock ticked. The morning's lessons dragged. Victoria read her passages; she spoke her answers and wrote her essays. She exerted herself to keep from glancing at Jane. But when she did look, she saw Jane scowling at her fancywork, the book and, oddly, her pink reticule.

What does she have that for? Her maid should have taken it away with her coat and bonnet.

"Victoria! You do not attend!" snapped Mama.

Some days Mama was content to sit through Victoria's lessons at her desk, working with her own correspondence. Not today. Today Mama sat directly behind her, sniping at the tutors, finding fault with Victoria's posture, and berating her if she so much as took a breath to think. This, of course, made every lesson take twice as long as it should have.

The ache in her head and back returned. Victoria's temper strained.

In contrast, Sir John had settled himself contentedly at his own desk to read and write his letters, exuding warm satisfaction like some great cat.

Victoria tried to keep her thoughts where they should be. But they kept straying back to yesterday's ride, to Sir John's assertions—first, that she had lied, then that she had come across some unfortunate gardener. From there they skittered to Mama catching her out in the palace's dark spaces and that furious recitation of all her fears as she dragged Victoria back to their bright, safe rooms.

Aunt Sophia going from insisting she would have known if a gardener had died to whispering secrets with Uncle Sussex.

Jane Conroy, stabbing pointlessly at her crumpled fancywork and trying to hide the fact that she finally had something of her own to say.

The rumors sent by Lehzen's friend that Victoria was finally to be given her own household.

It was a random, ramshackle collection of things. Victoria felt herself piling them all together like a bored child trying to make up a new game from broken toys.

And yet she could not make herself stop. She wanted too badly to make these jolts and jots into something—something that was hers alone and owed nothing to Mama and Sir John or even to Lehzen.

Something that came into being despite all of them.

Even with all these thoughts boiling beneath the surface, Victoria managed to keep most of her mind on her tasks, and her temper largely under control, until the time came for Mama to inspect her journal.

Victoria's first journal had been a gift from Mama herself for her twelfth birthday. She'd been so excited. She had mistakenly thought that this lovely book with its creamy blank pages could be a kind of friend. She could pour out confidences here, and no one would censure her for what she thought or wondered or doubted. It would be like listening to music—a moment when it would be safe to be herself.

That had lasted all of one day.

The next morning Mama had demanded to see the book and what she had written.

"Shame on you," cried Mama when Victoria burst into tears. "To say you want to keep secrets from the one who loves you most in the world!" And she, too, started to cry.

Left with no choice, Victoria had surrendered the journal. Once Mama had read her writing, she made Victoria erase it all and replace her thoughts and feelings with several simple sentences detailing what she'd done that day.

Instead of a friend, Victoria found the journal was a new front in her war with Mama and Sir John.

Today, when the time came, she stepped smartly up to Mama's desk, laid the journal down, and folded her hands behind her back as Mama flipped the pages to her most recent entry.

April 2, 1835
  I awoke at seven and got up at eight. Breakfasted with Mama and the dean. Lessons. Practice. Went riding with Jane Conroy and found dead man on the green. Prince startled and shied. . . .

Mama took up her pencil and crossed out the lines.

"Erase that," she said. "Start again."

Victoria did not move.

"It is the truth. Even Sir John said it was the truth." She felt, rather than saw, him raise his head at the sound of his name. "I wrote down exactly what he said last night at—"

"It is not a subject for you to write upon!" Mama shouted. "You are to know nothing of such things! What will people think when—"

"I'm to know nothing of death?" Victoria snapped back. "How many funerals have I attended? How many lectures have I endured about what must happen when my uncle king dies?" She paused. "Or perhaps you are worried because you do not wish me to write honestly about what you and Sir John—"

Sir John stood up. Mama's face went hard as stone. In one abrupt motion, she tore out the page and crumpled it in her fist. Victoria stared, mute, her fists clenching around the empty air.

"Begin again." Mama snapped the book shut and pushed it back at Victoria. "And this time remember who you are."

There was a cough. Everyone jumped. The footman stood beside the door, and Dr. Clarke stood with him.

"Your Highness. Your grace. Lady Charlotte. Sir John." The doctor bowed. "How does Her Highness today?"

"She should be bled," said Mama. "Her brow felt distinctly warm this morning, and her spirits are unusually heightened."

"Well," said the doctor, "we shall see about that."

In the privacy of her boudoir, Dr. Clarke settled into the business of taking Victoria's pulse, examining her eyes and the back of her head, and asking her about her pains and blurred or double vision. When it was through, he once again pronounced her sound.

"She should be bled," insisted Mama again. "At least an ounce. She barely slept at all last night."

"I see no occasion for such interference," replied Dr. Clarke. "Should the aches become too severe, I recommend a warm compress and two tablespoons of brandy." He packed his bag.

The doors were opened. Dr. Clarke paused in the sitting room to bow to Sir John and Lady Flora. Jane had not moved, but Victoria was certain she was attending to every detail. She wondered what Sir John had said and how Flora had answered.

Victoria found herself reluctant to let Dr. Clarke leave so soon. While he was here, Mama had to show at least some modicum of courtesy.

"Dr. Clarke, do convey my best wishes to Dr. Maton," she said. "How is he doing?"

Dr. Clarke paused. Dr. Clarke looked at Mama and at Sir John. He cleared his throat.

"Ah. There we have very sad news, ma'am. Unfortunately, Dr. Maton has succumbed to his ailments."

For a moment, Victoria felt as dizzy as she had when Prince shied.

"That is very sad news," she said slowly. "Is it not, Mama?"

Mama's face remained stony. Her attention, however, was focused not upon the doctor but upon Sir John.

"Indeed it is." Her voice was low and steady.

Victoria's sensibility—trained by hours at dinners and in drawing rooms, where there was nothing to do but watch the adults in the room—leapt up. *Pay attention to this*, it told her. *Pay attention to how she looks at Sir John right now.*

"Did Dr. Maton have family?" inquired Victoria. Jane was watching them now, too, frowning and listening hard. She did not know Dr. Maton had died. And from the displeasure in her expression, neither did Mama.

Did Sir John?

Pay attention!

"Dr. Maton has left a wife and three sons," said Dr. Clarke. " All the boys have followed him into the medical profession. A fact of which he was very proud, you may be sure."

"Well," said the duchess, "we shall be sending our condolences to his family."

"I know that will be most appreciated, ma'am." Dr. Clarke bowed. "I shall return again tomorrow, but as ever, do not hesitate to call me if there are any changes."

And he bustled away.

Victoria turned on her toes to face Mama, her head cocked, her eyebrows raised.

Which, it seemed, was more than Mama was prepared to stand.

"You are a ridiculous child! Your imagination has done enough damage, and if you are not able to properly command your thoughts, I will *order* Dr. Clarke to bleed you to bring down this fever. Now you have your journal to write, Victoria," she said. "I expect to see you busy."

Victoria folded her arms around the book. "I will go to the—"

"You will stay here!" snapped Mama. "You have more than fully demonstrated your judgment is not to be trusted."

"I may not go to the next room?"

"You may not."

"Not even if I take Jane and Lehzen?" Victoria blinked her eyes in a great show of innocence. "Not even if I leave the door open? That way I will remain safely under your watchful gaze."

This was a dangerous game, and she knew it. She was pricking Mama just to provoke her. It was childish and disobedient and would create a scene, and she could not stop.

You will hear me. I will make you. You will admit he lied to you, just like he did to me.

Chapter 15

Mama was going to scream. Victoria knew it. She saw the muscles cording in her mother's neck and the white lines that appeared around her mouth. She steeled herself, ready to answer shout for shout. Dash knew it, too. She could feel him tremble as he pressed closer to her.

Jane's gaze, as always, shot to Sir John to see how he regarded the scene. This time she and Victoria both got a surprise.

Sir John looked embarrassed. He'd been caught out, and he knew it. Victoria pressed a hand over her mouth to stifle her laugh.

Mama realized something was amiss, and she swallowed all her anger in a single hard lump.

"Very well, Victoria," she said, but she kept her gaze fixed on Sir John. "If it will give me a moment's peace. Lehzen, see that the door is left open."

"Jane, come," said Victoria, scrambling to be gone before Mama had a chance to change her mind. "And bring that book you were talking about. And your workbasket. I want to see how your stitching is coming along."

Jane got up and turned. Victoria could not help but notice she angled herself so that her body was between the stool and her father's searching eyes. *What is she doing?*

There was no way to tell. All Victoria knew was that when Jane turned back, she had her book and basket. She slunk obediently behind Victoria and Dash into the smaller of the two sitting rooms.

The princess chose the settee, which was big enough for them both. Dash curled up at her feet, perfectly content as long as no voices were raised.

"Now, let us see that book you brought." Victoria extended her hand.

Jane gave her the book and sat down beside her. Lehzen settled herself into the straight-backed chair beside the hearth and took up her sewing. It just so happened that she now faced the open door, which would allow her to see the moment anyone approached the threshold.

Victoria dropped her voice to a murmur. "Did you . . . did you have something you wished to say to me?" She turned a page in the book.

"I did," said Jane. "But . . . I don't know if it matters."

"I would like to hear it, anyway."

Jane stared at her hard. Victoria could read the question in her gaze as plain as the words on the page in front of her.

Does she mean it?

Victoria cringed inwardly. Jane had reason to wonder. Victoria had not exactly hidden her feelings. Jane had always been a piece of the daily puzzle that must be worked around or avoided altogether. Occasionally, Victoria felt sorry for her. After all, it must be very hard to be Sir John's daughter. But there was nothing more than that. Not since they were children.

Back then they had played together and laughed together. Then it had all changed. She tried to put her finger on when and how and, disconcertingly, found she could not.

"I walked home across the green last night," Jane breathed. "To look at the place where you fell. I found these."

Jane opened her basket. Using the basket lid as a screen, she handed Victoria a sadly battered pair of pince-nez spectacles. A wrinkled black ribbon stained with dried mud dangled from the frame.

Victoria received the spectacles into her hands as if they were precious jewels. Jane, who never spoke out of turn, who sat and sulked and slunk, who always did exactly what she was told, had gone walking where she should not. Jane had doubted her father and had gone out to search for answers.

"But with Father changing his story and saying the dead man was a gardener, it can't mean anything."

Victoria closed her fingers around the pince-nez.

"No," she said to this new, strange Jane. "It means a great deal. Because that story is a lie, and now we have proof."

Proof that she had seen what she had seen. That this time she had not seen a ghost. That she was not mad.

"How can this be proof of anything?" Jane's question cut through Victoria's triumphant thoughts. "Anyone can wear spectacles. Even a gardener."

How?

Victoria closed her eyes. She willed her anger and her imaginings away.

I will see what is in front of me. Only that.

She opened her eyes.

"This ribbon is silk." She smoothed the bedraggled black scrap. "A gardener would not have a silk ribbon. They couldn't afford it. And if somehow they did own such a thing, they wouldn't use it on a workday. They would save it for best." She looked again. She saw again. "And the rims on the spectacles. They're gold. A gardener would have steel. Or wood."

"Maybe he stole them."

"What for?"

Jane had no answer for that.

"The man I saw wore a black coat, as well," Victoria went on. "How could the dead man be a gardener who wears a black coat and gold-rimmed spectacles on a silk ribbon? Such a thing does not exist." She threaded the ribbon through her fingers. "That wasn't a gardener. It was Dr. William Maton. I thought it might be. Now I'm certain. He wore spectacles like these. He put them on so he could read his watch when he took my pulse."

"But why would Father lie about such a thing?" asked Jane.

"I've been wondering the same thing," Victoria admitted. "At first, he didn't lie. He just didn't believe me, because he didn't want to. That was probably just a reflex."

Jane nodded. She had to be as familiar with this aspect of Sir John's behavior as Victoria was.

"Then, when he found out it was true, his next instinct would be to make it go away as quickly and quietly as possible, which he did by making his announcement at the concert last night." Victoria smoothed her hand across the specticles. "Now, with these, we have solid evidence that the dead man was Dr. Maton. So, what we need to ask is, why didn't Sir John want anyone to know it *was* him?" Victoria took a deep breath. "Jane, will you help me find out what's happened?"

Jane looked nakedly, openly shocked. "What help could I be? I don't know anything, and . . . and I'll only make a mess of things."

"But you found these." Victoria held up the spectacles and then tucked them into her sleeve. "That's a great deal. All I ask is that you try."

Jane groped for what to say. Victoria seized her hand and pressed it, willing some strength into her, willing her to understand that this once they had a chance to *do* something.

Jane looked at their hands clasped together. Her cheeks flushed. When she met Victoria's gaze again, Victoria felt she was looking at a stranger.

All at once, Lehzen coughed. Victoria's gaze jerked up; so did Jane's.

Sir John stood framed in the open door. Mama sat at her desk in the other room, watching him. Sir John looked at Jane and gave a very slight nod, the tiniest sign of approval.

Good girl.

Victoria's skin crawled. Sir John beamed and shut the door, showing how much he trusted Jane.

What does he think is happening? What has he set in motion? Victoria felt something like panic brewing inside her. Had she mistaken Jane's motives?

In her mind's eye, Victoria saw Sir John standing over his daughter. Saw him raise his fist and Jane's head snap back. Such a blow could terrify anyone into obedience, no matter what the scheme.

Jane was staring at the book, which was still open on their laps. Her breath was heaving, as if she'd just run the length of the palace.

"It doesn't matter about the spectacles," Jane said through clenched teeth. "He'll just come up with another lie. He has an answer for *everything*, and no one will believe me if I contradict him. They won't even believe you. They'll just say . . ."

That I'm making it up. That I'm mad.

"It does matter." Victoria faced Jane fully. *I will not let the possibility of you slip away so easily.* "And you know that it matters. That's why it frightens you. It frightens me, too," she admitted. "But that is exactly why I mean to keep going."

"How?" demanded Jane.

A fresh thrill ran through Victoria. This was not a refusal. Jane was listening. Jane was considering the possibilities.

"We must establish two things," Victoria said. "We must establish what happened to Dr. Maton before his death. Why was he out on the green? Where had he been? Where had he planned to go?"

"And the other thing?" asked Jane.

"What was Dr. Maton's full connection to Sir John? Of course, they knew each other because Dr. Maton attended my parents and me. But was there more than that between them?"

Jane didn't look at her. Jane turned over a page in the book and frowned. Victoria held her breath.

Finally, Jane spoke. "I . . . I suppose I could talk to my sister, Liza. She knows everything that goes on in the house and in the town."

"Excellent," said Victoria. "And if you learn anything, and we can't talk, you can leave me a note." She furrowed her brow at the volume between them. "Perhaps in a book? But not this one. Sir John might see it as his property. We'll use Wordsworth's poems. Mama is used to me reading those and won't wonder at it."

"But—" began Jane.

"But what?"

"Why are you doing this?" Jane spoke the words in a rush, as if she did not want to give herself time to take them back. "What could it possibly matter to you whether it was Dr. Maton or a gardener or Father Christmas who died?"

"Because Dr. Maton's death is not a small thing," Victoria whispered. "This is not one of Sir John's usual lies about my temperament or why Mama was late for the reception. This is about the security of the palace and the security of my person. If I can prove Sir John was involved, that would mean that he meant to deceive me, and that he schemed to deceive Their Majesties. I can tell Queen Adelaide, and she can tell my uncle king. They can use it to force the hands of the Kensington board into giving me my own household."

"That is why I am doing this," she said. "And why I intend to succeed."

Chapter 16

"How did matters progress with the princess today?" Father asked Jane.

They sat in the stuffy carriage again, facing each other. This time, instead of gazing out the window, Father leaned forward, watching her with greedy expectation.

How do I do this? She'd known that Father would quiz her when they were alone, but she didn't expect him to start the second the carriage door was closed. They hadn't even reached the palace gates yet.

"She liked the book," said Jane, to gain herself a little extra time.

"What else?"

She'd imagined all manner of answers. Now that Father was actually in front of her, all those ideas flew away. Did the princess realize what a position she'd put Jane in? Probably not. But what if she did? What if she knew full well she was effectively asking Jane to choose the princess's hopes or her father's.

Choose her trust or his.

Anger burned inside Jane, at them and at herself. After all, she'd started this mess when she walked out across the green. It had seemed like a good idea at the time. Now she had no choice but to play the cards she had laid out for herself.

"Come, come, Jane, don't sit there like a block."

Jane lifted her eyes. She saw her father and thought of all the stories she'd heard him spin to get what he wanted.

She took a deep breath. "She knows you lied."

Father frowned. "What do you mean?"

"The . . . the corpse on the green. He wasn't a gardener. She knows it. She knows you lied to her."

She expected him to deny it. She braced herself for his angry shout. But instead, he was silent, regarding her without seeing her. That felt worse somehow.

"Does she know who it was?" he asked finally.

Jane's heart thudded hard. She had this single moment to decide whether she would turn over the next card. This one moment to decide what she would try to make him believe.

"Not yet," Jane told him. "But she means to find out."

Father smirked. "Has she said exactly how she means to do that?"

Just say it. He'll take any hesitation as you being afraid of him. You are always afraid. You are poor, whey-faced, slow-poke Jane. And he knows that.

She watched her hands twisting together in her lap. "N-not exactly, but she seems very sure she can."

"And that is entirely like her," said Father. "She is a thoroughly spoilt young woman. Although I do not have to tell you that." It was a mark of confidence in her—a shared secret, a shared contempt. Jane felt her cheeks heat up. "She constantly overestimates her own capabilities."

Jane made herself turn up one corner of her mouth in a small smile.

"And what did you say to her about it? When she told you she meant to solve this troublesome riddle?"

Another heartbeat. Another decision. A flicker of power and possibility warming a place in her that had been cold for so long.

"Jane?" She did not look up to see his frown deepening, but she heard it clearly as he spoke her name. "What did you say to her?"

"You'll be angry," she whispered.

"I will be angrier if you do not answer me."

Jane regarded her father, aware of a shriveling misery inside her. *What am I doing? He'll know I am not telling him everything, that I'm burying the lie inside the truths. He'll see it instantly.*

"I said I would help."

"You did?"

Jane made herself nod the same way she had made herself smile.

Father laughed. It was a long, full-throated sound. It was real. Jane's heart and breath stopped entirely.

"Oh, Jane! You clever girl!" Father beamed, and his smile was as genuine as his laugh. "It's perfect! It's a game of 'Let's pretend,' and it will keep her distracted and out of trouble. And, when the time is right, I will be able to tell the board and . . . others . . . what silliness she's been engaged in and how my dutiful daughter has been trying so hard to keep her distractions from showing. Yes, Jane." He reached over and patted her hand. "You've done very well."

"I . . . I'm trying, Father."

"You're succeeding." He beamed. "And that means we will all succeed."

How was it possible she was doing this? She was telling the truth and yet somehow transforming that truth into a complete lie. And Father believed. He believed, and he laughed.

"What is it now, Jane? There's something you are not saying."

Jane's mind suddenly felt very crowded. She heard the princess saying, *What was Dr. Maton's full connection to Sir John?*

Don't risk it. He'll know. That voice gibbered. *He'll know. He'llknowhe'llknowhe'llknowhe'llknow!*

"We heard today that Dr. Maton is dead."

"Yes. I heard that, as well." Father's voice was bland, dismissive. "What of it?"

The only question that remains, said the princess from memory, *the only lie that remains, is that the dead man was Dr. Maton . . . Why didn't Sir John want anyone to know it was* him?

"I only thought . . ."

"What did you think?" Father's habitual cold was creeping back into his voice. Jane knotted her fingers together.

"I thought you were friends with him. He's been to dinner . . ." A twist of guilt seized her. This was something she had not said to the princess. Father frequently hosted dinners for the men of the Kensington board and other people in the princess's household who could be useful to them. Dr. Maton had been among them.

All the goodwill she'd gained from Father drained away. She felt it as clearly as if it was water running from her cupped hands.

"Dr. Maton did his duty as a physician in the medical household," he said. "And yes, he came to dine with us, along with other members of the Kensington board, all of whom are responsible for the princess's welfare. You didn't say that to the princess, did you?"

"No, Father." *But why shouldn't I? She knows you talk to the men of the board.*

"Who dines with us is of no concern to her, you understand that?"

"Yes, Father," whispered Jane.

He reached out and patted her hand. "Good girl."

He was not watching when Jane curled her hand into a fist.

Chapter 17

Supper was over. Sir John had taken Jane home hours ago and was not expected to return. There was no concert or special occasion tonight, so Victoria and Mama sat together in the larger sitting room. Lehzen and Lady Flora occupied their places in the sitting room. Lehzen sewed. Lady Flora played patience, drawing and laying down the cards without making a single sound. Mama was writing letters, the scratching of her pen clearly audible in the silence.

Victoria was meant to be reading. But she stared at the page without seeing it.

"We must establish two things," she'd said to Jane. "We must establish what happened to Dr. Maton before his death. And what was Dr. Maton's full connection to Sir John?"

It seemed a logical place to start trying to unravel this strange riddle. But how could she find anything out? There were people who should know the answers, but how could she reach them?

Victoria closed her book. Dash, who had been curled up at her feet, raised his head and wriggled, asking with his whole body if they were going somewhere.

Mama did not look up. She did not even pause in her writing.

Mama must be writing to one of her relatives. Her face was relaxed, and her pen moved quickly. Mama always found it easiest to write in German. When she wrote in English, it was hard labor. Victoria had seen her close to tears as she sorted through her limited grammar to find the correct words.

Victoria stood and all but tiptoed over to Mama's desk. Dash, amiable and vigilant, trotted beside her. She stopped at the corner of the desk and waited. She also read Mama's words that sprawled unevenly across the creamy paper.

Dearest Brother Leopold (Mama had written):
As I write, you may be assured that I and Vickelchen are both in good health.

Reading letters without appearing to do so was an art, and Victoria had applied herself conscientiously to mastering it. She could read what Mama and Sir John and the rest of her attendants wrote from almost any orientation, including upside down.

You will by now have heard rumors that His Majesty is not well.

Victoria's heart thudded hard against her ribs. What was this? Was the king ill? Why hadn't Lehzen told her? She'd spoken to her friend Mrs. Wilson only recently. Surely, *surely* if the king were ill, she would have said something.

All such rumors are currently being contradicted by the palace, and we must take them at their word, as the queen has long since disdained to speak to me directly.

Victoria's breath had gone short. *Uncle can't die! Not yet.*

If he died before she turned eighteen, Mama would be appointed as regent. Parliament had made that decision years ago, and Mama and Sir John had made sure Victoria knew about it. Mama would rule in her name until she was eighteen.

Which meant Sir John would rule in her name.

Which meant Sir John would rule her.

> *It is also true that a dead man has been discovered on the grounds of the palace. Sir John says he is a gardener and that it means nothing. But I am sure he just means to soothe me. The closer our Victoria comes to her eighteenth birthday, the more desperate our enemies become.*

"What is it, Victoria?" Mama dipped her pen into the ink and wiped its tip.

Which enemies? Victoria wanted to shout. *What do you know about Dr. Maton?*

But to ask this would be to admit she had been spying on her mother as she wrote.

"Mama, I was thinking we should visit Mrs. Maton," she said.

"Who?"

Do not pretend you have forgotten. You are writing to Uncle Leopold about him! Victoria bit back hard on her anger. She would get nowhere if it showed.

"Mrs. Maton," Victoria repeated. "Dr. Maton's widow? I wish to condole with her regarding the loss of her husband."

"Impossible. We will send a letter. Perhaps a small gift. That will be more than sufficient. Lady Flora can select something suitable. Lady Charlotte can deliver it."

Victoria let herself be silent for a moment, as if considering this.

Mama wrote: *I fear the coincidence of his appearance at such a time, and I fear also Sir John is not being entirely open with me. What does Baron Stockmar tell you? Send word by him, and him only.*

Mama dipped her pen again. "Was there something else you wished to say, Victoria?"

"Mama—" *Go carefully.* "You have told me many times that appearances are of the utmost importance."

"Yes, of course," said Mama, as if Victoria had mentioned the importance of breathing.

Carefully. "And you have said I must cultivate the goodwill of all the people around me, and of the people in general. Isn't that why we take our tours across the country? To show me and create sympathy with the people?"

Mama's sigh was sharp. "And what has that to do with Mrs. Maton?"

Victoria tilted her head a little to one side. "It is only that I was thinking how Dr. Maton served us for so many years. And served my father before that. Would it not look well for me to visit his family and thank them? Offer them some comfort in their time of mourning? It would be perfectly private, if you thought it best." *Of course it would.* "But if the Court Circular made mention of it, it would, I think, reflect credibly on, well, on all concerned."

Mama frowned at her letter. "Well . . . a brief visit . . . if you are suitably attended, of course. Perhaps yes." She pressed the blotter over the letter, which, frustratingly, hid it from view. "That is well thought of, Victoria. I will make the arrangements."

"Thank you, Mama." Victoria kissed her mother's cheek, and Mama patted hers in return.

Victoria went to her own chair and brought out her

sketchbook. She opened to a fresh page and began to draw Mama. She filled in her basic form and then began the tricky business of hands, of the folds in her skirt, the curl of her hair. She worked quietly, drawing no attention to herself. Mama worked at her letters. The ladies moved about the room, busy with their own little works.

What do you think Sir John is keeping from you? she asked silently as she drew. *What are you afraid of? What do you know about Dr. Maton?*

Was it possible Mama did not trust Sir John as much as it seemed?

Victoria stared at the page, her quick sketch, drawn almost without thought. Her hand had given Mama a frowning face and had spilled the ink across her desk.

It was a picture of discontent, a picture of someone trapped.

Is it possible? Victoria stared at the woman she had drawn. *Are you trapped, Mama?*

All at once, a vision rose up in front of her. Victoria saw herself telling her mother the truth about Dr. Maton. She saw Mama turning to Sir John and ordering him to leave—leave at once, leave for good. She saw Mama wrapping her arms around her, sobbing, calling Victoria her dear girl, and promising everything would be different now.

Saw them moving together to her new home, learning how to be mother and daughter together, truly this time.

Victoria bowed her head and watched as a single tear splashed onto her sketch.

Chapter 18

Dinner was excruciating. Father was at his most expansive, talking about what fools the other members of the Kensington board were and how easy it was to flatter them into agreeing to positions they had declared themselves dead set against. This much was familiar and required only that they listen and occasionally agree. Jane doubted Mother or Liza absorbed a single word that was said. Ned certainly didn't. He spent the meal with his head resting on his fist and scowling into his wineglass.

But then Father turned toward praising Jane and her attendance on the princess. He spoke glowingly of how she was bringing Victoria into tractability and dependence, a sign that he was correct in deciding that Jane should be the one sent to the palace.

"The duchess has agreed that Jane should come with the princess on the tour," Father concluded triumphantly.

This made Mother and her siblings turn and stare at her. Jane suddenly wanted nothing so much as to crawl under the table. She couldn't make herself lift her gaze from her plate, either. She was afraid if Father saw her eyes, he would see all her dissembling, and he would know that his sunny vision of Victoria finally coming under his sway was a complete fantasy.

Under normal circumstances, Jane would have felt a surge of relief when the meal was finally over and she could escape back to her rooms. But not tonight. Tonight she still had to face Liza, and she had no time to waste.

Liza had an invitation to a rout at a friend's house. As soon as dinner was finished, she dashed upstairs. Jane came in just as she was being done up into her rose-pink tulle gown with ballooning skirts and sleeves that puffed up to the level of her ears.

"I'll help her, Meg," said Jane. "I think Mother wants you downstairs." Meg looked dubious, but she did not argue, and Jane took her place behind Liza.

"What's this for?"

"I need to talk to you." Jane worked the hooks up the back of her sister's gown. As she did, she glanced at Liza's reflection in the looking glass. Her hair had been braided, beribboned, and looped into a tight, tall coronet. She looked bang up to the minute in terms of fashion.

She also looked vaguely ridiculous, but Jane kept that to herself.

Liza squirmed and shimmied her shoulders, trying to settle the pads beneath the great puffs of her sleeves. "Well, what is it you want to talk about? I haven't got forever, you know."

What can I say that she'll believe? "The princess . . . she asked me who from the palace has been here for dinner. She wants to know who Father's cultivating."

Liza's duties as the older sister included being Mother's social stand-in. When Mother could not—or, more frequently, did not wish to—attend one of Father's dinners,

Liza played the role of hostess. Jane would not be brought down unless she was needed to balance the number of men and women at the table, which was seldom. Father's dinners were not the kind where men were introduced to the daughters of the house to size them up as partners for marriage. They were not social gatherings with friends of the whole family. They were for men Father was courting and planning to use.

"Jane." Liza frowned at their reflection in the mirror. "You didn't say you'd get her father's guest lists, did you?"

"She asked me to. What could I tell her?"

"You might ask if she's lost her mind, because you have clearly lost yours! What will Father say when he finds out you're spreading gossip about what goes on in our house?"

"It's just a guest list. What does it matter? Everybody already knows Father hosts members of Parliament and the royal household. He brags about it himself!"

"That's his decision. Our job is to do what we're told and keep our mouths shut."

Liza was growing nervous and angry. Jane couldn't blame her. These were not things they ever talked of. It was all simply understood.

"Are you going to tell him? That I asked?"

"Serve you right if I did. What are you even thinking, Jane?"

The door was closed. The room was empty except for the two of them. But Jane's mouth was still dry, and she could not raise her voice above a whisper.

"I'm thinking that maybe Father's right. Maybe we should be trying to win the princess over."

"By gossiping about what goes on in this house? He'll be *livid*!"

"I didn't say we should try to win her over to Father's side, did I?"

Liza drew back. Liza stared. A hundred different expressions flickered behind her bright blue eyes.

"Jane, what are you playing at? No. Stop." She held up her hand. "I don't want to know."

Good, because I'm not sure I could answer you. "So, will you tell me who's been here? I mean recently."

"Good Lord, how am I supposed to remember? The whole of the Kensington board has been at one time or another. Their wives. Lord Melbourne. A dozen other very dull officers, politicians, and m'lords."

"Dr. Maton?" ventured Jane.

"Him?" Liza rolled her eyes. "Yes, he's here every time the board is, with that little rat-faced accountant, Father's friend from his army days. What is his name?" She frowned. "Rea. Mr. William Rea."

This name was new to Jane. "What does he do?"

"Tries to keep Dr. Maton from drinking the cellar dry and talking his head off, as near as I can tell."

Liza gathered up her skirts and perched gingerly on the chair in front of her vanity table.

"You should wear your topazes," Jane suggested. It was a sort of peace offering. "They'll go perfectly with that dress."

"Get them, will you?"

Jane opened up the jewel cabinet. Liza's topazes were pink and blue, making a chain of sparkling flowers for her white throat. There were earbobs with brilliants that matched, and a comb decorated with more pink brilliants for her hair.

"Well?" Liza eyed her reflection critically. "Do you think I'll do?"

"You're beautiful," said Jane honestly. "Liza . . ."

Liza rolled her eyes again. "What on earth is it now?"

Jane swallowed. A month ago, a week ago even, she would have left this alone. She would have been sure there was nothing that could be done. But, somehow, watching Victoria so determined to unearth her answers had caused a shift inside Jane. It made her wonder if she might try to change at least some small thing in her own life.

"I was just . . . I wondered if you know where Susan's gone."

"What an odd question." Liza selected a perfume bottle and dabbed some scent behind each ear.

"I just thought . . . she might need help."

"Why on earth do you care?"

"Because Ned's not going to," said Jane flatly.

"But it's not your *business*," Liza insisted. "And not something Father . . ."

"Do you know or don't you?" She met Liza's gaze, aware that she was showing an unusual amount of stubbornness. She'd always thought Liza was the brave one, the worldly one. Had she ever paid attention to how much Liza referenced what Father would or would not want?

Liza opened her bottom drawer and took out the rouge pot she kept hidden there. With her little finger, she dabbed a minute amount on her cheeks and her lips, then took plenty of time to blend it in.

Jane handed her sister her powder box. Liza powdered her cheeks as carefully as she had rouged them.

"As it happens," she said at last, "Susan has not even left Kensington."

"You're sure?"

"I saw her just yesterday, walking past while we were out in the carriage. It was a great surprise, I can tell you. I asked little Thomas to follow her, to see where she went."

Jane must have looked surprised or confused, because Liza

gave her a sharp sigh. "You're not the only one worried about Ned producing a by-blow, you know. I don't need my chances at getting out of this house ruined because Mama was too lazy to hush things up properly and Susan decides to take him to court for breach of promise or some such."

"Anyway," Liza went on, "Thomas said she went to a house at the end of Lower Market Street. He thought it was her house rather than just one she was working in, as she went in through the front door."

"Thank you, Liza."

Liza did not turn from contemplating her own face in the mirror. "I've some money in my writing desk. Take that for Susan, and tell her there will be more, provided she keeps quiet, all right? And make sure she knows it comes from *me*, not from Father or Mother. Now, help me find my slippers and my reticule. I *cannot* be late."

"Is there something I should know, Liza? Or someone I should . . ."

"Save your breath," said Liza. "There's nothing and no one, yet. But I am not about to leave matters up to Mother or Father." She paused. "And you shouldn't, either."

They stood there in silence for a long moment, each watching the other and letting the space between them fill up with all the things they were not saying.

Jane took a deep breath. "You know if I can help you, I will."

"No, I didn't. But I do now. Thank you, Jane."

Jane nodded.

The first slipper was under the bed. The second was under the washstand. Liza's reticule, at least, was in the wardrobe where it should be, along with her gloves and her fan. Liza took one more look at herself in the mirror and then gathered up her hems and hurried out the door with careful, mincing steps, so as not to disturb her sleeves or her skirts or her hair.

Jane closed the door behind her sister. She stood in the middle of the empty room for a long time, just breathing. Just listening.

Just trying to understand what she was turning herself into.

Chapter 19

When the weather allowed, the Kensington System called for Victoria to spend from half ten to eleven o'clock in the morning walking about the gardens. It was very decorous and very dull, which made it her least favorite form of exercise.

This morning, however, she was grateful for it, because it meant she had time to talk to Jane without being overheard.

There was always a crowd at the gates, eagerly craning their necks to get a look at her and cheering when they did. Victoria was very used to them by now. As she passed, she smiled and raised her hand, and they cheered all the harder.

That small duty done, Victoria linked her arm with Jane's and drew her farther along the path. Lehzen, who followed behind with shawls and parasols and other such accoutrements, promptly began to engage Lady Flora in conversation.

I will thank her later.

"Tell me quickly," murmured Victoria to Jane. "Were you able to learn anything?"

Jane looked troubled, as if some uncomfortable memory had caught her. "I spoke with my sister. Dr. Maton has, had, been to the house for dinner several times."

"Why didn't you tell me before!"

"I am not generally allowed at the table when Father has guests. I'm too young, and well, Liza's prettier," she whispered.

Victoria touched her hand in sympathy. Jane composed herself.

"So, I don't usually know who's coming. I mean, I knew that Father invites people from the palace regularly—"

Victoria froze. "Who?" *Who from the palace is friends enough that he sits down to dinner with them?* "Do they talk about me?"

Belatedly, Jane seemed to realize that this revelation was not a small thing to Victoria. A look of utter panic crossed her face.

"I don't know. I told you, I'm not allowed at the dinners. But I made a list of who Liza said has been there most recently." She glanced quickly behind and then pulled a paper from her sleeve.

Victoria took the list, willing her hands not to tremble. She unfurled the paper and read it.

Lord Melbourne
Lord Duncannon
Lord Dunfermline
Earl of Dunham
Mr. Rea
Dr. Maton

"This is the board," she breathed. "This is the Kensington board. These are the men who oversee . . ." She swallowed.

They were the men assigned to oversee her welfare. They

ultimately controlled the budget allotted for her maintenance. They crowded into the room on examination days as her tutors quizzed her, listened to her answers, and made reports to Parliament. They had final say over who did or did not serve in her household.

Victoria's knees wobbled. Thankfully, there was a stone bench near at hand. She sat down abruptly.

"They all dine with him?" *The men who decide where and how I live have all become Sir John's friends?*

What would they do when they heard the king was contemplating that she be removed from his care?

Victoria crumpled Jane's list between her hands.

"Did you know?" she demanded. Her anger was ridiculous. Jane had no say in her father's doings. But Jane was the one beside her, and she had nowhere else to direct her anger or her fear.

"I didn't think about it," said Jane. "It doesn't pay to think too much about what Father is doing. It's better to let it go on over your head."

"Yes," murmured Victoria. *I will control myself.* She and Jane had only just renewed their friendship. She could not let her temper break them apart. "I have been tempted to do so many times."

"But you don't."

"I suppose not."

"Why not?"

Victoria looked across the expanse of the lawn, toward the pond and its clusters of geese and swans. "I don't know. I've tried. I know things would be much easier."

"We should walk on," murmured Jane. "I think Lady Flora is growing concerned."

Lady Flora was indeed watching them intently. Victoria could just imagine what she would report to Mama. She got to her feet and resumed her stroll, with Jane close beside her.

Victoria stretched out the list and looked at it again.

"Who is this man, Mr. Rea?"

"I don't know," said Jane. "I think Liza said he was an accountant and a friend of Father's from his time in the army. He's not one of the counselors?"

Victoria shook her head. "They've all come to inspect me at one time or another, but I don't know him."

"Does it matter?"

"It might. Sir John surely finds him useful for some reason. But if he's not a board member, then what is it?"

She waited for Jane to suggest that as Sir John had known Mr. Rea from his time in the army, he might simply be a friend. But Jane was not so naive.

"I don't understand . . . ," began Jane, but she let the sentence trail away.

"What, Jane? You can say anything."

Jane looked doubtful, and Victoria found herself torn between guilt and impatience.

"What use did Father have for Dr. Maton? Why was he at these dinners with the Kensington Board? Liza said he always drank too much and Mr. Rea was the one who had to keep him from talking. Father hates a man who can't hold his liquor." He had, in fact, complained about Ned's failure in this area more than once.

"Perhaps we'll find out this afternoon. I convinced Mother to pay a condolence call on Mrs. Maton. You'll come, as well, and together we should be able to learn something from the family."

But Jane hesitated. "May I ask a favor, ma'am?"

"What is it?"

"Instead of my accompanying you to the Matons, would you . . . send me on an errand?"

"What errand?"

Jane shrugged. "Any errand. Something away from the palace."

"Why?"

Again, Jane hesitated. "It's private."

Victoria's brows arched, but she nodded.

"Very well. Let's think. What could we—"

"No, there. You see there? Those are diseased!" The booming voice reached them from up ahead.

Victoria turned, so did Jane. Aunt Sophia, in a billowing linen smock and straw hat, stood with a cluster of gardeners. She leaned on her cane and pointed emphatically at one of the flower beds.

"You see? There, and there?" She stabbed toward the nodding flowers. "They must be pruned at once, or it will spread everywhere!"

The under-gardeners looked bemused. But the head gardener nodded energetically.

"Of course, ma'am," he said. "It will be attended to immediately. I apologize we did not do so before."

"Well, now, no harm done. Yet," added Aunt Sophia ominously.

Excellent! Victoria felt herself grinning. She'd been searching for an excuse to speak with Aunt Sophia alone.

She picked up her hems and hurried across the lawn.

"Aunt Sophia!"

"Vickelchen!" Aunt Sophia kissed her on both cheeks. "So, her grace let you out this morning? Did she not fear you would get your feet wet?"

"It was time for my walk. I am glad to see you, Aunt. There has been some news, and I was not sure anyone would have thought to tell you."

Aunt Sophia shoved her bulbous spectacles up on her nose and craned her neck, as if she needed to get a better look at Victoria. "What news?"

"I'm afraid Dr. Maton is dead."

Victoria expected some strong reaction, at the very least an exclamation that her aunt had known Sir John was a liar.

But all that happened was Aunt Sophia's face went blank for a moment.

"Maton?" her aunt murmured. "Well, well."

"He is the one who was found on the green," Victoria prompted.

"Not a gardener, then?" Aunt Sophia was looking out across the gardens, toward the lawn and the green.

"You knew it was not. How did you know that?"

"Well, as you have seen, I know the groundskeepers well." She waved back toward the cluster of gardeners, who were now busy at work around the flower bed and its companion hedges.

"Is that what it was? You expected they would tell you if one of their men had died?"

"Oh, they would not have had to tell me. I know all the secrets of the flowers and the hedgerows." She beamed.

"I'm serious, Aunt. How did you know?"

"Perhaps I did not," said Aunt Sophia owlishly. "Perhaps I just wanted to make a scene to see your mother and her lapdog jump."

"You're teasing me."

"That also could be. But you mustn't mind it."

"I don't. But I do mind that you won't answer me." *And that you and Uncle Sussex really are keeping secrets. No matter what Lehzen says.*

Aunt Sophia sucked her cheeks in, making her face even more hollow. She stooped slowly, brushed three leaves off the gravel path, and straightened just as slowly.

"Did you consult Dr. Maton?" Victoria asked her.

"Occasionally, yes."

"Was that how you knew something was amiss? He did not call on you when expected?"

Aunt Sophia's face spasmed. "Yes, yes, that is fair. He did not behave as expected, not as he had or as I thought. Old fool, if you miss one blossom, the disease spreads." She stopped and swayed on her feet. Victoria tensed, ready to catch her in case she began to fall.

"Vickelchen, you mustn't mind me," murmured Aunt Sophia. "You mustn't take what I say or do seriously. No one does." She blinked, and her low voice grew ragged. "I am an old woman. I have lived most of my life behind walls. In the royal nunnery, they called it. Ha! If only they knew. Not that they would believe, because I am not to be believed . . ." The brittle bitterness in those words stunned Victoria. "I'm wandering. I'm wandering. Pay me no mind, Vickelchen." She beamed and blinked.

She wants to appear foolish. She does not want any more questions. That heartbreak she'd felt when she realized that Uncle Sussex was keeping things from her returned.

Victoria decided to try a different approach.

"Mama and I are going to call on the Matons this afternoon," she said. "Shall I add your condolences?"

"Yes, do. He was a good friend once, when I needed one." Aunt Sophia's voice softened, and her gaze grew distant. This time, Victoria decided, the emotion was real. "I do not blame him," Aunt Sophia murmured. "Say that. Be sure to say that there is no blame on him."

"For what, Aunt?"

Aunt Sophia still did not look at her, but the set of her jaw changed. Her hand closed and opened again. Victoria held her breath.

But then, all at once, Aunt Sophia slumped. "Ah, ah, my knees!"

She staggered, banging against Victoria, and almost knocked them both over. The waiting women, who had been waiting at a respectful distance, ran forward and caught her.

"Damned old knees!" bellowed Aunt Sophia. "They hurt! I hurt! Take me home, take me home!"

"Yes, ma'am. Come away now," murmured her woman. "We will take you home."

The woman turned Aunt Sophia to face the palace, but as she did, the old woman's gnarled hand shot out and snatched Victoria's sleeve, tearing the delicate gauze.

"Learn to live inside your walls, girl. Do not fight them. They will destroy you."

Victoria covered over the tear in her sleeve as if it was her skin that had been scratched. She watched her aunt's attendants lead her gently but firmly away, as they had led her out of the salon the other evening, after she had made her scene with Sir John.

After she had told one and all that he was lying.

After she told me he was lying.

Victoria felt Jane step up beside her. She'd almost forgotten the other girl. Now she was very glad she was there.

"We were talking about an errand you might go on, Jane," Victoria said. "I've heard there's an apothecary in the village, a Mr. Oslow, I think. His wife makes a lemon and verbena cordial that is said to be very soothing."

"She might," said Jane. "We use Mr. Cummings."

"Well, go to Mr. Oslow and see if you can get a bottle of cordial. I want to give it to Aunt Sophia. I think she has not been sleeping well lately."

"Yes, ma'am. Of course."

Jane clearly did not understand everything that was happening, at least not fully. But Victoria was not thinking about her now. She was consumed by memory. Her mind's eye showed her Mama at an evening party, laughing and tossing out careless, devastating insults to the lords and ladies gathered around her. "Oh, but you must not mind me!" Mama would say afterward. "You know I take nothing seriously!"

Except Mama took everything seriously, and the people around her knew that. But in those moments, she could make them believe the opposite. It was a performance, polished and perfected by repetition. Just like her own performance as the demure princess. Or Jane's as the dullard.

Just like Aunt Sophia's as the doddering old woman.

"I do not blame him," Aunt Sophia had said. "Say that."

Blame him for what, Aunt? Victoria wondered. *What were you going to tell me? And why did you change your mind?*

And why that warning about my walls? What happened inside yours?

Chapter 20

Rooms told stories, Victoria knew. Houses, however, spoke volumes.

When compared with the grandeur of London, Kensington was a modest village. But Dr. Maton's establishment was a luxurious one, clearly meant to convey that he could easily have settled into the city's rarified atmosphere had he chosen to do so.

It was a tall, modern house on the high street, built of warm red brick with fresh white trim. The windows sparkled in the blazing summer sun, and the marble steps were immaculate. The house had two doors, the first being plain and black and leading to a low wing off the main residence. This would be the entrance to the surgery. The second, painted green, led to the house itself.

The knocker had been muffled in black crepe. Lady Charlotte went up the stairs first and knocked for Victoria and Mama. They were admitted at once by a footman dressed all in black, even to the ribbon in the queue of his powdered wig.

All of them stood aside and made their reverences as Victoria climbed the steps and crossed the threshold.

Dr. Maton, or his wife, it seemed, had a taste for the dramatic as well as the expensive.

The entrance hall was tiled in marble, paneled in immaculate white up to the chair rail, and painted a pale blue above. The effect was airy, modern, and very uncomfortable.

Like walking into a cave of ice.

In that stark space, the man in black frock coat and trousers stood out as sharply as a silhouette on white paper. She could see at a glance that this must be one of Dr. Maton's sons. He had thinning hair, a round face, a form that was already sagging toward middle age, all of which reminded Victoria sharply of her former physician.

He bowed deeply to Victoria.

"Your Highness, your grace," he said. "It is a great honor to receive you. If I may present myself? I am Dr. Julius Maton."

"Thank you, Dr. Maton," said Mama. "Her Highness wished to deliver her condolences to your mother personally, and to express her gratitude for your father's excellent care of her and of all our family."

"Yes, of course. My mother and brothers are in the parlor. If you will step this way?"

They followed him. The theme of pastel walls, marble tiles, and white trim was carried through the ground floor of the house. The black crepe around the banisters and picture frames made midnight slashes across the icy background. Gray outlines on the painted walls showed where mirrors had been removed.

In the parlor heavy drapes had been drawn. The hot, still air was thick with dust and a dragging chemical smell, which Victoria knew meant death itself. Heavy carpets had been laid down to muffle their footsteps. The only light came from the candles at the coffin's head and foot.

Victoria tried to picture this room filled with light and laughter and the sounds of company, perhaps with tea or music, and found she could not.

Chairs draped in black cloth had been set at an angle so the persons sitting vigil could stand to greet the mourners as they arrived but not block the coffin. As Victoria entered, Mrs. Maton and her two remaining sons rose at once and made their reverences.

The Matons were a pale family. Victoria thought that when they were not in mourning, they must fade away in all these pastel rooms.

As a girl, Mrs. Maton had doubtlessly been the perfect English rose—all pink and white, with golden hair and sparkling sapphire eyes. Now the blush had faded from her cheeks, her sapphire-blue eyes were watery, and the hair under the black cap was turning white as the marble tiles. But there was still a strength about her. Mrs. Maton held herself stubbornly straight, as if she refused to be bowed by her grief.

A grim face, thought Victoria. *She is grieving, yes, but there's something else . . .*

"Your Highness, your grace," Dr. Julius Maton was saying, "may I present my mother, Mrs. Phillipa Ashdowne Maton?"

Mama approached Mrs. Maton and touched her hand.

"Mrs. Maton, I am sincerely sorry for your loss. Your husband was a good man and a dedicated physician. I always felt myself in the very best of hands when he was with me."

Mrs. Maton lifted her gaze, took a quick glance at Mama. There. Victoria saw a flash in the widow's eyes. It was not grief. Not in the least.

It was resentment.

And it was gone. The widow dropped her gaze.

"You are most kind, your grace."

"May I also present my brothers?" said Julius Maton. "Dr. Marcus Maton and Dr. Gerald Maton."

Ironically, both of his brothers were taller than Julius, who Victoria assumed was the eldest, since he had taken the duty of performing the introductions. All three brothers shared the same round build, pasty skin, faded eyes, and thinning fair hair. Had these men been in a ballroom with five hundred other guests, one would have known instantly they were all from one family.

The middle brother, Marcus, was staring at Mama. There was something hungry in that look, and Victoria did not like it. Mama did not even seem to notice.

By contrast, the youngest brother, Gerald, was watching his own mother. Was he afraid she might commit some impropriety? That, perhaps, she might break down and cry? He had the same round face as his brothers, and his double chin had already begun to form. It was a face made for joviality. But there was nothing jovial about him. Neither was there any sign of grief.

Gerald Maton was quietly, unmistakably furious.

He did not approach his brother or his mother but stayed beside the coffin, as if he thought the ladies from the palace were resurrectionists come to steal his father's body. Victoria could not help noticing the ribbon attached to Gerald Maton's watch chain, with the end tucked into his waistcoat pocket. She felt sure there must be a pince-nez attached to that end.

Mama was assuming a sympathetic air. "Your sons will surely be a great consolation to you," she said to Mrs. Maton.

"Yes, indeed, ma'am. They have ever been my comfort. My husband was often from home, you see, with the medical household."

"Men have many calls to answer. We can only wait and be patient."

"Yes, your grace." There it was again, that flash of resentment. A prickle of cold skittered across Victoria's skin.

"It was your husband who attended mine during his final illness," Mama told her. "No one could have been more diligent."

Gerald Maton did not like this remark. He, of course, said nothing. But the sharp, bright flush on his round cheeks betrayed the intensity of his unspoken feeling.

Mama had fallen silent, which gave Victoria space to speak. She had spent all last night and much of this morning trying to decide how to proceed. She could not count on a moment alone with any member of the family, but that didn't mean she couldn't discover anything.

She could begin by making a statement she knew to be untrue.

"But his end was a peaceful one," she said. "That must be of some comfort."

Victoria waited to be contradicted, but to her surprise, Mrs. Maton simply lowered her gaze.

"Yes. Dr. Maton died in his bed, in his sleep," she said. "It had been a long and troubling illness, but we all believed he would pull through."

The words were pious, and unexceptional. But they were also oddly bland and stilted.

Studied?

"What a comfort that all his family was able to be with him," Victoria prodded.

Mama was not happy with her little sallies. Of course, she could not silence Victoria in front of the Matons, but Victoria felt the smothering weight of her silent disapproval.

"Yes, indeed, ma'am," said the widow, and the words were still bland, still oddly stiff. "A great comfort." There was a pause and a glance toward her husband in his coffin. A wistful, beseeching expression flickered across her pale face. "He had planned to retire, to assist our son in his practice, and write his memoir."

It was the first genuine thing she'd said. Victoria was sure of it.

Gerald's hand twitched, like he wanted to reach for something. Or perhaps make a fist.

Mama, it seemed, had had enough of Victoria's curiosity. She grabbed Victoria by the elbow and steered her toward the coffin.

"Come, Your Highness. Let us pay our respects."

Dr. Maton lay inside the padded box, immaculately dressed and carefully posed, his eyes closed and arms folded. Victoria tried to picture him on his side in the rain, deflated and cold. It was growing increasingly difficult. Was that really the curve of the shoulder she had seen? And was that the hair—thinned and gray, showing that mottled scalp? Doubt assailed her again.

Mama bowed her head in prayer. Victoria did, as well, but she also shot a sideways glance toward Gerald Maton.

The youngest Maton son glowered at the remainder of his family. They all ignored him. His older brothers flanked their mother, looking more like guards than consoling sons. Mrs. Maton kept her hands folded in front of her and her eyes pointed rigidly ahead.

Mrs. Maton refused to be cowed either by the fact of her husband in the coffin or by the undisguised anger of her youngest son. But just in case, her older sons meant to make sure she did not put one foot out of line.

Odd that they were so concerned about their mother breaking down—*or breaking ranks?*—but that they did not seem to spare a thought for their brother.

Why is that? She had no answer, but Victoria knew what she must do next.

Mama murmured, "Amen." Victoria lifted her head.

Before Mama could turn her away, Victoria faced Gerald Maton.

"Dr. Maton, I hope that you will accept this small token." She pulled the little paper bundle from her reticule and held it out to him.

"Oh, Your Highness . . ." Mrs. Maton stepped forward.

Victoria did not acknowledge her. Instead, she pressed the packet into Gerald's hands, and of course, he could not refuse to receive it.

"I shall keep you and your family in my prayers," she told him before he might feel he had to say something. "Good-bye and may God bless you. Mrs. Maton." Victoria faced the widow. "Thank you allowing us to pay our respects today. We will not intrude upon your grief any further."

Since she had announced that they were leaving, there was nothing for anyone in the room to do but make their reverences and murmur their thanks. Victoria snuck one more look at the youngest Maton brother. Gerald had already put the packet into his coat pocket.

Julius Maton showed them to the door and stood on the step while the footmen helped Victoria and Mama back into the carriage. Lady Charlotte and Lady Flora were handed into their separate vehicle.

The door closed. Mama turned to Victoria. She was not pleased. Victoria braced herself.

"What did you give that man?" Mama demanded.

"A sketch I made of Dr. Maton. I thought the family might like to have it." *Please, don't let her have noticed the odd shape or that the packet was too thick just to be a paper sketch. . . .*

"Humph," Mama snorted, but Victoria could see her anger had already deflated. "Well, you should have given it to the widow or at least the eldest son."

"I'm sorry, Mama," Victoria murmured. "It was only

that he looked so very distressed. I wanted to do something for him."

"Sympathy is not a reason to ignore proper conduct," said Mama sternly. "Still, that was very thoughtful." She gave Victoria an indulgent smile. "This has been a good day's work." She patted Victoria's hand. "I'm proud of you, dearest."

Victoria let herself smile. She hoped she looked modest. She hoped she did not show any sign of the triumph she felt. The truth was she had picked Gerald because the grieving Mrs. Maton and her eldest son were so very clearly working to conceal . . . something.

Gerald Maton, on the other hand, burned to talk.

And now I must arrange a time for him to do so.

Chapter 21

♛

Oslow's Apothecary was a popular and busy shop. Despite this, Jane was able to procure the lemon cordial after only a short wait.

"We have one more stop to make," she said as Betty tucked the bottle into her market basket.

She started walking again before Betty could ask where or what it was for.

In Kensington a family's status could be measured by how close their house was to the palace grounds. The farther away a residence stood, the less consequential it could be considered.

The direction Liza had given Jane was not quite on the fringe of the village, but it was close. Lower Market Street itself was little more than a rutted lane, and the "house" was a cottage that squatted in a tangled yard where a few scrawny chickens were watched by an even scrawnier cat. Two old men occupied a bench under the cottage's broad eaves but did not rise as Jane approached the door. A crockery jug sat on the bench between them.

Betty eyed the men, the jug, and the house, as if she expected to be snatched up and spirited away to the West Indies.

Steeling herself, Jane knocked on the battered door. At some time in the distant past, someone had painted it a cheery blue, but now the paint was badly chipped, and the color faded by sun and dust.

No one answered. Jane knocked again. The men on the bench watched this performance with great interest.

Jane was ready to turn and ask them if the mistress of the house was at home when the door flew open and she found herself face-to-face with Susan.

Susan was tiny, thin, and watchful, like a sparrow. Mama liked her servants to appear delicate. *I cannot abide a raw-boned woman.* But if you looked closely, you saw the muscle cording her neck and her forearms, as well as the chapped and reddened skin on her palms and fingertips. Her sleeves were rolled up past her chafed elbows. Large brown eyes looked out of a pale face, but everything about her suggested a knife's sharpness rather than porcelain delicacy. She had little humor about her, and she set her tiny chin in such a way that suggested that any speech would have to be dragged out of her, possibly by force.

But Jane had always liked that determined silence. Long days in the palace had taught her to distrust quick speech and quick wit. She was permanently sore from the jokes made at her expense. Despite that, she found she was unprepared for the contempt that glittered in Susan's eyes. Jane had always known Susan as a servant. As long as Mother and Father paid her salary, Susan had to be at least polite and attentive to Jane's requests.

But now that there was no salary to be considered, Susan clearly saw no need for deference or even courtesy. Instead, she folded her arms and glowered.

"What do you want?"

"I wanted . . ." Jane bit her words off. The old men were listening, and so was Betty. "May I come in?"

Contempt glittered like ice in Susan's brown eyes. Jane thought she might refuse, but in the end, she turned and walked away into the dim house, leaving the door open behind her.

"Wait here please, Betty," said Jane, indicating the tiny flagstone foyer. She followed Susan into the depths of the house, not bothering about bonnet or coat.

The house was a low, cramped place. The wood was chipped, and the plaster cracked or simply missing over the lath. There were few windows, and the floors were flagstone or dirt. A baby wailed in another room. Jane looked at Susan. There was no sign of a thickening waist or the reddened face that came with pregnancy.

The kitchen was narrow and worn, as chipped and splintered as the rest of the house. The dirt floor was packed hard as macadam. The yard out back was a maze of wash-lines. The acrid smells of bleach and farm animals filled the air. Geese mingled with the chickens, and pigs lounged in their pen. Everything, even the clean wash, was speckled with soot.

Susan stopped in the middle of the room. She didn't sit and didn't invite Jane to. "What is it? I'm busy."

Jane felt as if her tongue were sodden, thick wool. "I wanted to make sure you were all right," she said.

Susan shrugged. "See for yourself, can't you?"

She did see. But she also saw the bitterness in Susan's demeanor. "Is there anything you need?"

"Why? You going to get me a job at the palace?"

"I, no. But I—" She opened her purse and took out the packet she'd made up.

Several years ago, the question of pin money for Liza and

Jane, had been raised. Father had not intended to give them any, but for once, Mother had intervened.

"Let them have it," she'd sighed. "Otherwise they shall be forever pestering me about dresses and ribbons and slippers, and I couldn't bear it!"

Of course this was not said when the girls were in the room, but by that point she and Liza had learned exactly where to stand to overhear conversations in any part of the house.

Jane found she spent next to nothing. She saved it instead. And she'd been frankly stunned at the amount she had found in Liza's desk. Liza was always overrunning her allowance and begging Father for a little extra.

Except now Jane understood that this was another one of Liza's domestic deceptions. She wondered how many others had gone entirely unnoticed.

Jane held the packet out. Susan eyed it suspiciously.

"What's that for?"

"Well, I, the baby—" she stammered. She meant to go on about how it came from Liza and that there would be more, but Susan cut her off.

"What baby?" demanded Susan. "Who's saying there's a baby?"

Jane felt her eyes bulge. "I . . . Liza said . . ."

"You can tell Miss Conroy thanks very much for her concern, but she can mind her own business from now on."

"I . . . if it wasn't . . . then why were you dismissed?"

"Because I broke an entire tea set! Or so I'm told."

"Then, you didn't?"

"I never. That was an excuse to get rid of me."

"But why? I mean, if you weren't . . ."

"How on earth should I know? They told me I was done, and showed me the door. Was just lucky I had a home to go back to, wasn't I?" She plucked the packet from Jane's fingers. "Since your fine sister is in a giving mood, I'll accept, as I don't expect Lady Conroy to bother about getting me the wages I'm owed." She tucked the packet away in her apron pocket and folded her arms again. "Was there anything else you wanted? If not, I'll thank you to be about your business, so I can be about mine."

"No, nothing," said Jane. "Except, well, if you need a character reference, I can write you one."

Susan's jaw shifted, as if she was grinding her teeth. Or maybe she was just trying not to laugh.

"Well, I thank you for that. You can see yourself out, I expect?"

"Yes. Thank you, Susan."

Susan nodded once. Jane took her leave and did not let herself look back.

Chapter 22

It was sometimes easy to forget that Kensington Palace was not the center of the stately world. It was more like a dusty box on a shelf, remembered only when its contents were wanted.

Lehzen had had to leave Kensington quite early so she could complete her errand and be back before the late afternoon, but she did not mind. After the stifling silence of the royal apartments, Lehzen found London's crowd and noise invigorating. She had not lost her ability to marvel at the green parks and great houses. The royal governess who had traveled across the country in the princess's retinue might be jaded, but the schoolmaster's daughter still looked at this great city with wide-eyed amazement.

Her destination today could not be classed as a great or even a stately house. It was a modest private residence in a square that was entirely respectable but not at all fashionable. The door was opened for her by a footman in plain livery, and she was shown at once into a charming little parlor that overlooked a simple, sunny garden.

"Louise!" Frau Schumacher rose and came forward to take both her hands. "How are you, my dear?" she asked in her comforting German.

"I am well, thank you," replied Lehzen in the same language. "And thank you for allowing me the use of your parlor."

"Ah, what else are friends for? The tea is being prepared, and I believe we expect Mrs. Wilson soon—" The front door's bell sounded in the distance. "So. This may be her now."

The footman opened the door to admit Martha Wilson. In her plain gray dress, with its simple lace collar and cuffs, Martha looked more like a Quaker housewife than one of the queen's attendants. Which, of course, was the point.

"Good morning, Louise. Good morning, Frau Schumacher." Martha greeted them in English and pressed their hostess's hands. "Tell me, how does your son?"

"Very well, thank you." Frau Schumacher's English was fluent but accented, like Lehzen's own. "He writes the university is miserably hard, but he enjoys the work. He says he is daily grateful for all that Herr Lehzen put him through in preparing him."

"I shall write to my father and tell him," said Lehzen. "He will be glad to hear it."

"But now here is the tea," said Frau Schumacher as the footman entered with the tray. "You must both sit and have a good visit. I beg you will excuse me, but I have a thousand letters to write."

It was a polite fiction, but a familiar one. There had been a number of times over the years when Lehzen and Martha needed a place to talk where they would not be seen or overheard. Frau Schumacher had kindly volunteered her house for their meetings.

Their hostess and coconspirator bustled away, leaving Lehzen and Martha facing each other.

"Shall I pour?" asked Lehzen in French. Martha had no German, but her French was excellent. Frau Schumacher's staff was trustworthy and discreet, but experience had left them both wary. Conducting their meetings in French reduced the chances their conversation might be discussed out of hand. The precautions might have seemed excessive to some, but the war of influence between St. James's Palace and Kensington was genuine, and if they were found to be in communication, the consequences could be severe.

Martha took her chair, her teacup, and a shortbread biscuit.

Lehzen fixed her own cup and drank. It was a relief to be able to make a really strong cup of tea. The duchess insisted on a brew that was little better than tepid water.

"What is the news from St. James's?" Lehzen asked.

"Do you mean to ask how the king is doing?" inquired Martha.

Lehzen nodded. "Word has gone abroad that he is ill."

"He is, and he is in bed. But the doctors are no more than usually concerned. You know I would have written if it were otherwise."

"You must forgive me. We are very unsettled in our household at the moment."

"So I am hearing. We have heard the princess had a bad time while out riding."

"Yes. The princess, or rather her horse, did stumble over a dead man on the green. It seems it was Dr. Maton, who is, or was, attached to the medical household."

"It is a shocking thing. How has the princess responded?"

By believing some skulduggery is afoot. By believing Sir John Conroy is behind it. For which he has only himself to blame. "She is a young woman who does not have enough to occupy her natural energies or intellect, and she is beginning to chafe at the system of living imposed upon her."

"To hear you tell it, she has chafed against that harness since she was a little girl."

"That is my point," Lehzen told her. "She is not a little girl anymore. She has grown and changed, but the system has not." *And it will not, because its aims have not been achieved.* "Tell me, Martha, when may we expect a decision soon regarding her new household?"

"I cannot say." Martha set her cup down and leaned forward. "What is worrying you, Louise?"

I must go carefully here.

Lehzen and Martha were both creatures of the court. There was no such thing as complete confidence between such persons. But Martha was the one sure source of information Lehzen had from St. James's and Queen Adelaide. She could not risk losing her trust.

"The princess is a strong-willed, intelligent girl who is ready to become a woman. She longs for variety, and to test her mettle. She is sick of being told that any thought of which her mother and her mother's companion do not approve is a sign of madness, or that her smallest gesture of independence is not only ungrateful but hopelessly reckless."

"Oh, la la," Martha breathed.

Lehzen nodded. "Any girl raised in such a state might well become angry. She may begin to give in to her less healthy impulses simply because she is bored or because mischief is a way to lash out at those she sees as her jailers."

Martha did not reply immediately. Lehzen refilled her cup. *How very English I have become*, she thought. *Discussing the future of the kingdom over a cup of tea.*

Martha reclaimed her cup and sipped. "I can see where that girl's true friends may well become concerned for her health."

"They might, perhaps, suggest that a . . . a separation

would be beneficial. A change of . . . What is the English phrase . . . ?"

"Scene and society?" Martha nodded. "And it might be as well if the girl's friends conveyed this to her relatives?"

"I would say so." Lehzen took a swallow of tea. The lemon had sat too long. The liquid was thoroughly bitter now.

"I understand there is to be another tour beginning shortly," ventured Martha.

"Yes. Of the northern counties."

"His Majesty objects to these productions."

To the casual observer, it might seem strange that the king could not simply forbid the princess to be taken traveling. But the situation was far from simple. Parliament had declared the Duchess of Kent to be Princess Victoria's legal guardian. Therefore, she was the one in charge of the child's movements. If the duchess declared the princess would travel, then she traveled. If the members of the aristocracy wished to open their homes to receive the princess, and if towns wished to mark the occasion of her visit with speeches and celebration, that, too, was perfectly natural. And if the king tried to forbid it, people would wonder why. They might even wonder if there was something wrong with the princess or her mother.

Or the king.

"Her Highness does not undertake these tours willingly. She finds them exhausting and a great strain upon her nerves." Lehzen paused. "Perhaps if it were put to His Majesty that the business of moving to a new establishment must necessarily supersede the tour . . ."

Their eyes met for a long moment.

"Hmm. Yes. That is a thought. I shall bring it up to Her Majesty."

"Most urgently," said Lehzen.

Martha nodded. "Most urgently, you may be sure."

"Because, Mrs. Wilson, I believe Sir John may have multiple reasons to want the situation to remain exactly as it is. And I believe if he gets word that the princess is to be removed from his influence, he may well grow desperate," she said. "I cannot say what may happen after that."

Chapter 23

When Jane entered the royal apartments, carrying her basket with the bottle of cordial, she saw Lehzen sitting beside the open windows. A welcome breeze stirred the draperies. A table with a tea tray had been placed in front of her, along with a second chair.

"Miss Conroy." Lehzen folded the letter she had been reading. "I see you have completed Her Highness's errand."

"I, um, yes." Jane fumbled with the basket. "This is the cordial she asked for." She held it out. Lehzen took it with thanks.

"Her Highness and her grace are still on their visit to the Matons. But I have some fresh tea here, as you may see." She smiled. "Will you take a cup?"

Jane wanted to refuse. She did not like Lehzen's smile or the light in her eyes. But what excuse could she possibly give? And besides, she was thirsty.

So, Jane sat down and accepted the cup. Lehzen pushed the milk and the sugar bowl toward her. She also glanced at the door, which was open, so that they might be plainly seen and, incidentally, see anyone who came in.

Jane added milk and a sugar lump to her cup.

"Things have been strange the past day or so, would you say?" Lehzen remarked.

Jane added a second lump to her cup. And a third. Mother would have sighed dramatically and rolled her eyes. Lehzen, however, seemed to have things on her mind beyond Jane's overindulgence.

"I think we may even call them unsettled," Lehzen went on, her tone somehow both bland and pointed. "And yet it all seems to have created a new sympathy between you and Her Highness."

Jane kept her attention on her teacup. Silence was the habit of a lifetime. She had waited out her father hundreds of times when he was in a talking mood. She could wait out Lehzen.

"What was behind this business with your errand this morning?"

That surprised Jane. She jerked her head up and sloshed her tea. "She didn't tell you?"

Lehzen shook her head.

I thought she told you everything.

Jane shifted. She looked out the window; she looked into her tea but found no answers. Father hated Lehzen. He would go on at length about her duplicity, her sneaking ways, her gossip, her bribery of the servants.

As near as Jane could tell, Father's real objection to the woman was that the princess trusted Lehzen and did not trust him

Jane made her decision. "I had someplace I wished to go, but I did not want my father to know," she said. "A servant of ours had been dismissed without wages. I didn't think she deserved it. I wanted to see if I could help her and to give her some money. I couldn't let Father know, so I asked Her Highness to send me on an errand."

"That was very thoughtful of you." Lehzen cocked her

head toward Jane, and Jane got the impression the governess was trying to see her with fresh eyes. "Miss Conroy, I realize that despite all the time we have spent together, we do not know each other well. That is in part my fault, and I find I regret it now."

"You regret it because now you don't know if you can trust me."

"Yes," replied Lehzen. "Just so."

The calm answer surprised Jane. She assumed Lehzen would try to cover up her true meaning with some platitude about wanting to be friends.

"But it is more than that," Lehzen went on. "I don't know if Her Highness can trust you."

"She believes that she can."

"She has been very sheltered."

Jane felt her mouth twitch. "Has she, ma'am? Has she really?"

They sat like that for a while, holding each other's gaze, cups and saucers forgotten in their hands, the table and their mutual silence between them.

Jane drew a sharp breath. She braced herself. "Ma'am, what do you think is happening?" She spoke quickly, as if she needed to get the words out before someone caught her. "Why did my father lie about Dr. Maton?"

"I don't know," said Lehzen. "I was hoping you might."

Jane shook her head. "All I know is that he came to dinner at our house with the men of the Kensington board. But you see everything. You watch everyone for the princess. What was Dr. Maton's relationship to my father?"

"Well, let me see. I know that Dr. Maton was always the duchess's first choice to attend the princess, which, I admit, surprised me."

"Why?" asked Jane.

"Because he attended her husband on his deathbed. I am

not sure I would choose the doctor who failed to save my husband to look after the health of my child."

Jane hadn't known Dr. Maton had been there when the duke died. "Was it my father's idea? To have Dr. Maton look out for the princess?"

"He did not object certainly."

"But did Father want him? Did he choose him?"

"Is the distinction important?"

"It could be." Jane knew she was betraying her father a little more with each word. She was explaining him to his enemy, talking out loud about things that weren't even supposed to be whispered.

But she kept talking.

"If Father just lets a thing happen, it's because he believes it's harmless. If he encourages it, it's because he believes it will help some plan of his. So, if he urged the duchess to make sure it was Dr. Maton who attended the princess . . ."

"It was because he personally had reason to trust or to use Dr. Maton," Lehzen finished for her.

Jane nodded. "Father gossips to people about the princess's behavior, about her weakness."

"And perhaps he believed that Dr. Maton was one who could be counted on to agree with his assessments?"

"Or at least that he could be convinced not to contradict them," Jane said.

"Convinced," echoed Lehzen. "An interesting word."

"Did you ever hear Dr. Maton go along with my father's lies?" She felt reckless speaking this way. Dangerous. She was appalled. She was also elated.

"There was one time," said Lehzen. "I came upon them unexpectedly. I had been looking for her grace . . ."

You wanted to eavesdrop.

"And I found Sir John was speaking with the Earl of Dunham. Dr. Maton was there with them. I remember Sir John said, 'It is a deep shame, I tell you, but her legs are terribly weak, bordering on a true malformation.' "

Jane's whole face puckered.

"Sir John turned to Dr. Maton and said, 'Would you not agree, Doctor?' And I remember Maton replied, 'She is badly undergrown for a girl her age. The consequences may become more evident and more severe as she matures.' "

"Father would not have liked that," said Jane. "He would have wanted something more definite."

Lehzen shrugged. "But it does sort with your theory that Maton was your father's creature."

Jane found this idea left her very cold.

"Ma'am . . . ," she began.

"Yes?"

Everything in her screamed at her to keep quiet. If she spoke, she would be laughed at. She would be shouted at.

"I haven't said this to the princess yet. But . . . what if Dr. Maton was talking about her with someone else? Or what if he was talking to Father about . . . well, other people?"

"You mean what if the good doctor was trading secrets about the household?" Lehzen's voice dropped. "About the princess herself?"

"Yes. If he was getting information for Father and then spreading around what Father wanted known or believed—"

"Gossip is the currency of all courts," said Lehzen. "Even when it is counterfeit. That is something worth thinking about." Lehzen set her teacup down and did not refill it. Nor did she offer Jane anything more. "For years, I have looked after Her Highness, have tried to be her friend and to care for her as if she were any other young girl in this world. But that is not possible, because she is not any other girl and never will be."

"I understand."

"Do you?" Lehzen cocked her head toward Jane. It was a

quizzical look and highly skeptical. "I confess I am at a loss, Miss Conroy. It was my intention to ask you to stop acting as the princess's aide in this . . . this dangerous campaign she has begun. I had planned to threaten you with exposure—to the duchess, to your father. To say to them it was all your idea and you had put Her Highness in jeopardy."

Guilt and anger shot through Jane. She kept still and kept her gaze steady. She could hear what Lehzen had to say. She would endure it, with her head up.

It's time I learned how to do that.

"Now I do not think I will do this," Lehzen went on. "Now I think I will ask you to keep me informed as to what you learn."

Jane's jaw dropped open. She closed it hastily and swallowed all her surprise. Lehzen smiled, but it was a kind smile that acknowledged a silent shared joke.

"And we must find a way to make sure the princess has heard what you have suggested to me about the late Dr. Maton," Lehzen went on.

Jane's mouth twitched. Then, slowly, as if unused to this particular exercise, her lips bent into a smile of their own.

"Her Highness has already thought of that."

Chapter 24

By the time Victoria and Mama returned from their call to the Matons, both Jane and Lehzen had already settled themselves in their usual places in the larger of the sitting rooms. Lehzen rose at once to help Victoria with her coat and bonnet.

Victoria looked to Jane and saw she was reading Wordsworth's poems.

"I'm sorry," said Jane at once. "It was only there was that particular passage you were reading out to me, and I was not sure I understood. I wanted to review it. I should have waited..." Jane spoke in her usual hesitant, complaining tone, but Jane's eyes held hers.

Pay attention. Something's changed.

"Not at all," said Victoria at once. "You may borrow whatever book you wish, mayn't she, Mama?"

"I always recommend a young woman improve her mind through a rational course of reading. However, it must wait until tomorrow."

"But...," began Victoria.

Mama ignored her. "Miss Conroy, you will not be wanted anymore today. You are dismissed."

Victoria's first instinct was to protest, but Jane shook her head minutely, and Victoria subsided. She was right, of course. What reason could she give for making a fuss?

Wouldn't that please Sir John? To know that I am taking Jane's advice? Of course, he might not be so pleased if he knew on what subject.

"Before you go, Jane, bring me the cordial," said Victoria.

"Of course, ma'am." Jane went at once to retrieve the basket and ring the bell for her maid.

"What cordial?" demanded Mama. "What is that?"

"I told you, Mama." Victoria accepted the brown bottle from Jane. "I asked Jane to get me some of that soothing cordial from Mr. Oslow's in the village. I thought it might help Aunt Sophia. She has not been sleeping well."

Mama made a noncommittal noise. Victoria decided she could take a chance.

"I will just go take it to her before—"

"No. Lady Flora will take it, if it is to be done."

"But—"

"I said no, Victoria," snapped Mama. "I have indulged your whims quite enough today. There is a dinner tomorrow and a concert. We will prepare you for those. Now, come here and sit down. Jane, we will see you tomorrow, as usual."

And so Lady Flora was dispatched with the bottle, and Victoria found herself under her mother's most impatient scrutiny.

The rest of the afternoon was spent writing letters as Mama dictated and then sitting in the red salon, memorizing the latest guest list for dinner and then practicing the new piano piece she had been assigned, because Mama wanted her to play for the ladies she had invited for luncheon on Saturday.

That, at least, should not have been any kind of trial, but Victoria was so impatient for a moment alone that her fingers grew clumsy and she made any number of ridiculous mistakes.

Finally, Mama's patience reached its end.

"What on earth have I done to earn such a daughter!" She lapsed into German, the surest sign that she was genuinely angry. "I've tried. God in Heaven, I have done nothing but try, and this is what I get in return!"

"I'm sorry, Mama." She was. She did not want to be stupid or clumsy. She did not want to have secrets. She wanted to be able to tell her mother what she was doing, what she thought and felt.

When I know what's happening. When I have proof . . .

But she didn't. Not yet. Now she could only sit and look as stupid as Mama accused her of being. Anger boiled inside her.

"You will go sit on the sofa and not stir for an hour while you think about what you have done."

"Yes, Mama."

Victoria sat on the sofa by the windows. The breeze smelled of dust and soot. Mama dropped into her chair at her desk and began shuffling through her letters.

Jane had left Wordsworth's poems on the sofa. Victoria looked to Lehzen. Lehzen nodded.

Victoria waited until Mama had settled on a letter to read. She let her hand slip across the sofa to the book. Lehzen moved just a little to obscure the view. Mama frowned at her letter, her mouth moving as she read. It must be in English or in French.

Victoria flicked her finger against the book so it flopped

open and, as she hoped, showed the paper stuck between its pages.

She grabbed the note. Lehzen moved away, retrieved her workbasket, and settled herself in her usual spot by the fire.

Mama glared at Victoria. Victoria bowed over her hands. Mama turned back to her letter.

Victoria opened the folded scrap of paper. She knew the handwriting at once. It was from Lehzen.

A possibility to be considered: JC used Dr. to spread rumors and paid to keep him complacent.

Victoria read the note again and a third time. Her breath quickened, and she had to swallow several times to get herself under control. She glanced up. Mama was absorbed in reading her own letters. She met Lehzen's gaze, and Lehzen nodded. Victoria sucked in a deep breath.

It would make perfect sense. A doctor, a member of the medical household who had attended to her for years, would be listened to. He could tell anyone anything, and he'd be trusted. Sir John could take him to a dinner, to a board meeting, to a club where members of Parliament gathered. . . .

Why would he do such a thing?

Gossip was a fact of life. It could not be silenced. But it was also a fact that those who were caught talking out of bounds were dismissed. If Dr. Maton had been talking where he should not, he had taken an enormous risk. Sir John and Mama might run her life, but theirs were not the only voices when it came to the sprawling staff in and around the household.

Did Mama even know? Victoria's breath hitched. *That he used the doctor to spread his lies about me?* The doctor she'd sent for, the doctor who had attended her through her fevers and her hurts large and small.

Did she go along with the plan?

"Victoria, stop frowning. You'll wrinkle."

"Yes, Mama."

Victoria's quick, clever fingers shredded the paper into bits. She spent the rest of her hour's punishment slowly dropping those bits out the open window one by one for the breeze to carry away.

Chapter 25

"Jane?"

Jane froze. The voice was Mother's, coming from the blue salon.

Her head was full of everything that had happened today—seeing Susan, being quizzed by Lehzen, passing the note to the princess. The possibility that Dr. Maton had been used to spread not just rumors but rumors selected by Father and maybe the duchess.

That she had actually sat with Lehzen and aired her ideas and been heard as if she was a rational being.

"Goodness!" Mama raised her head from her silk pillow as Jane walked into the salon. "You look like I caught you sneaking in from meeting a sweetheart! Where's your father?"

"He's needed at the palace tonight. He said you should not wait dinner. "

"And here I had Cook make his favorite. Ah well. I suppose it does not matter." Especially as Jane very much doubted Mother had done any such thing. Jane found herself wondering if her mother even knew what Father's favorite meal was.

I certainly don't. Is that odd?

Mother gestured to the stool beside her. "Sit and talk to me, Jane."

Jane sat down and clenched her hands tightly together in her lap. Mama was indolent, but she was not a fool. Had she heard something? Did Liza let something slip?

"Now then, miss," Mother said with mock sternness. "You didn't go to the palace with your father this morning. No, don't bother to deny it. Where were you off to?"

How did she know? Jane thought. This was followed quickly by, *Why does she care?*

"I'm waiting, Jane."

Jane swallowed and prayed that her voice could remain steady. "The princess asked me to fetch her some of Mrs. Oslow's lemon and verbena cordial for the Princess Sophia. She has been . . . agitated lately."

Mother regarded her from under her fluttering eyelids. "Your father says you're finally making headway with our little princess. In a rather . . . unexpected fashion."

"I'm just . . . She wants someone to talk to. I'm there."

"You've been there for years, and she's never wanted someone to talk to that badly." Mother tilted her head. "I do wonder what's changed."

Jane twisted her hands. Mother smiled.

"Cat got your tongue?"

"I don't know what you want me to say."

"What I want you to say. Yes." Mama sighed deeply and let her sleepy gaze wander to the mantelpiece, to the portrait of Father, to the ceiling. "That's always the question, isn't it?"

Yes. Yes it is.

"Perhaps you should tell me whatever it is you've told

your father," Mother suggested. "It's much easier when you have to remember only one story, don't you think?"

Panic threatened. Jane clutched her hands together so tightly that for a moment she thought she might break her own fingers. "It's . . . it's complicated."

"I'm sure it is." Mother's voice was amused, as if she'd just heard some bon mot during a party. Her whole attitude was full of charm and ease. But there was something there beneath all this, something calculating.

Something that reminded Jane of Father.

"Did Father tell you about the corpse?"

"Oh, that." Mother's sigh was long and ever so slightly bitter. "This to-do is about that?"

"The princess is sure there's something behind it. Some story or something, and she wants to find out what it is."

"What an odd notion! How does she plan to go about this extraordinary endeavor?"

"That's what she's talking to me about. She wants me to help her, and Father says I should play along. So I am."

Mama laughed. It was a strained, weary sound, not like anything Jane had heard from her before. "And this is the indulgence that finally brings you into the princess's good graces?"

Jane smiled. She didn't know what else to do.

"Well, it does seem to be working. It was most amusing to hear your father singing your praises at the table the other night. So. You will be Her Highness's pet for as long as her interest lasts."

Jane felt oddly offended at this assessment, but then she saw her mother's face. The comfort and charm had shifted, had turned into something much sadder and more speculative. "For all our sakes, Jane, do remember that you are a pet, and nothing more than a pet." Mother spoke urgently. Jane couldn't remember ever having heard her do so before. "And be very careful not to let her think you'll bite her hand. That girl forgives even less readily than the duchess."

Mother was remembering something specific. Jane was sure of it. She wanted to find a way to ask what it was, but the moment passed. The unfamiliar seriousness of her manner drained away, leaving behind the bored and exhausted beauty she knew so well.

"Go away now, Jane." Mother's eyes drooped. "I'm tired."

But Jane found she was not yet ready to leave.

"Mother?"

Mother pressed the back of her hand to her brow. "Mmm?"

"Mother, did you know the dead man was Dr. Maton?"

"Yes, of course," said Mother. "Your father told me."

"He did?"

"Yes." Mother opened her eyes and lifted her hand away. She was definitely not pleased. "What's the matter, Jane? You look like you don't believe me."

"No, well, I . . ."

"Jane, you know how I hate it when you stammer so stupidly. Speak clearly, or do not speak at all." Mother let her head flop back onto the pillows. "Ugh. Why must everything be so difficult?"

Jane took a deep breath. "Father lied about who it was to the princess. Do you know why he did that?"

For a moment, Jane thought Mother would simply dismiss her. But Mother shifted uneasily.

"Your father, Jane, is one for grand schemes." She spoke to the ceiling, but Jane had the sense that she was speaking to her memories, as well. "He dreams of so much *more*, and not just for himself but for all his children. The difference between him and other men is that he actually works to make those dreams come to pass. He works for all of us, Jane." Mother turned her eyes toward Jane, but the distance in them remained. "Unfortunately, he is not always careful with the little things. Small details, small men ... He leaves them scattered about."

Understanding drifted past Jane. She knew she was being told something true, and it was important. But there was some piece missing—some final meaning in her mother's words and lazy, arch looks that she could not entirely grasp. Without that piece, she could not hold on to the rest.

Chapter 26

Victoria's day dragged on. Mama's temper did not improve. She found fault with Victoria, of course, but also with each of the ladies in turn—berating them all for being slow, for not attending, for general sloth. But Victoria was not permitted to so much as go to the other side of the room. She must sit beside Mama's chair, so that Mama could watch over her shoulder as she wrote in her journal and read her letters and made her comments on each one.

Dinner was a relief, because at least it gave Mama something different to complain about.

Afterward, she was content to let Victoria practice her piano while she sat with her letters. This at least allowed Victoria some occupation for her restless thoughts and feelings.

But Victoria could not help noticing that Sir John did not make his customary appearance.

Is that what's got you in such a stew, Mama?

So when the door opened, the entire room jumped. But it was not Sir John.

It was Mrs. Bingham, Aunt Sophia's favorite waiting woman. She handed Lady Flora a paper note.

"A note for Her Highness from Princess Sophia, ma'am," Lady Flora announced.

Mama held out her hand. Victoria would have liked to object, but it was useless. Of course Mama must read it first.

Mama scanned the lines and muttered something.

"What does she say?"

For a moment, Victoria thought Mama would refuse to tell her. "She asks you to come up and have a glass of that ridiculous cordial with her before bed."

"May I? She has been so troubled of late. Perhaps I can help soothe her mind."

Mama sighed. Victoria watched her look for reasons to refuse.

"A half hour," she said finally. "No more. Lady Flora will go with you."

Victoria swallowed her protest. What protest could she reasonably make? That she had things to say to her aunt that she did not want Lady Flora to hear?

"Thank you, Mama." Victoria kissed her cheek and let Mama pat her cheek in return.

"One half hour. You must not be up too late. I want you at your best tomorrow."

Victoria knew that Lady Flora did not like the dark. She did not so much walk through the long line of empty rooms as march, as if the deliberate belligerence of her movements would keep any waiting goblins from catching up with her.

She didn't like Aunt Sophia, either. She regarded her as a pathetic old woman who should have been put out to pasture years ago. Somehow, she managed to ignore the fact that as far as the rest of the court was concerned, being housed in Kensington Palace was being put out to pasture.

But then Victoria could understand how a lady with such a high opinion of herself as Lady Flora might not want to consider that fact too closely.

They had almost reached Aunt Sophia's private apartments. Lady Flora opened the door to the "queen's writing room." But the room was already occupied. Uncle Sussex stood at the mantel, a lamp burning beside him. He had the mantel clock turned around and its back open.

"Ah! Vickelchen and Lady Flora." He smiled but barely spared them a glance. "Don't you mind me. Some fool has forgotten to wind this one. I'm just setting it to rights." He fussed with something in the mechanism, and the clock chimed gently. "There we are!" He closed the back carefully and turned to them. "Now." He pulled out an enormous handkerchief to wipe his hands. "What brings you to these distant domains?" He spread his hands, indicating the tiny, dark room.

"A royal invitation from the Princess Sophia herself," declared Victoria.

"Truly? Well, well, such an honor. If you will step into my antechamber, I shall go and see if Her Very Royal Highness is receiving." Uncle Sussex held out his arm.

Victoria giggled at the little game. Uncle Sussex beamed. Lady Flora's smile said she was tolerating this show, because really, what else could she do?

This side of the room had two doors; Uncle Sussex pushed open the one at his right hand, which led to what had once been a private study. It was an odd choice, but he was smiling so genially, Victoria let herself go along with the game.

But then the other door opened, and through it walked Sir John. He was accompanied by another man. This one wore a clerk's black coat and stock.

Victoria stared. So did Sir John. So did the man in the black coat.

"What are you doing here?" demanded Sir John. "Ma'am?" he added belatedly.

"Aunt Sophia invited me," Victoria answered. "What are you doing?" She said this to Sir John, but she kept her attention on the man in the black coat. The man bowed and slipped his gaze sideways to Sir John.

"There was business to attend to," said Sir John. "I am surprised your mother permitted you to come so near your bedtime. I shall speak with her about it." He turned to the man beside him. "You may go on now, Rea. We will talk tomorrow."

Victoria felt her heart thump. This tall, bright-eyed man with his head thrusting forward was Mr. Rea? He smiled at them all, bobbing his head randomly, as if agreeing with each of them in turn. Victoria was so busy watching him that she forgot to speak. Her silence gave Sir John room to usher orders.

"Lady Flora, you may thank Princess Sophia for her invitation but tell her it is too late for the princess to be out of her rooms. Assure her that Her Highness will attend her at some more appropriate time. I will escort Her Highness back to her rooms." He helped himself to the lamp that Mr. Rea held.

"Aunt Sophia invited me," protested Victoria. "I want—"

But it was already too late. Lady Flora had curtsied, and Mr. Rea had bowed, and they had all begun to move in the directions Sir John had pointed them. Sir John turned to her and held out his arm.

Victoria looked to her uncle. But Uncle Sussex just shrugged apologetically.

She could call Lady Flora back, give orders, insist she would go to see her aunt, but what good would it do? She could not now see Aunt Sophia alone. Sir John would doubtless insist on coming in with her, whether she wanted him to or not.

She had been checked, and she knew it.

Victoria looked down at Sir John and the arm he held out. She had two choices—take his arm or walk away into the dark on her own and risk making a fool of herself by running into a door or tripping over something unseen.

She took his arm.

They walked down the long straight row of rooms. Sir John led, his long strides forcing Victoria to scurry to keep up and leaving her breathless and awkward.

He does it on purpose.

Well, if he would insist on keeping her close, he could suffer the consequences. "Why were you in Aunt Sophia's rooms?"

"Logic would suggest I had business with Her Royal Highness."

"What possible business could you have with my aunt?"

"Ma'am, despite your hurtful resentment of me, I have served your family faithfully for much of my life, and I shall continue to do so as long as I am able. Your aunt has very few people to whom she can turn for help with practical matters. Your mother some time ago suggested I should help her, and so I do."

"Practical matters? You mean with her money?" *Sir John handles Aunt Sophia's money?*

"I assist her, as I assist your mother," said Sir John. "As I will assist you as your private secretary when your time comes."

"Whether I want you to or not," muttered Victoria.

Sir John halted. He faced her, holding the lamp up high over them both. The shadows flickered, sharpening the bones and planes of his long face but turning his eyes to nothing but empty black holes.

"One day," he breathed, "you will find yourself alone, surrounded entirely by wolves, all eager to tear out that dainty throat of yours. And on that day, you will turn to me, as your mother did, as your aunt does. You will acknowledge that we are bound together, that you need me and you will always need me, because I am the only one you can trust to save you."

He stepped closer. He was tall and broad. He smelled of sour sweat and old wine. Victoria's mouth had gone dry. She tried to back away and stumbled, and Sir John smiled.

"You do not believe me, because you are stubborn and childish, but your day will come." His voice was harsh and muffled. The wooden walls deadened all the echoes. Victoria was suddenly painfully aware of the vast chain of empty rooms around them.

"But don't worry, child," said Sir John, his tone a sick imitation of gentleness. "I will be just as faithful to you as your secretary as I have been to the other women who have trusted me to be their champion. And you will be very glad to make me your man."

She couldn't breathe. She was afraid. Of what exactly, she could not say—of his touch, of his grin, of the shadows behind him, of the thoughts swirling behind the empty holes of his eyes.

Then, as if that fear were dry kindling, anger burst into flame. She wanted to scream. She wanted to demand he say what he knew about Dr. Maton and about the rumors he helped spread.

Was he your man? Did he carry your tales to the board, to Parliament, and St. James's? Were you using him to keep me and Mama under your thumb?

She could lash out now, let him know she would not be fooled.

I know what you are. I know what you are doing!

Then, past Sir John's shoulder, she saw the ghost. It was

Elizabeth, the tall and red-haired queen, with her lace ruff, pointed chin, and angry, penetrating gaze.

The regal ghost put one long white finger to her lips. *Hush,* the gesture said. *Keep your secrets.*

Sir John was watching. Victoria dragged her feelings back and bundled them up tightly in her chest. She shrank down, made herself small, made herself into the humble, tiny thing he so loved to see.

Made him smile his thin, satisfied smile.

"I should be back with Mama," she murmured.

"You should." He gave her his arm again, and she took it and watched the floor all the way back to her rooms.

And all the way back, she knew the ghost followed.

Chapter 27

Queen Adelaide emerged from the king's bedchamber. Doors were opened and closed. Candles moved to provide better light as she sat in the chair before the fire. A glass of wine had already been placed on the table. It was rich red. French, no doubt. She missed the ice wines of home sometimes. She wanted something clear just now. Something strong that would fortify her spirits, not depress them.

It was Mrs. Wilson who approached her first.

"How does the king, ma'am?"

"Better," she said, loud enough so her whole suite of ladies and servants could hear. "His fever is lessened, and he took some broth and watered wine." She took a drink of her own wine. It wasn't what she wanted, but it was far better than yet another cup of tea. William had croaked multiple complaints about the wine and demanded rum, like the sailor that he was. Adelaide told him not to be ridiculous.

"If you want to be on your back for three more days, you will go on and drink your ridiculous rum ration. If you would rather be out of this room and back about your business, you will listen to your doctors and me."

William had, thankfully, decided to humor her. "No need to give the troublemakers more time to be about their business," he muttered.

Mrs. Wilson had not yet retreated.

"Was there something more?" Adelaide asked.

"You know that I have been to speak with the Baroness Lehzen."

"And?" Adelaide finished off her glass. The footman moved forward with more wine, but she waved him back. *You received a note from Lehzen, but nothing from Lady Charlotte, our official state governess. It is a wonder we bother to keep her there at all.* "What does Lehzen have to say?"

"She says rumors of the king's illness have reached the duchess and Sir John."

"Damn." Living so long with a naval man had caused a certain deterioration of the queen's language, at least in private. "Well, tell Lehzen that it's a mild cold."

"I did, ma'am."

"And also tell her she should repeat that as often as she feels will be helpful, and perhaps even laugh over . . . others' concern for His Majesty's health."

"I am sure she will do so, but I will write and remind her."

Adelaide nodded. *God, I am so tired.* "How is the princess? She is recovered from that fall?"

"Much recovered," said Mrs. Wilson. "Dr. Clarke is visiting her daily. But there is something else."

Somewhere outside, morning was dawning. Adelaide knew she ought to tell Mrs. Wilson that whatever she had to say could wait. She needed sleep. She would do her husband no good if she was so tired she could not think straight, could not fend off all those vultures from Parliament. . . .

Instead, she asked, "Well? What is it?"

"Lehzen indicated that rumors have also reached Sir John and the Duchess of Kent that His Majesty means to change the princess's establishment."

"What? Who told them that?"

"I don't know, ma'am. But she suggests that a final decision be made quickly, before Sir John is able to muster support . . ."

*Before he is able to create controversy. To raise a stink in
Parliament and in the newspapers.* There was nothing that
man was better at than making a mess of simple things. Of
course it was ridiculous that the king could not house his
niece and heir as he saw fit. But there it was. She supposed
she could not entirely blame Parliament for making Victoire
the girl's guardian when Fat George was alive. That man had
been no proper guardian, and his court no fit home for a
pretty little girl. But since then . . .

Well, there was no use in railing against what could not be
helped. Parliament controlled the civil list and, therefore, the
household budgets of all the royals. If Their Lordships
would not allocate money to set up a new house, hire new
servants, or appoint new attendants, it could not happen. If
Parliament would not change the guardianship for the heir
to the throne, then it was Victoire, not William and not her,
who would say where the princess lived and how.

Sir John had been nothing short of masterful in charming
those men who were best placed to sabotage any such change,
and of course, Victoire had done nothing to stop him.

*Oh, Victoire, what has become of you? How did you let
that man get such a tight hold on you?*

But Adelaide knew. Her own pride had helped drive Victoire away. They had been friends when they both arrived in
England, but since then . . . First, there was the animosity
between their husbands. Then there was Victoire's refusal to
come to court or allow her daughter to have any contact
with William's children by Mrs. Jordan. Adelaide did understand. She might have done so had she had any choice in the
matter. But as it was . . .

Then there was the simple, devastating fact that Victoire's daughter had lived and not one of Adelaide's had.

Adelaide wanted to believed that she had never truly resented Victoire's little daughter. She wanted to explain to her former friend how it had been so hard, how much her heart had bled with each child she and William lost, until it seemed there was nothing left in her but grief—and yes, anger against any child who lived and breathed while her own lay buried in the cold clay.

She wanted to tell Victoire about the nights when she woke from dreams of her little ones crying in that endless dark.

Slowly, the dreams had faded. Slowly, the pieces of her heart had knit themselves together. But by then it had been too late. Victoire had decided not to forgive, and she had turned instead toward the ready smile and—if rumors were to be believed—the waiting arms of Sir John.

Yet Victoire declares she will not have her daughter brought to court, because there is a grievous moral taint to William's children.

And once again, Adelaide found herself unable to see past her anger.

"Is there anything else?" she asked Mrs. Wilson.

Mrs. Wilson correctly interpreted her tone as indicating there should not be. "No, ma'am."

"Very good, then. I will lie down for an hour. If there is any change from the king, or anyone else, I am to be woken at once."

"Yes, ma'am."

Chapter 28

Thankfully, the next day was a sunny one. Victoria was able to sit through her lessons and Mama's interrogation with patience because she knew at half ten she would be required to take her morning walk through the gardens.

Victoria had never been so glad for the system's rigid schedule in her life. When the time came, she all but leapt out of her chair.

"Let us walk out to the round pond," she said to Jane. "I want to draw."

So, Jane dutifully gathered up both her and Victoria's sketchbooks and pencil boxes. She even remembered Dash's favorite ball. Dash barked and ran for the door, more than ready to be outside.

The summer morning was oppressively hot and still. Even the geese and ducks huddled under the shade trees, leaving the water to the swans. Victoria had been dressed in her lightest muslin, but she still felt unbearably sticky underneath her shift, corset, and stockings. Her hair under her bonnet was growing damp with perspiration. The roses drooped, and the green lawn was burnt as brown as the gardeners who dug in the borders by the hedgerows.

A stone bench waited near the pond. Victoria sat down, and Jane handed her, her sketchbook and opened her pencil box. *The very image of the waiting lady.* Victoria quirked a brow at her. Jane shrugged with one shoulder and nodded toward Lehzen and Lady Flora, who stood some little distance away, but not too far, holding shawls and fans and other such things that might be called for at a moment's notice.

Also close enough to hear the conversation if they raised their voices. Victoria nodded.

Jane sat beside her and opened her own sketchbook. Anyone who came across them, or who took it into their head to watch from a window, would see a perfectly peaceful scene without a single aspect out of place.

"I got the note." Victoria took up a charcoal stick and opened her book to a clean page. "That Sir John was making use of Dr. Maton. But there's more to it."

Jane's brows rose. Victoria nodded. Then, making sure to glance occasionally out at the pond and its inhabitants, she told Jane about her attempt to visit Aunt Sophia the night before and all that happened afterward.

She did not mention the ghost.

"She wanted me to see Sir John and Mr. Rea together. I am sure of it," Victoria concluded.

"But why would she?"

"She knows something about Sir John. She knows he has some closer connection to both Dr. Maton and Mr. Rea."

Jane didn't answer. But her face twisted tight.

"What is it?"

"Nothing," said Jane quickly, and Victoria rolled her eyes.

"It is something. You thought of something or remembered something. What is it?"

"It's . . . it's not something we talk about."

"We?"

"The family. My family." She paused. "My father."

"Something to do with Dr. Maton?"

"Something he might have known about my mother." She stopped. "And your father."

"*What*?" Victoria cried. Lehzen and Lady Flora both came to attention. Victoria blanched. She also swatted playfully at Jane's hands. "Oh, Jane! You ridiculous thing!" She laughed.

Jane ducked her head, as if hiding a blush.

"I shouldn't have said anything. I'm sorry," she whispered. "It's nothing. A delusion, a lie. I'm not sure which, but it has to be—"

"Jane Conroy. Stop it."

Jane shut her mouth.

"Now. You've already gone too far," whispered Victoria harshly. "Tell me what it is you're talking about."

"My father," said Jane. "He says my mother is . . ."

"What is she?"

"A natural daughter. Of your . . . of the late Duke of Kent."

"That is not true," said Victoria, her voice flat, cold, and hard. "That cannot possibly be true."

You will acknowledge that we are bound together . . .

"I only know it's what he says," Jane told her miserably.

"He is a liar!"

"Ma'am?" Lehzen came closer. "Is something wrong?"

"No," said Victoria. "Nothing."

Lehzen retreated. Victoria sat very still. She stared out, seeing nothing. Or, perhaps, everything.

"I don't think it's true," Jane said. "I think it's just something he says to us, so that we would agree to come and be your ladies . . ."

"And to spy for him," said Victoria through clenched teeth.

"Yes," said Jane. "But if Dr. Maton or Mr. Rea knew that it was something he believed, or something he had said, and perhaps used to convince somebody of his importance . . ."

"They could hold that against him," said Victoria. "Mother would tolerate almost any lie from him, but not him saying that . . ." Mama believed bastardry was a sin, that it irrevocably tainted the person. She would not tolerate knowing Sir John had married such a person, had fathered her children. . . .

"He would do almost anything to keep that rumor from her."

The words fell heavily, and Jane sucked in a sharp breath, as if she wanted to take them back into herself. But it was too late.

Victoria looked down at her book. "You were right to tell me. I'm sorry I shouted."

Victoria quickly sketched a little duck flapping its wings and frowning at the world. Jane smiled just a little. She reached across with her own pencil and added a speech bubble so that the duck was quacking at the top of its lungs.

Victoria added three ducklings in the water. Jane added a fourth caught in the act of diving down, so its tiny bottom pointed to the sky. Victoria grinned and wrote, *Let's walk on. There's something I want to do before I'm called back indoors.*

Jane looked at her.

Victoria smoothed the page down and wrote, *We need to talk to the groundskeepers. Let me have Dash's ball.*

Thankfully, the men were still about their business in the gardens. Getting close to them was easy enough. Victoria took Dash's ball and tossed it for him to chase. The spaniel loved his toy, but he loved new people more and quickly abandoned the ball in the grass to go and make new friends, and also to investigate what fascinating mysteries surely awaited in the herbaceous border.

"Oh dear!" Victoria hurried to fetch her truant dog, with Jane at her heels.

The groundskeepers took off their hats as she reached them, and bowed.

Victoria beamed at them. She also picked up Dash, who wriggled and licked her chin.

Victoria turned to the head groundskeeper. Richards was his name, she remembered. He was not an old man, but a life outdoors had left him tough, tanned, and wrinkled, despite his broad straw hat and loose smock. He was tiny and wiry, but she had the impression he was perfectly ready to move a mountain with a shovel and barrow if the job required it. "I do apologize for Dash, Richards," she said. "I hope he did not do too much damage."

"No harm done, ma'am," the man said calmly.

"I'm glad," she replied. "I appreciate you have been given more than the usual amount of trouble of late."

This puzzled him. "Well, now, ma'am, I would not say so. 'Tis always a busy time of year. Must make hay while the sun shines, if you understand me, but—"

"But this business with Dr. Maton. It is very hard."

"Ah. Yes." Richards scratched his stubbled chin. "Very sorry about it, I was. Always very gentlemanlike, Dr. Maton. Heard young Simpson there coughing one day and gives him a going-over on the spot. Says he'll send round some special syrup, and he did that the next day. Did the lad a world of good. Thoughtful like that, he was."

Victoria nodded. "It must have been a shock to find him so."

"Well, it was, and it wasn't. I mean, it's sure a shock when Sir John comes to get us, says, 'Bring a barrow.' Says Dr. Maton has dropped down, God rest him, and he must be got home. 'Mustn't be any fuss,' he says. So, we gets the barrow, and pon my soul, ma'am, we took as much care as we could."

"I am sure that you did." *That explains the wheel marks Jane saw.*

"Coulda told him so much walking wasn't good for a gentleman his age," Richards went on. "Not bred to it, like."

This startled her. "Did Dr. Maton walk on the green that much?"

"Oh, yes, he was always back and forth across there. All weathers. At least once a week, if not more. Not a problem for someone like me." He chuckled and flexed his wiry arm. "Used to it, you know, but he was a city man, if you understand me."

"I do indeed," said Victoria solemnly. "Now, I must not keep you from your work any longer."

The men all bowed, and Victoria strode back to the path, with Jane right behind her. Victoria put Dash down, retrieved the ball, which Jane had remembered to collect, and tossed it. Dash barked and ran, and Victoria watched.

"Which of us will say it?" breathed Jane.

"I will, if you like." Dash had caught up with the ball and now galloped back to them.

Jane nodded.

"Dr. Maton was walking the route that would take him to your house." Victoria threw the ball again. Dash barked and ran, delighted.

"We know he was working closely with Father, so that's really not a surprise," said Jane.

"And if Father wanted to dictate what rumors the doctor was spreading or find out what new gossip he was hearing, that would not be a conversation they could safely have in the palace."

"So was Dr. Maton keeping your father's secrets or spreading them?" muttered Victoria.

"Perhaps both," whispered Jane, glancing over her shoulder. Lehzen and Lady Flora were still there, of course, but too far away to hear. *Hopefully.* "Perhaps that's why he was so dangerous."

"Sir John is much with my mother, of course, but during lesson time, he is frequently about his own business. They could have met then." Victoria paused to take the ball from Dash and toss it out again. "Would your sister have seen them? Might she have overheard something?"

"She might. I can ask. Although, if it was in the morning, she would generally be out of the house on Mother's errands, if she's awake at all."

"Mmm. Yes. There's that. But would you ask, anyway? Just in case?"

"Yes, ma'am," said Jane, but her mind was not on the words. She had gone distant and grave.

"What is it?" Dash was barking at a bee in the clover. "Dash! Leave it!" Dash gave the insect one more good bark and turned back to hunting for his ball.

"It's just . . . Something happened yesterday," Jane said. "My mother, she called me into her, and she tried to get me to talk about you. She never does that. She talked about how well I'm getting along with you and how pleased Father is."

Victoria laughed. "If he only knew."

A smile flickered across Jane's features. "But then she said something about Father. She said, 'He is not always careful with the little things. Small details, small men . . . He leaves them scattered about.'"

"Do you think she knows something?"

"Or suspects something. Maybe. It's difficult to tell with her. She makes such a show of not wanting any bother."

"You must talk to her if you can." Motion caught Victoria's eye. It was Lehzen, signaling it was time they returned to the palace. Victoria nodded and walked on. She must be back for luncheon and afternoon lessons and afternoon exercise and a nap and then to dress for the dinner and all the rest.

"But our most urgent task," Victoria said, "is to contrive a way for me to speak with Dr. Gerald Maton."

"You can't possibly," said Jane. "You even aren't allowed to go downstairs without someone holding your hand. They'll never let you out to see a strange man. And there's no reason for him to come to the palace . . ."

"There will be a way," said Victoria. "I've spent half my life finding the cracks in Sir John's system. This is just one more."

Jane fell silent, but Victoria knew what she was thinking.

But none of the other times involved sneaking out of the palace.

It makes no difference. Victoria lifted her chin. *There will be a way.*

Victoria repeated that to herself several times to make sure she believed it.

Chapter 29

In the end, slipping the net took far more people, and far more time, than Victoria would have liked. Indeed, it took several days to arrange matters properly. And then two more after that for a frustrating rainy spell to let up sufficiently to allow Mama (and the system) to agree it was acceptable for Victoria to take a carriage ride through the village.

Sir John, Mama, and the system permitted these on occasion for the same reason they permitted the crowds to gather at the palace gates: they believed it was good for people to see Victoria and be reminded that she was their future queen.

Dull routine had never seemed to gnaw so painfully at her patience—standing still to be dressed; sitting still to have her hair done; reading; writing; sitting to dinner; listening; writing; reading; walking in the garden; parading before the ladies and their lords, reciting pleasant, approved answers to their questions, and then standing in silence while Mama extolled and lamented.

Fancywork, drawing, sitting to dinner.

Being put to bed and rising in the morning to begin it all again.

She had heard nothing from Aunt Sophia. Several times she had sent Lehzen to her with a smuggled note. Each time word came back that her aunt was not feeling well. It was a summer cold, Victoria was told. Nothing to worry anyone, but she was choosing to stay in bed.

But all these messages came from Uncle Sussex.

What is he doing? Is he trying to keep me from her? Why would he do such a thing?

Yet more questions she did not know the answers to.

At last, the sun shone, and Sir John was away to meet with the master of the horse about the baggage carts needed for the September tour, while Mama was meeting with the household chef about the next dinner.

So, it was for Lehzen to remind Lady Flora that it was time for the day's drive.

"If you're ready, ma'am?" Lehzen said to Victoria. "Miss Conroy?"

Lehzen held her hand as they went down the stone stairs, as required. Jane followed behind, and Dash scampered beside her.

As they all emerged into the sunny courtyard, Victoria wasn't sure if she wanted to skip or simply be sick. *Perhaps both.* There was so much that could go wrong. Lehzen had made that very plain as soon as Victoria had told her she wanted to go speak with Gerald Maton.

"Who would drive you? Any of the grooms might talk," Lehzen had said.

"Then you must find those who won't."

Victoria had apologized later for her imperious tone.

"It is not safe," Lehzen had said. "Let me go instead."

"No. I will do this myself."

"Why?"

"To discover if I can."

"Again, ma'am, why?"

Victoria met her gaze directly. "Because there may come some other time when I have to."

Lehzen had turned away.

The open carriage waited in the yard. According to a note Lehzen had left in Wordsworth's poems, their driver was Arthur Saddler. Saddler was the head groom and had taken Hornsby's dismissal personally.

Because of this, and because it runs afoul of Sir John's plans, he has agreed to help and not ask too many questions.

The outriders, presumably chosen by Saddler, took their places, and Saddler himself climbed onto the box. He touched up the horses. The usual cluster of onlookers were shooed back by the footmen so they could open the gates, and Saddler drove them smoothly through.

It was the same when they reached the village proper. The onlookers cheered. Hats were tossed in the air, and ladies curtsied deeply. Victoria waved, and the crowd waved enthusiastically in return.

"Beg pardon, ma'am," called Saddler from the driver's box.

"What is it?" answered Lehzen.

"The off horse has come up lame. There's a livery stable in the next street. If we stop there, we can change him out, and one of the boys can walk him back."

"Very well," agreed Lehzen.

Despite the sun, Jane looked pale. Victoria itched to ask if she was sure her woman would be waiting, as promised.

"You'll need a maid," Jane had pointed this out. "You're

still a gently bred young woman, no matter what bonnet you're wearing. You can't be out alone. It would look very odd. People would remember you, and you don't want that."

Jane was right. Victoria did not want her to be, but some facts were inescapable. A young woman driving alone would draw attention.

"Who then? Lehzen must stay with the carriage, and I cannot ask anyone of the palace staff."

"I might know someone. She's in need of work, and, well, she has no particular love for my family."

The livery sprawled between two brick warehouses—a rutted dirt yard populated by a series of wooden sheds. The air was thick with barnyard smells. Men led horses to and fro. Men stood around horses. Men bent to examine horses' hooves and reached up to feel their withers. Men shouted. Horses neighed and whickered. It was a managed and energetic chaos, and Victoria loved it on sight.

A brown-skinned man with a fringe of tightly curled hair outlining his bald scalp hurried up to the carriage. He and Saddler conferred for a moment, and then Saddler drove them around to a corner of the yard enclosed by a high wooden fence. Saddler drove them through the gate, which was then closed behind them.

The little space was filled with carriage bodies with missing wheels, broken traces, loose doors. All manner of bits and pieces for their repair had been neatly stacked against the fence.

In the middle of it all stood a petite young woman with a gaunt, freckled face. She wore a drab coat and bonnet. Beside her stood Hornsby, looking as cross and pinched as ever.

Jane looked ready to melt with relief.

"Quickly now," said Lehzen.

Victoria and Jane were helped down from the carriage.

Dash put his forepaws on the rail and watched this new game with great interest and much wagging of his tail.

"This is Susan," said Jane, introducing Victoria to the young woman.

Victoria beamed. "Thank you for your help, Susan. And you, as well, Hornsby." She touched his hand. "I'm sorry for what happened, and I will not forget this." She smiled a little. "And I am truly sorry about 'Pinch-face.'"

"All forgotten, ma'am." Hornsby bowed stiffly. Victoria decided to pretend that was true.

With silent efficiency, Lehzen swapped the bonnets, coats, and gloves, so that now Victoria wore Jane's and Jane wore Victoria's.

By the time this was done, Saddler and Hornsby had brought a second carriage into the little yard. This one was battered and in need of polish and was pulled by a dispirited chestnut mare who looked more than ready to be put out to pasture. Saddler and Hornsby also swapped coats, so that Hornsby wore Saddler's scarlet livery with its gold braid, and Saddler wore Hornsby's dusty buff and drooping black hat.

Saddler helped Victoria and then Susan into the drab carriage. Now Dash began barking, anguished to see that he was being left behind. Victoria ran to hug and soothe him, but he whined in his distress.

In the end, all she could do was hand him to Lehzen, who, thankfully, was familiar with his ways. Keeping wriggling Dash firmly in the crook of one arm, Lehzen laid her hand on Saddler's arm. She murmured something. Saddler choked hard and then bowed.

He closed the door, climbed up on the box, and drove out the gate and the yard and turned into the street.

"What did she say?" called Victoria.

"That if I let anything happen to you, she'd have my guts for garters and then turn what was left of me over to the duchess."

Victoria laughed, and when the new maid, Susan, stared at her in open surprise, she laughed again. But no one admonished her, and no one asked her what people would think.

In fact, no one said a single word.

Dr. Gerald Maton's surgery was a fine brick house with a gleaming brass plate on the door. A page in neat livery let them in, and a footman accepted the card Susan laid on his tray. While he took the card into the doctor, Susan took Victoria's bonnet and coat. The footman returned to show her into the consulting room. Susan followed, as calm and quiet as if she'd been waiting on Victoria for years.

Gerald Maton sat behind a broad desk with papers and books heaped untidily across its surface. Victoria wondered if he would recognize her from the condolence call she had paid his family.

A heartbeat later, she had her answer. The youngest Dr. Maton looked up as she entered, and his smile of welcome faded away into a blank stare of shock.

In the next second, he shot to his feet.

"Your . . ."

"Miss Kent," Victoria said quickly. "I am Miss Kent."

"I don't understand, ma'—"

"Miss Kent," said Victoria firmly.

"Miss?" he said weakly.

"Yes." Victoria took the chair that had been set in front of the desk. "Please sit down."

He did so, but he did not cease to stare. Another girl of sixteen might have been disconcerted by such scrutiny from a man at least twice her age. But Victoria was perfectly accustomed to the company of older men, and to being examined by them either openly or with sneaking sideways glances.

"I can only apologize for this highly irregular situation," she told him. "And I must beg for your discretion."

"I, but, that is . . . ma—miss," he sputtered. "Please. What is happening?"

"I am here in the hope I can persuade you to speak with me about your father's death."

The effect was immediate. Gerald Maton's mouth snapped shut. His cheeks colored, but it was not from shame or bashfulness. It was from that same anger that she had seen in his mother's parlor.

But he still struggled to find words. Victoria felt impatience building.

"If it will aid matters, you may ask me anything you wish first," she said.

"How is it you came to have my father's spectacles?"

Victoria nodded. The package she had passed him at the vigil had indeed been a sketch of his father, just as she had told Mama. But that sketch had been wrapped around the ruined spectacles, and she had written on it, *You may expect a visit from me.*

"They were found on the palace green, where he himself was found," Victoria told him now.

He slumped back in his chair, as if he no longer had the strength to hold himself upright. Victoria tried to be patient with this man, whom she had already begun referring to as Dr. Gerald in her private thoughts.

"Why did your family say your father died at home in his bed?"

Dr. Gerald's hands gripped the air, as if he was looking for something to tear apart.

"He was brought home to us in a cart," he said finally. "I

was not there when it happened. I was summoned by one of the servants. When I arrived, he had been laid out on his bed but not yet washed. I saw . . . I saw he was covered in mud and soaked with rain. My mother and oldest brother had locked themselves in his consulting room. When they came out, I demanded to know what had happened." Dr. Gerald stopped. His hands clenched again. Victoria waited, her face calm but her heart hammering. "They would not say a word about what had really happened. The only reason I know anything at all is because I asked one of the footmen."

"What did he say?"

"First, he begged me not to tell anyone he'd spoken to me, because my brother and my mother had threatened to sack anyone who spoke about how my father's body had been brought home. It was only when I swore I'd take him into my own household that he agreed to tell me anything at all."

Victoria nodded.

"He said that before they had sent for me, my mother and brother spent half an hour in private with a gentleman who did not give his name. It was when he left that they ordered silence and secrecy." Dr. Gerald looked at his hands on the desktop, clenched so tightly the knuckles had turned white. "The gentleman apparently spoke of a pension owing to my father that would only be paid upon condition that the . . . correct story was given out."

"How did they—your mother and brother—explain the necessity of this . . . story?"

Dr. Gerald snorted. "They said we must keep up appearances, that any rumors of irregularities—I believe that was the word my brother chose—would damage his ability to absorb and maintain my father's private practice."

"What did this gentleman look like?"

He shook his head. "I did not think to ask."

Victoria was silent for a moment. The case clock in the corner ticked insistently. She did not have much time. But there was one more question she very much wanted the answer to.

"Did you ever hear your father speak about the Princess Sophia?"

"Was she a patient of his?"

Victoria considered. "I don't know. Possibly. She said . . . that he was a good friend when she needed one." She did not tell him the other thing her aunt had said. *He did not behave as expected, not as he had or as I thought.*

Dr. Gerald contemplated the consulting room past Victoria's shoulder. What memories did he see there?

"I think you will have to ask Her Highness," he said slowly. "My father did discuss his cases—more than he should have perhaps—but he was always careful to refrain from using names. He might say, 'I know a lady,' or 'A certain gentleman in my care.'"

Dr. Gerald looked away. Victoria swallowed the spasm of anger. She did not have time for proprieties or hesitations. But neither did she have time to shout. Instead, she made herself small, made her eyes wide. Made her voice soft. *I am helpless, and I need you.* "I am sorry that I must intrude so callously on your grief. But I . . . I can only beg you, if you know anything that might shed light on this matter, that you will tell me." She reached her hand out and touched the back of his lightly, briefly. "Please."

Something she had not seen before overtook Dr. Gerald then. Something beyond his anger and his confusion. It was grief, and it was bone-deep shame, and it robbed him of the dignity he had so far maintained.

His hands clenched empty air again. "Ma—Miss. Was my father going to be dismissed?"

This startled her. "I had not heard that. Why would you think it?"

"My father owed so much money . . . ," Dr. Gerald whispered. Victoria had to lean forward to hear him. "He could not pay, but he would not stop . . . I was afraid . . ." He swallowed. "I was afraid he'd begun to embezzle from the medical household. To steal from you."

Chapter 30

"What makes you think he was stealing?" Victoria asked.

The idea left Victoria shocked. But as the possibility settled into her mind, she found also that she was not surprised.

She had been convinced for some time that Sir John was paying Dr. William Maton to be his talebearer and possibly his spy. This talk of a gentleman arriving with an offer of a pension for the family in return for their silence seemed to cement that conclusion.

A man willing to sell lies for money might well turn to outright theft.

"I'd been suspicious for some time," Dr. Gerald said. "I knew he had mountains of debt. My mother had been very upset about it. So upset that my brothers and I—Well, you must believe me when I say nothing less than the possibility of ruin could have united the three of us enough to go speak with our father and find out how he meant to extricate himself, and us, from his troubles.

"However, when we did, he told us not to worry. He said that he knew his affairs had gotten out of control, and promised solemnly that all would shortly be put to rights. And for a time it seemed he was telling the truth. Julius said that he had begun to pay down the bills, and that when tradesmen came to the door, they were no longer being sent away empty-handed. So, I was hopeful. That was, I think, a month before he died."

Dr. Gerald paused. He was gathering himself, forcing down anger, disappointment, and grief so he could speak plainly. "Then father died so suddenly, and we looked into his account books, or, I should say, Julius looked. But it was Marcus who told me Julius found some strange entries in his ledgers." *Marcus is the middle brother.* "There were large amounts of money, one hundred pounds and more, that had no obvious source. None of us could understand it. They weren't gambling wins. He marked those differently. That was when Marcus raised the possibility our father had been stealing. Then you came here and . . ."

Victoria nodded. He assumed that was what she wished to talk about. Which brought them to what might be the most important question. Unfortunately, there was no easy or diplomatic way to ask it.

"Do you know what caused your father's death?"

For one moment, Victoria thought the man in front of her was going to cry.

"My brother said his heart must have stopped. I only saw his body briefly." His words were thick, harsh, and bitter. "If there was a wound or a blow of some sort, I saw no sign. So I suppose in the end, it truly was his heart. But as to what caused it to stop—" He closed his mouth.

Victoria watched him for a moment—watched the way his gaze shifted, the way his whole demeanor hardened.

"You may say anything," she told him. "I will respect your every confidence, as I am trusting you to respect mine."

I am not just a young woman you need to protect, and I

am not a patient you need to humor, she thought toward him. *I am someone quite different, and you know it.*

But which way would that difference push him?

"We know so little. Physicians," he said bitterly. "We spout our Latin and our Greek and talk so gravely about humors and heartbeats, bleeding and cupping and scarring, and we know *nothing.* Sometimes I swear the oldest country midwife knows more about the secrets of the human body than we do."

Victoria let Dr. Gerald have this moment with his anger. She understood what it was to have knowledge withheld and to be helpless because of it. Sometimes the only remedy was to shout at whoever was nearest.

"When my father was brought home, when I heard about this mysterious pension that would be distributed in return for silence, the first thing I thought was that he had been murdered."

Victoria's mind went utterly blank. Certainly, she had whispered the word to herself as she mulled over what she might find. Now that it was spoken aloud, however, she felt startled and coldly frightened. It was a moment before she herself could speak.

"But if he was killed, if there was no wound or blow, how could it have been done?"

Dr. Gerald deflated, and Victoria regretted her question. It was heartless. She was speaking of his father, after all. She, of all people, should have some understanding of how much that loss could hurt.

But she did not apologize. She needed his answer.

"He cannot have been choked," said Dr. Gerald slowly. "There would have been a bruise. He might have been smothered." He stopped. "Or poisoned."

"Dr. Clarke said he had been suffering from a stomach ailment."

If Dr. Gerald had looked uncertain a moment before, now he appeared truly shaken.

"My mother mentioned he had not been well, but she did not say—" He stared blankly at his desktop. "My father and I didn't speak often. I . . . disagreed with how he conducted his affairs, and we quarreled." He pulled a handkerchief from out of his pocket and wiped at his face. "There was a case once . . . I consulted on it for a friend of mine. A man with a stomach ailment that would not yield to any treatment. He could keep nothing at all down. He began to experience seizures . . . In the end it transpired that his daughter was mixing arsenic with the sugar she put in his coffee, several spoonfuls a day, morning and evening."

Victoria must have looked a bit green around the gills, because Dr. Gerald instantly apologized. "I'm sorry. I should not say such things in front of . . . in front of any patient."

"There is no need for apology. After all, I am the one who asked the question."

Dr. Gerald spread his hands. "But even if my father was poisoned, what could I do? There is no definite way to differentiate between a stomach illness and poison. There's a man named Marsh who is said to be working on a way to test for the presence of arsenic in a solution, but he has published no results yet . . ." He let his hands fall into his lap. "And my family, they would never agree to a coroner's inquest. Especially now." He lifted his gaze to her. "What should I do?"

Years later Victoria would remember this moment. This was the first time someone had openly appealed to her for help because she was Her Royal Highness, Princess Alexandrina Victoria, heir to the throne. Even though Dr. Gerald could plainly see she was a young girl, he believed there must be something she could do. Because she was the princess. *His* princess. Because she would be his queen.

She felt elated. She felt terrified. She could not fail to rise to this occasion, but she did not know what to do.

All at once she found herself thinking a thing that would never have occurred to her under normal circumstances. *What would Mama do?*

Victoria raised her chin. "You may leave the matter with me. I will make the necessary inquiries and determine what can be done."

For a minute, she thought he'd laugh at her. That was also something Mother would do.

But he did not. If anything, he seemed truly relieved. "Thank you . . . miss. I—" He wiped his face again and his hands. "Well, thank you."

"I will send word as soon as I am able," she said. This seemed a safe promise.

"If . . . if I should learn anything that might be relevant, how may I send word?"

Victoria found herself at a loss. It was very unlikely she could arrange to come here again. It was as much by luck as by planning that she had been able to come at all. And Dr. Gerald could not write to her. Even if his letter made it through the layers of palace clerks and secretaries to get to her, Mama opened all her correspondence first. Mama and Sir John.

Susan coughed, startling them both.

"If I may," she said. "Perhaps a letter taken to the post office, to be left until called for?"

"Addressed to V. Kent," said Victoria. "Yes. That will answer very well." At least it sounded as if it would. "Thank you for your time and your confidence." She stood, which caused him also to stand.

"Miss," he said. "What is happening here? What did my father do?"

"I am trying to find it out." She paused. "Your mother,

I think, mentioned your father was planning on writing a memoir?"

"He has always said he would."

"But had he begun? Have you seen the manuscript?"

"I believe that he had started, but no, I never saw it." He tapped the desk a moment, considering. "He kept a journal, however, and notes on his prominent cases and so forth."

"Do you think you might be able to look at his papers? To see if there are hints of new trouble or anything of the kind?"

"I should think so. Julius will have kept all that. I can offer to help go through them."

"Excellent. You can then write and tell me what you find. Thank you." She extended her hand, and he, a little startled, took her fingertips and bowed carefully over them.

"That was an excellent suggestion, Susan," said Victoria as soon as the two of them once again settled in the carriage. "Thank you."

"You're welcome, ma'am." Contradictory emotions warred on Susan's face. She looked pleased at the compliment but also angry at the fact of being pleased. Victoria had seen this before. There were people who were very determined not to be persuaded by rank and courtesy.

"I'm sure I must appear very foolish not to know anything about . . . post offices," she said.

"Not at all, ma'am. The toffs, that is, the quality, I mean—"

"We sad creatures who mope about abovestairs?"

Susan had now turned beet red.

Victoria laughed and then pressed her hand. "Oh! I shouldn't tease you. I am sorry. Please, forgive me."

Susan's high color subsided. "What I meant to say is that if you've never had to do a thing, you can't be expected to know how it works, can you?"

"Just so," said Victoria. "But thank you, anyway."

Susan dropped her gaze and mumbled something. Victoria sat back and let her breathe.

The carriage rattled and jolted its way across the cobbles. Mr. Saddler, she observed, had a deft and patient hand with their underfed and clearly dispirited horse. She idly wondered if she might convince Saddler to purchase the poor creature. Surely it deserved a better life than it had now.

"Ma'am?" said Susan hesitantly.

"Yes?"

"What was said in there"—she flicked one finger vaguely toward the passing street—"about the doctor being murdered . . . was that true?"

"I don't know. It may be."

Susan was no longer blushing. In fact, she no longer had any color to her cheeks at all.

"Are you quite well?" Victoria asked.

"Yes, ma'am," Susan said weakly. "Don't like doctors that much and all the talk . . . Why would anyone want to murder Dr. Maton? I mean, Dr. Maton's father?"

"I don't know," said Victoria. "But that is exactly what we must find out."

Chapter 31

It was possibly the strangest moment of Jane's life. She sat in Victoria's place in the shining black and gilt carriage. She wore the light silk bonnet with pale blue ribbons, the white coat of superfine wool, and spotless kid gloves. When they drove past, people took off their hats and bowed. She raised a hand, and people cheered.

None of them noticed how badly the ensemble fit or that she couldn't button the princess's white gloves fully, because they were too small. They saw the carriage, the tall woman in tidy gray, and the girl in white, with a spaniel in her arms. It was enough.

Jane thought about Father and all his dreams, about the story he told about Mama's secret parentage, and how they deserved so much, how they were as highborn, as worthy, as the royals.

She wondered what he'd say if he saw her now.

It was all very odd and, in some crooked way, terribly funny. Jane found herself smiling.

"Miss Conroy," said Lehzen.

Jane's tentative enjoyment dropped straight through the carriage floor. How long had Lehzen been watching her without speaking? Jane didn't know. Lehzen had allowed Jane to forget she was there.

Jane cringed. Dash whined and wriggled to complain he was being held too tight.

"Keep your head up, Miss Conroy," said Lehzen coolly. "We do not want people thinking the princess is not well."

"Yes, ma'am." Jane dutifully raised her chin. Lehzen nodded her approval, and Dash settled more comfortably into her lap.

They passed a cluster of men standing around a stout woman who held a cow by a rope halter. They pointed, and they bowed, and the men took off their hats. Even the cow dipped her head. Jane raised her hand. One of the men grinned and waved his hat in the air as he cheered.

But even in the middle of the cheers, Jane saw the crowd shift. All at once, a young man shoved his way onto the cobbles, splashed through the gutter, and sprinted down the street.

Recognition jolted Jane. *Ned?* She twisted in her seat.

It was Ned. She knew him even from the back. Her brother bolted through the streets, hanging ridiculously on to his hat, while the boys and old men jeered.

Another young man—this one a roughly dressed stranger, his hat sliding back and threatening to fall off—shoved his way through the same crowd. He pelted hard after Ned, fists clenched, face red with exertion and anger.

Ned disappeared around the corner. The other man shouted and ran after him.

"What's the matter, Miss Conroy?" asked Lehzen.

"Nothing." Jane swallowed and faced forward again. "Nothing."

Lehzen kindly let Jane have her silence until Mr. Saddler

drove them back into the livery yard. The princess had arrived before them, and it was immediately evident she was most satisfied with her visit to Dr. Gerald Maton.

"I sent Susan home," she said as Jane climbed down so Lehzen could help them swap coats, gloves, and bonnets and return them to their proper selves. Dash was delirious to see his mistress. He barked, wagged his stumpy tail, and bounced up and down until the princess cradled him in her arms again. "Thank you for bringing her to us, Jane. She was perfect, and I'm certain we will have more use for her."

Jane wondered what Susan had thought of all this. She also remembered Ned escaping from the other man in the street. She wondered if Susan might know who the stranger was, if Ned had told her anything when they were . . .

Not now, she told herself. *That's for later.*

"But what—" began Jane.

The princess, however, put a finger to her lips. Jane fell silent, glancing left and right. She squashed her impatience. She wanted to know if all this trouble had been worth it. The light in the princess's eyes said she thought so, but Jane felt impatient and irritable.

She knew this feeling had more to do with seeing Ned than with anything the princess had done or not done. Normally, she would not care what her brother was up to. But if word of Ned's latest antics made it to Father, Father would take his displeasure out on the rest of the family. He might become more suspicious about the time she spent with the princess, and she could not afford that.

We cannot afford that.

Hornsby was left to settle things with the liveryman man while Saddler drove them out through the yard and onto the street, then turned the horses toward the palace.

It was only then that Victoria spoke.

"You were right," she said to Jane and Lehzen. "The late

Dr. William Maton was being paid by someone. Dr. Gerald Maton told me that his father was heavily in debt. He said that after he died, a gentleman came and promised his mother and older brother that there would be a pension, but only if they agreed to say that William Maton died quietly at home."

"Did he say who this gentleman was?" asked Lehzen.

The princess shook her head. "But we can guess, I think."

Lehzen pursed her lips. "I would rather not guess in this matter. It is too serious. It would be better to know."

"It would, and I did ask," said the princess. "But Dr. Gerald, as I will call him, was not there when the gentleman came. He got the story from a footman, who also said that his eldest brother, Julius, and Mrs. Maton had threatened to sack any servant who gossiped about their master's death."

"What do we do now?" Jane was painfully aware how petulant she sounded.

The princess, however, had a ready answer. "I have been thinking about the money. I wonder what Mr. Rea might be able to tell us."

"Mr. Rea?" said Lehzen. "Do you mean William Rea, the clerk of the accounts? What has he to do with this?"

"He is a friend of my father's," said Jane. "They were in the army together."

"Yes, I had heard," replied Lehzen, in such a way that made Jane think she had heard it a great many times. "But how is he involved with the business of the late Dr. Maton?"

"Mr. William Rea and Dr. William Maton both come—both came—to dinner when the members of the Kensington board are, were, are invited," said Jane.

"Do you know Mr. Rea, Lehzen?" asked the princess.

"He is the one who keeps track of the incomes and outflow of the money for Your Highness's household. I have tried to get to know him, but . . ." Lehzen paused, searching for the correct words. "It seems he has taken careful note of Sir John's dislike of me."

Victoria's face creased with disappointment. "I had hoped to ask you to speak with him, but now I see we will need to find another way, and it must be soon."

"Why?" asked Lehzen. "If Sir John is paying bribes, he would hardly consult with a household clerk about it."

"But he might tell a friend," said Jane. "Father talks. He likes to let people know how oppressed he is or how clever." *Whichever might be useful.*

The princess nodded. "We don't even have to begin with the possibility that Sir John has done any wrong. Dr. Gerald said his father might have been embezzling from the household. Who better to inquire into that possibility than the head of accounts?" She spoke more quickly now, warming to her own ideas. "Add to that that he and William Maton sat down to dinner together. They talked. Mr. Rea may know something of the late doctor's character that he kept from others, and he might be more willing to talk about it than the Maton family. *And* he also might have access to the appropriate account books to track the embezzlement."

"Unless—" Jane dropped her gaze and closed her mouth.

"Now, none of that." The princess reached out and tapped her once on the back of her hand. "You can say anything."

Which in itself was an extraordinary idea. Jane lifted her gaze. "What if Mr. Rea was a part of it?"

"What do you mean?" asked the princess.

"Well, it's only that if the late doctor wanted to steal from the household, he could do worse than having help from the man who keeps the ledgers."

Victoria fell silent for a moment. "I had not thought of that. But that is all the more reason to speak with Mr. Rea."

"But even if Mr. Rea was willing to talk to you, even if you are not accusing Father of paying bribes, he remains my father's friend and confidant," said Jane. "How could we trust him?"

And what if he decides to tell Father what's been said?

"I don't know," the princess admitted. "But we would get his measure at least and perhaps find the chink in his armor." The princess petted Dash restlessly. "We do not have many ways to pursue this. And we must pursue it."

"There is something more, isn't there?" asked Lehzen.

The princess's face hardened. "Dr. Gerald says that his father may have been poisoned."

"Poisoned!" cried Jane.

The princess nodded. "He says that the late doctor's stomach complaint could have been poison. He said he had seen a case with similar symptoms where a daughter put arsenic in her father's coffee."

Jane's breath hitched.

"Are you in earnest, ma'am?" Lehzen spoke so softly, she could barely be heard above the rattle of the carriage wheels on the cobbles.

"Dr. Gerald was," said the princess. "Don't tell me you can't believe it, Lehzen?"

"I can," Lehzen replied. "But I do not wish to. Especially as I have encouraged you to move forward with this . . . inquiry." She shook her head. "Was he sure? Was your Dr. Gerald sure?"

"No," admitted the princess. "He said there was no way to tell." She stopped. "Wait. What if we asked Dr. Clarke?"

"Dr. Clarke?" echoed Lehzen.

Clarke, Jane recalled, was the new physician, the one who was willing to speak plainly with the duchess.

"Yes. He worked with Dr. Maton. Perhaps he could tell us something useful, either about the state of his health or about his actions before he died. He might even know who Dr. Maton's close associates in the household were."

"Aside from my father," muttered Jane.

"Yes," agreed the princess, apparently unbothered by her tone. "Dr. Maton may have had friends and colleagues who could tell us more."

"How would you go about speaking with Dr. Clarke?" asked Lehzen. "You would never be permitted to see him with any kind of privacy."

"But you could, Lehzen," said the princess. "You could complain of a cold or some such and ask to see him. Will you?"

"If it is what you wish."

The princess tilted her head, regarding her governess carefully. "You still do not think we should be doing this."

The palace was in sight now. Saddler had turned them onto the carriage road. Gravel crunched beneath the wheels.

"I do not know anymore," Lehzen said. "I cannot deny there are questions . . ."

The princess reached out and pressed Lehzen's hand. "Speak with Dr. Clarke. It will be the easiest to arrange and can do no harm. And it will be something useful that can be done until we hear from Dr. Gerald again. He promised me he would go through his father's papers and look for information, but that may take time. We do not wish this trail to grow cold."

"Trail," sniffed the governess.

"Lehzen," said the princess, "we cannot shrink from this now."

Lehzen did not answer.

"We *must* find out what happened," the princess insisted. "I promised Dr. Gerald I would."

"How can he expect such a thing from a *child*?" blurted out Lehzen.

"He can expect it from the person who will be queen."

Lehzen fell silent again.

"I admit, I thought I knew why I was doing this," said

Victoria. "I thought it was to spite Sir John. I thought it was to defy the Kensington system and, well, and Mama. But then . . . in speaking with Dr. Gerald . . . I saw that this thing matters to more people than just me. It matters because his father, William Maton, was a man who lived and breathed and walked, and because he may have died because someone took it upon themselves to decide he should not live, and that is a breach of the king's peace, and that will be *my* peace, and . . . that matters." She stopped. "I am not making my point very well."

"No, you are," said Jane.

But I am like Lehzen, and I wish you weren't. Because William Maton was possibly being paid by my father to lie for him. Because Mr. Rea is my father's friend, and if someone was stealing from the household and Mr. Rea was involved, my father could have been involved, as well.

And all of that might mean it was my father who killed William Maton.

Chapter 32

King William IV strode down the corridors of Whitehall, his boots ringing hard against the marble floors. Persons of various stations stared and whispered as he passed. He ignored them all. He knew what they were saying.

They called him Silly Billy and wondered what had gotten him into a temper today. They compared his head to a pineapple and said his narrow brow was an outward sign of some inward mental impediment.

They thought he didn't know. As if he had not come up in the Royal Navy, which drank down rumor and gossip along with the rum ration. As if he wouldn't recognize an insult because it was disguised by a smile and a fluttering fan.

As if he had learned nothing as a prince in his father's—and then his brother's—vicious, deteriorating court.

Indeed, something both the navy and the court had taught him was the importance of good intelligence, not to mention the vital importance of maintaining the element of surprise. Which was why he had not given the men of the Kensington Board any notice that he planned to attend their Whitehall meeting.

"My lords! The king!" bellowed the footman.

All the men in the room scrambled to their feet. Lord Dunham actually dropped whatever papers he'd been holding, and they scattered about the floor. He was red as a beet when he bowed.

William pretended to ignore it.

"No, no, no ceremony, no ceremony!" he declared, although no monarch had ever actually meant those words, and he certainly didn't mean them now. "Sit, sit, all of you."

William dropped into the chair at the head of the table and looked directly at the brandy decanter. "Drink? Very good." He held out his hand, which sent Dunham and Dunfermline both scrambling to get a glass and fill it with brandy. DuncanNon looked pained.

God's teeth, how is it we wound up with a set of lords all titled with Ds for this ridiculous committee?

The glass of brandy was put in his hand. "Your health, my lords!" William drank. Which meant they all had to drink with him.

He slammed his glass down on the table.

"Your Majesty, we had no word . . . ," began Dunfermline, his nervousness deepening his Scotch accent.

"No?" William twisted in his seat to glare at his secretary Marsters, who stood hunched behind him like a particularly tidy crow. "No?"

"An oversight, sir," replied Marsters. "I am sorry." The man was amazing. William almost believed him, even though he knew for a fact the fellow was lying through his teeth.

"Oh well, nothing to be done about it now."

"Sir John has just left, I'm afraid, sir," said Lord Dunham. "We can perhaps still—"

William swept all this aside with a single gesture. "No need, no need. You're the fellows I want to talk to. You're the ones in charge of my niece's household, after all, and it's the household I'm here about." He watched them shooting glances at each other, shuffling their papers, trying to work out exactly what was happening.

They should know, b'gad. And they would know if all of them weren't under the spell of that Conroy fellow. Conroy had them all convinced he would have the last word regarding little Victoria.

Well, time to put paid to that nonsense.

"Now. Let's go straight at it, shall we?" The king planted his elbows on the table. "My niece is now sixteen. It's time, past time, that as heir to the throne, she was given her own establishment."

"But she is well established at Kensington," said Lord Duncannon. Duncannon was a ginger-haired, sharp-faced little fellow with startling black eyes. Looked like a ferret, with his long hands and his tiny ears.

"You mean that mother of hers is," William snapped. "It is time the princess had her own house, with her *own* ladies about her." Meaning ladies chosen by Adelaide, not that double-damned duchess. "If she were a prince, it would have happened years ago. My brothers and I were barely breached when we were taken out of our mother's house. It may be different for girls, but still, for Victoria, it should have happened years ago. Yes, yes," he said before anyone could speak. "There were other considerations at the time. Let that pass. Now. We consider that Buckingham House would be a suitable residence. You, my lords, will consult with the accountancy department to draw up a decent allowance to put before Parliament . . ."

"Sir . . . forgive me," said Dunham. "But why now?"

Yet another Lord D. and yet another Scot, b'gad!

"I told you. It's time. And frankly, I've never liked the way the girl's mother schemes with that fellow Conroy."

"Sir John was a trusted assistant to your late brother the Duke of Kent, sir," said Dunfermline. "It is natural that the duchess should also place her trust in him."

"Well, she places too damn much trust in him and always has," growled William. "And he's been allowed too much influence over the girl. It ain't seemly." Let them hear his definite opinion, just in case they weren't already aware of it.

Let them see it was time for a prudent man to turn his coat.

But Dunfermline, it seemed, was unwilling to take the hint. "May I ask, sir, are you hearing these rumors from the Baroness Lehzen?"

"It makes no difference where the information comes from."

"I beg your pardon, sir. But I fear it does." Dunfermline smoothed down his bristling whiskers.

Like he needs to calm the unruly things.

"As Your Majesty is well aware," Dunfermline went on, "things between the palace and Parliament are at a very delicate point. And the health and well-being of the princess is naturally of great concern to the whole of your government. If it seems that you are taking the word of a jealous servant over that of the girl's mother and a baronet and the whole of the Kensington Board . . . Your Majesty runs the risk of looking ridiculous, or envious."

"Because I've no legitimate children of me own?" bellowed William. "That what you mean to say?"

Dunfermline's eyes widened, and all his whiskers bristled. "I only wish to present—"

"Yes, yes, I see very well what you wish. Now, sir, you will hear what *we* wish." William slammed his hand on the table, rattling the glasses, the papers, and the whole gathering of mealymouthed men. "We wish that our niece have an establishment and income suited to her age and her position as the next queen of the United Kingdoms. We do *not* wish to be pushed aside by some lackey whose only claim to our regard is that he once served our late brother. What have you to say to that, eh? What?"

Lord Duncannon cleared his throat. "Well, yes, of course Your Majesty's wishes in regards to the heir are paramount." William felt his temper swell. Did the little weasel think to *manage* him? "Perhaps if we were to wait until after the coming tour, to give Your Majesty's councillors time to formulate a full plan . . ."

"Tour?" barked William. "What tour?"

Duncannon shrank backward, his ferrety little eyes darting in all directions as he looked for some way out. "I . . ."

"*What tour?*"

Dunfermline soothed his agitated whiskers. "Your Majesty was surely informed that the Duchess of Kent and Sir John have planned a new tour in September to take the princess into the North."

"The devil I was informed! Why the bloody hell should I be informed? I'm only the fucking king of England! Why the fucking hell should any of you bloody, sodding, poxy, shit-eating, flabby-arsed buggers tell me anything!"

"Sir . . . ," tried Dunham.

"What!" William surged to his feet, which forced them all to stand. "You want to tell me something now, do you? What is it? Eh? What?"

But Dunham just closed his mouth and bowed.

"Quite right," growled the king. "Now, my lords, I shall tell you something. You will write up a bill for Parliament detailing the requirements of a new household for the princess. You will inform your peers and whoever else you think necessary that it is done by the king's express wish, and you will do it before the month is out. And you will none of you go babbling to Conroy or the duchess. Is that clear? I'll tell them what they need to know, or the queen will. Good? Yes?"

That should have been the end of it. But Lord Dunham didn't have the sense God gave a goose. "The Duchess of Kent will not agree to the princess—"

"The duchess will do as she is told, or she will find herself out on her arse! Is there anything else? No? Good!"

William turned and barged out of the room, his secretary and retinue of footmen following behind in neat formation.

"Marsters?" he snapped without breaking stride down the wood-paneled corridor.

"Sir?" His secretary stepped up beside him.

"You'll tell me which of them runs tattling to Conroy and the duchess, as soon as it happens."

"Of course, sir."

"Good man."

Chapter 33

"Speak with Dr. Clarke," the princess had told her. "It will be the easiest to arrange and can do no harm."

Lehzen felt an unaccustomed surge of impatience with her charge at this confident pronouncement. She felt an even stronger surge of impatience with herself in that she had not refused the task.

Because the princess was right. There was something going on. It was serious, and Sir John was doubtlessly involved. All the events surrounding Dr. Maton's death pointed to it.

So. As soon as I can discover whom to trust with this information, I will put it into their hands, she promised herself. Because this . . . thing, whatever it turned out to be, was driving the princess to a level of sneaking defiance even Lehzen had never seen from her before. Secret letters. Secret meetings. A sense of power that was making her careless of her position and her person. What would come next? There was no way to know.

But what Lehzen did know was that if she tried to steer

her charge from this course without being able to suggest another one, the princess would shut her out entirely. If Lehzen wanted to be able to protect her, she must, however reluctantly, continue to help her. Which meant finding a way to speak privately with Dr. Clarke.

Having spent much of her adult life in the claustrophobic courts of Germany, Lehzen knew perfectly well how scarce true privacy was inside even the largest palace. But like all those who waited on the great families, she had learned how to scratch out small moments for herself.

So the next day she made sure she had a chance to sit at the worktable with Lady Charlotte.

"I'm having headaches," she said softly. "And I need some privacy to speak with the doctor."

When Lady Charlotte was in waiting, she lived in the palace, but not in the royal apartments. She had her own little suite of rooms in the same wing. She and Lehzen were not friends, exactly, and Lehzen was very careful about what she let that lady see, but Lady Charlotte was a good woman and sympathized with the fact that Lehzen had no place in Kensington she could call her own. She readily agreed to loan Lehzen the use of her private apartment.

So it was that when Dr. Clarke answered her summons, Lehzen was sitting alone beside a table with a tea tray, for nothing could be done between the English without tea. She clutched her handkerchief in both hands, trying not to tie it, or herself, into knots.

Dr. Clarke made no remark about her demeanor or their surroundings. He simply set his bag down and bowed.

"How may I be of service, ma'am?"

"Won't you please sit down?" answered Lehzen. The doctor bowed again and did so, although he refused the cup of tea she offered.

Lehzen took a deep breath. "You must forgive me, Dr.

Clarke," she said. "I am afraid I have asked you here under false pretenses."

"There is no need to worry, ma'am. You would hardly be my first patient who was a trifle reticent regarding a medical question. If it helps, you may be assured of my absolute discretion." He was looking at her with gentle sympathy.

My God! thought Lehzen suddenly. *Does he think I've fallen pregnant?*

She downed a gulp of tea to keep from laughing out loud. When she could speak again, she said, "I do thank you, Doctor, but my question, questions, they are not medical ones."

"Then I'm afraid I do not understand."

And how do I explain?

Lehzen took a deep breath. As she had many times before, she pushed her uncertainties aside. She had been given a task. She must complete it. She squeezed her handkerchief, as if it was a friend's hand and she was seeking reassurance.

"I wished to speak to you about the late Dr. Maton."

"I still do not understand."

"Were you acquainted with him?"

"We were colleagues," said Dr. Clarke. "We consulted on each other's cases. Members of the medical household frequently do."

The "medical household" was an association, not a place. A select group of surgeons, physicians, and apothecaries would travel with the royal family to be on hand should the need arise. When on duty, they lived in proximity to the palace but not inside it. Naturally, they talked among themselves about their patients. Who else would they talk to?

"What was your opinion of Dr. Maton?"

"As a doctor, he was a sound practitioner in the conservative and traditional vein."

A highly diplomatic answer, sir. It sounded like praise and yet did not commit him to a detailed opinion.

It also did not offer a clear conversational opening through which one might gain a wider assessment of Dr. Maton's character or habits.

"Did you agree with his . . . method of proceeding?"

This was entirely the wrong question, and Lehzen knew it as soon as the words left her. Dr. Clarke's entire demeanor snapped shut.

"Are you asking me to pronounce judgment on my late colleague's practice and methods?"

Scheiße. "Dr. Clarke. The princess is much affected by the loss of Dr. Maton. She knows he attended her father, and that gives her a . . . a sentimental attachment. She is disquieted by having discovered him when he died alone and out of doors."

"*What?*"

Lehzen feigned her surprise. "You did not know? When the princess fell from her horse, the horse had shied because they came across a dead man on the green. It was Dr. Maton."

"No, I most certainly did not know!" cried Dr. Clarke. "Why was I not told of this?"

"It was not my decision, Doctor."

Dr. Clarke jumped to his feet. He commenced pacing—to the window and to his bag and back again, his hands folded behind him. His speech was as quick and unnerved as his manner.

"I certainly would have recommended rest and quiet after such a shock. No wonder Her Highness was agitated!" He faced Lehzen again. "She must be kept as quiet as possible. She must not be presented with any circumstances that could call the events back to her mind, or she will surely suffer the strongest relapse. She may even fall into hysteria!"

Lehzen bowed her head humbly before this assessment. "As you know, sir, it is difficult to persuade a naturally energetic young woman to rest quietly. If I could tell her I had answers to her questions, she would surely agree to sit and listen—"

"No." He held up his hand to stop her. "I will speak to the duchess directly."

"I beg you, sir, do not do so."

Dr. Clarke drew himself up. He was now very much on his dignity, and Lehzen felt something close to panic nibbling at the back of her mind. "What exactly is the matter here, ma'am?"

Scheiße, she thought again. "Questions have been raised about Dr. Maton. About his conduct in the medical household."

"*This* is why I am here? To spread gossip about my late colleague?" Dr. Clarke demanded. "You have much mistaken me, ma'am, if you believe I would do any such thing."

"Please, Doctor . . ."

But he had already picked up his bag. "You may call me when you have a legitimate medical concern. Otherwise, I will bid you good day." He did not bother to bow but simply strode out of the room, leaving Lehzen behind to curse fruitlessly in German.

Now what do I do?

Then, slowly, it occurred to Lehzen that she had been granted a wonderful opportunity.

She could lie.

She could tell the princess that Dr. Clarke had assured her there was nothing untoward regarding Dr. Maton's career and conduct or, indeed, his death. His debts were of an ordinary kind, and his son Gerald had been over-worried, as a loving child could sometimes be.

She could say that Dr. Clarke and his other colleagues had warned Dr. Maton to take his indisposition more seriously and that he had brushed their warnings off. That he had been in the habit of taking long walks across the green. Ironically, she could say he had done so for the sake of his health.

The princess would believe her. After all, it was very like how her father had died.

Lehzen could end this dangerous quest in five minutes.

Lehzen pressed her hand over her eyes. She sat there for a long moment, confused thoughts swirling darkly through her mind.

How does one become a good queen? Victoria's voice rose up from the depths of memory.

The princess was ten years old. It had been a worrisome day. She had found a genealogy of English kings in her history book. It was a new one. Lehzen knew because she had placed it there the day before. The old king had just been laid to rest. It had been decided that it was time for the princess to know certain truths.

Victoria read the genealogy, one tiny finger tracing the lines that ran from name to name. She found herself, and she frowned.

"I am nearer to the throne than I thought," she said.

Lehzen had long determined to treat this moment casually. It was simply another fact of the girl's life—like how grown men bowed to her or how she must wear her tiara during formal occasions, even though it rubbed her forehead badly.

The princess seemed to take this new knowledge quietly enough. Indeed, during that day she seemed not only solemn but also sullen. Lehzen found herself wondering if Victoria was coming down with a fever.

Then the princess asked the question she had been brooding over.

"How does one become a good queen?"

Aware, as she must always be, of listening ears and speaking tongues, Lehzen answered, "One reads much, especially history. Queen Elizabeth, she was a great monarch and much loved by her people. One might study her example."

The princess listened intently, her brows knitted together,

as if by straining her body, she could hear better. She nodded rapidly. "Then that is what I will do. I will be good."

And the princess turned back to her pencils and her puppy, and just like that, the moment passed. At least it did until later that night.

The duchess was still at dinner. Where the other ladies were, Lehzen could not recall. She had put the princess to bed and then sat beside her in the darkened room.

Victoria lay on her back, her face still pinched and serious even in sleep. Her dainty hand dangled over the side of the bed, as if she had just been petting her dog.

Gently, Lehzen lifted the girl's hand and tucked it under her coverlet.

"Sweetness, you asked me, how does one become a good queen?" Lehzen whispered. "This is what I would tell you if I could. I would tell you it means understanding that you are the prize and they all want you—all your uncles, as well as your mama, the men of Parliament and, most of all, Sir John Conroy." She felt tears prick behind her eyes. Cold crawled up the skin on her hands. "I would tell you that as queen, you must grow eyes in the back of your head."

She touched the girl's brow and the lace ruffle on her cap. "You must always pay attention, and you must always be wary, because the one who wins you will win the throne. And they will never stop trying to win you. They do not care that you are child, and they will not care when you are a woman. They do not care for the good of the nation, and God knows they do not care for your happiness. You cannot change this, because you were born who you are, and the choice to be otherwise is not one you have. So you must watch, little one, and you must find ways to fight."

Find ways to fight. Lehzen felt herself looking from the present day back at her earnest, worried self in the shadowed past.

"And all that time you must remember that you are a symbol," said that past self to the sleeping girl. "And that you are an example. That the people look to you for comfort and certainty when it seems as though the world must fall apart around us all, and they have nothing to offer you in return. I will help. I will try, I promise. But in the end, the only one you will have is yourself, and I am sorry for that."

Memory faded. The present returned. Lehzen knew she could not sit here drinking cold tea and feeling sorry for herself like some hausfrau when her man was away.

"I will help," she had said. "I will try."

With a sigh, Lehzen got to her feet. Her knees had begun creaking. It was too soon for that, but so much standing, so much walking across the hard floors . . . Well, it was no matter.

She had promised she would help the princess, had promised she would protect her, no matter what, or who, threatened her.

The problem was, she did not know how.

Chapter 34

Getting to the post office was easier than Jane had feared it might be. All she had to do was tell Father that she wanted to stop and purchase a volume on the "language of flowers" that she thought might amuse the princess, and he was happy to let her walk to the palace that morning rather than ride in the carriage with him.

Getting rid of Betty was just as easy. Jane suggested that Betty might not want to waste her morning lingering about a bookshop and gave her a few shillings to go buy herself some buns at the baker instead.

"Then just walk on ahead. I can meet you at the palace gates," she said with an awkward wink. "And none the wiser."

Betty met her gaze, and Jane looked back, unblinking. Betty pocketed the coins. There was a silent agreement in her curtsy before she turned to walk away.

Betty understood, and Jane understood. This payment was for Betty's silence, and it would not be the last.

Mr. and Mrs. Carey, the couple who ran the post office, knew Jane, of course. They also considered Father a snob and far too standoffish, so she had no fear they'd chatter awkwardly or ask him who this "Miss Kent" might be.

It's far too soon, she told herself as she waited, shifting from foot to foot, while Mrs. Carey rifled through her pigeonholes. *The princess only spoke with Dr. Maton two days ago. I should have waited. I shouldn't have wasted the excuse . . .*

"Here you are, dear." Mrs. Carey handed Jane the letter sealed with a plain blue wafer. "Dropped off yesterday, it was."

Jane stared. She barely remembered to thank Mrs. Carey. She practically ran the rest of the way to the palace.

When Jane reached the royal apartments, the princess was at her lessons, singing scales of increasing speed and difficulty under the careful direction of her music tutor and, of course, under the duchess's watchful eye. Father was at his desk, reading some papers. He looked up as Jane came in, and frowned at her empty hands.

Jane just shook her head. She'd tell him that the shop owner had sold the last copy on hand but had promised to order another.

When did it become so easy to think of lying to Father?

Jane moved quietly to her corner and picked up Wordsworth's poems. When she was sure Father's attention was fixed on his papers, she opened it, intending to slip the letter inside.

But there was something already there. A neatly written note on a slip of paper.

C. knows nothing. Must try elsewhere.

Jane glanced up and found herself looking directly at Lehzen. Lehzen watched as Jane pulled the letter from her sleeve, tucked it into the pages, and carefully closed the book.

After that, there was nothing to do but wait.

* * *

At half ten it was time for the princess to take her exercise. "May I walk in the garden, Mama?" she asked humbly. Too humbly, in fact. Fear rippled through Jane. *The duchess will suspect something.*

But the duchess, it seemed, was involved with her own cares and simply nodded. "Lady Flora can take you."

"Yes, Mama," said the princess dutifully. "Come on, then, Jane."

Jane rang for Betty to bring her bonnet. She grabbed her sketchbook and pencil box and Wordsworth's poems.

They were well into the dog days now. The sun was bright and the day was rapidly becoming uncomfortably hot. Sweat prickled under Jane's bonnet and trickled down the back of her neck. She was grateful that the princess decided to stick to the formal pathways between the hedges so they could walk in the shade. Dash was having a splendid time running this way and that on the grass, shoving his nose into the hedgerows and flower beds.

The real reason the princess chose to stay in the gardens, of course, was that the tall formal hedges provided a screen between them and the palace. Even if someone decided to watch from the grimy windows, they would be unlikely to see Jane pull Gerald Maton's letter from the book or the princess's face light up as she broke the seal and shook the page open.

Jane and the princess put their heads together until their bonnet brims touched. Together they read.

> *My Dear Miss Kent,*
> *I trust this letter finds you in the very best of health and spirits.*
> *For my own part, I scarcely know what to write or how to tell you what I have learned.*

Following our consultation, I found myself so agitated that I was barely able to continue to see my patients for the day. Please do not think this was your fault! It was entirely my own doing and brought on by a rational review of all that had passed between myself and my family since my father's death.

So often, we see our family through a kind of hopeful haze. This means that actions they take can seem quite harmless to us, even if that same action would seem deeply nefarious or ill-advised if taken by a stranger.

Victoria and Jane paused and shared a long look of mutual understanding.

When I was at last able to close my surgery, I went to my brother Julius's house. I spoke with him and my mother together. I said I wished to see Father's papers, his case notes and journals and the like. I said I wished to review these things to satisfy my own mind on some points that his death had recently returned to the front of my memory.

I attempted to speak lightly, to pass it off as agitation brought on by grief, and as something that could be quickly alleviated. I am not sure how well I succeeded. After all, they already knew I was bitterly angry over the treatment of Father in death and the haste and silence surrounding his burial.

But it transpired that I could have spared myself the effort. Upon my mother's signal, my

*brother Julius informed me that all my father's
personal papers had already been burnt.*

Jane pressed her hand over her mouth to stop her exclamation. Victoria clenched the edges of the letter, wrinkling
the paper.

"Why would they . . . ?"

*I demanded to know why they would do
such a thing. Again, they spoke of the promised
pension and of the necessity for "all our sakes"
that the family reputation be preserved. Julius
spoke firmly for several minutes about how any
controversy could damage my practice and
Marcus's, as well as his own. Therefore, he had
no choice.*

"I don't believe it," muttered the princess. "About the
reputations. It is about this money, the pension they were
promised. It must be."

"That depends what they were afraid those papers said,"
breathed Jane.

Victoria frowned.

*I left feeling depressed and angry, but also
uneasy. Unease turned to suspicion with uncomfortable speed. So, taking a great chance, I
waited near to the house until I saw that same
footman I had spoken to before leave on an errand for my mother. I took him up into my
closed carriage, and I quizzed him about the
fate of my father's papers.*

Jane realized she had stopped breathing.

He said that it was true they had been burnt. That my mother and Julius had seen to the matter personally. But, he said, he had been called in to help, as there were a great many boxes and files to be dealt with, including some that had to be brought down from the attic. As a result, he was able to overhear some of what passed between Mother and Julius.

They were, he said, particularly agitated about the manuscript of my father's memoir, and as they emptied each drawer and box into the fire, they were constantly asking each other, "Did you get it all?" and "Are you sure there's nothing more?" and "Could there have been a fair copy made?" and other such questions. He said that their depredations extended to Father's case books and appointment books, going back some years.

Remembering your questions when we met, I asked him about the gentleman who came to the house to inform Mother and Julius about the pension. He said the gentleman left no card, and he was unable to hear the name. He did, however, give a description of a tall man with military bearing, dark, curling hair, and bright blue eyes.

"Sir John," said the princess.

At the same time Jane said, "Father." Of course it would be. Father had gotten the gardeners to fetch the cart. He would naturally have gone with them to make sure their burden reached its destination and so he could speak with the Matons immediately.

"We knew he had something to hide," said the princess. "Oh! I could scream."

"Well, it's over now," said Jane. She was disappointed, which shocked her. She should have been relieved. "Whatever there was to find, the Matons must have destroyed it." Jane looked over her shoulder toward the clock tower. "We should be getting back. They'll be calling you in soon."

"You don't believe we should keep asking questions," said the princess.

"I don't believe we can find proof of anything wrong," Jane said flatly. "And without proof, we're just two silly little girls playing an absurd game."

The princess wanted to be angry, Jane could tell. But she couldn't quite muster a retort.

At last, the princess sighed. "You're right, Jane. We should get back." But even as she said this, she set her jaw, and Jane knew she was not ready to stop.

And as she trailed behind the princess, Jane found, oddly, that she had begun to smile.

Chapter 35

"Ah, there you are at last, Sir John."

Victoire was so attuned to the man's presence, she did not even need to look up to know it was him. She could tell by the rustle of his coattails and the soft fall of his footstep against the carpet.

"I was not aware I had kept you waiting, ma'am." She heard the smile in his voice. He was humoring her.

She was in no mood to be humored.

"You are so often absent these days." She kept her attention on her letters, sorting them into piles according to how urgently they needed to be answered. "I almost think you are avoiding me."

"You know how busy matters are at present." There it was, that first touch of impatience. She was not responding to his presence with proper warmth and gratitude. He was very sensitive to that. "Our departure date is scarcely a fortnight away." He paused. Perhaps he looked around the room or glanced at the clock. "Is Victoria on her walk? Who is with her?"

"Your very own Jane, of course." Victoire looked over her latest letter from Leopold. It was filled with his usual long paragraphs of sound and excellent advice, exhortations to trust herself to his adviser Baron Stockmar's excellent judgment, and so forth. It begged for news of the king and Parliament and whether they meant to continue paying his pension. Being king in Belgium, it seemed, was an expensive proposition, and he needed the money.

She laid that letter down on the least urgent pile.

"She has begun badgering me to let her go out riding again," Victoire said. "I suppose I will have to. We have told so many people she took no hurt from her fall, and . . . what happened."

"As it happens, I agree that she should go riding as soon as possible." He paced around the desk, then came to stand within her field of vision. He wanted her undivided attention. "It will help dismiss any lingering gossip about what happened, and I'm sure you agree that now more than ever, it is important the princess be shown in the best light. We want buoyant crowds on her tour, not fearful ones."

Victoire looked up at Sir John. How many years had he been at her side now? How much had she relied on him because her husband had urged her to? And because she desperately needed an ally—any ally?

Was it possible she had made a colossal mistake?

"The king does not approve of this new tour."

He chuckled. "The king has never approved of any tour. With any luck, he will give himself an apoplexy."

Victoire permitted herself a tiny smile to indicate she understood the joke but did not approve. One should not joke casually about the death of kings. Not even Silly Billy.

"What is bothering you, Victoire?"

Victoire stood. She walked to the window, indicating that he should join her. The windows had been opened wide to catch the slightest possibility of a breeze. Therefore, it was easier than usual to see down into the gardens. There Victoria walked arm in arm with Jane Conroy, with Dash gamboling at their heels.

From the corner of her eye, she watched Sir John smile down on the little trio affectionately. Indeed, triumphantly.

"What a remarkable change you have wrought, Sir John," said Victoire. "My daughter, who was so indifferent to yours, has now clasped her close."

"And I have explained it to you," he said oh so patiently. "Victoria has turned her fancies to this business of Dr. Maton. She has always had a girl's love of the dramatic, and this engages her overheated imagination. She wants to uncover a great scandal. Jane is humoring her, which is why they are now friends. Jane is also keeping me informed of what Victoria is up to. There is no reason to be concerned. You know I will not let the matter go too far."

"And you are certain that's what she's doing?" inquired Victoire.

"I don't understand you."

"No, I expect you do not." She turned abruptly and stalked away. She did not know where she planned to go, but she could not be so close to this man anymore.

"Ma'am, what is the matter?"

"Sir John, I have trusted you all these years."

"And you can always trust me." He was coming close again. She could feel his warmth, his worry. She could all but hear the wheels of his mind turning as he tried to guess what she was about to say.

She whirled around suddenly and was rewarded by the sight of him taking a step back in surprise.

"Trust you? When you have made such a terrible blunder!"

"What blunder?" he demanded. "Who have you been talking to?"

"I have been talking to my daughter, Sir John, and my friends in the palace. They inform me that you have been entirely taken in by a little girl, and it may cost us everything we have worked for!"

Sir John drew himself up, silent, furious, astonished.

"Did you know that the king is planning to demand that Parliament give the money to create a separate household for Victoria? And that the queen supports this?"

"Of course. It is of no matter. You are the girl's legal guardian. Nothing can be done about her living arrangements without your permission. That is the law."

"The law, the law," she mocked. "What your English law gives, it take away."

"You cannot believe that the king or Parliament is interested in going to war with us over custody of—"

"The sole heir to the British throne?" inquired the duchess sweetly. "Especially now, when the king's health is failing? Especially when the men of your great English Parliament believe that I am morally unfit to be her mother?"

"What?"

"They believe we are lovers, Sir John," she snapped. "You have *permitted* them to believe we are lovers."

It was true. She watched his face—the ways his eyes darkened, the way his busy mind searched frantically for some lie. But there was no lie that could brush away this truth. He was a man like all the others. He preened and swaggered in front of his compatriots, and each of them tried to outdo the others with their claims about which grand lady they had managed to fuck.

That she had teased and flirted, that she had worked to wrap him around her little finger, that was beside the point. She pushed it all to the back of her mind and locked it away.

"Victoire," he began. "I promise . . ."

I find I am uninterested in your promises just now. "And

you have permitted Victoria to go gallivanting about with no one but your daughter and that traitorous Lehzen to protect her—"

"Victoria is playing a *game*. She thinks she is on the cusp of unearthing some great mystery behind Maton's death. If she's occupied with that, she cannot be focusing on this nonsense about the new household . . ."

"Unless she's using this freedom to press her case to be removed from my care!"

Again, Sir John fell silent. Victoire took a perverse satisfaction in having shocked him twice within the space of a few minutes.

"I know my daughter, Sir John. I have watched her. Despite all our efforts—all your efforts—she has not grown more biddable or dependent. She has grown ever more defiant, and she is more clever than her antecedents would suggest. And . . ." Victoire paused to make sure she had his full and undivided attention. "She hates you."

"Ma'am—"

"She hates you, and she hates me." Tears sprang into Victoire's eyes. Not the pretty, playful tears she used with courtiers and men of influence. These came from her sore heart. "She is working with the queen to get herself removed from our care."

Victoire watched Sir John begin to realize the extent of what he had missed.

"How can she be in communication with the queen?" he demanded. "She is constantly watched. We read all her correspondence."

"She uses Lehzen, of course." Every one of Victoire's words dripped with sugar and acid. If Sir John had been raised in a court, it would have been as obvious to him as it was to her. But for all his machinations, Sir John was an interloper in these halls where she was the native. "Lehzen has been having secret meetings with Mrs. Wilson, who waits on the queen. Victoria has blinded you with this ruse about chasing after phantoms and dramas on hillsides. The truth is much simpler. She is conspiring with the queen to get her own household, and she has flattered your daughter into helping her."

"No," said Sir John. "She is a tiny fool of a girl. She is not capable—"

But the doors opened, and the footmen entered, and they had to close their mouths and turn to see the Earl of Dunham rush into the room.

"Dunham!" cried Sir John. "What brings you here at this time?"

"Forgive me for barging in on you like this, your grace, Sir John. I . . ." He bowed hastily. "There has been a development with the board." He cleared his throat. "And the king."

Chapter 36

Much to Victoria's surprise, the rooms were empty when she and Jane came in from the garden. To be sure, Lady Flora and Lehzen were there to take their bonnets, but neither Sir John nor Mama was in evidence.

A stroke of luck at last.

But it did not make up for all they had just learned from Gerald Maton's letter. The truth was, despite her determined words to Jane, Victoria felt dispirited. She had been counting on Dr. Maton finding *something* in his father's papers. People wrote the most amazing things in their private letters, somehow believing that no one else would ever see. . . .

Victoria froze.

"Letters," she breathed.

"What did you say, ma'am?" asked Jane. But she was not looking at Victoria. She was looking across the room at Lehzen and Lady Flora.

"I was just saying I had some letters I wanted to finish," Victoria announced. "Come help me, Jane."

"Yes, of course."

Victoria's table sat next to Mama's desk. Dash had a basket beside it. He hopped into it now and turned himself around, nosing his blanket until everything was to his liking.

Victoria also made as great a fuss of settling herself. She took out her paper, pen, and ink. She found her latest letter from Feodora and one from Uncle Leopold. She unfolded them and bent her head, as if studying the pages. Then she picked up her pen and addressed the paper.

Sir John and Maton were friends, she wrote. *May have written letters.*

"But the doctor's letters were burnt," breathed Jane.

Victoria smiled and wrote, *Sir John's were not.* She underlined it.

Jane clapped her hand over her mouth.

Victoria nodded. *Item: Search Sir John's desk at home.* She drew an arrow toward Jane.

Jane blanched. She swallowed. Victoria held her breath. Then, slowly, Jane nodded.

Victoria beamed. She wrote, *Item: Search Sir John's desk here.* She drew an arrow pointing toward herself.

Jane frowned. She mouthed, *How?*

Victoria grimaced, dipped her pen in fresh ink and wrote, *It only wants a little caution.*

But Jane shook her head minutely. She made a twisting gesture with her hand. For a moment Victoria could not understand. Then she realized Jane was pantomiming the turn of a key.

Oh, damn!

Sir John kept his desk locked. Victoria knew that. She'd seen it herself. Every day he came in and sat down and pulled his chain of keys from his waistcoat pocket and opened the drawers.

What can we do? There must be a way . . .

But her mind remained stubbornly blank. She must think

of something quickly. Wherever Mama and Sir John had gone, they would be back soon, and it was not the time for writing letters, and she hadn't done her journal yet for today, and . . .

All at once Jane got to her feet.

"What is it?" whispered Victoria.

Jane didn't answer. She just went to the bell and rang. Lady Flora looked at her curiously. So did Lehzen, but neither moved to stop her.

The footman walked in and bowed. "Miss Conroy?"

"Yes, Phillips." She twisted her hands awkwardly. She looked, Victoria realized, every bit her old limp self. "My father has lost his desk key. He asked me to find out if there might be a spare . . . ?"

"I'm sure there is, miss," Phillips replied. "Mrs. White will know for certain. Shall I go speak with her?"

"Yes, thank you. And you needn't bother my father with it," she added. "Just leave it on the mantel. He knows to look for it there should it be needed."

"Very good, miss." Phillips bowed and retreated without any hesitation. Because how could anyone suspect Jane of any deception? They all knew her far too well. She was shy and downtrodden and possibly a little stupid.

Jane returned to Victoria's table, and Victoria seized her hand, then squeezed it hard. Jane grinned. Jane Conroy actually grinned.

Victoria picked up her pen, but before she could write anything, Dash barked and jumped to his feet.

Because Phillips had opened the door again, and there stood Mama and Sir John. Victoria's tongue froze to the roof of her mouth.

"Well, did you girls have a pleasant walk?" Mama sailed into the room. "What are you writing there, Victoria?"

Victoria realized she had made a fatal mistake. She had left something written right out in the open. Mama would see it in a moment and know it was not a letter or anything like it.

"Oh, this . . . ?" Victoria reached for it, and Jane reached at the same time.

It was impossible to say which of them knocked over the inkwell, but in the next instant a black pool of ink spilled across the whole of her writing table. Jane leapt to her feet and Victoria with her, but the ink had already poured across the table and begun to to drip onto the table and the rug. And Dash.

Dash immediately began to bark and rush in circles, trying to get at whatever it was that was soaking through his coat.

"*Ach, mein Gott!*" screamed Mama.

"Oh, Dash!" Victoria snatched him up.

"Victoria! Your *dress!*"

After that, no one paid attention to what might have been lost on the writing table. And as Dash was being taken away by Lehzen to be bathed, and Phillips was shouting orders about the table and the carpet to a small army of servants, and Victoria was being hustled away by Mama and Lady Flora to be changed out of her ruined dress, no one had a spare moment to see how Victoria looked to Jane and smiled.

Chapter 37

Jane knew something was wrong the moment Father climbed into the carriage. His face was flushed, but his expression was ice cold. He pounded on the carriage roof with his closed fist to signal their driver to go but afterward sat rigidly upright, saying nothing.

This silence was a familiar tactic, and the one Jane feared the most. It never failed to set her mind racing. Usually, she asked herself, *What have I done?*

But now that she had done so much, all she could think was, *What does he know?*

Perhaps it's nothing to do with me. Perhaps he's had some bad news. He and the duchess were shut away so long with Lord Dunham . . .

Lord Dunham was one of the Kensington board. He might have come to bring word that the princess really was being moved out of the palace and away from Father.

That would more than explain his temper. It's not me. It's not what—

"Jane."

Jane froze. Her hands clenched together.

"What have you and the princess been up to?"

Answer him, she ordered herself. *Don't sit there like a stupid block. Answer!*

"Just what I told you." She kept her voice low and her eyes down. She was humble. She was uncertain. "She's worrying at the death of Dr. Maton. You said that I should play along and keep her distracted . . ."

"And that is everything?"

Jane looked up, made mute by her confusion. It was a mistake. Father's anger skewered her.

"Because I have reason to believe you are hiding things from me."

"I'm not!" cried Jane. "I promise I'm not. Only it's difficult to remember every tiny thing that happens in a day, and it's not as if I can sit and take notes in front of the princess!"

That seemed to dampen his temper, but only for a moment. "Then tell me now. What is she doing while she plays her little game?"

What do I do? What do I do? He'll know if I lie!

But an unexpected voice answered this gibbering with calm. *Then tell him the truth.*

"She . . . she spoke with Gerald Maton."

Father went very still. "What? How?"

How?

Jane wanted to cry. She wanted to shrink away, to bow her head and confess her sins before Father's righteous anger. He would be angry, but he would finish shouting eventually. Then he would go away. He'd forget about her again. That was how it always was.

Inspiration, bright and unfamiliar, struck. She knew how it always was. She knew how *he* always was. For seventeen years, he had been the driving force of her life.

She knew him far better than he knew her.

"It happened after the vigil," Jane said, which was true and gave away nothing at all. "I was going to tell you, but I'd had no chance yet. She saw Gerald Maton at the vigil and made shift to speak with him. She thought he might know something you weren't saying . . ."

"Why would she think that?"

Jane swallowed. He had stopped asking how the thing happened. That was good. She must keep him away from that. She must bow her head. She must twist her hands. She must tremble and hunch her shoulders. She must remember he might hit her, snap her head back, make her taste the blood in her mouth. . . .

"She knows his father came to dinner at our house."

Silence. If she looked up, she'd see the ice and calculation in his eyes. "How could she know that?"

"I told her," whispered Jane.

"You fool! You talking fool!"

He was yelling, and she had expected it. Had deliberately brought it down on her own head to get him away from wondering how the princess had slipped through the bars of his perfect system. She had meant to cringe and cry and plead for forgiveness, like she always did. It would work. She knew it would.

"But . . . but . . . you told me to help her," she whined. "You said to entertain her suspicions and keep her busy, and I have been doing just that."

"You were not to share my private business with her!"

Why should she not speak to Gerald Maton, Father? Why should she not know it was Dr. Maton who was found dead out on the green? Why do you care?

It took everything she had to hold those questions inside.

Do not let him see what you've become. Do not let him know what you are. Hide, Jane. Hide everything!

But there were other voices, voices from the mists and the

shadows, and they were louder and clearer, and oh, Jane wanted to listen to them.

"I tried, sir," she said. "But what can I do? You won't tell me ends and aims, so how am I to know what I should say and what I should keep secret?"

It was a mistake. It was too much. He was going to hit her again.

"God preserve me from the imbecility of women!" he growled. "Since you are incapable of understanding on your own, I will spell it out for you. You are to indulge the princess. You are to play her little games and flatter her and pretend to run her errands, but whatever she has you do, you come straight to me and you *tell* me, and I will decide how you are to proceed. Now, do you understand?"

"Yes, sir."

Why am I angry? Why am I even disappointed? He does not change. He will not. I knew that. I know that. I used it. I should be happy that my distraction worked.

But Jane could not be happy. She was angry and sorely disappointed. She hated the scene she had just so successfully played out.

"Now." Father made a great show of being patient. "You say she talked with Gerald Maton? What did she tell you about that?"

"She said his mother and brother had burnt the late doctor's papers." Jane kept her gaze focused on her hands. She did not dare look up, or he might see the blazing anger she carried inside. "She's not sure what she can do next." Jane paused. She let her brow furrow. "I think she may be getting tired of the whole thing."

Which was as blatant a falsehood as Jane had ever told.

"And that's all?"

Jane nodded fast, like a little girl being questioned about her lessons.

"She's said nothing to you about any communication with the palace? With the king or queen?"

Jane looked up, genuinely startled. "No. Why? Is there—"

But Father was frowning because she had dared to ask anything at all. Because it was what he did and always would do.

"I'm sorry, sir." Jane ducked her head.

"You will keep a close eye on the princess, and especially her doings with Lehzen," he said. "It may be she is trying to send messages behind her mother's back, and Lehzen is helping her. If such a thing is happening, we need to know how it's being done, do you understand?"

Jane nodded.

"Whatever you learn, you are to come tell me *at once*, do you understand?"

"Yes, sir."

"Very well. And you will never again repeat any piece of our private household business to anyone in the palace."

"No, sir."

And that was the end of it. He had said all he wished to say, and was satisfied that she would do as she was told. He could gaze out the window and plan his plans.

Jane watched him, and Jane burned.

As soon as they arrived back home, Jane escaped upstairs. She needed to talk with Liza.

If Father's told Mother anything about the new household, Liza will have heard . . .

But when she reached their rooms, Jane found that Liza was very much occupied.

The wardrobe's doors were thrown open. Liza's bandbox and portmanteau were on her bed, and her small trunk waited beside it. When Jane walked in, Liza was standing at her dressing table, closing her smallest case.

"Liza, what are you doing?"

Liza jumped and whirled around. When she saw it was Jane, she pressed her hand to her heart.

"Jane! You startled me. What are you doing back so early?"

"The princess has a dinner tonight. I was dismissed early. What—"

"Oh, this?" Liza waved at her luggage. "I've been invited to stay with Miss Schumann and her family for a few days. I told you about it. You remember."

Liza had not told her, and there was nothing for Jane to remember. But her sister's expression was intense, and it was pleading.

"I hope you have a good time," said Jane slowly.

"I'm sure I shall." But there was a hitch under Liza's breath. "Miss Schumann is so amusing. And her brother is coming up, as well. Which reminds me, Jane. I need a favor. Have you any money?"

"Money?" Jane echoed.

"I hate to ask, but there's sure to be cards at the Schumanns', and I must have something to play with, and with the expenses earlier—and then Ned came begging earlier today—well, I've nothing left."

Expenses. She means the money we gave to Susan.

"Ned borrowed money from you?"

Liza laughed bitterly. "Well, *borrowed* is something we say only when there's a chance of getting it back, isn't it? Ned scrounges. In fact, while I'm gone, you should probably put anything you've got somewhere safe. Sooner or later, he's sure to remember you get pin money as well as I do."

Jane remembered sitting in the carriage, disguised as the princess. She remembered watching Ned flee through the streets like a cuckold in a farce. "Is Ned in debt?"

Liza shrugged. "Probably. The way he gambles, it would be a surprise if he wasn't. Why?"

"I was . . . out the other day, and I saw him," Jane told her. "He was being chased down the street by some man."

"Probably it was either someone he owed or someone he cheated. With Ned, it could be either." She paused. "That is, if it wasn't somebody whose daughter he got up to mischief with."

Jane felt her cheeks heat up.

"I know what you're thinking," said Liza. "And yes, he gets away with it because he's a man, and it's not fair, and it never will be, and there's nothing we can do about it but get on as best we can." That wasn't at all what Jane was thinking, but Liza clearly was not interested in hearing anything from her. "I'm in a dreadful hurry, Jane. Miss Schumann's sending round her carriage, and I have to be ready to go. Can you loan me anything?"

Jane looked at Liza and saw she was lying. Whatever she had planned, it was much more than going to stay with her friend and her friend's family for a few days.

Liza looked back and silently begged her not to ask any questions.

Jane went to her wardrobe and opened the bottom drawer. She pulled out a roll of itchy wool stockings, the sort meant to be worn only on the very coldest days. Inside that roll was a small, plain bag, and inside the bag was five years of unspent pin money.

She'd never been quite sure what she was squirreling it all away for, but it had always made her feel obscurely better to know that it was there.

She counted fifty pounds and held the notes out to Liza.

Liza looked at the money and swallowed. But she took it and folded it into her reticule.

"Thank you, Jane," she croaked without turning around.

"If there's anything—"

Liza shook her head. "No. There's nothing you can do. Well, you can ring the bell. These things have to be gotten downstairs." She paused. "Oh, and be careful of Betty, won't you? Mama pays her to spy."

"I know," said Jane. "I'm paying her to keep quiet."

Liza blinked. "So am I."

They both giggled. Jane turned away to ring the bell before Liza could see the tears that had begun to form.

Now Liza seemed to be having trouble with her bonnet's ribbon. Jane rolled her eyes and took charge, tying a pretty bow under Liza's chin.

"Will you write?" Jane asked. "Between card games?"

Liza smiled and pressed her hand. "I'll leave something at the post office, all right? And I will pay you back, I promise."

Jane nodded.

There was no time for anything else. Meg and Paul, the footman, arrived to take the luggage downstairs. Liza embraced Jane quickly, picked up her reticule, and scurried out the door.

Jane's ears had begun ringing. She felt oddly light. She floated to the door and closed it and then drifted to the sofa and sat softly down.

Alone in her empty sitting room, Jane opened her bruised heart as wide as it would go and wished her sister good luck.

Chapter 38

Another dinner. Another concert. Another night when the ability to simply enjoy the performance—to dream and to soar for the length of the concerto—was denied.

The guest list was familiar and expected—visiting princes, selected lords of Parliament and their wives. A friend of Mama's. A friend of Sir John's.

What was different was that Mama was not enjoying herself, either. Usually she was firmly about her business during dinner. She talked, laughed, and expertly directed the chatter and gossip where she wished them to go. She showed off Victoria from all her best angles.

Tonight she was distracted and distant. So much so that Victoria overheard Lady Cowper asking if the duchess was quite well.

Victoria watched, and she wondered about it. Lord Dunham had been to visit earlier but had not waited to say a word to her. The only reason she knew he had come at all was that Lehzen had managed to slip a note into Wordsworth's poems.

Had he told Mama about the possibility of a separate household for Victoria? Was Mama afraid of being set aside? She had always said Their Majesties hated her. All of Father's family hated her. Did she think Victoria would not be able to stop her from being left behind?

Does she think I won't even try to stop that? Because I would. Of course I would. I love her. It's only that I need to get her away from Sir John.

These thoughts circled round Victoria's head, drowning out the music and distracting her from other important facts. Like the fact that Aunt Sophia came to the concert and brought Uncle Sussex with her.

Aunt Sophia sat in the corner, as usual, right beside her maid and waiting woman. When the recital was over and everyone was mingling to talk, she ricocheted from group to group, as she always did.

But tonight Uncle Sussex stayed at her elbow. Where Aunt Sophia barged through the crowd, Uncle Sussex tripped lightly. He laughed, told absurd stories, and generally exerted himself to please.

It took almost an hour, but Mama moved away from Victoria's side to speak privately with Baron Stockmar, who had arrived late. This gave Victoria space to signal Lady Charlotte from across the room. Lady Charlotte understood her and went over to her aunt and uncle, who let themselves be steered over to Victoria.

"Hullo, Aunt. I'm glad to see you are feeling better." Victoria kissed both her cheeks. "Hullo, Uncle. How nice to see you, as well." She repeated the greeting with him and thought she felt an extra trembling in his shoulders.

"Yes, yes," sighed Sophia. "My brother has decided I am making too much of a nuisance of myself and must be watched over." She slapped his arm with her fan.

Uncle Sussex just chuckled. "My sister sees every man as a jailer. I found myself in the mood for a little noise and society for a change. I love my books, but they are very quiet companions!"

"Well, I hope you enjoyed the music," said Victoria politely. They were being watched, of course. Every guest in the room was glancing in their direction, taking note of how Victoria dealt with her family.

Victoria chose her next words carefully. "I had hoped I might be able to accept your kind invitation soon, Aunt. I tried to come see you the other night, but you were . . . occupied."

"Oh, yes. Sussex told me you'd arrived. That was some poor planning on my part. This old head of mine!" She sighed and tapped her temple.

"I didn't know you knew Mr. Rea," Victoria remarked.

"Oh, yes," said Aunt Sophia airily. "Keeps the accounts. Has done for years. He and Sir John between them have me on quite the short leash. Probably for the best, eh, brother?"

"It's not just you, sister." Uncle Sussex's smile was meant to be indulgent, but his eyes remained worried. "Managing money has never been one of our family's strong suits."

By now Mama had noticed whom Victoria was speaking with, and sailed back to her side.

"Well, well, Sussex and Sophia, how very good to see you both." Naturally, Mama did not mean a word of it, but they all knew that.

"And you, sister!" boomed Sophia. "So good that I am overwhelmed with feeling. Come, Sussex. Take me back to my rooms. I find I'm quite faint." She clutched his arm, and he winced but obeyed, steering her slowly through the crowd.

Mama leaned down and whispered sharply in Victoria's ear. "What did she say to you?"

"She talked about the concert, and how she thought Uncle Sussex was being too managing."

Victoria was not sure if Mama believed her, but at least she did not ask any more questions.

Now Victoria lay in her bed and waited for Mama to return. She wondered about Aunt Sophia and Uncle Sussex, tucked away in their own wing, where they might as well be on the moon for all she could see or speak with them.

"What did she say to you?" Mama had asked.

Nothing she wanted to. Nothing she hoped to. Why did Uncle Sussex come with her tonight? What was he afraid she was going to do?

She turned these questions over, looking for answers, but to no avail. However, the exercise kept her mind occupied for the time it took for Mama to return, for her to be undressed and settled into bed. For the waiting women to depart to their room, and for the boudoir to finally settle itself.

At last, the sounds of sleep—the slow breathing, the soft rustles, the low snores—rose up around her. Victoria could move now.

The thrill of petty disobedience was unexpectedly heady.

Stop it. You are not a naughty child, Victoria scolded herself. *This is serious business.* She made herself picture Gerald Maton and his searching confusion. She pictured Dr. Maton collapsed, alone, on the green. She pictured Sir John dealing out his smooth reassurances and confident lies, convincing everyone that he would rule her life, even when she came to rule a kingdom.

The sense of mischief died.

Victoria shoved her covers back and planted her stockinged feet on the carpet. The room was black. She could see nothing but vague shadows, even though her eyes were well adapted to the dark. Still, she moved with confidence and practiced silence. If anyone peeled open an eye and saw her now, they would think she needed to use the commode waiting in its cabinet. Not even Dash stirred in his basket.

Running on her tiptoes, Victoria made for the door. Her dance master would be pleased at how lightly she crossed the floor. The door handle turned. Thankfully, Mama had hectored the staff so that the hinges on all these doors were well oiled and did not squeak, as they did elsewhere in the palace. Victoria slipped from the boudoir into the dressing room, and from there into the sitting room and then into the morning room.

Now the risk set in. There was no reason for her to be here. No excuse she could offer. If Mama woke and saw she was gone . . . if Dash woke, uneasy at some sensed movement, and barked . . . they would discover that she crept out at night, and that she knew how to do so. Mama would lock all the doors and hide all the keys. She'd set maids and footmen to stay awake all night to watch.

Don't think about it. Be quick.

With the door closed behind her, Victoria did not need to be as cautious. She could draw back the curtain. The blurred moonlight fell across the carpet. It wasn't much, but it was enough.

She'd berated herself several times today for not thinking of searching Sir John's desk sooner. Of course a man's secrets were kept in his desk, and Sir John's desk was part of her daily life. He sat there, writing his letters and sending them off with a crisp precision that she assumed came from his days of writing military dispatches. When his work was finished, his papers vanished. They went into the hands of various aides and clerks or into these drawers, locked away until their master returned.

Victoria crossed to the cold hearth and put her hand up on

the mantel. Her fingers touched metal, and she picked up the key. Phillips had kept his promise.

Sir John's desk was as square and sturdy as a coffin. It stood in the corner, so Sir John's back was always to the wall and nothing in the room could escape his searching eye. Victoria slipped between it and the stout wooden chair.

Each side of the desk had three drawers. There was another drawer in the center.

The center drawer would be for immediate business and tools—pens, blotters, fresh paper. She could ignore that. She sat in the chair and pictured Sir John. It was the end of the day. He was satisfied, humming slightly, shuffling his papers, opening . . .

She put the key into the lock of the lower right-hand drawer. The clock's ticking sounded very loud. Someone might wake up at any moment. Dash might wake and miss her and bark and wake the whole room. . . .

She flinched when the lock clicked, told herself not to be ridiculous, and pulled the drawer open.

Inside, she found files and folios, all neatly labeled. There were bound ledgers, bills of sale tied with ribbons and labeled according to the provider's name. It was all very tidy, very efficient, entirely impersonal.

The upper right-hand drawer held more of the same. Victoria glanced at the door and at the clock. What was happening in the boudoir? Had Lehzen woken up and decided to check on her? Lehzen wanted her to stop her questioning but would never betray her. Not even now.

But Lady Charlotte would. So would Lady Flora.

Victoria opened the lower left-hand drawer. Here, at last, she found the letters. They were bundled together and tied with ribbons.

They were all from women.

Here were stacks of letters from Princess Lieven, and here
was a stack from Lady Cowper, and another from Lady
Palmerston, from half a dozen others whose names she did
not know.

Why keep personal letters here? In the next heartbeat she
had the answer. *So Lady Conroy will not find them.*

There were—one, two, three, four—stacks from Mama,
tied in pink ribbons. Victoria felt the full stomach-roiling
strength of temptation. She could take these, sit in the moonlight with them, read them all.

*And why shouldn't I? They don't tell me the truth. Why
shouldn't I find it out for myself?*

But what if they told each other something else? What if
all those whispers and meaningful looks and pressed hands
were explained in these letters? If she read confirmation of
her worst suspicions, she'd never be able to forget it.

And what will I do then?

But something else caught her eye. A much smaller bundle lay at the bottom of the drawer, tied with a blue ribbon.
She lifted it out and squinted at the little tag.

Pss. Sophia.

What is Sir John doing writing to Aunt Sophia? Then she
remembered what Aunt Sophia had said after the concert
about Mr. Rea. About Sir John.

*He and Sir John between them have me on quite the short
leash. Probably for the best, eh, brother?*

*It's not just you, sister. Managing money has never been
one of our family's strong suits.*

Sir John had told her as much when he spoke of handling
"practical matters" for Aunt Sophia. But how was this possible? Aunt Sophia was cold, teasing, and deliberately ob-
streperous whenever Sir John was near. In return, he was
condescending and unctuous. Mama hated her, and Sir John
belittled her for Mama's sake.

At least, that was what Victoria had always seen.

"I will be just as faithful to you as your secretary as I have been to the other women who have trusted me to be their champion," Sir John said. "And you will be very glad to make me your man."

Victoria looked at the stacks of letters from all those women, from Mama, from her aunt.

You will be very glad to make me your man.

Suddenly, all Victoria wanted to do was to run away to some corner where she could be violently ill.

The clock was ticking. She must set aside feeling. She could do that. She had had years of practice. She must decide what to do before someone woke to use the commode, before Dash got restless and noticed she was gone, before any of a thousand things happened that would cause somebody to wake up and find her here behind Sir John's desk with a packet of his letters from Aunt Sophia in her hands.

I'll read one.

She bit her lip. She closed the desk up carefully, put the key back on the mantel, and crossed to the window.

I can read one. If there's nothing to the purpose, I'll put them back and not risk any more . . .

Victoria sat down tailor-fashion on the carpet, awash in moonlight. She pulled one letter from the packet, unfolded it carefully, and began to read.

And when that was done, she read another. And then another.

And then another.

Her neck ached and her eyes blurred and her breath came fast, as if she'd been running.

The curtains stirred, and her head jerked up. There in the shadows stood a tiny woman in a black dress. She scowled at Victoria, and Victoria's throat closed.

This one was Mary Tudor, Bloody Mary, and she pointed toward the boudoir with one heavily beringed finger.

Victoria scrabbled at the letters, gathering them up, and stuffed them into her night robe. She ran—lightly, silently—back to her bed and dove under the covers.

"Vickelchen?" murmured Mama sleepily.

"I'm here, Mama," she answered. "Right here."

Chapter 39

Jane decided that morning was actually the safest time for her to search Father's desk. The servants would be busy getting the house ready for the day, and Father would be dividing his time between reading his newspapers in the library and having breakfast. Mother, of course, did not rise before ten. Ned might be up earlier, but if he was, he'd be about his own business.

Where Liza was and what she was doing was something Jane tried very hard not to think about.

Jane left instructions for Betty to rouse her at six. Betty did, although it came with a running stream of complaints about Jane and her erratic habits. Jane apologized while she stood to be dressed. She apologized again while her hair was being done. She gave Betty an extra five shillings for all her patience.

Meg brought her tray with chocolate, tea, and toast because breakfast would not be fully ready for at least another hour. Jane apologized again.

The maids left. Jane swallowed her chocolate and wolfed a

piece of toast. Then she sat for a while, waiting for something terrible to happen. Because it must happen. Despite her newfound ability to look Father in the face and lie, part of her still could not accept that she planned to break into his desk and rummage through his private papers.

But nothing did happen.

Jane descended the stairs to the first floor. The corridor was empty. The sound of the servants laying out breakfast drifted up from the ground floor.

Father would still be in his bedroom. He woke at half seven, unless there was an urgent summons from the palace. And there had been nothing. Betty would have said. Or Meg would have.

Surely, they would have said.

Jane gritted her teeth and walked down the corridor.

Father's study was the last door on the right. It was the farthest from the street, because Father required perfect quiet for his work. The door, Jane knew, would be unlocked. Why would it be locked? No one in the house would disobey Father's wishes and come in here without being explicitly sent for.

Jane did not let herself hesitate. She opened the study door, stepped over the threshold, and closed the door softly behind herself. She stood in the dim, still room, trying to breathe. For an absurd moment it seemed impossible that she was still in the same house or that she could be the same person.

Stop it, Jane. Look around you. It's just a room.

It was paneled in dark wood. It was spread with good carpets. The draperies were pulled shut, but there was enough light to see by. A full-length portrait of Mother and Father hung over the fireplace mantel. Mother sat unusually upright in a richly upholstered chair. Father stood beside her in his scarlet and gold uniform, looking every inch the soldier he used to be. He had a hand on Mother's shoulder. Jane had always thought her face looked like he was squeezing her just a little too tight.

No dawdling.

Although Father did not lock the study door, he did lock the desk, because he kept a strongbox with the household money in there. There was no need to go hunting for a copy of the key, however. Jane had found it years ago. She'd been a little girl, playing hide-and-seek with her dolls because neither Ned nor Liza would play with her. At that moment, she'd been acting as her doll Flossie, who was very mischievous. Flossie had decided to hide in Father's study, up on the mantel, behind the clock. She'd knocked clock and the key off, and Jane had been caught trying to put them back.

She'd been shut in her room for three days with only bread and milk for meals. She never saw Flossie again.

Jane realized was shaking.

What am I doing? What am I thinking? What will I tell him when he finds me?

Mother and Father watched her with their painted eyes — Father in command, Mother in pain.

I'll say I'm doing what the princess asked me. That the princess knows you lie. The princess doesn't trust you. She will never trust you and is looking for an excuse to have you thrown out.

That's why I'm doing this.

The key was on the mantel, underneath the clock, right where she remembered it. She snatched it up and hurried to the desk. She'd been in here before when Father was working. When he was angry with his children, he would call them in singly or together. They would then have to stand in front of the desk in silence while he finished with whatever matter currently occupied him, and could then turn the full force of his attention on them.

As a result, she had seen him put away his files, his ledgers, and his letters.

Jane unlocked the lower drawer on the left-hand side. As she expected, it was filled with individual packets of letters. Jane sorted through them as quickly as she could. Some were from men she recognized as lords of Parliament or members of the Kensington Board. There were some from relatives, and some others with names she did not recognize.

Then, at the bottom, she found two packets stacked together. One for Mr. William Rea. One for Dr. William Maton. *The Two Gentle-Williams of Verona . . .*, thought Jane absurdly as she pulled them out of the drawer.

The door opened.

Jane slapped her hand over her mouth to stifle a scream. A man cursed roundly and slammed the door, shutting them both in together.

But it wasn't Father.

It was Ned.

"What the devil are you doing here?" he demanded in a harsh stage whisper.

Jane was so relieved, she forgot to be afraid. "I could ask you the same thing! What are you even doing up so early? Do you have another horse to go look at?"

The truth was, her brother didn't look as if he'd ever gone to bed. His trousers and coat were rumpled; his hair was uncombed. The stubble of his beard made his face look like it was smeared with ash, and his eyes were as exhausted as they were bloodshot.

"Your new position as favorite minder to our shrimp of a princess has made you saucy," he sneered. "And you still haven't said what you're doing here."

"Father sent me to retrieve a letter he needed."

"Did he? Perhaps I'll go ask him about that."

Jane shrugged. "Go ahead. You'll have to explain what

you were doing in his study without permission. I wish you luck with that."

"Puts us in the same boat, doesn't it? Difference is, I've got nothing to lose, and I rather suspect you do."

Jane held on to her determination for a full minute. The difficulty was, Ned was right. She did have something to lose. If Father ceased to trust her, he'd banish her from the palace and the princess's company. There was a time when she would have liked nothing better. Now it was exactly what she feared.

"What have you got there?" Ned made an impatient gesture with two fingers. "Come on, give over."

Jane could see nothing else to do. She scowled, but she held out both packets of letters. If she was lucky, Ned would just be confused, and she could tell him some story. . . .

Ned snatched them away and looked at their neat labels. And blanched. And swallowed.

He recovered fairly quickly. He also pocketed the letters.

"Give those back!" Jane hissed.

"No. They are none of your business."

"They are. Dr. Maton, from the medical household, is dead. He may have been poisoned—"

Ned folded his arms. "I know."

"You . . . know?"

"And I know that whatever is in these letters, you do not want to be involved with it." Ned's voice and his expression were disconcertingly mild. Sympathetic even. "Go on, now, Jane." Ned stepped aside to make a clear path for her. "I'm sure the princess is expecting you."

But Jane remained where she was. "Why should you even care what I'm doing? You never have before."

He held her gaze for a moment longer, then, to Jane's surprise, her brother smiled. It was a tiny, bitter expression, and the sight of it made something twist inside her.

"You're right," he said. "After all, we're all doing the same thing, aren't we? Trying to work out some kind of life for ourselves. Only we all keep getting caught." He shoved his hands into the pockets of his rumpled coat. "You must believe me, Jane. I am protecting you." He nudged the door open. "Go back to your princess, and if you find your way out of this house, I wish you Godspeed, and I swear I will not get in your way. All I ask is that you do the same for me."

There was nothing she could do. Jane gathered up her skirts and strode out into the corridor. Ned pulled the door shut behind her.

Jane had thought she would just walk away. She should. She should go back to her rooms at once, finish her chocolate, get ready to go to the palace. She could come back later in the day, when the house was quiet and Ned was gone. Ned would surely return the packets to their drawer. He must be doing that right now.

Because what else could he still be doing in there?

Jane turned again and faced the door. She steeled her nerves and crouched down and put her eye to the keyhole.

There on the other side was Ned. He was behind Father's desk. He pulled open a drawer and brought out a metal strongbox. He took something from his pocket. Another key? She couldn't tell, but he struggled with the box, jiggering and shaking it, his mouth moving in silent curses.

At last, he threw the lid open and dipped his hand inside. He came up with a wad of what could only be banknotes and stuffed them into his pocket. He snapped the lid shut.

Jane straightened. She flew down the corridor and ducked into the empty morning room. Once inside, she held the door open just a crack so that she could see out. She held her breath, too, so that Ned wouldn't hear her panting.

She needn't have bothered. Ned strode past without turning his head and all but ran down the stairs. She heard the door below slam.

Ned was gone.

Ned had robbed Father.

Ned—their brother, Father's heir, the young man who came and went as he chose, who flirted with and flattered Kensington society, who had been abroad in the army, on tour, at the consulate—had just stolen a handful of banknotes from their father.

Liza had said he'd taken her money, as well.

Whatever is in these letters, you do not want to be involved with it . . . I am protecting you.

She thought about him running through the streets, with the other man hard on his heels.

Jane had spent much of her life deliberately trying not to hear other people's secrets, but she was still a denizen of the palace and the parlor. Everyone knew there were a thousand ways for clever, ambitious young men to be ruined.

Which of those ways had caught up with Ned?

Jane slipped out of the morning room and raced up the stairs. She needed coat and bonnet. She needed to be out the door before Father came downstairs and asked about her. She needed to make her way across town.

And if luck was with her, she would find Susan at home.

Chapter 40

The morning brought a gloomy, determined gray rain. And Jane was late. Victoria struggled through her lessons. What she wanted was to grab up her pencil box, where she had hidden Aunt Sophia's letters, and run all the way to her aunt's rooms so she could wave the pages in her startled face.

Look! Look at this! Why didn't you tell me!

What was Dr. Maton to you? she would demand. *Why were you so determined to get him more money?*

She wanted to show the letters to Jane, to explain to her what she had found, to ask her opinions. She even wanted to tell her about the ghost.

Victoria believed she was well used to keeping her own council. But these few days with a friend of her own to talk to had changed her absolutely. Now sitting in silence and muffling her secrets felt like a form of torture.

All through her morning lessons, Victoria kept looking toward the doors, waiting for Jane to slip through. This, of course, earned her a scolding from Mama and repeated gentle reproofs from her tutors.

Now it was half ten, and according to the system, it was time for her lessons to pause so she could take some exercise or engage in other improving activity. Jane still had not appeared. But Sir John had.

He surveyed the room, counting its occupants the way Victoria used to count her dolls in their boxes.

"Where is Jane?" he asked.

"You don't know?" said Mama, surprised.

Something was clearly wrong, and now Jane would be in trouble when she did appear.

"I sent her on an errand," said Victoria quickly. "To the bookshop. I'm sure she told you about it."

"Again?" Sir John frowned, and Victoria wished she could kick herself. But she kept her countenance and answered him easily.

"I want to make sure I have plenty to read when we leave on the tour, and Jane has such amusing taste, don't you find?"

Sir John could not exactly fault her praise of Jane when he was the one who had pressed her on Victoria as a friend and companion. He gave an irritable shrug. "Your mother and I will have to approve these books."

"Oh, of course."

If her amiable acquiescence raised any suspicion in him, he did not show it. He just settled in behind his desk and opened the first of the folios laid there for his attention.

Victoria glanced out the window. Rain drummed hard against the glass. Dash caught her agitation and whined. She ruffled his ears, but it did little to soothe either of them.

She could not just sit here. She was so filled with nervous energy, she felt she might scream. So, with Dash at her heels, Victoria walked over to her mother's desk.

Mama was not writing letters this morning. She was making a list. Victoria tried not to squint as she skimmed it. It was the names of ladies and of prominent families.

"Mama?"

"Mmm?" She added the Marquess of Exeter.

It's the tour, Victoria realized. Mama was writing out the names of the people they were to be staying with.

"May I go see Aunt Sophia? Just to—"

"After the way she behaved last night?" Mama dipped her pen again. "I should say not. I will not have her influence spoiling you at this time."

"What time?"

Mama wrote, *Countess of Leicester.* "Go read your book, Victoria, or write your journal. As you can see, I have work to do."

Yes, but what is that list for? "Please, Mama. I'm worried about her."

Mama sighed and laid her pen in the holder. She turned to face Victoria. Sir John looked up, as well.

"Your aunt has her brother and her waiting women," he said. "It is their duty to look out for her, not yours."

"Yes, but—"

"But what, Victoria?" said Mother.

"Old people begin to wander when their time is near. I do not want her to . . . well . . . I want to be sure I've told her I love her, Mama."

Naturally, Mama looked to Sir John. Victoria wanted to stamp her foot and shout. *Look at me! I am the one talking to you!*

"I have warned you against too much sentimentality, Victoria," said Mama. "Especially toward your father's family."

"She may seem a harmless old thing," added Sir John, "but she has all their spirit, and their ill feeling toward your mother and toward you."

Then why are you handling her money for her? Why do you call yourself her champion?

"Please, Mama. This once. I will ask for nothing else all day. I promise. Please."

Mama was looking at Sir John again. Victoria bit the inside of her cheek to keep quiet. She hated begging like a child, hated having to gain permission just to leave a room in her own home. But it worked. Sir John must have signaled some sort of approval, because Mama threw up her hands.

"All right! All right! But you will take Lady Flora with you. I need Lehzen here."

Mama needed Lehzen? That could not be. Mama did not like her and definitely did not trust her.

Mama was making lists of the families they were to meet on tour. Mama was keeping Lehzen away from her with flimsy excuses.

Something is happening. Victoria felt suddenly torn. But having successfully pleaded her case to go see her aunt, she couldn't suddenly decide to stay so she could eavesdrop.

She had no choice now but to leave Mama and Sir John to their own devices.

Chapter 41

Susan was home.

All was as it had been the last time Jane arrived at the cottage's doorstep. The two old men sat on their wooden bench beneath the eaves with the jug between them. They watched with interest as Jane knocked on the door and Susan opened it.

"Thought I should see you again sooner or later," Susan said, wiping her hands on her apron. "You'd best come in."

Betty stayed in the foyer. Susan took Jane through into the low, cramped kitchen. Despite the fire in the hearth, the gloomy day filled the place with an unseasonal twilight. Susan waved Jane toward the long wooden bench. Jane sat down and took off her damp bonnet and set it on the end of the thoroughly scrubbed board table.

Susan folded her arms and rubbed her raw elbows. "Is there work?" she asked. "Or is it something more about that doctor fellow?"

"It's about Ned," Jane told her.

Susan's expression turned thunderous. "You ain't about

to say I was up to no good with him again, are you? Cuz I already told you—"

"No, no, it's not that. I just wanted to ask if you ever knew Ned to have any dealings with Dr. Maton? Not Gerald Maton. I mean his father. Were they ever at the house together that you saw?"

Jane watched Susan screw up her face, watched her get ready to lie. Or perhaps to order Jane out of the house.

"I wouldn't be asking, but the princess needs to know," Jane added hastily.

She felt like she was being unfair somehow by invoking the princess. Perhaps she was, but it did work. Susan's expression softened, and she sat down across the table from Jane. She ran her hands across the pitted surface, as if smoothing an invisible cloth.

"We wasn't friends, me and your brother," she said. "Not real ones. He wasn't as bad as some, I'll give him that much. He teased, and he pinched a bit, but nothing worse. And when he found out my uncle"—she nodded toward the foyer, and Jane realized she must mean one of the two men on the bench outside—"had drunk away the rent, again, he gave me the money and asked for nothing in return."

Jane found herself staring. Ned had done that? Careless, drunken Ned?

"And, well, he talked," Susan went on. She rolled her eyes at Jane's fresh confusion. "It's that way sometimes. The family, they'll say all sorts of things to a servant, because they think you don't matter, and they believe you're somehow too loyal or too stupid to tell anybody important." She shrugged. "So, I knew about his going to the gaming parties, and I knew how he said he lost so much money only because the other gentlemen cheated and . . ." She shrugged again.

"Well, one morning I'm bringing up the coal so I can lay the fires in the parlor, and there's a great banging in the scullery and the door flies open and there's a man in a black coat with a doctor's bag. He and this other gentleman are dragging Mr. Ned between them, and his shirt's all covered in blood. They're yelling at me to bring hot water and clean towels, only I'm not to wake the house. I don' t know what's happening, but I fetch what I'm told to, and they lay him out on the kitchen table, and . . ."

She shuddered. "Well, they asked me to stay while they sewed him up, in case they needed anything. And I gathered from their talk that there's been a duel and Mr. Ned was wounded. Bullet grazed his side. Not serious, the doctor didn't think. Just messy. They could get him patched up. But they said that other man, the one Mr. Ned shot at—he was killed."

Jane's mouth went dry. There was a roaring in her ears. The sensation of lightness had returned. This time, she wished she really could just float away. But she remained tethered here, forced to hear what Susan said next.

"That doctor? It was Dr. Maton?" asked Jane.

Susan nodded. "It was after that, that Mr. Ned started giving him money, too."

Chapter 42

When Victoria reached Aunt Sophia's sitting room, it was to find a waiting woman holding a tray with a pot of chocolate and a rack of toast on it.

"I'm sorry, ma'am." The woman's curtsy was slightly awkward because of her full hands. "Her Highness has not yet risen for the day."

"Oh, I'm sure she won't mind me visiting," said Victoria. "Is that her chocolate? I'll take it in."

Victoria took the tray out of the woman's hands and breezed toward Aunt Sophia's boudoir, with Dash scampering behind. What could the woman do but open the door for her?

And close it right behind her.

Because Victoria—a Royal Highness and a member of the blood family—could enter Princess Sophia's bedchamber when she was en déshabillé. Protocol dictated, however, that Lady Flora must wait outside until invited. Victoria felt quite sure Aunt Sophia would not be inclined to include one of Mama's spies in their conversation, however trivial that conversation might be.

And what Victoria had to ask her aunt was far from trivial. Aunt Sophia lay in her broad carved bed, under a tapestry canopy. In her nightclothes and cap, she was a tiny, pale, ruffled doll in a sea of brocade silk and velvet.

"Vickelchen!" Aunt Sophia cried. "What a lovely surprise!"

"Good morning, Aunt! I came to see how you are." Victoria set the tray on her aunt's lap and kissed her cheek. "I hope you do not mind Dash."

"Not at all. Put him up here." She patted the bed beside her. Victoria complied, and Aunt Sophia rubbed the spaniel's chin. "There's a good doggy!"

"Should I pour you some chocolate?"

"Yes, yes, and I'll ring for a cup . . ."

"Oh no," said Victoria as she poured the rich brew into the gilt-rimmed cup. "I've had mine. But I'll steal a slice of your toast."

"Greedy girl." Sophia laughed.

Victoria hopped up on the bed, just as she had when she was small. Now she and Aunt Sophia sat side by side, propped up by the silk bolsters. Dash lay between them, looking mournful and thumping his tail hopefully against the covers until Victoria fed him several bits of toast.

Her aunt took a long, guzzling swallow of chocolate. "Ah! Now. To what do I owe the pleasure of your company on this horrid morning?" She waved at the windows. The rain had stopped, but the day remained thoroughly gray.

Victoria thought about saying she'd just wanted to visit. She didn't have to disturb her aunt or herself. She could find another way. She could let the . . . the . . . other matter go.

Because if she spoke, she might very well break something precious, and she knew it.

"Vickelchen?" said Aunt Sophia. "*Was ist los?* What is it?"

Victoria took a deep breath. She patted Dash's back. She

found she could not look her aunt in the eye. "Aunt Sophia, I have to ask you about Dr. Maton."

"Which Dr. Maton? I understand there is an entire flock of them."

"Dr. William Maton. The household physician." Now Victoria was finally able to lift her gaze. "The one who died."

"Yes, yes, I know. I'm teasing." Aunt Sophia selected a piece of toast from the rack and gnawed at it.

"Aunt . . ."

"Out with it, girl." Aunt Sophia waved her toast, scattering crumbs across the bedcovers. "I'm too old for all this foot-dragging."

"Was Dr. Maton your son?"

Aunt Sophia put down her toast. She drained her chocolate cup and set that down, too.

"My son?"

"Yes." Victoria did not let herself look away. She had said this thing, and she would face what came next. She would look her aunt in the eye, and she would hear whatever she had to say. Even if she fell into one of her screaming fits. Even if she burst into tears. "You . . . you had a child when you were younger." *Out of wedlock and out of sight. You had a secret lover and a secret bastard. Just like your brothers did.* "And you'd been working to make sure Dr. Maton was paid extra beyond his stipend from the household, and Sir John and Mr. Rea were helping you."

This was what she'd learned from the letters she'd stolen. Aunt Sophia had been a young and lonely woman. Her father's madness had kept marriage out of reach for her and her sisters. The fact of her being a woman had kept her from having her own home, a luxury that all her brothers had been allowed.

There had been a great deal of sighing over the boredom and isolation of that time, of the endless days with nothing

to do but sit with her sisters and her mother and embroider
or play solitaire, waiting—for hours, for days, for years—for
their father to get better.

There had been more. Victoria had read veiled hints about
what King George III did in his madness and about her
brother the Duke of Cumberland. Things she could not
quite understand. *Or perhaps I don't want to.*

What she did understand was that Aunt Sophia had fallen
pregnant and she had given birth. It was all meant to be in
secret, but that secret had escaped. That was why she was ex-
iled here to Kensington Palace, with no one except one dis-
graced brother to keep her company.

Victoria waited for Aunt Sophia to shout or cry or accuse
her of being ungrateful, selfish, and a host of other epithets.
But she just sighed.

"I would ask how you found out about my son, but I have
a feeling I don't want to know." She shook her head sadly.
"But to answer your question, no. Dr. William Maton was
not my son. However, he was there when my son was
born."

Victoria's breath hitched.

"I had wondered when you'd find out about Tommy.
That's his name, by the way. Thomas Garth. Would you like
to see his picture?"

Victoria nodded. Aunt Sophia reached beneath her wrap-
per and pulled out a gold locket that hung on a chain around
her neck. She opened it carefully. Inside waited a painted
miniature. The man it depicted was round-faced and pop-
eyed and was wearing an officer's scarlet coat. His brow, his
eyes, and the dark waving hair all declared he was related to
Sophia, to the rest of the royal family.

To me. It was the first time she had seen any of her illegitimate cousins, and Victoria felt a strange frisson inside. Because
he looked exactly like the few legitimate ones she had met.

Aunt Sophia seemed to be waiting for her to say something. What could she possibly say?

"He's very handsome."

"Thank you." Sophia gazed at the portrait, her wide eyes swimming with tears.

Victoria knew she should cringe back from her aunt. There could not be any sympathy. Aunt Sophia had permitted herself to be ruined. She deserved her lonely life and should be grateful that the family had continued to support her at all. The man in the portrait—despite how normal he appeared—was tainted by the nature of his birth.

Mama had said all this and more about Uncle William and his mistress and his children.

But somehow, as Victoria sat here beside her old aunt, with the chocolate pot and toast crumbs and her spaniel dozing between them, the outrage and horror she knew were proper responses refused to manifest.

"Do you ever speak?"

"Oh, not directly. Not in years." Aunt Sophia snapped the locket shut. "My brothers were all allowed to raise their bastards, at least until they had to join the race to produce a legitimate heir. I was never even permitted that much time with my son. I gave birth in a public house, and within hours he was taken from me to be raised elsewhere." She closed her bony hand around the locket and held the image of her son close for a moment before she hid it away again. "Every so often a letter still finds its way to me. Mostly asking for money."

"Do you give it to him?"

"When I can. I have a bit of my own, you know. Living locked in a tower is a marvelous way to husband one's income." She chuckled, and she pulled a handkerchief from her sleeve and wiped at her eyes. "I'll have some more chocolate, there's a good girl."

Victoria filled her aunt's cup and put a slice of toast on the saucer. She kept her gaze averted while Aunt Sophia mopped her eyes and her nose and generally pulled herself together. In fact, she did not look up at all until her aunt took her cup and downed half the contents in a single gulp.

"Ah!" Aunt Sophia threw her head back and sighed harshly up to the canopy. "Say what you will about tea, but it's chocolate that saves one at such times."

Victoria smiled, but just a little, and only for a fleeting instant.

"Aunt, I have . . . I have another question." She stopped. She steeled herself and began again. "Aunt, did my father . . . Were there any outside children?"

"Like that whole litter of Fitzes belonging to dear William?" Aunt Sophia's mockery was sharp. "Or Sussex's pair away off in Germany or Italy or wherever it was?" The sneer slid across Victoria's skin, and it felt prickling. Dangerous. Victoria reminded herself that Aunt Sophia had a right to her anger, particularly on this subject. "What makes you ask now?"

Sir John says his wife is my sister. Sir John tells his children that they are my blood relations because she is my father's natural daughter. "It's simply that . . . when I am queen, I should not like to be . . . surprised."

"Mmm . . . yes. There's sense in that. No other reason?" She cocked her head. "A reason from Sir John, perhaps?"

Victoria froze. Aunt Sophia patted her hand.

"You found out his ridiculous delusion about his wife, didn't you? *That's* what's behind this sudden interest in all our bastards."

Victoria swallowed. "Jane said . . . said her father said . . . about her mother . . . I wanted to know if it might be true." She blushed. This stammering was not like her. She had come here determined to face any and all truths she might learn. "Jane told me that Sir John thinks his wife is . . . is my half sister. Could it be true?"

"Well, now, Vickelchen, I'll tell you." Aunt Sophia leaned back on her bolsters and regarded her seriously. "Your father was a cunning, careful man, and he kept a close eye on his future. He knew there was a chance he might come to the throne, and he didn't want any complications from the wrong side of the blanket to follow him there."

Perhaps she should not be so relieved. Perhaps she should have been more confident that the story about Lady Conroy was just another lie, as Jane had suspected. But Victoria was relieved. So much so, in fact, that for a moment she could do nothing but gather Dash up and hold him close.

Aunt Sophia gave one of her deep chuckles and rubbed Dash's head.

"I'm sorry to have disturbed you with such talk," said Victoria.

"You do not disturb me, my dear. As it happens, I'm rather impressed you asked the question. I was sure that your mother had quite destroyed your ability to think of your own future."

"Did you ever?" she asked curiously. "Think of your future?"

"Oh, my dear, we had no future, and we knew it. Marriage was one escape available to any of us, but the law said that the king must approve any proposal before we could accept it, and the king's illness left him unable to approve anything at all." She shook her head again. "There, at least, my brother George did what he promised. When proposals were made for my sisters, he agreed to them. I, alas, had taken matters into my own hands by then."

"Why did you do it?"

"I fell in love. Or I told myself that I had. The truth was, I was desperate for some shred of a life that was my own. Something unconnected to the tangle of my family, of my rank and title. And there were other reasons . . ." Her words and her gaze drifted away.

She is not here. She is in the past. Heaven help her, it is an ugly place.

"Let it be a lesson to you, my dear," whispered Aunt Sophia. "Whatever dream of the future you nurture, keep it free of romantic notions. Love can only ruin the lives of women like us." She took up her handkerchief and blew her nose hard. "Ach! I am a mess. An old, sentimental mess." She dropped the kerchief onto the table beside her bed. "Now, was there anything else you wanted to know?"

"Yes, in fact. Why did you make sure I would see Mr. Rea and Sir John together? Leaving your room?"

Her aunt squinted at her. "What is this?"

"The day you invited me up here. I know what you said at the concert . . ." *Sussex told me you'd arrived. That was some poor planning on my part. This old head of mine.* "But you really wanted me to see them leaving your rooms, wasn't it?"

"Good God! How suspicious you have become!" cried Aunt Sophia. "But since I see I must allay these worries, I will tell you, I didn't expect them. They came to me. There were papers they wanted me to sign. Mr. Rea helps with my money, and Sir John directs Mr. Rea."

"But why would you let Sir John near your money? You hate him!"

"Because, my dear, Sir John hates my brothers and will exert himself to the utmost to make sure they cannot get their hands on any part of my allowance. Now, he may take something for himself as a sort of commission for his services and his silences, but he at least knows enough not to kill the golden goose. I could not expect so much forbearance from any of my brothers."

Victoria made no answer. She only stared at her aunt in mute horror.

Aunt Sophia made a dismissive gesture. "We all do what

we must, Vickelchen. You know this already. Don't pretend otherwise."

Victoria petted Dash. She watched her hand moving across his silky back.

Aunt Sophia caught her hand and squeezed. "No tears, child. No regrets. We will not be conquered, not even by our own families." She grinned, and it was a terrible expression showing all the gaps between her crooked teeth. "It is your turn to answer some questions. Why come to me with this now, hmm? Why are you nosing about in these murky waters?"

"Because Dr. Maton may have been poisoned. Because someone offered his family a pension to keep certain facts about his death a secret, which made them burn all his papers." *And that someone might have been Sir John, and he could have been following your instructions, because Dr. Maton knew about your son, and you wanted to make sure that secret did not get out again.*

"And you think perhaps I decided Dr. Maton could no longer be trusted to keep quiet? So I sat scheming in my tower like Eleanor of Aquitaine and ordered my minions to poison his port wine?"

"You think I am ridiculous."

"I think you are an intelligent young woman. I think you look and you see and you listen. And our family has done far, far worse than cause the death of one greedy man. But no, Vickelchen. If someone tired of Dr. Maton's threats and made an end of him, it was not me."

"But why does Uncle—"

But Aunt Sophia cut her off. "No more. You have tired me out, my girl. Go back to your own country. Leave me to mine." She settled back and closed her eyes.

"But—"

Aunt Sophia held up her hand, gesturing for silence. Then she pointed toward the door. She did not open her eyes.

What else could Victoria do? She kissed her aunt, picked Dash up, and went back out into the gaudy, crowded sitting room.

Lady Flora stood and shook out her skirts, every inch of her betraying her profound irritation. Victoria ignored her. She was too lost in her own thoughts. She did not believe Aunt Sophia was tired. She simply didn't want to answer any more of Victoria's questions. As soon as Victoria brought up Uncle Sussex, she had been dismissed.

She remembered Aunt Sophia's admonishment. *Good God! How suspicious you have become!*

But it made no difference. The questions she did not ask followed her like the ghosts all the way back to her rooms.

Chapter 43

If Victoria had had any thought to spare, she would have expected to find her rooms much as she had left them. Mama would be writing, Sir John reading, and the waiting ladies working quietly at their mending.

She did hope that Jane would be there. *I have so much to tell her.*

But when the footman opened the door to the private rooms, Victoria found everything in chaos.

"No! No! You! Put it down there! Lady Flora, make him understand! Lady Charlotte, get that open—"

Mama stood on the threshold of the dressing room, directing half a dozen footmen, who were all carrying trunks. Lady Charlotte and Lady Flora were huddled with at least as many maids, murmuring and pointing at the wardrobe, at the jewel case, and the dressing table. Sir John stood beside his desk with a pair of men in clerk's uniforms, issuing orders for them to write down.

Jane had indeed arrived in the middle of all this disorder. Her skirts were damp, and their hems muddy. She huddled on her stool in the corner, as bedraggled, ignored, miserable, and pale as the day they had found Dr. Maton's corpse.

"What on earth!" Victoria cried. "Jane! Mama! What has happened?"

"Everything!" Mama cried. "Sir John tells us the departure date for your tour has advanced. We must all be ready to leave in two days!"

"What!" Victoria's mind reeled. It was too much to take in. She was still dizzy from everything she'd learned sitting by Aunt Sophia. She could not grasp this new shift.

"We are invited by Lord Liverpool to his house at Tunbridge Wells," Sir John said. "I have already accepted on your behalf. We will stay there several days. Then we will travel on to the Midlands, as previously planned."

"But I am not ready . . . !" *I need time! I need time to hear word from St. James's, to convince Mama! I need time to discover how you're involved with the Matons and what happened to the doctor and why his papers were all burnt—*

"You will be made ready," said Sir John. "Your mother and your very capable ladies have already begun."

"And I want no fuss, Victoria," said Mama. "I have a thousand things to do—all on your behalf, may I add. There's no time to waste arguing."

Victoria stared at her. *This is why you were writing that list. You were going to alert the other families who will be hosting us that the time frame of the tour had changed. You knew all morning this was happening, and you did not tell me!*

"Lady Flora," said Mama. "Take the princess and Jane into the rose room. Her lessons for the afternoon are canceled, but she can write her letters and her journal and stay out of the way there. Lehzen, I will need you to help me with checking through the trunks and the wardrobes. There are surely items that will need repair, and you must tell me which dresses no longer fit—"

"No, Mama!" cried Victoria.

"Yes, Victoria!" shouted Mama. "Now!"

Victoria turned, searching desperately for support or for escape. Lehzen's expression was closed and dark. But Jane moved her hand just a little. That was when Victoria saw what she had failed to notice before—that Jane clutched Wordsworth's poems on her lap.

Victoria lifted her chin and pirouetted on her toes. "Very well. Come, Jane. Come, Dash." She strode out of the room. "Lady Flora, bring my writing desk."

The rose room was hung all pink and white. This was where Mama received ladies for tea. At one time, it had been Victoria's playroom. She remembered inventing whole countries with her blocks and her dolls on the pretty pink carpet.

Now the carpet had faded to a kind of dull gray. The toy box still waited in the corner for the same reason the dollhouse and dolls waited in the bedroom—to remind everyone that Victoria was still a child.

Victoria plunked herself down at the round table by the window. Lady Flora placed the writing desk in front of her and retired to a chair right next to the door.

Keeping watch like a good jailer.

"Jane, come sit with me."

Jane came and sat. Despite the stuffiness of the room, her fingers were dead white, and the ends of her hair were quite damp. She looked, in fact, like she'd been walking in the rain without a coat or bonnet. Victoria seized her friend's hand.

"Lady Flora, Jane is ice cold! We need hot tea and towels and something to eat."

"I'll have to ask—"

"Then do!" snapped Victoria. "At once!"

Lady Flora turned up her nose, but she did leave.

"Quick, Jane." Victoria took both Jane's hands between hers, then chafed them together to try to bring some warmth back. "What happened to you?"

Jane didn't answer. Instead, she pulled away and turned to Wordsworth's poems. She yanked a note out of the book and shoved it into Victoria's hands. Victoria, with a quick glance at the door, unfolded the paper.

It was from Lehzen. Victoria read:

> *Palace sent letter to duchess advising imminent establishment of Her Royal Highness to Buckingham House. Bill being drawn up in Parliament. Sir John wrote Lord Liverpool to ask to bring you to Tunbridge Wells early.*

Victoria stared at Jane. Jane nodded.

Victoria jumped to her feet.

"No, don't—" croaked Jane.

But Victoria had already grabbed up her skirts and bolted back to the sitting room. Mama was in the boudoir, lifting gloves out of a cedar box.

"Mama!" cried Victoria. "Why didn't you tell me?"

"Tell you what?"

"That the king has offered me my own household! That he has sent his intention to Parliament!"

Mama laid one pair of white gloves on the dressing table and picked up another out of the box. "Because it isn't important."

"Not important . . . !" Victoria choked.

"Yes. Since it is impossible that you would accept, it is entirely unimportant."

"Why wouldn't I accept? I'm *sixteen!*"

Mama laid the second pair of gloves down and picked up a third. "Their Majesties are desperate to gain control over you before you turn eighteen, and are resorting to blatant bribery to do it. Sir John is penning an appropriate reply."

"No, Mama. I will not agree to anything Sir John writes. Where is the letter from the palace? Let me see it."

"There is no need," said Sir John from behind his desk. "Your reply is almost ready."

He was writing. Victoria ran to the desk. He did not look up at her, did not acknowledge her in any way. But she could read what was there.

> . . . *cannot possibly accept Your Majesty's proposal as to the change in my situation, coming as it does with the insistence that I be parted not only from the invaluable Sir John Conroy . . .*

Victoria choked.

> *Rather, aware as I am of my youth, my feminine delicacy, and my inexperience, I fully intend to make it known to Your Majesty and the lords of Parliament that I desire her grace, the Duchess of Kent, should remain my legal guardian until I reach the age of twenty-one. Further, I use this letter to officially appoint Sir John Conroy as my private secretary and desire he should continue in that position when . . .*

Anger blurred Victoria's vision. She couldn't read any more.

"You will sign this," said Sir John. "And it will be delivered to St. James's."

"I will not sign such a ridiculous document." Victoria turned her back. Mama stood right behind her.

"Mama, think!" cried Victoria. "This is our chance to get out of Kensington Palace. You've wanted that for years!"

But Mama's demeanor did not soften at all. "The price is too high, Victoria. I do not choose to pay."

"But I—"

"It is not your decision," said Sir John.

"It is not yours!" shouted Victoria.

"It is," replied Mama with icy calm. "And it is made. You do not seem to understand, Victoria, this is not an act of love and respect. It is an act of greed and fear." Mama drew herself up to her full height. "If Their Majesties really cared about you and wanted your coming reign to succeed, they would not only approve of these tours but would insist you go."

"This has nothing to do with the tour!"

"Doesn't it? Then why does this letter come now? Why is it offering you the one thing you want? It's to keep you out of sight! It's so the people of this country will not see you or know you, and you cannot know them or have any understanding of the kingdom you will preside over! They mean to keep you hidden and spoiled until they are certain they have got control of you!"

"And what have you done!" demanded Victoria. "What has he done!" She stabbed a finger at Sir John.

Mama ignored this. "You will sign the letter. It will be delivered, and we are leaving in two days. That is all there is to it."

"I will not!"

Mama raised one brow. "What will you do instead, Victoria?" she inquired. "Lie on the floor and kick and scream like a baby? Walk all the way to St. James's?"

Victoria felt the fact of her isolation fall over her like a net dropped from a tree. She stood in the center of the room, unable to so much as breathe. But it was true. There was no order she could give that Mama could not contradict. There was nowhere she could go where she would not be followed and brought back. Her little jaunt to speak with Gerald Maton had taken days of planning and the help of half a dozen people.

She could not leave here, because she could not do what the scullery maid could. She could not so much as walk out of doors simply because it was what she chose to do.

She could shout. She could scream. She could throw books and hairbrushes and paperweights. She could throw herself on the floor, as Mama so icily suggested. None of it would make any difference. The trap of Sir John's system had been in place for years, and now it snapped shut.

Everything would remain as it was, and she would do as Mama wished. As Sir John wished.

She was helpless.

No, I am not. Not entirely.

"I will not sign that letter," she repeated. "You may drag me away on this tour, but I will not sign my name to lies and have them sent to my uncle king."

Mama pressed a hand to her heart. "Listen to the girl!" she cried to the whole room, and to Heaven for good measure. "Drag her away! I am her kidnapper now! I have given my life to protect you! To keep you from being fought over like the last bone with a pack of starving dogs! You know *nothing* of what I have done—what Sir John has done—for you!"

Mama's fury stunned Victoria into momentary silence. The whole of the day, all her crowded thoughts about Dr. Maton and his death, rose up in a whirlwind. It caught up Mama's shouts, turned them around, mixed them up.

Jane had come in at some point. Victoria had not even seen when. But now she slipped up to her father. She touched his arm, and he leaned down so she could whisper in his ear.

It was a fresh shock. Jane had never approached her father so easily, not when Victoria could see, and he had never given her such attention.

Sir John's face brightened. Jane stepped away.

"Ma'am, let Jane take the princess out into the garden. The rain is gone, and some fresh air and reflection will calm her spirits. The girls can take Lady Flora with them."

"Certainly not!" cried Mama. "Jane cannot manage her. She has proven that. She will wet her feet and catch cold and . . ."

"I will make sure she stays on the path, ma'am," murmured Jane. She folded her hands. She also looked at Victoria from under her lowered eyelids.

Victoria's chest was heaving from her anger and her fear. She could not think straight; she could barely see straight. But she could see that Jane was right. She needed to get out of here.

"I'll go," she announced. "Since I am not permitted to do anything else. Come along, Dash."

She walked away. She did not look behind her. Mama did not call her back. That was enough for now.

It had to be. It was all there was.

Chapter 44

It had taken Jane hours to recover enough nerve to walk across the green to the palace. She'd even welcomed the rain, because the cold and the wind and Betty's complaints helped drown out her own thoughts.

Ned had fought a duel. Ned had killed a man. Dr. Maton knew it. Ned had been paying Dr. Maton for years.

First, Jane had just gone home. Ned was not there, and she was relieved. She knew she would have to confront him eventually. But what on earth would she say?

She had no idea. She was so cold. So shaken. So afraid of all the things she did not know.

And now this.

The princess wasn't walking. She was marching. She stayed on the gravel pathways, but she splashed straight through the puddles. Her slippers would be ruined, and her feet soaked, and the duchess would need her smelling salts when she saw it.

It was childish defiance, but it was her own. It was the princess doing as she always did—making herself seen in whatever way she could.

Jane found herself wearily admiring those frustrated splashes. Then the princess stopped. She hung her head, and she turned. She came running back and grabbed both Jane's hands.

"Jane, I'm so sorry. Something's happened to you, and with that horrid letter and this business with the tour, I haven't even thought to ask where you were this morning. Are you all right?"

Jane looked down at their hands.

"No," she said. "I don't think I am."

"Did you find something in Sir John's desk?"

She heard the tight, hopeful note in the princess's voice. She wanted there to be something she could use against Father. Something that would allow her to refuse to leave on the tour and that would convince the duchess to take the king's offer.

"There were letters, but before I could read them, my brother found me. He took them. He—" Jane choked. She was going to cry.

"Jane?" said the princess gently. "I swear, you can tell me anything. Please."

Jane stared straight ahead, seeing nothing. She could lie. She could insist it was private. She could keep what she knew to herself, as she had always done. It would be easier. It would be better.

"I spoke with Susan this morning," Jane said. "After my brother caught me in the study. She told me . . ." She swallowed. The world seemed to blur at the edges of her vision. "I . . . I think my brother killed Dr. Maton."

Chapter 45

Victoria was aware she should be shocked. Perhaps she should even be morbidly, terribly delighted. This was, after all, what she had longed to hear. This was something Mama could never ignore or brush away.

But she looked at Jane's misery, and all she could think to do was enfold the other girl in her strongest embrace. Jane was so startled, she stiffened. Then, slowly, tentatively, she wrapped her arms around Victoria and hugged her back. She sobbed once. And then she stepped away.

Victoria yanked her handkerchief out of her sleeve and handed it to Jane. Jane wiped her eyes.

"Tell me what happened," said Victoria.

Jane looked behind them. Of course she did. They needed to be careful. Even now, even here, someone might be listening. *And we do not have much time.*

Victoria pressed her hand. Jane squeezed her fingers.

"My brother, Ned, he gambles. He . . . It seems, I heard, he accused someone of cheating, and they fought a duel."

Victoria held her hand firmly, willing Jane to be strong.

"The other man died. Ned was wounded. The doctor . . . the doctor they had on the site was Dr. Maton. They brought him home—" She stopped.

"Jane, what is it?"

"I remember that morning," she breathed. "The noise woke me. I remember them bringing Ned upstairs. Liza said he was drunk. And he was in bed for four days. They said it was a fever. And then he got his post at the consulate—" She stopped, voice and hands trembling. "It was to get him out of the country."

Of course it was. Dueling was illegal. If Ned Conroy had killed the man, he could be hanged for the murder. Of course his friends got him out of the country.

His friends. His family.

His father.

"But either Dr. Maton threatened to tell or Ned simply didn't trust him . . . I don't know which . . . Ned was giving him money to keep quiet."

"Good God."

"What?"

"Aunt Sophia was giving him money, too."

Jane giggled, a high-pitched, frantic noise. "And Father was paying him, too . . . Dr. Maton was bad as my maid Betty. It seems everyone in our family was paying her to keep quiet. Maybe even Ned. I—" Jane stopped dead.

"What is it?"

"We assumed it was Father who went to the Matons to offer the pension. But what if it wasn't?" She pressed her hand to her throat. "The letter from Gerald Maton said it was a tall man with dark hair and blue eyes. That could describe Ned as easily as Father. Ned's been taking money from our sister, and I caught him robbing Father's strongbox. I assumed it was to pay his gambling debts, but what if it was to keep paying the Matons?"

"That could be why William Maton was walking back and forth across the green so much," said Victoria slowly. "He was going to talk with your brother."

"Ned could have offered him a drink, a cup of tea or coffee," said Jane. "He could have slipped the poison in."

Would Dr. Maton's bad stomach have made it work faster? Or could Ned have given him several doses over several visits, like the daughter in Dr. Gerald's story? Was Ned Conroy capable of such dreadful patience?

"What do I do?" Jane stared wide-eyed at Victoria. There it was again, that desperate belief that she must be able to do something, because she was the princess, because she would be queen.

Victoria took her by both shoulders. "You remember what you told me," she said. "That there is no proof. No evidence. We're just telling a story right now."

"But it could be—"

"But we don't *know*. You said it. Lehzen said it. We cannot guess. It's too important. We must know."

"But how can we find out? You're leaving. *We're* leaving. We'll be gone a month. Anything could happen. We might never—"

"Stop!" snapped Victoria. "Let me think, let me think . . ." She gritted her teeth and willed her mind to be quiet. Willed all the anger, all the fear, to quiet itself. It was slow, but gradually, her whirling thoughts stilled. And new possibilities rose.

"I know," she breathed. "I know what we can do. Dear God!" She pressed her hand to her mouth. "Sir John has made a mistake, and he doesn't even know it!"

"I don't understand."

"While Sir John is gone, while Mama and I are gone, you won't be needed at the palace. You'll be free! You can talk to Mr. Rea, to the Matons, to *anyone*, and they won't even know!"

"But you're forgetting that since we're such good friends now, I'm supposed to go on the tour with you. Father decided."

"I did not forget anything," said Victoria. "But you forget Sir John and Mama think I'm childish, stubborn, and capricious." She felt herself smile.

"I don't—"

Victoria took Jane's hand and spoke solemnly. "I'm sorry, Jane. I'm afraid you and I are about to have a dreadful quarrel."

Chapter 46

Everyone looked up when Victoria marched back into the rooms. Everyone saw how Jane hung back, her cheeks flushed, her eyes frightened.

"What on earth!" cried the Duchess. "Victoria! Your slippers!"

Victoria ignored her. "Sir John, I want you to take your daughter away."

"What!"

"What has happened?"

"She's intolerable, and she lies, and I will not have her here anymore!"

"Jane? What did you say?"

Jane looked away. She twisted her hands. Her breath hitched.

"Victoria?"

"She lies, Mama. She says that Aunt Sophia . . . that she is a . . . that she had a . . ."

Sir John went dead white. Victoria did not finish her sentence.

"Jane did not say any such thing. Jane would not be such a fool."

"No, sir," said Jane. "I never. I was trying to say that it was strange Their Majesties waited until now to change the household, and now she says—"

"Fine! Believe that I'm the liar!" cried Victoria. "It does not matter. What does matter is that she is to leave this instant. I do not want to see her anymore." She faced her mother squarely. "You asked earlier, What did I plan to do? What is in my power to do? I agree, you have not left me much. But let me promise you this. If Jane Conroy comes with us, you will not have that smiling, pleasant, perfect princess you so dearly want to show off. She will be scowling, sick, lazy, and snappish. She will refuse to get out of bed and will say she is terribly ill. She will tell everyone about the neglect and horrors of her life under the Kensington System, and do not think she will be above inventing things."

"You would not dare," breathed Mama.

"I promise you, Mama, I would, and if I am forced to take this . . . this . . . *person* as a companion, I will."

Father stalked over to Jane. Jane did not look up. She shrank back, cowering, clearly, plainly waiting for the blow.

Sir John's lips curled into a smile. His gaze said he was surprised, perhaps even pleased. He touched his daughter's shoulder.

"Jane, go home."

Chapter 47

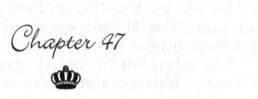

Mama was upstairs in her private sitting room when Jane got home. She sat at her untidy desk, with a pile of banknotes and coins in front of her.

Oh, yes, thought Jane wearily. *It's Thursday.* Mama would have been at her card luncheon. It was the one social event she never failed to attend. Liza had theorized she used it to supplement her pin money, and Liza might have been right. Their languid mother was surprisingly good at cards. However, considering how much artful feigning and sighing she practiced daily, perhaps it was not that surprising at all.

"Is it something important?" Mama asked as she made a note in her tiny account book. "As you can see, Jane, I'm very busy." But she did pause and look up and see the state of her daughter's dress.

"Again?" Mama groaned. "What on earth did you get into this time?"

"I've been sent home."

"That much is obvious. Was it for wrestling ducks in the pond?" She gestured at Jane's mud-spattered dress.

"I've quarreled with the princess. She says I'm not to come to the palace anymore."

"I did try to warn you, Jane. That one does not forgive."

Your son killed a man.

"I know."

Your husband helped cover it up, and they together might have conspired in the death of another man.

Mama sighed. "Well, there's nothing to be done now. You'd best go get changed."

Do you know what they've done? Would you care if you did know? Would you help?

Did you help?

"Have you . . . have you heard anything from Liza?"

"Mmm? Oh, yes. Did I not tell you? I had a letter just yesterday. It's here somewhere." She looked helplessly at the mass of unanswered correspondence spread out across her desk.

"What did she say?" asked Jane.

"As I recall, she says she's having a marvelous time and that Miss Schumann has invited her to stay a week longer." Mama sighed. "Do you know this disagreement of yours may turn out to be a blessing, Jane. Without your sister, I have no help at all. I shall drown from all there is to do. So, I shall be counting on you." Mama turned back to her winnings. "Now, run along, there's a good girl. We'll talk at supper."

Jane did as she was told. She returned to her empty rooms and sat on the chaise and stared out the window. Slowly, awkwardly, with no one to see or to stop her, Jane began to cry.

The princess had said they couldn't guess what had happened. They had to know. That they couldn't panic until they knew. Jane's fear had decided it was not willing to wait.

She was afraid for Ned, and she did not understand why.

She did not love her brother. At least, not with any of the perfect, unquestioning love she had been told a girl was supposed to feel for her brother. She barely saw him anymore. And if he had done what they said, if he'd killed Dr. Maton, if he'd killed a man in a duel . . .

But if he had, and if anyone found out, Ned would die. He'd be hanged by the neck until dead. Father would let it happen, because if he lifted a finger, he might be implicated in Ned's crimes.

No one would help Ned. Ned, who was as damaged as she was, as Liza was. He was as confused, as lonely, as desperate to carve out some kind of life that their father did not control. He'd given money to Susan when she'd needed it, and asked for nothing in return. He'd told Jane he'd stand aside and let her fly if she found a way.

Ned would die, and it might not be her fault, but she'd be responsible. She couldn't do it. She was not brave enough to live with the fact of having killed her brother. She did not hate him that much. She was saddened and sickened and sorry for him.

And Jane cried because it was not right. It would never be right.

But also because it was true.

Chapter 48

Victoria hated Sir John's system. She hated his hectoring and his rules, his observations and his lies. She hated his hold over her mother and her.

But of all the ideas he had instituted to shape her life, the one she hated worst was the "tour."

She hated the endless hours in jolting carriages with Mother rehearsing her fears, her jealousies, and all the disasters she anticipated in every town. She hated the endless parade of strange rooms in strange houses and the continual presence of strange, smiling, fawning people.

If she were allowed to ride horseback sometimes or even to walk out and really see the towns or the country they passed through, perhaps it would be different. But if anything, she was kept even more closely than she was in the palace. In addition to the usual list of dangers, Mama feared madmen and revolutionaries roaming the English countryside. So she made Victoria stay in whatever room had been set aside for her until a specific event required their presence.

Every town they stopped in had their public speeches.

That meant long hours in the blazing heat or freezing cold, sitting on a hastily constructed platform that creaked and swayed whenever anybody moved, while local dignitaries droned and flattered. When these men were done, it was Sir John's turn to stand up and smile out at the crowds and give an answer, which everyone pretended was hers.

These were the moments when Sir John was endlessly, entirely happy. He was constantly busy, consulting with everyone, orchestrating every detail, while Victoria was taken about like a parrot in its cage. Everyone jumped when he shouted, running this way and that at his slightest word. Even in the cold, on the platforms, when he sat behind the dignitaries, he seemed filled with energy and excitement.

And when the crowds cheered, his eyes lit up like a child's on Bonfire Night.

There were tours of local industries to be navigated, bouquets from schoolchildren to be received, fairs to be presided over. Victoria sat. She stood. She waved. She held the bunches of flowers in the crook of her arm and tried not to cry because she missed Dash so badly.

But the worst of it was how exhaustion drained all the enjoyment out of those things she normally relished most. When they did go to some grand house for a dinner, the meal could drag on for hours, until Victoria grew sleepy and stupid. Then they might go to see a concert or play. But by the time they reached the theater, Victoria was so tired she could barely sit up straight, and more often than not, her head ached so badly that her eyesight blurred and even the music became painful.

When at last she was allowed to crawl into bed, it could be as late as two in the morning. She hid under the covers, knowing that she would be woken at six so she could be dressed in time to be driven to wherever she was supposed to be next.

But she had been through all this before. She thought herself ready for it. But on this tour, she found, Sir John decided to introduce an entirely new horror.

They had spent the night in the Hotel Splendide, in York in a sprawling suite of rooms on the first floor. Victoria's bed had been set up next to Mama's, as usual. She had, it seemed, fallen asleep just minutes before.

"Wake up."

It was Sir John. Victoria blinked her eyes open, startled by his gruff voice.

He stood beside her bed. He had a folio tucked under his arm. A strange maid stood behind him with the tray of tea and toast.

Victoria struggled to sit upright. Where was Mama? Lehzen? Their beds were already empty. How could that be? Who had let Sir John into the boudoir alone?

Sir John took the tray and dismissed the maid. Instead of putting the tray across her lap, however, he set it on the table by the window. He did, however, pour her a cup and hand it to her.

Victoria drank. "Are you playing lady's maid now, Sir John?"

"I do whatever is necessary, ma'am. You should know that by now."

She took another swallow. The night had been dry and cold, and the tea was welcome. "It's too sweet."

"It will be a cold day, ma'am. Sweet tea is more warming. Now." Sir John opened the folio and laid it in front of her.

There was the letter. The one he had written to the king, in which "Victoria" pleaded to be allowed to stay under her mother's care until she was twenty-one.

The one that designated Sir John her private secretary.

"What is this?" Victoria demanded. "I told you I would not sign that thing."

"You will." Sir John brought out an ink bottle and pen. He dipped the pen and held it out to her.

"Why don't you sign my name for me?" she inquired. "You wrote it for me. Why not finish it?"

He smiled thinly. "Sign and be done. You will in the end."

"I want some more tea." She held out the cup.

"You can have it as soon as you sign."

Victoria closed the folio and shoved it toward him. Sir John shrugged. He collected ink and pen. He picked up the folio. He set them all on the tea tray and took the tray out of the room.

That was the first morning.

Chapter 49

Liza had tried to warn Jane that being able to stay home was very much a mixed blessing.

If you think running Mother's errands and paying Mother's calls and writing Mother's letters—not to mention giving the orders to Cook and Mrs. Pullet because she simply cannot be bothered—is a grand way to spend your time, you're welcome to try it.

Liza, as usual, had been right. Even with Father gone, there were a thousand household tasks to be done every day. There were all the orders for meals and laundry and shopping to be given, and Jane didn't know any of the routines, and the housekeeper's sympathies stretched only so far.

Then there were all the calls to be made, because the social ties had to be maintained, but it seemed that Mama did not actually like any of the ladies she called friends and so did not choose to exert herself on a regular basis. But, of course, it was vital that she be available for calls to be paid on her. So, for Mother's "at-home" days, Jane had to sit in the parlor, to pour the tea and usher the ladies in and out.

At another time, Jane would have found all of this insufferably dull, but now she threw herself into it. Because while she was doing Mother's work for her, she wasn't thinking about Ned and the duel and the blackmail.

Wasn't thinking about how she could find a way to talk to Mr. Rea or what she would say when she finally did.

Thankfully, with Father gone, Ned seemed to find he had an even greater license to do exactly as he chose. Most nights he did not come home at all. That meant Jane did not have to see him or sit with him and keep silent about all the suspicions that rubbed her heart raw.

Because I don't know anything.

And she wouldn't know anything until she talked to William Rea, and yet she was afraid what would happen once she did.

So, to her shame, Jane dithered. She told herself she had time. The princess would be gone for almost the entire month. She and Victoria had whispered about Jane trying to come and meet the tour at Ramsgate, the last stop before they returned to Kensington. There they could enact a tear-filled reunion.

"We'll have to make sure whatever we've quarreled over will keep you in your father's good graces," Victoria had said. "That way he'll permit you to stay with us at Ramsgate so we can talk and decide what we will do next."

But that meant that even if there weren't any delays during the princess's progress, there were two whole weeks until Jane needed to find a way to travel to meet the royal household. She could take her time. She could plan her own maneuvers.

Then Liza came home.

It happened remarkably quietly. Jane was in her sitting room, reviewing the dinner menu. Because the morning was fine, she had opened the window, and so she heard when a carriage pulled up in the street. She glanced out the window and then jumped to her feet and ran to see.

In the street below, Liza was climbing out of a private carriage. The footman came out of the house to collect her luggage, which the coachman had dropped unceremoniously onto the cobbles.

A scant few minutes later, Liza breezed into the sitting room.

"Hello, Jane!" She pulled off her bonnet and tossed it aside. "What's that? The dinner menu? Oh good. I'm sure I haven't had a decent meal in a week. I would cheerfully commit murder for one of Cook's apple pies."

What are you doing here? I was sure you eloped!

But no. Liza sat calmly on the lounge and began pulling her gloves off. She glanced up at Jane, and Jane saw the deep shadows under her eyes and the hollows of her cheeks.

She also saw her sister's silent plea that she not remark on any of this.

Jane swallowed hard. "How . . . how is Miss Schumann?"

"Oh, it was a marvelous time," said Liza brightly. "They would have kept me longer, but I thought I'd best be getting home. I knew the place would be in an absolute shambles without me. I think Mrs. Pullet is happier to see me than Mother is."

"What about Miss Schumann's brother?" asked Jane cautiously. "You'd mentioned him particularly before you left . . ." *And you said you weren't waiting for Mother and Father to make any kind of match for you . . .*

"Oh, well, that." Liza's voice shook. She cleared her throat and went on more calmly. "You know what young men are. Desperate flirts, all of them, but you can't take any one of them seriously. I'm sure I don't have to tell you that!"

Jane looked at her sister.

Liza looked back. *Don't make me say anything*, her weary eyes said. *Please.*

But Jane stood up and walked over to her. She sat on the lounge and took her sister's hand, and Liza did not pull away.

"Is there," Jane began, "anything you will . . . need help with?"

A single tear trickled down Liza's cheek. "No, Jane. I didn't . . . almost, but not quite. So, no." She smiled weakly. "But thank you."

After that, there was nothing for them to do but hold on to each other while they cried.

Chapter 50

The tour dragged on.

Every morning Sir John shook her awake, always before dawn, even if she'd only gotten to bed a few hours before. Some days he allowed her one cup of tea. Some he did not. Always, he dropped his folio onto her lap, handed her the pen, and waited for her to sign. When she did not, he took away the tray.

Victoria complained to Mama, but Mama said, "Well, then, sign the letter, as you know you should. It will save us all a world of trouble."

She asked Lehzen why she was not in the room in the mornings, and she thought Lehzen might cry. "He orders me out," she whispered. "If I did not go, he threatens to send me back to Kensington without you." Victoria gripped her hand. Lehzen kissed hers.

The third morning Victoria closed the folio and threw it across the room.

But then there came the fourth morning, the fifth, the sixth.

The tenth.

The fifteenth.

She was never permitted a moment alone with Lehzen. Her governess was kept awake until after Victoria was asleep, and shooed out of the room before she was awake.

She missed Dash. She missed Jane. She was so angry and so tired.

There was the concert in York where she pinched herself black and blue, trying to stay awake. There was the crowd in Doncaster that pressed so close they threatened to overturn the carriage and the horses reared in their traces. There was the storm in Leeds, where the thunder rattled the windows and the streets ran six inches inch deep in mud, so that the carriages stuck and had to be levered free.

And every morning Sir John woke her a little earlier, and every day Mama told their hosts that the princess must be kept on the strictest of diets to preserve her health.

"But I'm hungry, Mama," she said.

"You're fat," Mama told her. "You cannot be stuffing yourself."

At first, Victoria was able to keep her anger suppressed and her spirits up. She told herself that all she had to do was endure. Jane was at work. She would soon have news. By the time they reached Ramsgate, Jane would have *proof*. Then Victoria would be able to tell Mama what had really happened to Dr. Maton. It would be something that could finally be turned against Sir John. Something even Mama could not ignore.

But it was hard. She was so cold; she was permanently hungry; and she was continually exhausted by the noise, the faces, the carriages, the late nights and early mornings. By Sir John's hearty cheer. By the way Mama swung from tearful concern and gratitude in public to stern admonishments in private.

"Mama, my head aches," Victoria said.

"And whose fault is that? If you had not gone riding when you should not, you would not be feeling the effects."

"Mama, I'm ill," she said.

"Ah, now it comes. You told us yourself you would try this tactic. Perhaps you regret that particular bit of honesty now."

The days blurred. Victoria could no longer remember which town she was in. Sometimes she could not remember to whom she was speaking. When Sir John came into her darkened room to lay the letter down in front of her, she blinked at it stupidly.

One morning she found herself sitting up, with the pen in her hand and no memory of how it got there. She threw it away as if it were a snake.

Then came the morning when she could not sit up at all.

Chapter 51

In the end, Jane decided to tell Liza what was happening.

First, oddly, because Liza might laugh at her. She thought that if Liza scorned her fears about what Ned had done, she might find herself less worried about him.

Second, because she had to do something to bring Liza back to herself. Liza drifted around their rooms like an aimless ghost. Jane had expected her sister to fall quickly back into the old routines, but most days she could barely bring herself to walk down to the breakfast room.

"Were you in love with him?" Jane asked.

"I thought I was," said Liza. "But I think I was in love with the idea that I was leaving, and I've managed to break my own heart over it. Isn't that ridiculous?"

"No," said Jane. "Not a bit."

But what decided the matter was that Jane desperately needed someone to talk to. The princess had been gone three weeks, and although Jane had gone to the post office every day, no letter had arrived. Victoria had been certain that between her and Lehzen, they would be able to smuggle something out, and by now, the postmistress, Mrs. Carey, was very used to looking for anything from Miss V. Kent. But nothing had come.

She's just being watched, Jane told herself. *She said it would be difficult.* But that didn't help.

So, Jane told Liza what was happening to her. She brought up a tray with tea and a full sugar bowl and thick slices of bread and butter. She closed the door to their sitting room, and when Liza had fixed her cup of tea, Jane told her all about Dr. Maton and the princess's determination to find out what had happened. Told her out the circumlocutions that had allowed the princess to speak to Gerald Maton, the mysterious "pension," and the discovery that the family had burned his papers.

Jane told her the true reason Ned had given Susan money, about the duel and its consequences, about how she feared that Dr. Maton had been blackmailing Ned and perhaps Father, as well.

"Well," said Liza when she'd finally finished. "You've been having a busy time."

Jane giggled but quickly stopped herself. The sound was far too close to hysterics. "And now I've been left behind specifically to talk to Mr. Rea, but I don't know how to do that. I can't just turn up at the palace and ask to see him, and I can't invite him to tea."

In fact, she'd hoped to avoid the whole affair by retrieving the letters from Dr. Maton and Mr. Rea from Father's desk. Surely, she reasoned, there would be enough in those that she could put off talking with Mr. Rea until the princess returned. But it seemed Ned had realized she might come back, and had spirited them away entirely.

"But why not invite Mr. Rea to tea?" asked Liza. "Make it on Thursday, when Mother is out. I'll be in the house, so it will be perfectly proper, if that's what you're worried about."

It wasn't. "What if Ned sees him?"

There it was—the light in her sister's eyes, the easy, confident self that had been missing since she returned.

"Don't you worry, Jane. If it comes to it, I'll take care of Ned."

It did not "come to it." Jane invited Mr. Rea for one o'clock. By that time, Ned was out about his own business, whatever that might be. It was Liza who met Mr. Rea at the door and ushered him into the blue parlor. There Jane sat in the round-backed chair that was her post when presiding over Mother's teapot on at-home days. She had the tray ready, with the second-best cups and a plate of Cook's finest shortbread.

Jane found that William Rea did not suit her idea of an accountant. Accountants should be hunched, balding, pale, paunchy, ink-stained men with spectacles who carried fat, well-thumbed ledgers. Mr. Rea was a tall, lean man. His black coat fitted him well, and his black cravat was neatly tied. His dark hair was neatly styled, and his side-whiskers were closely trimmed. His breeches showed the shapely legs of a man who led an active life, and the smooth assurance of his bow spoke of a comfort with parlor manners. But this pleasant appearance was spoilt by his trick of walking with his head thrust forward and nodding at everyone and everything he saw. It made him look both too vague and too sharp at the same time.

"Thank you for coming, Mr. Rea," said Jane as she indicated he should sit on Mother's sofa.

"It was no trouble at all, ma'am. I'm honored that you asked for me. Honored." He nodded several times and accepted the cup of tea she poured. He sipped politely and nodded again. "Now, tell me, how may I be of assistance to such a charming young woman?"

Mr. Rea smiled.

Jane was familiar with this sort of look. Mr. Rea thought he could disarm her simply by being handsome and obliging. He was unlucky in that there were lots of men in the palace who held similar beliefs about themselves, and even Sir John's dreary daughter saw her fair share of flashing blue eyes and coy grins.

Jane took her time fixing her own cup of tea. As she did, she thought about Liza and the duchess and Mother. How would they speak to this man?

"Mr. Rea," she said, "I asked you here specifically on business for Her Royal Highness."

Mr. Rea drew his chin back in surprise. "Her . . . the Princess Victoria?"

Jane nodded.

Mr. Rea was silent for a minute, clearly torn between being flattered and being wary.

"Of course, I am glad to be of whatever use I can to Her Royal Highness," he said. It was the correct answer, while at the same time it committed him to exactly nothing.

Jane folded her hands, surprised to find them so still. She remembered the feeling of sitting in the princess's carriage and how grand it was to be someone else entirely. This was the same feeling. Sitting here, she was not Sir John's dreary daughter and spy. She was the princess's friend and her trusted confidant. She had planned this moment herself and was carrying it through.

For this one moment, she was finally fully Jane Conroy.

"You may have heard that the king has informed Parliament that the princess is to be given her own household."

Mr. Rea's expression turned owlish.

Father told you, didn't he? And I imagine he said he would be nipping all that in the bud.

Jane stiffened her spine. She set her jaw. And then she lied.

"What you may not know is that the matter has already been settled between the duchess and the queen."

That startled him.

Jane bit her tongue hard to keep from smiling. "I tell you this in strictest confidence, Mr. Rea." She waited while he nodded and nodded again. "As soon as Her Royal Highness returns from her tour, the arrangements will begin. At that time, the princess will be making her own decisions about her household staff."

She waited for Mr. Rea to make some remark. He remained silent.

"You'll surely be familiar with the rumors that Her Royal Highness does not share her mother's affection for my father." Jane smiled. "Father says this is because she is a silly, stubborn girl."

She could see that the accountant had heard exactly those words. *Probably more than once.*

"But it goes a little . . . further than stubbornness," Jane went on. "And I can promise you absolutely that when the time comes, Her Royal Highness will be consulting her own inclinations, not Father's. And she will most certainly remember anyone who was a friend to her."

Jane watched as this idea sank slowly into Mr. Rea's mind. She watched his gaze dart about the room.

What are you looking for? Answers? An escape?

Whatever it was, he apparently did not find it in the parlor, because Mr. Rea got abruptly to his feet. He paced over to the window, his head nodding in time with his footsteps, and stared out at the garden.

"Sir John has been my commanding officer and patron for years now," he said.

Jane gritted her teeth to remind herself to keep silent and let Mr. Rea talk.

"He's the reason I have this position at all. When he came into the duchess's service, he wrote to me and told me that I should join him."

And he's made use of you ever since. It's what he does.

"I cannot, I will not, betray his confidence."

"That's not what I'm asking," said Jane. *Although it is interesting that, that is what you're hearing.* "What Her Royal Highness wants to know is about Dr. Maton."

"Maton?" Mr. Rea turned, clearly surprised. "Sir John said he was taking care of the matter."

Jane fought to keep her voice steady. "Then there's no harm in the princess knowing what's behind it, is there? So that she does not mistakenly trust the wrong person in the future?" Inspiration struck. "I've heard that Dr. Julius Maton may be in line for a position in the medical household, or perhaps Dr. Gerald Maton." This was another lie, but surely that did not matter at this point. "If the princess needs to choose between them, she needs to know which one she can trust with her secrets."

Mr. Rea smirked. "I wouldn't trust any of Maton's sons."

"Really? Why not?"

Jane watched Mr. Rea consider. He'd already slipped. What would he do now? If he decided he needed to keep all the secrets and preserve his loyalty to Father, she was sunk. But if he decided it would be as well to ingratiate himself to the princess, even just a little, she would win.

Which is it? She clenched her hands together. *Which way do you choose?*

"Well, I tell you frankly, Miss Conroy, their father, William Maton, was an out-and-out scoundrel."

It seemed to Jane then that the heavens opened and the angels sang. She hoped that Mr. Rea mistook her stunned expression for one of simple surprise.

"But ... he was a part of the household for so long ...," she murmured.

"And I warned Sir John many times over the years that he was not to be trusted," Mr. Rea told her. "Not only did he drink and gamble, but he was not above using private information to extort money to pay his debts. I knew all this, and even I was shocked when I heard about his latest, well, his last, scheme."

"What was the scheme?"

Contempt twisted Mr. Rea's mouth into a sneer. "You heard, perhaps, that Dr. Maton was writing a ... memoir, I believe he called it?" Jane nodded. "Well, it seems that he was putting in all the secrets he'd been keeping about his patients and their households. All of them."

"All?" Now Jane was shocked. *All* meant the duke, the duchess, Princess Sophia, the Duke of Sussex.

The princess.

"All," repeated Mr. Rea. "That is, unless, they would pay him to keep them out. It seems he was making the rounds of all the affected households and informing his victims as to what it would cost to keep him from publishing their confidences."

"But ... he couldn't possibly publish such a book. It wouldn't be allowed. Someone would stop him."

"In an earlier age perhaps," said Mr. Rea. "But, alas, these are sadly degraded times we live in, and the press"—he waved vaguely toward the window—"may publish very much as it chooses. And scandal sells newspapers, and books."

"I see."

Liza had said he drank and talked too much. Gerald Maton had said he talked about his cases more than he should . . .

He'd been there when the Duke of Kent died. He'd taken care of the princess the whole time she was growing. He'd taken care of the duchess. He'd sat in on meetings of the Kensington Board. He'd had years', decades' even, worth of secrets he could threaten to publish about any and all of them.

Even about Father, if he chose to.

Dr. Maton had known that Father had been lying—to Parliament, to St. James's, to anyone who would listen— about the princess's health and the state of her mind, and that the duchess had been helping him.

What else does he know about the royals? About us?

He had known about Ned, and the duel, of course, but what else?

Jane was suddenly very glad she was sitting down, because her knees were trembling.

Jane picked up her teacup and gulped the contents gracelessly. "Well. That is very helpful. Thank you, Mr. Rea. I will make sure that Her Highness knows how ready you were to help."

"And your father . . ."

"Oh, this does not concern him," she said, giving her best imitation of Liza's breezy nonchalance. "I don't see any reason to mention it at all."

Mr. Rea smiled and bowed over her hand and took his polite leave with many more nods and many assurances that should the princess ever require anything further, he was, of course, entirely at her service.

He had not been gone half a minute before Liza came in. Jane grinned. Liza raised her brows.

"Did you hear?" Jane asked.

"What do you take me for?" Liza sat down and reached for the shortbread. "Of course I did."

"What do you think?"

Liza flopped backward, assuming a pose very much like Mother's and took a large bite of shortbread. "I think that the next thing we must do is work out how we're getting to Ramsgate."

Chapter 52

Someone was shouting.

"Wake up! Wake up, you spoiled brat!"

Sir John. It must be morning. Victoria needed to sit up. But she couldn't sit up. Her head hurt too much. She tried to roll over, and pain lanced up her back.

She tried to remember where they were. Ramsgate. Yes. In the cottage. At the seaside. She could smell the salt air. They were to rest now. She was promised rest.

Why can't I rest?

Her throat was aching and painfully raw. Her tongue felt like wet flannel clogging her mouth.

"Water," she whispered.

"You will have nothing until you cease your shamming and do as you are told!"

He grabbed her shoulders, and she shrieked as he hauled her upright. She tried to open her eyes, but the light was far too bright. She screwed them shut again, and even that hurt.

Anger washed through her, a weak tide, but it gave her just enough strength to lift her head.

"Is this how you killed Dr. Maton?" she whispered. "Did you poison his tea? Or was it his drink? I understand he drank to excess."

Sir John's face went utterly blank. "What in God's name are you talking about?"

"You killed Dr. Maton," she said. "You poisoned him, and now you are poisoning me."

"Is that what you think?" Sir John crouched down, bringing his face close to hers. "Is that the nonsense you've been relishing while you've run about with my daughter? Well, now, you deluded little creature." Her head sagged, and he put his hand under her chin to force her to look at him. "It's possible, I suppose, that one of Dr. Maton's victims may have done for him, but I don't really care. The man is proving more of a nuisance dead than alive. Now." He grabbed her hand and fumbled with her fingers.

What are you doing? Stop it! But she had no strength left to protest.

It was only slowly that she realized he was wrapping her fingers around the pen.

"You will sign what I give you to sign, and you will speak to me with respect, or you will lie here and burn to ashes for all that I care. Do you understand, you stupid little girl? Do you?"

The pen was in her hand. Sir John was shouting. The whole world shifted and blurred. She was hot. She could not see clearly. Her hand was being moved. She didn't understand.

She did know there was something important she must do, but she couldn't remember what it was.

I must . . .

I must . . .

I . . .

With a shuddering effort, she loosened her fingers. The pen slipped free and clattered onto the floor.

Darkness swallowed the world.

It took two days for Jane and Liza to get to Ramsgate. Betty drove a hard bargain but agreed to go along as their maid. The sisters pooled their money, what there was of it, to hire a carriage and horses. Jane sent a letter to Mr. Saddler at the palace, and Mr. Saddler, in turn, sent Clyde Hornsby to act as their driver and manservant.

Liza had suggested that Ned could drive them and that it might keep him away from fresh trouble. Jane had countered that they did not need a driver who might drink himself into a stupor at the coaching inn or gamble away their limited store of money in some tavern once they reached the town. Liza shrugged and admitted Jane had a point.

Mother probably would have protested the entire enterprise if they'd bothered to consult her. As it was, they simply left before she was awake, instructing Meg to say that they were visiting friends (which was true, after a fashion) and that they would write when they were safely arrived.

The journey was delayed only slightly by Jane's insisting they stop at the post office.

"I need to be sure this goes into the next post, Mrs. Carey," she told the postmistress as she handed over her letter.

"Of course, dear." Mrs. Carey squinted at the direction. "Your Miss Kent's in Ramsgate, then?"

Jane nodded. "It's to be left at the post office there until called for."

Because Lehzen or the princess might check, and she wanted the princess to know that she had kept her promise and that she was on her way.

*   *   *

334 Darcie Wilde

"Please, ma'am. Let me send for Dr. Clarke."

Lehzen.

"Don't be ridiculous. She's shamming. She warned us herself that she would, and now she is."

Mama.

"You would be of more use, Lehzen, if you exerted your influence over her and made sure she signed the letter."

"She's shamming? You truly believe with that fever and that cough, she's shamming?"

"Yes!"

Don't cry, Mama. You mustn't cry.

"She must be shamming! She cannot be so very ill. She is a naughty child who does not want to listen to what's best for her. Sir John has said—"

"Was his grace the duke shamming when—"

There was a short, sharp sound. Victoria winced.

Someone has been slapped.

She wanted to open her eyes, to ask for water, to see what had happened.

But she couldn't, and after a bit, the world went away again.

It was raining when Jane and Liza reached Ramsgate. This was not the steady southern-county rain they were used to. This was solid sheets of salt-laced water lashed by a wind strong enough to set the carriage rocking. They could progress only in fits and starts because Hornsby had to maneuver around puddles that had begun to blend into lakes. The horses balked, and in the end, he had to get off the box, take hold of the harness, and lead them on at a walking pace.

Jane, Liza, and Betty all huddled together, trying to keep each other warm. They could see nothing out the windows and didn't even know they'd reached the inn until Hornsby came round to open the door and let down the step.

Thankfully, the inn was a reputable place, and they were given a room with a clean bed and a private parlor. Jane handed over half the money remaining to them as a deposit and told herself they'd find a way to make up any shortfall when the time came. Surely the princess or Lehzen would loan them something.

She did not even consider asking Father.

The landlady brought hot water so they could scrub the travel mud off themselves. Betty helped them into dry things. Jane was exhausted, but she found she couldn't settle down. She went to the windows and peered out, trying to see up to the sky.

"Jane, for heaven's sake, come away," snapped Liza.

"I just wanted to see if it was clearing."

"It's not."

"I was hoping to go to the post office."

"Well, you'll have to hope we don't catch our deaths instead. Come back to the fire and let me brush your hair before we have to cut it short to get the snarls out. Betty, you go see if the landlady has any tea or if there is anything hot on the fire."

"Yes, Miss Conroy." Betty scuttled out.

"You and the princess can wait one more day, Jane," said Liza. "Everything will be fine."

It was the creaking step that gave Lehzen away. Phillips, who had been dozing by the kitchen door, shook himself and rose to his feet.

"I'm sorry, ma'am. Sir John said you're not to leave."

"But—" began Lehzen.

Phillips was already shaking his head. "He was very clear, ma'am. It's as much as my position's worth."

"Perhaps—" She reached into her bag.

But Philips shook his head again. "No ma'am. I'm sorry."

There was nothing left to do but to beg. "Please, Phillips. The princess is ill. She needs a doctor at once."

"I know, ma'am," he whispered.

"Then let me go."

"I can't. He'll sack me. I'm all the support my family's got."

I will not cry, Lehzen told herself. *I will not fall at this man's feet. I will think. There must be something. There must be . . .*

She looked around the darkened kitchen, saw the clock, saw the keys hanging on their hooks, saw the calendar on the wall, with the date circled.

Remembered the princess's whispered plans, and her heart squeezed painfully.

"If I cannot leave, perhaps you could send the boy with a letter? It's for a friend of mine. I just need it left at the post office. What harm can that do?"

Philips met her gaze. Lehzen did not permit herself to so much as blink.

"Right," he said. "A note to the post office. I'm sure that would be fine. Give it to me, and I'll see the boy's sent just as soon as the rain clears a bit."

It was the slimmest possible hope. It was almost certainly no hope at all. But it was all that she had.

"Oh, do sit *down*, Jane," cried Liza.

It was morning, although outside it was still nearly dark as midnight. The remains of breakfast sat on the table. The fire had been built up fresh, and the rain still poured down. Liza had joked about the necessity of building an ark, or perhaps they could simply trade the horses for dolphins.

Jane craned her neck, trying to see past the eaves, in case the clouds had begun to clear. "I can't." She squinted. Was that perhaps a tiny bit of blue?

"Why not?" Liza spread her toast with the landlady's surprisingly good marmalade.

"I don't know," Jane turned to face her sister. "I just . . . I feel like something's wrong."

"What could be wrong?"

"She didn't write, Liza." Jane's voice broke. She hadn't realized quite how that neglect had affected her until this moment. "She's always writing letters. But it's gone on three weeks, and there's been nothing."

Clearly, Liza wanted to snap back some bit of sarcasm, but something in Jane's face stopped her.

"Jane, you said yourself Father would be watching her particularly closely. She probably just didn't find a way to slip the net. That's all."

I've spent half my life finding the cracks . . . Jane turned back to the windows.

Behind her, Liza sighed. In the next moment, she tossed her napkin aside and yanked on the bell rope.

Betty appeared from the parlor. "Yes, miss?"

"Betty, get your stout boots on," said Liza. "It seems Miss Jane has decided we're going for a little walk."

The room was well lit. A good fire burned. The rain slammed against the windows, as if angry at being denied admittance.

Her daughter lay still in her little travel bed, her face nearly as white as the sheets.

"We should get the doctor," Victoire said.

"And what will the doctor do?" asked Sir John. "Bleed her? What she needs is a little rest. Some broth and tea, and she'll be right as rain in a few days."

Yes, that's it. That's all it will take. I am worrying too much. It is the mothering instinct. It is that I love her, that I need her—

Sir John was behind her now. He laid both hands on her shoulders and squeezed. Just a little too hard, but she could not seem to tell him to stop.

"You agreed with me that she was not ill, that she was just feigning. When the board asks, that is what will be said."

"By you."

What is the matter with me? Why can't I move? Why can't I think? Edward? Edward, my dearest, what have I done?

But the answer came from Sir John.

"It's the truth, Victoire. You know it is. She was feigning. Just as she did when we first left Kensington. How was it to be known that these symptoms were anything different?"

"I do not neglect my daughter," she breathed. "I have never neglected her!"

I am not making any sense. But neither is he. Worrying about what the board will say because she's caught cold!

Edward caught cold. Edward died of his cold.

"No, of course not. There is no more dedicated mother than you. I see that every day. But she is a stubborn girl, and she has a distressing tendency to falsehood when the mood overtakes her. She said herself that she would feign illness if she did not get her way."

"Yes." Victoire grabbed hold of his words like a lifeline. "Yes, she did do that."

It is not my fault. It cannot be. I have only done my best. Edward, you know that, my heart. You do know.

"She was trying to get sent home early to avoid her duties," said Sir John. "It was the king's letter that brought on this most recent burst of stubbornness. If he hadn't disturbed her with this talk of her own household, she never would have been tempted to make such childish threats."

The duchess rubbed her brow. "Yes, of course. Forgive me, Sir John. I'm simply tired and not thinking straight. She has worn herself out with her own stubborn behavior. That is what this is."

"Just so," said Sir John gently. "Get some rest, ma'am. I'll watch Her Highness."

She squeezed his hand. "Whatever would I do without you?"

*   *   *

Victoria drifted.

There was a great roaring in her head, and the light burned her eyes. But that faded. Now she was home, in her old rooms, with their green walls and the smell of damp.

There was someone with her. A young woman with red hair and a stiff green dress. She was standing in front of the dollhouse, arranging the figures inside.

"That's mine!" Victoria cried.

"That's mine," the woman sneered. "And do you know who this is?" She held up a doll in a blue dress.

Victoria moved forward. She looked at the doll and did not recognize her but felt very much that she should. The roaring redoubled. It hurt. She was so dreadfully hot, she could not understand what she saw.

"Pool little Victoria." The red-haired woman shook the doll hard. Its tiny legs rattled. "Poor little girl. She could not bear it. They will put her in a box now and take her out only on special occasions."

The woman laid the dolly in a black box all lined with velvet. She took a little white blanket and tucked her in.

Victoria looked at the doll and at the woman. The doll's face was a woman's face but was painted solid white, with the brows drawn on.

No, she had no face. Her face was a skull.

"I'm tired," Victoria told her. "I want to rest."

"Dolls who want to rest go into their boxes. They may be brought out later. If they are very good. If they do as they are told."

"No."

"Oh, yes. Are you a good dolly? Will you let them play with you?"

"Stop." Her head hurt; her eyes hurt. Someone was shouting. She did not understand.

"But they will let you rest then, dolly. You will have only

to do what you're told," said the skull, the woman, the queen. She was a queen. She had a crown on her red hair, on her naked skull. "So much easier that way. Just do as you're told." She picked up the doll again, then dangled it in front of her. "Come on."

"No."

"You must! You have no choice!" screamed the skull, screamed the queen, screamed the doll dangling in her hands.

Said Mama. Said Sir John.

"Take it, and do as you are told!"

The doll had a dull and stupid face and crooked legs, and the woman—skull, queen, death, life—shook it hard by the back of its neck. Like she meant to shake it apart.

"No!" screamed Victoria. "No! You will stop! Stop it!"

She lashed out with both fists. Something overturned. Something crashed to the floor. The pain exploded in a burst of noise and heat and dreadful burning light.

And she was in her bed and surrounded by wooden walls. Mama and Sir John were staring at the open door.

There on the threshold stood Jane Conroy, with Lehzen beside her.

"We've brought Dr. Clarke," Jane announced.

And there was nothing else after that.

Chapter 53

It was a full week before Jane was allowed back into the princess's room.

Thankfully, Father was too busy running about to pay her much attention. He was grimly, constantly busy—dispatching messages to St. James's, to the newspapers, to the prominent families in the area, to friends. All of them were briskly reassuring and said that the princess had been ill, but the fever had now broken, and she was perfectly well now. Her physician, Dr. Clarke, was in constant attendance and advised that she should stay in the healthy seaside air for just a while longer before returning to Kensington Palace.

With all this to do, he took only passing notice of Jane's story that she and Liza had come to Ramsgate because she planned to apologize to the princess for their quarrel.

Neither one of them spoke about her having brought Dr. Clarke, apparently against Father's and the duchess's standing orders.

"He thinks you managed it," said Jane to Lehzen. *Which you did, really.* "When he has a moment to spare, he's going to be terribly angry."

"And we will let him," she replied. "My appointment is from Their Majesties. He cannot dismiss me, a fact which, as you know, very much gets under his skin."

The duchess was the one now meeting with Dr. Clarke. Their conversation seemed to involve her alternating between quizzing him and berating him, with an occasional sprinkling of lamenting over her own suffering and mistakes while Lady Flora held her hand.

So, it happened that Lehzen was the only person in the boudoir with the princess when Jane slipped inside.

"Hullo, Jane." The princess's voice was a light, rasping sound.

"Hullo."

She The princess was pale. The bones of her face pressed against her skin. Blue veins stood out clearly on the back of her hands.

Jane's heart squeezed tight. "How . . . how do you feel?"

"A little better, I think. Dr. Clarke says my convalescence is likely to be a long one." She rolled her eyes, and Jane suddenly did not think she could be happier. The princess was ill, she was weak, but she was still herself, and Jane had missed her.

"Did . . . What does the doctor say?" Jane asked.

Lehzen was the one who answered. "Dr. Clarke is quite certain it was typhoid fever."

"Then it wasn't . . . ," began Jane.

"Poison?" whispered Victoria. "I thought it might be, too, but no."

Jane knew it was not truly possible to melt from relief, but at that moment she believed she might.

"Jane," breathed the princess. "Lehzen says you probably saved my life."

Jane felt herself blush. "You should rest now."

"I could have died, Jane. He . . . he was ready to let me die."

She turned her face away, but Jane saw what she did not say: *Mama was ready to let me die.*

"No." Jane shook her head. "With you dead, what power does he have? Who will keep him at court?"

"Unless he was more afraid of what we might know than he was of being powerless. What did you find out from Mr. Rea?"

Lehzen looked ready to panic at this, and honestly, Jane could not blame her. She took the princess's hand and pressed it gently.

"Get better," Jane said. "Then I'll tell you."

"No, tell me."

"Get better," Jane said. "If you don't, you'll never find out, will you?"

The princess frowned, but there was a light in her eyes. Jane grinned.

"Miss," said Lehzen, "the doctor said it could only be a few minutes."

But Victoria clung to her hand. "Don't leave me, Jane."

"I won't." She covered Victoria's hand with her own. "I promise."

After that, Jane rejoined the household. Liza took Betty, Hornsby, and the hired carriage and returned home.

"I'm sorry to abandon you," Liza had said. "But it's that or start borrowing. Betty doesn't trust me, and she won't go a day without her sweetener."

It was another two weeks before Dr. Clarke declared the princess was fit to travel. The journey that had taken Liza and Jane two days took the household five. The carriages crawled at a snail's pace to minimize how much the princess would be jolted. They stopped at every coaching inn on the road to allow her to rest.

Jane didn't think it possible she could be so glad to see the gates of Kensington Palace. The only thing that seemed more welcome was watching how Victoria beamed when she settled onto the sofa and Dash leapt into her arms.

"Yes, yes, Dash!" the princess croaked as the spaniel alternately barked and joyfully licked her face. "I have missed you so much! Yes, you are my very best friend." But she lifted her bright eyes and looked at Jane where she stood next to Lehzen. "Well, almost."

That evening Jane climbed into the carriage with Father. He banged on the roof and sat back, staring out the window. Jane looked from him to the passing lawn, the gates, the cobbled streets.

The world should have changed, she thought idly. *He should have changed. I should be able to see it.*

But study Father's face as she might, there was nothing new there.

Or perhaps there was. "Jane. Did the princess say anything to you about poison?" he asked.

"No," said Jane. "Why would she do that?"

He made no answer, and Jane was happy to let him have his silence.

Mother received them home with a declaration that they all looked as exhausted as she felt, and promptly decided she would take her dinner on a tray. At the table Father scowled at Ned, and after the meal concluded, he called him into the study and slammed the door.

He need not have bothered. His voice was clearly audible in the corridor. Jane knew because she stood outside the door to listen.

"What have you done, you bleating young fool!"

Father was still enumerating the various unfavorable aspects of Ned's personality when Liza came up the stairs.

"He found out about the banknotes Ned took," she told

Jane. "And about the gambling debts." Jane raised her brows. Liza shrugged. "Ned talks when he's in his cups, and I may have mentioned one or two things I learned where Father could hear."

"Remind me not to tell you secrets," muttered Jane.

"Too late, Jane."

That was, of course, true. "Does Father know about the duel?" she asked. "That Dr. Maton was there?"

"Oh, he's known about all that for quite some time," said Liza. "I rather think he respects Ned more for it than otherwise."

"Yes," murmured Jane. "He would, wouldn't he?"

Liza threaded her arm through her sister's. "Come away, Jane. Get some rest. There's nothing new for you to learn here tonight."

"And tomorrow?"

Liza shook her head. "That I don't know."

Chapter 54

It was indeed a lengthy recovery. But every day Victoria found herself able to stay awake a little bit longer. Her headaches were absent more often than they were present, and sitting in the sunlight was no longer a torment.

Slowly, she was able to rise from the couch. At first, it took both Lehzen and Jane to support her as she tried to cross the room. Soon, however, it was just Jane, with Lehzen following behind and Dash scouting officiously ahead.

Of course, she was inspected. The Kensington board all came and stood about her couch and looked down at her, trying not to frown. Victoria felt a terrible urge to let her eyes roll up in her head and fall backward, just to see what all these solemn men would do.

She told Jane about that later. Jane said this was surely a sign of her returning health. Victoria found she tended to agree.

They saw very little of Sir John. He was constantly at Parliament or at St. James's, delivering his reports and soothing tattered nerves.

Mama, of course, stationed herself at Victoria's side and would not be shifted. When she was not giving orders, she was complaining or despairing. At last, it reached such a stage that Dr. Clarke suggested—very solicitously—that the duchess's extremity of feeling could lead to a case of nervous exhaustion.

"I must insist, ma'am, that you lie down in your bed, quite still and in perfect solitude, for one hour every day. It is for your daughter's sake," he said solemnly. "You must remain strong for her. Lady Flora, will you please take her grace to her room?"

As he packed his bag and left, Victoria saw him wink.

The door was shut behind him and Mother.

"Quick, Lehzen," Victoria croaked. Her throat still had not fully recovered. "Take me into the rose room. I want to talk to Jane."

Jane looked to Lehzen, who nodded her agreement. There followed the endless fuss of moving Victoria to the new couch, of covering her properly, of touching her forehead and hands to make sure that the fever had not returned.

Victoria tried to bear it patiently, but she felt her patience straining. At last, Lehzen retired to her chair by the hearth, where she could simultaneously keep an eye on Victoria and Jane and the door.

"There's word from the palace," Victoria told Jane as she made room for Jane to sit next to her. "The board delivered a letter from Uncle King."

"Are you being moved soon?"

It took Victoria a minute to be sure her voice would not shake. "It seems that due to my recent severe illness, it has been decided that establishing any independent household should be postponed at least until I am stronger."

This was the real result of Sir John's long days closeted

with the board and the lords of Parliament. She knew it. So, clearly, did Jane.

Jane licked her lips. She looked out the window. "Will you tell them?" she asked. "What he did to you?"

"Who would believe me? No one else saw it."

"But Lehzen—"

"Did not actually see it," said Victoria. "She was kept out of the rooms most of the time."

"Oh."

"Yes. Oh," she agreed heavily.

"I'm sorry," said Jane.

Victoria reached up. She wiped her hand across the fogged window so she could see the autumn garden that much better. "Don't be," she said. "It won't be forever."

Jane bowed her head.

Victoria tapped her on the back of her hand. "None of that, Jane Conroy. You promised that when I was better, you would tell me about your conversation with Mr. Rea. Now I am better, so you can begin." She folded her hands with exaggerated patience.

She expected Jane might smile, but she did not. She looked at the door, and she twisted her hands together.

"It seems Dr. Maton was not making enough money by blackmailing only one or two of his patients," Jane said. "Mr. Rea said that his memoir was going to be filled with all the secrets he knew, or at least that's what Dr. Maton was telling people."

Victoria listened with growing horror as Jane described how Dr. Maton had concocted a scheme to extort money from his wealthy, and royal, patients by telling them he would keep their follies, their crimes and sins, and—most importantly—their names out of his memoir.

All they had to do was pay him the amount he asked.

"That's why they wanted his papers burned," Victoria breathed. "Whoever 'they' are."

"That's just it," said Jane. "There could be dozens of people who wished those papers destroyed and Dr. Maton dead. How are we to even begin to find out? Anyone from Kensington to Gravesend might have killed him."

"No," said Victoria. "Not anyone."

"Why not?"

"Because he was walking on the green. Because that was where he died. He was between your house and the palace."

"That might just be coincidence."

"But it might not."

"But even then, there are so many possibilities," insisted Jane. She started ticking off possibilities on her fingertips. "Princess Sophia, the Duke of Sussex, if he thought it might save Princess Sophia. And then there's Father—"

"This is going to sound odd coming from me, but I don't believe it was your father."

Jane stared at her. Victoria felt herself smiling. "I know. But when I was falling sick, I accused him of having poisoned Dr. Maton." *And of trying to poison me.* "What he said . . . He said he knew about the blackmail scheme. He said that one of Dr. Maton's victims might have turned to poison, but it was not him."

"And you believe that?" asked Jane.

"Oddly enough, I do," said Victoria. "But that does leave your brother as a possibility, I'm afraid."

"And your mother," said Jane.

Victoria bowed her head. *Do I believe that?* Victoria found she did not know, but it was fair that Jane should say it.

"There's Dr. Maton's own family, as well," said Victoria. "His oldest son, at least."

Jane frowned. "Why them?"

"To save themselves." Victoria remembered Gerald Maton and all the anger in his demeanor when he spoke of his father. "Debts can be repaid, but what happens to the family if their father's scheming destroys their reputations? And a doctor would know how to handle poison."

Jane nodded. "Mr. Rea already said he would not trust any of the sons, because of their father." She rubbed her eyes. "But that's not even a full list. It could be any of a hundred people in the palace. For all we know, Lady Flora has some dreadful secret. Or Lady Charlotte. Or someone whose name we don't even know."

"It would have to be someone Dr. Maton would sit with," said Victoria slowly. "Someone with whom he might share a drink or something to eat." She paused. "Someone who he could reasonably expect to be able to call on in the middle of the day. Someone he trusted and yet had a secret he could make use of."

She waited for Jane to argue, but she did not. Victoria closed her eyes.

Think, she ordered herself. He walked during the day. Otherwise the groundskeepers would not have seen him. He walked regularly. So, whoever he was visiting, he expected them to be there during the day. . . .

If it's not all a coincidence. If it wasn't really his heart. If . . . if . . . if . . . Victoria ground her teeth together. Frustration rose in her, and she suddenly wanted to break something.

Break something. The words repeated themselves inside her. *Break something.*

Victoria's eyes flew open.

"Jane," she said. "Tell me again how Susan was dismissed."

Confusion filled Jane's eyes. "My mother said she broke the best tea set . . ." Her words trailed off. "You can't suspect Susan!"

"Not Susan," said Victoria.

Jane blanched. "*Mother?*"

"She had a secret she very much wanted to keep. She was home during midday, which was when Dr. Maton was out walking. She would be expected to serve tea to any guest. And as hostess, she would be the one to fix his cup."

Jane sat stupefied. Slowly, her mouth began to move. She wiped her hand across it, as if seeking to wipe some stain away.

"What day was it?" Jane asked suddenly.

"I don't understand."

"The day, what day of the week was it when we found Dr. Maton?"

"It was Thursday afternoon," said Lehzen. Lehzen, of course, had been listening. She had heard everything and had said nothing. Until now.

Jane's face twisted up tight. Her mouth moved again, but it was a long moment before any sound emerged.

"The card luncheon," Jane said.

"I don't—"

"My mother attends a weekly card luncheon. The ladies there play very deep, and Mother wins a great deal. So, on Thursday afternoons she always has money, and she is alone in the house. Dr. Maton could walk over then and receive his payment."

"And she would serve tea," said Victoria.

"But . . . she had no secret," stammered Jane. "I mean, the one she did have, it wasn't real, and it seems that everybody knew that, anyway."

Victoria shook her head. "No. Don't you see? The real secret was that she was *not* my father's natural daughter. She was *not* related to my family. That was what she needed to keep from your father."

Because Sir John valued his status and his consequence. Sir John would not forgive anyone who took that away from him.

And he most certainly not forgive anyone who had spent years successfully deceiving him.

"But we can't know," Jane whispered urgently. "We've said all this time we have to *know*. We have to have proof! What proof is there? No one saw! Liza was paying calls, and Susan said she wasn't even there."

"Someone saw," said Victoria. "It is not possible your mother was truly alone. There was someone there—" She stopped. She blinked. She shifted herself so that she faced Jane fully.

"Jane," she said. "Where's Betty?"

Chapter 55

"Mother?"

Jane stood on the threshold of the blue parlor. Mother sat on her sofa, a magazine spread out on her lap and a cup of tea cooling on the table beside her.

She didn't even look up. "Jane? Good Lord, what is it this time? Another quarrel?" She turned a page.

"Mother . . . I've brought a guest home."

"And what has that to do with me?"

"Good afternoon, Lady Conroy," said the princess.

Mother looked up. Mother gaped. Jane realized it was one of the few times she'd ever seen her mother lose her countenance.

Mother rose and dropped into a curtsy. "Your Highness! Well, well. Such an honor!"

"Thank you." Victoria walked into the room as if she owned it. Which, Jane supposed, she did in a way. "May we sit down?" she inquired rather pointedly.

"Oh, yes, ma'am. Please." Mother was glowering at Jane. Jane found she could not muster the strength to care. Victoria sat first, of course, and Jane took the chair beside hers.

"Let me ring for tea." Mother moved to the bellpull.

"There is no need," said Victoria. "I was hoping to speak with you in private."

"With me!" Mother laid one long white hand on her bosom. Her gaze flickered to Jane.

Have you guessed yet? Jane wondered. *Do you know what's about to happen?*

"Are you sure we should not wait for Sir John?" Mother was saying. "Surely whatever you have to say—"

Jane found she couldn't stand any more. "Mother, we are here to talk about Dr. Maton."

Mother drew back just a little, but her expression remained perfectly, politely bland.

"Lady Conroy," said the princess, "Dr. Maton was killed. He was poisoned, possibly very slowly, over the course of several weeks."

"Good heavens," murmured Mother.

Do you know? Do you see it yet?

"It was your doing, Lady Conroy," said the princess.

Jane did not know what reaction she expected to this blunt statement. She could not even fully believe that the words had been spoken out loud, that they reflected any possible version of reality.

Mother's response was to arch her delicate brows. "I poisoned a man? Goodness, ma'am! I'm afraid such a thing would be far too much trouble for me."

"But you did do it," said Jane. "You poisoned his tea. Then you upset the tray and broke all the china so it could not be used again. You sent him away to die." She swallowed. "And you did it because otherwise he would have written in his memoir that you have been lying to Father all these years and letting him believe you are related to the Duke of Kent."

"Unfortunately, he is not always careful with the little

things," Mother had said. "Small details, small men . . . He leaves them scattered about."

"What an amusing story," murmured Mother. "But you should know, Jane, your father will not be very pleased when he learns you have been spinning such ridiculous fancies for Her Highness. I do apologize, ma'am," she added to the princess. "My daughter's imagination seems to have become overwrought from your recent kind attentions—"

The princess did not let her get any further. "I notice, Lady Conroy, you do not ask where Betty is."

"Betty?" Mother echoed.

The princess inclined her head. "Betty is on her way to Sheffield. She will collect her family and from there proceed to Leicestershire. A very bad time of year to have to travel, but there's a living there for her brother. A gift of the countess. While we visited her home on the tour, she mentioned the position had recently become open."

"I'm afraid I don't understand what that has to do with me. Other than the fact that this largesse has left me short yet another servant!"

"Betty overheard your last meeting with Dr. Maton," said the princess. "She saw you break the tea set and go on to blame Susan for it. You were paying her for her silence, and to keep an eye on your daughters, just in case they said anything odd."

"I see," said Mother.

Jane had not known what she would feel at this time. She had not expected it to be so much heartbreak or so much silent rage. The blood drained from her face as she watched Mother sitting quite still and poised, calmly listening to the princess speak about her guilt.

Her beautiful, languid mother, who hated any sort of bother. She had poisoned a man. She had watched him walk out the door to die.

Mother sat, beautifully composed, her hands perfectly folded, her skirts spread out prettily around her, her dark curls falling across her sloping shoulders.

"Well," Mother said, "I am certain that upon reflection, ma'am, you will see that this story is one best forgotten as quickly as possible. That is sure to be my husband's view of the matter."

Do you honestly think you can scare her by mentioning Father?

"I'm sorry, Lady Conroy," said Victoria. "I cannot let this matter go."

Mother laughed just a little. "But, ma'am, surely my daughter's hysterics—"

The princess did not allow her to finish. "What would be best, Lady Conroy, would be for you to leave."

"Leave?" echoed Mother.

"Sir John still has family in Ireland, I believe. In fact, he has a sister—Cathleen is her name, is it not? You can go to her. It can be said that you require a rest and are on an extended visit."

"Ma'am, you will forgive me—"

"I will not," said the princess. "It is only out of consideration for your daughters that I am here now, rather than informing my mother and your husband and the many, many others who would turn this matter into public business."

"If you go to Sir John and tell him this fantastical story that I"—Mother laid her hand on her breast—"poisoned poor, drunken little Dr. Maton, he will never believe you. Either of you. And if Sir John does not believe you, the duchess will not believe you, and there's an end to it."

"I'm afraid not," said the princess. "Because there are those who will believe this story." She paused. "Or perhaps it would be more accurate to say there are those who will find this story useful because they do not like Sir John. They do not like his influence over my mother, and they do not like his hold over me. These men will go to my uncle king and to the queen, who, as I am sure you know, lately indicated a wish to remove me from Sir John's influence. The utter ruin of his family reputation would be a very good excuse to do just that."

Mother laughed, a glittering sound like a breaking bell. "And this will happen on the word of two little girls!"

"But by then it will not be just two little girls," said Jane. "You can take Ned with you. He's getting himself in trouble here, and it really would be best if he was out of the country for a while."

This was not how it should be. Jane should not be turning on her mother like this. It should not be her responsibility to say what was the right punishment for her crime. This was a question for courts, for magistrates, for the whole mechanism of public justice.

And yet Mother was right. She had pointed out what had been the sticking point all along. They were just girls, and all that vast, churning machinery of justice would not hear them. Not even when one of them stood poised to become the queen.

So this was what they could do.

"And who will run this house?" demanded Mother. "Who will see to the properties and care for your father and for you and your brother . . . ?"

"I will," said Liza.

Mother twisted herself around, surprised to find Liza there at all. Jane certainly was. She had not even heard her sister enter. But, of course, Liza knew what was happening. They all knew exactly where to stand to hear what was being said in any room of the house.

Mother sighed and blinked at the ceiling for a long moment. Jane felt the seconds crawling across her skin. She had no notion what her mother would do. Or how the princess would respond.

Mother sighed once more.

"Oh, very well," she said. "I suppose it's for the best."

"Excellent." The princess's declaration was firm and cold as ice. She stood. "I trust I will hear of your having sailed quite soon. Jane? We should be going." She started for the door.

Jane followed, but then she hesitated. "Ma'am, I think . . . May I stay for a moment? I have some things . . ."

The princess touched her arm. "We'll wait for you in the carriage."

Jane nodded.

"I'll show you out, ma'am," said Liza promptly.

When the door closed, Jane turned. Mother had fallen back on the sofa. She stared up at the ceiling.

Jane wanted to scream. She wanted to throw something. But all she could do was stand there, her hands hanging limp at her sides.

Mother closed her eyes. "Go away, Jane. I'm tired of this."

Jane stared. Her jaw was open, and she could not seem to close it. She could not move any part of her. She just stared at her mother, stretched back on her sofa. A perfect picture of elegant ennui.

"I just want to know how keeping this . . . story about you being a royal bastard could possibly be worth a man's life?"

"Oh, Jane, you must understand, your father is exposed to so many temptations. If I wanted to keep him with me, to keep his material support, it was necessary that I give him something no one else could. This was the simplest way to do that."

All her life Jane had believed her mother to be a frail creature. That all she did or failed to do came from her bone-deep indolence. But now she saw there was so much more beneath her mother's flawless skin than that pretty sloth. She wanted things easy, yes. She wanted things smooth and pleasant.

And she would move mountains or destroy lives to keep them so.

And when whole worlds collapsed, no one would know quite how it happened. Because it could not possibly be the doing of shallow, fainting Lady Conroy.

You sent him away to die.

Go away, Jane. I'm tired of this.

"Mother?" she whispered.

"Yes, Jane?"

"Was it Father who went to the Matons to offer them money to burn his papers?"

"Mmm? Lord! Have we not had enough of this? Yes, if you must know, it was. It seems Dr. Maton had a few little secrets that belonged to your father that he was not willing to give back."

"What secrets?"

Mother smiled lazily at the ceiling. "Well, my dear, that is something for you and our little princess to find out for yourselves. Now, go away, Jane." She sighed. "I am dreadfully tired, and it seems I shall shortly have a great deal of packing to do."

Chapter 56

Victoria sat in the enclosed carriage and watched Jane descend the steps from her house, pale and silent as any ghost could ever be.

Mr. Saddler did not need any instruction. He came forward at once to open the carriage door and help Jane inside. Lehzen moved to cover Jane with the second carriage robe.

Victoria took Jane's hand. It was cold as stone.

Lehzen signaled for Mr. Saddler to drive on. A tear dropped from Jane's eye and splashed on the back of her hand. And another. Victoria pulled her handkerchief out and wiped at her friend's face.

"I'm sorry," Jane whispered. "Truly."

"Dear, silly Jane," murmured Victoria. "What do you have to be sorry about?"

Jane shook her head. "I don't know. I just am."

"I understand," said Victoria.

She did. She knew what it was to feel so much responsibility, even when there was no fault on her part, nor any power to prevent what happened.

"She said it was Father who had the Matons burn the papers. That Dr. Maton was holding some other secrets about him."

"Yes, well, that was rather to be expected."

Jane lifted her head. "What will you do? Will you find them out?"

Victoria contemplated this for a quiet moment. "In time, I'm sure I will." She paused. "Or perhaps I should say we will. These things have a way of escaping eventually."

"But her grace—" began Jane.

"I've already spoken to Mama."

She had. This morning. Mama had been at her desk, writing yet another letter to Uncle Leopold. Victoria had stood beside her desk and swiftly read her looping handwriting. She'd read . . .

Stop, Victoria told herself firmly. *No need to distract yourself with that.*

But even as her heart had thudded heavily at the sight of what Mama had written, Victoria had mustered her courage and told Mama what happened on the tour, had told her about Sir John's shouting, his bullying, the way he tried to force her to sign his foul, lying letter.

"You misremember," Mama had said.

Victoria had felt her jaw fall open.

"Close your mouth, Victoria," Mama said immediately. "If you cannot control yourself better, you can leave this instant."

"Mama—"

Mama laid down her pen. "Sir John was out of his mind with concern for you," she said. "You know the Irish tendency toward sentiment and emotion. They are nearly as bad as the English. He shouted at the doctors. *That* is what you heard."

"You're lying!"

"You were delirious, Victoria. You do not know what you really saw or heard, and you cannot pretend that you do."

Victoria knew then that she was too late. She could see how it was that Mama had already reworked the scene in her mind, how she had erased or torn or burned the facts that were not useful and written in others that were more to her liking.

"Why are you doing this, Mama?" Victoria asked. "Why are you letting him have his way?"

Mama shrugged. "The English have a saying about the devil you know. Sir John is the devil we know. Now, go lie down, Victoria. We do not want you making yourself ill again."

But Victoria did not move.

"Do you know what I truly don't understand?" she said. "You spend so much time wailing about how weak I am, about all your fears that I'll fall ill. Then it happens. I am ill. And you did not believe me. You did nothing."

Mama picked up her pen and dipped it in the ink. "I can only pray that one day you will understand exactly what I have done."

"Then we have the same prayer."

And Victoria turned, and she walked away. But instead of the way in front of her, she saw the words from Mama's letter shining in front of her eyes.

Dearest Brother, she had written in German.

Some pleasantries. Inquiries after his health and that of his wife. Inquiries on how he found the Belgians and the work of building his still new kingdom. And then . . . and then . . .

She had paused, letting the words shape themselves in her mind before committing them to paper.

> *It seems to me the time has come when we*
> *must begin to turn our thoughts to a proper*
> *marriage for our Victoria. It would not do to*

have a repetition of the sort of mad, jockeying
scramble that afflicted my late husband's family
not so very long ago. Nor should I wish for any
great mismatch of age or temperament. Neither,
of course, would I wish for a stranger who may
not understand—or care for—our family's in-
terests.

    I understand via Baron Stockmar that you
have been training up our young cousins Ernst
and Albert with an eye to the match.

    How soon, do you think, will you be able to
bring them to us?

Now, sitting in the carriage with Lehzen and Jane, Victoria shook this memory off. She could not, she would not, let despair take her. If Mama thought she would tamely submit to her choice of a match, she was very much mistaken.

"You're doing it, aren't you?" said Jane abruptly.

Victoria blinked. "Doing what?"

"Finding the cracks. Right here, this minute. You're finding the way to slip the net."

"It is the devil I know," Victoria said lightly. "And look what we have done with that knowledge, Jane, you, and I together." She took her governess's hand. "And you, Lehzen."

"And Miss Liza," said Lehzen.

"And Susan," added Jane. "And Betty."

Victoria laughed. "Oh, yes, definitely Betty. We must hold on to that."

"But you do think we'll find out then?" asked Jane. "What it was Dr. Maton was holding over Father's head?"

"I think we will," said Victoria. "You and me, and Lehzen and Liza, too. Indeed, I expect we can do whatever we want." She smiled. "And then I think the devil might discover he does not know us at all."

Epilogue

SIDMOUTH
1820

He's dying.

Victoire, Duchess of Kent, sat on a hard stool at her husband's bedside and willed him to keep breathing.

The room was dark, except for the fire that sputtered fitfully in the hearth, trying in vain to match the roar of wind and surf outside, trying also to warm the room and bring some small chance of life to the man who lay so still in the narrow bed.

John Conroy stood back and watched the duchess and the dying man. A strange mixture of hope and fear twisted in his guts.

The doctor—William Maton—was speaking to them both. Dr. Maton was a fussy, fat, pale, bald man. He had spent the past four days swearing as to the unfailing efficacy of his knives, cups, and leeches. Now he was saying something far different.

"Your grace, I believe we have done all we can at this time.

Your husband is strong. We have every reason to hope, with the help of the Almighty, he shall make a full recovery."

The duchess's English was terrible. If she understood any of what Maton had said, she gave no sign. Her jaw moved back and forth. She had the habit of grinding her teeth when she was upset. The duke had sounded him out on several schemes to break her of the habit.

The doctor fell silent, but a fresh noise insinuated itself into the room's chill—a thin, insistent bawling. The baby, tucked up in her cot in the adjoining room, had begun to cry.

Again. Conroy had three children of his own, and he'd never known an infant so demanding of everyone's constant attention.

Drafts curled around Conroy's neck and the backs of his hands. He watched the duchess. She was a beautiful woman, determined and quick, nothing like his own wife at home. But she was dulled by grief and confused by the danger that her husband and protector found himself in.

She is alone, he thought. *And she knows it.*

Dr. Maton looked up at Conroy. "Does she understand what I'm saying?"

"I'm sure she does," he answered, although he was not sure at all.

"I think we will know for certain in another hour. I have every hope that this crisis is nearly past us."

The duchess had turned her face toward the window, not that there was anything to see. The shutter had been closed. For all the good it did in keeping out the cold or the sound of the storm.

The baby was still crying. Where was the blasted nurse? Or that dratted Lehzen? Or even useless little Feodora?

"Victoire."

It was the duke. His eyes were open, but the light in them was not a healthy spark. It was flickering, fevered.

Dying. Conroy's heart thumped.

The duchess seized his hand. "Yes, my heart, I am here."

"Victoire," Edward said again.

"Rest, my heart. You must regain your strength."

Victoire pressed her hand against her eyes.

The baby was still crying.

"Conroy," said the duchess.

"Yes, your grace?"

"Go see to the baby. Go talk to the nurse. See that Feodora and William are still asleep. I . . . I cannot."

"Yes, ma'am." He bowed. He also caught Maton's eye and jerked his chin, indicating that the doctor should accompany him.

Dr. Maton nodded, and together they left the room. The duchess did not look up to see them leave.

Like the rest of the house, the front parlor was dark. The storm rattled the shuttered windows and drew moans from the chimney.

"Doctor," said Conroy, "you must tell me. I have to be ready for whatever comes next. What is your real prognosis?"

Dr. Maton drew himself up. "The duke is a strong man—" he began.

Conroy held up his hand. "I asked for the real prognosis."

Dr. Maton glanced over his shoulder. "I don't know," he admitted. "It could be hours, or he could hold out for days yet."

Conroy's heart thumped again. "Hold out?"

"The fever remains very bad," said Dr. Maton. "I have already done all I know how to do."

Conroy rubbed his chin. He thought of all that the duke had trusted him with, and yet the man had never spoken of their closer bond, had never even once so much as hinted at the relationship they shared via his natural daughter, Conroy's wife, Elizabeth. They, and that squalling baby in her cot.

He thought of the duchess, lost and confused in the other

room. He thought of God in his Heaven and the knives in the doctor's bag.

He dug his hand into his inner coat pocket and brought out several folded banknotes. He pressed them into Maton's hand.

"The duchess is suffering." Conroy closed Maton's fingers around the banknotes. "She will not be able to stand this uncertainty. Not for days. She will go into hysterics and be unable to care for the little princess. She must not be left in this state. Do whatever you can." He gripped the doctor's arm. "*Whatever* you can."

Dr. Maton drew his hand back and tucked the notes into his own pocket. Conroy clapped the man on the shoulder. The doctor turned his back and returned to the sickroom.

Conroy stayed where he was, listening to the voice of the wind mingling with the baby's cries. Then, Conroy slipped up to the door. He listened while the doctor said, "I think we may bleed him one more time."

Alone in the dark, Conroy smiled and turned toward the nursery.

Now. Let us see about that girl.

Acknowledgments

No book is the work of just the author. I'd like to thank my editor, Wendy, for her hard work and patience, along with the whole fabulous team at Kensington Books; my agent, Jessica; the Untitled Writers' Group, who read everything; and most of all my husband, Tim, and my son, Alex, for all their love and support.

Further Reading

Williams, Kate. *Becoming Queen Victoria: The Unexpected Rise of Britain's Greatest Monarch.* Ballantine Books, 2016.
Baird, Julia. *Victoria the Queen: An Intimate Biography of the Woman Who Ruled an Empire.* Random House, 2016.

The following two titles are harder to find, but if you want to read more about the tangled relationship between Princess Victoria; her mother, the Duchess of Kent; and Sir John Conroy, they're worth looking up:

Hudson, Katherine. *A Royal Conflict: Sir John Conroy and the Young Victoria.* Hodder & Stoughton, 1995.
Ashdown, Dulcie M. *Queen Victoria's Mother.* Robert Hale, 1974.

For a look at what life was like for the daughters of George III, including Princess Sophia, this book sheds light on their lives:

Fraser, Flora. *Princesses: The Six Daughters of George III.* John Murray, 2004.